# THE LAGARTO STONE

# THE LAGARTO STONE

Gordon N. McIntosh

iUniverse, Inc.
Bloomington

# The Lagarto Stone

iUniverse books may be ordered through booksellers or by contacting:

iUniverse
1663 Liberty Drive
Bloomington, IN 47403
www.iuniverse.com
1-800-Authors (1-800-288-4677)

ISBN: 978-1-4620-0981-7 (pbk)
ISBN: 978-1-4620-0982-4 (ebk)

Printed in the United States of America

iUniverse rev. date: 06/15/2011

To Meridyth, for many wonderful years.

*What are fears but voices airy?*
*Whispering harm where harm is not;*
*And deluding the unwary*
*Till the fatal bolt is shot!*


William Wordsworth

# PROLOGUE

▼

He is in that place again, shivering in the dark, choking back his sobs. Goose bumps ripple his skin, tears sting his eyes. Gunshots and a man's scream echo outside the closet. His tiny hands fumble with the knob and the door opens. Candles in the distance draw him nearer. Approaching the light, he sees a body on the floor, a stranger with a dark stain spreading around him. To one side a woman in a white slip lies sprawled on a couch. She is still, but he can hear her heavy breathing. Something about her seems familiar, but tousled black hair conceals her face. He reaches out and pushes a few strands aside. He recoils and tries to cry out, but no sound escapes. Instead of her face, there is emptiness, a deep, swirling void. From behind him, he hears a footstep. Turning, a man with fiery red hair grabs him. He kicks and squirms, terrified the man's flaming hair will burn him, but the man is too strong and he's carried and flung back into the closet. Through the keyhole he watches as the burning man wrestles with the woman. Then he stiffens, preparing for what always follows when the door reopens—the wild flight, the crash, and the descent into the black water.

# CHAPTER ONE

▼

Doug Sutherland lay face-up and spread-eagled, his fingers digging into the mattress. The room had stopped spinning, but the bed rocked under him like a boat at anchor. Uneasy, he listened. Sensing only his rapid breathing and the central heat, he stretched into Kelly's territory and confirmed that he was alone. So what had dragged him from his stupor? As if in answer, his telephone rang.

Opening one eye, he peered into the darkness. The digital clock said 1:10. It had been thirty minutes since he'd crawled out of the cab that brought him home. He reached for the handset and knocked the phone to the floor. Groping around the carpet, he found it.

"Yeah? What?" His voice sounded like gravel in a steel drum.

"Mr. Sutherland? Jimmy here." It was the doorman. "Sorry to keep calling, but you got a visitor."

"She forget her key?" Kelly must have decided to come after all.

"It's not Miss Matthews. It's a guy."

"Who the fu…" Sutherland muttered.

"You all right, sir?"

"No." His throat felt hot, his tongue dry. Who the hell visits at this hour? "Tell him to go away."

"He won't leave. Some Latino." Someone said something in the background. "Name's Primo or something."

Sutherland turned on the reading light and squinted toward the bathroom. He needed cold water and aspirin.

"Can you talk to him?" Jimmy said, a note of urgency in his voice. Or was it something else? Maybe fear?

"Gimme a minute." He stood up and stumbled to the bathroom. He frowned at his bleary-eyed image in the mirror—five o'clock shadow, faded tan, eyes more red than blue. No photos please. He filled a glass with water, fumbled three aspirins from a bottle, and washed them down.

Returning to the phone, he said, "Put him on."

"*Buenas noches. Soy Javier, su primo.*" It was the anxious voice of a young man.

*Primo?* Cousin? Sutherland was perplexed. "Sorry, wrong guy." After midnight, still half in the bag, and some *chico* wanted to test his Spanish. He tried to concentrate, searching for the words. "I'm not your cousin. *No soy su primo.*"

"*Sí, señor.* My mother she is *Isabela Castellano.*"

The name stopped Sutherland. His own mother was a Castellano. She could have dozens of relatives with that name. But who cared? He'd seen her once in thirty years.

"Look, it's late. *Demasiado tarde, comprende?* Come back tomorrow, okay?"

"*Por favorrr,*" the man begged. "*Es muy importante.*"

"Give me the doorman. *El portero.*" He heard some mumbled words and then Jimmy spoke again.

"This guy's sick, Mr. Sutherland. Or hurt. What the? Jesus…blood…"

Suddenly, a sharp clatter forced Sutherland to jerk the phone from his ear. Had the doorman dropped his phone?

"Jimmy," Sutherland shouted. No answer. "Shit." He hung up and stared at the rumpled bed, tempted to fall back in. Instead, he dialed the lobby number. Busy. Should he call 9-1-1? What could he tell them?

Cursing, he grabbed his pants from the floor and struggled into them. He found his tuxedo jacket on the doorknob and pulled it on over his bare torso. After slipping on his loafers, he scooped his keys off the dresser and trudged out of his apartment to the elevator. When the doors opened onto the lobby, no one was in sight. With the lights dimmed for the night, the large space felt like a mausoleum, its granite walls and marble floor cold as death itself. The only movement was a soft snowfall beyond the windows that spanned the front of the building.

The reception desk sat in the center of the rectangular lobby, opposite the entrance. Sutherland moved cautiously, approaching it from the side. First he saw the cowboy boots sticking out from behind the desk. Edging closer, he saw the jeans and then the body lying on its side. The legs were bent and pulled up into the belly. Long black hair stuck to the face, covering it. Blood-slicked hands clutched the stomach. If that was his visitor, he was having a bad night.

Behind the desk on the floor, he saw the blue uniform, the brass buttons and the ample gut. The face was as gray as the marble tile, but there was no mistaking Jimmy, the doorman.

For a moment, Sutherland was dazed, standing in the darkened lobby with two bodies sprawled on the floor. But he was jarred alert when he realized that whoever did this might still be there. He glanced around, but didn't see anyone else. Outside the window, the driveway was deserted. Whirling snow formed halos around the streetlights.

He called, "Jimmy?" His voice echoed from the granite walls. The doorman didn't move. He was on his back, his eyes rolled upward and vacant. But there was no visible bleeding.

He studied the other man, Javier. His hands were clutched to his stomach. Blood seeped through his fingers, shiny in the dim light. Suddenly, his torso heaved, and his head snapped around to face Sutherland. His eyes were red and pained.

"*Señor* Sutherland?" His voice was weak and raspy, like glass shards scraping. He was young, no more than eighteen, with the round face and thick lips of an Olmec statue.

"*Sí. Qué pasó?*"

"*Me pegaron un tiro.*" He glanced at his stomach and lifted one hand to show where "they" shot him. Sutherland could only see a large, dark stain on the already stiffened shirt. Who were they? Had they shot the doorman as well?

He circled the desk and stepped over Jimmy while looking for the phone handset. He had to pull it from under the man's leg where it had fallen. Dialing 9-1-1, he took a deep breath, trying to control his shaking. When the woman answered, he gave the address and said a man was dying and another might be dead. Jimmy certainly looked dead. There was no blood, but his eyes were blank, and drool trickled from his gaping mouth. Sutherland checked for his pulse, pressing on his neck where the artery should be. With so much flesh there, he couldn't feel anything.

Then Jimmy belched, and his eyelids flickered. A second later, Javier groaned. Which one was he supposed to help?

"*Señor!*" The desperate cry and the blood decided for him. He sprung over to Javier and knelt by his shoulder.

"The ambulance is coming," Sutherland said. "What can I do? *Cómo puedo ayudarte?*" He pushed the wet hair away from the boy's face. Fear-filled eyes stared back.

"*Mi bota. Quítemela.*"

"Take off your boot?"

"*Sí, la derecha.*" The kid wanted his right boot removed. What for? A last wish to avoid dying with his boots on? There must be a better way to help the poor kid. The metallic odor of fresh blood and the spreading dark stain indicated a serious injury. But Sutherland's only training for that much bleeding was a tourniquet.

Not knowing what else to do, Sutherland grabbed the right boot. Pulling it from side to side, he eased it off and was hit with a foul stench. "The other one? *La otra?*" he asked.

"No," Javier wheezed. "*Dentro.*"

Sutherland held his breath and peered inside the boot. Nothing there but dark streaks on the lining where blood had run down Javier's leg. "*Nada,*" he said.

"*La…*" The boy's chest heaved. "*La punta.*" The point.

Sutherland reached into the toe of the boot, felt something moist wedged there, and pulled it out. It was a wad of paper inside a plastic wrapper. He held it so Javier could see it. "*Éste?*"

"*Síí.…*" He exhaled. "*Para usted. Muy importante.*"

Sutherland heard Jimmy cough. He stood up, jammed the small package into his jacket pocket, and returned to the doorman. Jimmy stared at the ceiling. He was alive, thank God, but Sutherland doubted he knew where he was.

He heard sirens and rushed back to the boy. Javier's eyes were squeezed shut, his face contorted in a grimace. He wasn't going to make it.

Flashing lights lit up the driveway. A red-and-white ambulance from the Chicago Fire Department slid to a stop on the snow outside. Doors slammed, and two men hurried through the revolving door. Their rubber soles slapped against the marble floor as they approached.

Sutherland sat down with his back against the reception desk. He shivered and pulled his tuxedo jacket tighter, trying to ward off the drafts from outside. He hugged his knees and thought of his warm bed only twenty floors above him. If only he was there and this was only a dream.

The aspirins were losing to the cognacs Sutherland had downed three hours earlier. It seemed like the bass drum in his temples was playing background to the voices of the policemen around the reception desk. Maybe they were making sense of what just happened. He certainly couldn't.

He sat on a bench in the alcove off the lobby with his elbows on his knees and his head in his hands. The lights had been turned up, and the glare wasn't helping his headache. If only he could go back to bed. He heard footsteps approaching across the marble floor and looked up. It was the detective again, a stocky, red-faced blond in his thirties. His name was Dugan, Deegan, or something like that.

"Can't we finish this tomorrow?" Sutherland said. Another icy gust from the door hit him. Why hadn't he put on a shirt under his jacket?

"Just a couple more questions." The detective sat across from him in a Barcelona chair. "If you never heard of this guy, why'd he ask for you?"

"A mistake."

"He knew your name."

"The phone book? I don't know. Look, officer, I was asleep. Hell, I'm still asleep." And half in the bag to boot. Better say as little as possible until he could think straight. "The doorman called. That's all I know. Is Jimmy okay?" he asked.

"The doorman? Fainted is all. The kid's bad though." He looked down at his notebook. "No ID. What'd he say his name was?"

"Javier Castellano…I think." He spelled it for him.

"You sure?"

"Just a guess." He stood and buttoned his jacket, as if that would make him respectable. "It's after two. I gotta crash," he said. "Call tomorrow if there's anything else. Apartment 2001."

The detective raised his hand. "Just a minute."

"Aww, come on."

"Was his boot off when you came downstairs?"

His boot? Sutherland vaguely remembered tugging on it, but the image was whirling in a blur of blood and contorted faces. "I might've pulled it off."

"Why'd you do that?"

His stomach turned with a hint of nausea and he swallowed hard. "I think he asked me to." Feeling another wave of queasiness, he held up his hand. "Sorry, gotta go. I don't feel too good." He hurried to the security gate leading to the elevators and opened it with his coded key fob. It closed behind him and locked.

"Wait!"

Inside the elevator, Sutherland pushed the button for his floor and watched as the detective hustled toward him. His index finger was raised, indicating yet another question.. He was stopped at the security gate, unable to pass. His face reddened, and he grabbed the gate's vertical bars. "You can't! Godammit!"

As the cop rattled the gate, Sutherland said to himself, "*Mañana*. Everything will be better *mañana*."

# CHAPTER TWO

▼

Enrique Arias slammed his Corona bottle on the bar with a resounding whack.

*"Me lleva la chingada*! I'm fucked," he barked, loud enough that a pair of patrons looked up and squinted at him through the smoky haze. One blinked and slumped back into his stupor. The other stared in Arias' general direction, eyes too glazed to see. At two o'clock in the morning, *El Chapulín Verde* was nearly deserted. Only a handful of neighborhood Latinos remained hunched over beers that had gone warm and flat. Behind the bar, the television soundlessly aired a soccer match. A faded Mexican flag hung over the row of dusty liquor bottles.

Arias glared at his nephew who stood next to him brushing melting snow from his leather jacket. *"Cómo?"* he rasped in his native Spanish. "How the fuck can you hide a whole truck? *Un chingado camion?* Tell me, Marcelo. How'd that *hijo de puta* hide a whole fuck'n truck? And how'd he get away?"

*"Quién sabe?"* Marcelo shrugged and signaled to the bartender, tipping an imaginary beer to his lips. "The *pendejo* took a bullet in the gut. We didn't think he could split. Who can run with a thirty-eight in the *vientre?"*

*"Idiotas.* Did he tell you anything?"

Marcelo gritted his teeth, expecting another rebuke. "We didn't have a chance."

*"Estúpidos.* What did he have on him?"

"Pesos, dollars, and paper with some names and numbers. Oh…a key."

"What addresses? Let me see them."

"He took his stuff with him," Marcelo mumbled, glancing away from his uncle's cold stare.

*"Chingada madre!"* Arias roared, pounding the bar with his fist. "All of it? The names? The key? Where is he now? What about the taxi?" Arias grabbed

his pack of Marlboros from the bar and fumbled out a cigarette. His hand shook as he tried to fire up his gold Dunhill. Finally having it lit, he drew in deeply.

"Took him to some apartment on the north side," Marcelo said. "We found it, but the *policía* are all over. Ambulance too."

"What are you doing about it? Where did they take him? Who did he go to see?" Arias lifted his tequila glass, his hand still shaking. He downed the contents and closed his eyes as the liquid warmed its way down. Then he turned to his nephew, trying to control his anger. "Come here. Sit a minute." He patted the seat of the adjacent barstool, and Marcelo eased onto it. "Look, Marcelo," he said, "I can't tell you why, but this is no ordinary shipment. I put you in charge, and look what happened. You blame me for being angry with you?"

Marcelo thrust out his chin. His eyes were hot with defiance. "I took care of the *campesinos*, no? Those stupid farmers."

Arias waved his hand in irritation. "*Sí,* but you did not need to kill them."

"They were just *indios*. Indian peasants."

Arias scowled and took hold of Marcelo's jacket lapel, rubbing the leather between his fingers. "The fact that you wear these expensive clothes and I send you to good schools means you are less Mexican than them? Look in the mirror, Marcelo. You are just as much *indio* — pure native stock. Save your hostility for your real enemies."

The bartender, a slender Latino with a ponytail, walked over and slid a bottle of *Negra Modelo* across the bar. Marcelo reached for it, but Arias grabbed his wrist. "How did the Castellano kid steal the truck in the first place?" Arias asked. "Where were you? With one of your *chicas*?"

Marcelo winced and tugged his arm free. "He must have been hiding in the back."

"Now you want to get drunk and let the *policía* find that truck?"

Marcelo rubbed his wrist. "What can I do now? It's late."

"Talk to the ambulance driver and the hospital. The apartment has a directory and a doorman. Do something."

Marcelo looked at his Rolex and sighed. He stood, zipped up his jacket, and slipped on his gloves. Turning for the door, he glanced sadly at his untouched beer, then walked past the empty restaurant tables and out into the snow.

Arias gestured to the bartender. "*Otro, Patrón,*" he said while pointing at his empty tequila glass.

It had been a disastrous few days for Arias. Good things were going bad at every turn. First, there were the complications with the *campesinos*. Then this

Castellano kid hijacked his shipment. The *joven* had been right under his nose, and Arias didn't know he was that *puta* Gabriela's nephew. She was another of the half-whites trying to claim Mexico's pre-Hispanic heritage for themselves, but she couldn't have known the true importance of the shipment. The rest of the discovery was nothing compared to a single piece of broken limestone. No one except the professor and Arias knew about it. If the professor had only come to him earlier, none of this would have happened.

He pulled off his glasses and rubbed his eyes, smoke-reddened and tired from days of tension. Now the *joven* is in some hospital and the *policía* are involved. Could he depend on Marcelo? His nephew was savvy enough, but he was also mean and impetuous, much like Arias at his age. Anyone seeing them together would take them for father and son. They shared the dark eyes and skin as well as the wide face and flat nose of their Olmec ancestors.

Years before, Arias promised his dying brother he'd take care of the eight-year-old Marcelo. He couldn't say no. It was his fault. His stupidity had caused his death. Arias had been too drunk to drive and hadn't seen the other car in time.

At first, the role of surrogate father wasn't easy for Arias, but, as if his brother was watching, he'd committed himself to it. The boy was hungry for love and attention back then and Arias gradually warmed to him. Before he was married, he took him on business and pleasure trips, spending his free time with him until Arias retired to his own room and his latest *chica*. Spoiled as he'd been, Marcelo expected to rise fast in the organization. However, Arias wasn't going to jeopardize a business that had taken years to build. He had a niche operation that was small enough to stay off the radar of the cartels and feds. Marcelo needed to grow up. As much as it pained him, Arias had to be tough on him.

"Enrique?" A slender woman with a blue-and-white bandana stretched tightly over her bald head came up behind him. She laid her head on his shoulder and rubbed his back. *"Podemos irnos?"* Can we go?

He relaxed with her touch and turned to look into dark eyes that struggled with pain. Esmeralda was the best thing to happen to him in this country. Friend, confidant, and his mistress for five years, she asked nothing for herself. Now she was dying.

"You were sleeping," he said. "I didn't want to wake you." Her cancer had spread and was deemed inoperable. The doctors gave her a few months at most.

"I couldn't sleep. You need a new couch in your office."

"We'll go in a minute. You rest while I have Paco warm up the car. You want a glass of water?"

"*No gracias*, I go use the *servicios*." She patted his shoulder and labored slowly to the women's restroom. Every step was a heroic feat of will.

Arias couldn't bear to watch. Wanting desperately to deny the inevitable, he focused again on Marcelo and the shipment. He threw back his tequila and made a decision. He'd give Marcelo until noon the next day. After that, he'd call on more experienced hands. Too much was at stake. Besides, he wanted Marcelo in Mexico taking care of Gabriela. Dealing with her was thirty years overdue.

# CHAPTER THREE

▼

The next morning Sutherland awoke with a Death Valley thirst. He felt as if an ax had hit him between the eyes. He was still wearing his tuxedo jacket and pants, but he'd somehow had the sense to kick off his shoes before falling into bed. Undressing, he noticed dried blood on his coat sleeves and he tossed the tux in the hamper. As he brushed his teeth and shaved, details from the previous night seeped through the fog in his head. He recalled Jimmy's phone call and the young Mexican with his pained face and bloody hands. He remembered the ambulance, the police, and the angry expression on the detective's face as he shook the security gate. Sutherland didn't look forward to talking to him again.

What a contrast to the early part of the evening. The black-tie ball had been held for his girlfriend Kelly's favorite cause. Despite his aversion to formal events, Sutherland would have suffered through it with a smile if he hadn't run into one of her board members. Sutherland couldn't let the man's patronizing attitude go unchallenged. Something he said prompted Kelly to leave the hotel ballroom—early and alone. Afterward, Sutherland ran into a buddy and closed the bar before finding his way to his empty bed.

He couldn't remember his last hangover. Thinking food was the best antidote, he pulled eggs from the refrigerator and made an omelet with jalapeño pepper, onion, and pepper jack cheese. After the eggs, two cups of coffee, three aspirin, and four slices of toast with peanut butter, he felt better physically. His head still felt spacey, as if his mind hadn't caught up with the rest of him.

So what about Javier Castellano? It had to be a mistake, even though it was a stretch to think someone else named Sutherland had a maternal connection to a Castellano. His mother, Gabriela, had left them thirty years ago when he was too young to remember. She returned to Mexico, and his father never spoke of her.

He pulled on jeans, hiking boots, and a sweater. As he brushed his hair, he thought a workout might return his normal color and eliminate the rings under his eyes. At thirty-five, he was too young to look fifty. Resolving to go to his club and exercise after he stopped at his office, he threw on a ski jacket, rolled up his tuxedo with the other dry cleaning, and took the bundle to the elevator.

The first floor showed no signs of last night's events. In the light, its high ceilings, gray marble floors and granite walls looked as elegant as a four-star hotel. After dropping off his laundry in the dry cleaning shop behind the lobby, he went to the management office. The secretary said Jimmy was fine, but she couldn't tell him anything about the Mexican. He'd have to ask the police.

On his way to the door leading to the garage, someone called his name. "Mr. Sutherland!" Angie, the old Korean woman who ran the dry cleaning shop, was shuffling after him. "Again, you no empty pockets."

In her hands, she held a cocktail napkin, three swizzle sticks, and a wad of paper with dark stains that looked like dried blood. "How in hell did I forget that?" he thought.

"You no look good," she continued. "You go slow. Marry nice girl I see you with."

He thanked her without commenting on her grandmotherly advice. He wondered what Kelly, that "nice girl," would think of Angie's suggestion. Sutherland hoped it wouldn't come up. Things were just fine the way they were. Only fools rush in.

The building garage used a valet parking system in which the attendants parked and retrieved the cars. When Aziz, one of the valets, saw Sutherland coming, he disappeared and returned a minute later with a green Jaguar sedan. Sitting in the driver's seat, Sutherland unfolded the paper he had taken from the young Mexican's boot. It was the top half of a packing slip addressed to The Chapultepec Gallery on Milwaukee Avenue. He turned it over and found a hand-scrawled message.

*"Las cosas están en el ático. La llave es para su madre. Está en peligro."*

The things are in the attic? The key is for your mother? She's in danger? Or was it meant to say Sutherland was in danger? In Spanish, it wasn't clear. He examined the wrapper, then looked around the car seat. He couldn't find a key. If the image of the young man's pained face and his bloodstained hands wasn't so fresh in his mind, he would have written this off as a joke. If it wasn't a joke, what was it? A mistake? After all these years, why would his mother suddenly appear? In danger or not? And why would anyone think he cared?

He started the engine and thought a moment. It had to be a mix-up. It had to be. He'd hand the note over to that detective and forget the whole thing. Last night would fade away, just like his hangover.

The trip down Lake Shore Drive to his Loop office took fifteen minutes. Chicago's downtown didn't see much traffic at 10:00 AM on a wintry Saturday. He parked on the street, signed in at the security desk, and took the elevator up to his floor.

The name on his office door said "Sutherland and Associates." It was a slight exaggeration considering his associates consisted of Julie, his part-time secretary, and an accountant who came in three days a month. He'd started the company nine months earlier and had contracted outside architects, engineers and attorneys. He wouldn't need more internal help until his first real estate development, a townhouse complex, took off. If everything went well, that could be soon. Even though he had little choice, the prospect of hiring more people worried him. He'd always been more successful working alone.

His subleased space was small. It had a reception desk, a copy and fax machine, coffee room, two empty cubicles, a small conference room housing his computer design system, and his corner office overlooking Madison and Clark. It wasn't impressive, but it was cheap. If he stood against the window, he could make out a sliver of the lake. His office walls were covered with renderings of a twenty-unit townhouse complex to be constructed in Lakeview, a neighborhood a few miles north of the Loop. His attorney had advised him against starting with such a large project, but Sutherland couldn't be deterred. He'd been successful as a commodities trader and real estate broker, two demanding, but unfulfilling occupations. For once, he wanted to sell something he had created himself. In a week, he expected the zoning would be approved, allowing his architect to finalize the design and the demolition crew to tear down the old buildings on the site.

He sorted through his mail and reviewed an engineering report, but he couldn't focus. It would have to wait until Monday. As much as he wanted to put the matter of Javier Castellano behind him, something about giving up the note bothered him. He made a photocopy and decided to give the original to the police. Next, he needed to sweat out his twenty-four-hour flu with some exercise.

The University Club was a five-block walk from his office. As a downtown club with most of its membership working in the Loop but living in the suburbs, the facilities were hardly used on weekends. When Sutherland arrived, the locker room was deserted except for Francisco and Juan, two Latino janitors. They were having a discussion in Spanish about the previous night's boxing match between a Mexican and a Puerto Rican. Sutherland had known Juan, a handsome, middle-aged man, for years. Francisco was new and about the same age as Javier, last night's visitor. During their good-humored argument, the way Francisco disagreed, crying *"por favorrr,"* struck a chord, like Javier's plea for help while lying there bleeding. Sutherland wondered if they were from the same region.

"Francisco, where are you from?" he asked.

The young man froze while holding a laundry bag over a bin, as if he couldn't let go. He stared at Sutherland with wide, frightened eyes.

*"De dónde eres?"* Sutherland asked.

Francisco looked to Juan, as if an answer was there, but Juan turned away. *"Michoacán,"* he finally said, dropping the bag into the bin. He picked up another from the pile, avoiding eye contact.

It then struck Sutherland that such a question could mean trouble to someone from a Latin-American country. Immigrants to the United States, legal or not, had learned to be wary of authority.

"Francisco," Sutherland said. "Don't worry, I was curious, that's all. *Que tengas un buen día."* Have a good day.

Francisco's face brightened. *"Igualmente, señor."*

Just then, a tall, sweaty, redheaded man with a squash racket rounded the corner and walked between them.

"Sorry," he said and hurried past them into the washroom.

A few minutes later, Sutherland was standing in his gym shorts in front of his locker when someone spoke from behind.

"Hello."

Sutherland turned to see the squash player. His white headband pushed his orange-red hair into a carrot top.

"I'm John Winthrop, the new pro." He had an English accent. A mustache even brighter than his hair capped his thin-lipped smile.

"Doug Sutherland. Welcome to Chicago." They shook hands. "British, are you?"

"London." His gaze darted from Sutherland's eyes to his bare torso. "You look fit. You play?"

"A little. Not in your league though." He pulled his racket from his locker and stroked a slow-motion backhand.

"Happy to give you some pointers. Where'd you learn Spanish?"

"Mexico mostly," Sutherland said. "Hung there for a while before finishing college."

"So you understand those buggers?" He hooked a thumb in the direction of the janitors. "You Yanks call them Beaners, right? Ask me, they should speak the language or go back where they came from."

Sutherland clenched his jaw and felt his stomach muscles tighten. "Those Beaners are Juan and Francisco. But why stop with them? Why not all foreigners?"

Winthrop must have sensed the negative vibes. With a strained smile, he said, "*Righto*. I better shower. Cheerio." As he slipped away, he glanced back, as if he was afraid of being followed.

Sutherland found himself gripping his racket like a club. What had pissed him off? Why did he have this strong reaction to that redheaded asshole? Did this thing with the Castellano kid remind him of his Mexican heritage? His father's parents came from Edinburgh, and jabs about Scotsmen never bothered him. He was Mexican and Scottish. What did that genetic fusion make him? He tried picturing a mariachi band playing "Yankee Doodle Dandy" on bagpipes.

His workout with the free weights was cut short when he felt a twinge in his back. With so many questions vying for answers, he couldn't concentrate on proper form, which was essential if one wanted to avoid injury. So he ran five miles on the treadmill instead, mindlessly watching CNN and telling himself he was sweating out all the bad of the last twelve hours along with the cognac. After his sauna, Sutherland called his voice mail from the University Club and picked up the message he'd hoped wouldn't come. The detective's name was Duncan, and he wanted to finish their interview. He didn't say "please" or "thank you." He also didn't sound friendly. Sutherland returned the call and agreed to come to the Western and Belmont station.

"I'll be there in a half hour," he said. "How's the kid?"

"He's hanging on, but no help," Detective Duncan said. "I hope your memory is better today, Mr. Sutherland. There's been a serious development, and it wouldn't be smart to withhold anything."

"Great," Sutherland thought after he hung up.

Retrieving Javier's note from his pocket, he turned it over and held it to the light, hoping for a revelation. Nothing. Undoubtedly, the detective would consider the damn thing "withheld evidence," but it wasn't intentional. Besides, what good would it do? The bloodstained paper meant nothing to Sutherland. What could it mean to the police? He stuffed the note back in his pocket and zipped up his jacket, confident Detective Duncan would see it his way.

As Sutherland headed across the Loop to his car, the gravity of Duncan's last words stopped him in the middle of a sidewalk crowded with weekend shoppers. What development could make the case of a mortally wounded young man even more serious?

# Chapter Four

▼

The view from Enrique Arias' twenty-fifth floor apartment took in Grant Park and Lake Michigan as far as the gray horizon. Through the floor-to-ceiling window, the panorama was like a huge black-and-white photo with the Art Institute and Aon Building bordering the snow-covered park on the right and left. Arias lounged on his leather sofa in front of the window as his nephew reported his morning's progress over the phone. Esmeralda, wearing a wig the color of her once-luxuriant black hair, was nestled beside him in the curve of his arm. She wore a heavy terrycloth robe over her pajamas. With both hands, she cradled Arias' second Bloody Mary of the morning.

Suddenly Arias bolted upright and blurted, *"Sutherland, me dijiste? Sutherland?"* After so many years, he was hearing that name again. Castellano first, now this. He put his hand over the mouthpiece and turned to Esmeralda who was looking quizzically at him.

"It's okay, *mi amor,*" he said. "Isn't it time for your medicine?"

She shrugged, then nodded, as if to say, "I'll take it, but what's the use?"

"Marta?" Arias barked in the direction of the bedroom. As if the nurse had been waiting, a plump woman wearing white hustled into the living room.

*"Sí, señor?"*

"Help Esmeralda back to bed and see she takes her pills."

Esmeralda gave Arias a kiss on the forehead, set his Bloody Mary on the coffee table, and struggled to her feet. On Marta's arm, she shuffled out of the room.

Sadly, Arias watched her go, a ghost of what she'd been. Her figure was gone, and her dark eyes had lost their sparkle. Amazingly she could still smile, that simple movement of the mouth that melted him and made him feel safe.

"*Tío Enrique?*"

Marcelo's shout over the phone line broke the spell. Arias stood up and walked to the window.

"This Sutherland, what's his first name?" he asked.

"Douglas," Marcelo said. "Lives on the twentieth floor. And there's a doorman."

"How old is he?" Gabriela had a son back then. It would make sense.

"The doorman didn't say. Just said that's who the kid asked for."

"What about the Castellano kid? *Dónde está?*"

"We tracked him to the hospital, but police are watching, and no one is talking. We tried the receptionist, but…"

"*Estúpido.* If the police are watching him, you call too much attention. What about this Sutherland? Are there police there? Can you slip by the doorman to get at him?"

"*No policía*, but there's a security gate and cameras."

"*Basta.* Enough." Arias checked his watch. It was only ten o'clock, but Marcelo's time was up. "Send the men to *El Chapulín*. You go pack. I have something you need to do in Mexico."

"Don't you want me to get to the kid?"

"I want you in San Miguel."

"But the action's here now," Marcelo whined.

"Just pack and get over here," Arias barked. "I'll have your tickets and instructions." He hung up.

If this Sutherland was the same person, he'd be in his thirties now. Once Gabriela learned the truck was coming to Chicago, she would have sent the Castellano kid to him for help. Why hadn't Arias seen this coming? It began when the *campesinos* went to Gabriela and she approached the professor. Arias knew that. When she started asking questions about the missing *campesinos* and artifacts, Arias should have taken more precautions. It was no coincidence that the kid didn't show up for work the day the shipment left San Miguel. Gabriela was the problem from the beginning, playing the Mexican heroine, protecting a heritage that wasn't hers. Getting revenge on Arias must have been like a bonus for her.

He was on to her now, and she had to know it. His men were watching her place, and the local police weren't going to raise a finger for her. Now it was up to Marcelo to redeem himself. Gabriela should know something. Even if she doesn't, she'd be useful if the Castellano kid or Sutherland weren't cooperative. The *joven* must have told or given this Sutherland something. Why else would he seek him out?

Arias lit a cigarette and watched the smoke drift upward in lazy coils. The movement, a column winding slowly to the recessed ceiling lights, inspired an idea for where to hide Gabriela while matters were resolved in Chicago. It should only take a few days. Getting to the kid might have to wait until the police eased up, but there was no reason to delay going after Sutherland. He lifted his phone again and dialed the number for the Chapultepec Gallery.

# CHAPTER FIVE

▼

Driving to the police station, Sutherland reflected on Detective Duncan's words. The implication that Sutherland was withholding something troubled him. True, he hadn't given up the note, but that was due to the late hour and his groggy condition. It wasn't an intent to hide anything, but the detective's accusatory tone set off a danger signal that was hard to ignore.

Sutherland wasn't a stranger to the law. He held a law degree, though he'd hardly used it. His deceased father was a disbarred attorney who'd been sent to prison. He knew his rights, but he also knew mistakes happen. That's what made him nervous.

He hadn't been in a police station for years and never for anything more serious than reporting an accident. Yet stepping through the door, he felt uncomfortable, as if he might not be able to leave. He assumed the assortment of humanity hanging around were the bad guys, but who knew? There were a couple hard-looking women in miniskirts, two tattooed young Latinos, and some banged-up college types who could have been on the losing end of a bar fight. Some might have been undercover or just cops in need of fashion consultants. He soon realized the good guys wore IDs and if a gun wasn't in plain sight, it meant the bulges under the clothing weren't wallets.

A uniformed officer at the reception desk made a phone call and directed Sutherland to the second floor. Detective Duncan met him at the top of the stairs. He was a little shorter than Sutherland's six-foot-one frame, but he outweighed him by a solid forty pounds. The blond hair and blue eyes gave him a clean-cut look, and his gray plaid jacket, blue shirt, and maroon tie were matched well. Duncan nodded, and his mouth twisted into what could have been a smile.

"Maybe this wasn't going to be too bad," Sutherland thought.

He motioned Sutherland to follow him down a corridor to an interview room. The walls were brick on three sides and painted green. The other wall was dark glass, probably a one-way window for observation. The metal table in the center was anchored to the floor.

After they sat facing each other across the table, Duncan said, "You can get yourself in a lot of trouble walking away from a crime scene like that."

"I was dead tired. Couldn't keep my eyes open."

"I know booze when I smell it. That don't mean you can walk away."

"Look, I came here to cooperate. I have something for you." He held up the note. "This was in his boot."

Duncan's lips drew tight. "I thought you were hiding something." He snatched the paper out of his hand.

"You gotta understand. I just woke up. Then there was all that blood. I nearly passed out right there. I stuffed that in my pocket and forgot about it. What's the big deal?"

"It's called obstruction of justice." He glared at Sutherland a second, then opened the note. He turned it over, frowned, and then turned it over again. "What's it mean?"

"Nothing to me."

"You understand this?"

"It says the things are in the attic. The key is for your mother, and she's in danger. Maybe it means I'm in danger. Either way, it's gotta be a mistake."

"So your mother's not in trouble." Duncan said.

"No idea. She lives somewhere in Mexico. I don't know where."

"You don't talk to her?" Duncan asked.

Sutherland shook his head. "Saw her once since she left. Over ten years ago." He recalled it wasn't a pleasant reunion. During their short time together he'd borne his resentment like a shield. She hadn't tried much harder at reconciliation. Maybe she still felt guilty for leaving. Maybe she didn't care.

Duncan scowled, a disapproving look. "What's her name?"

"Gabriela Castellano." Sutherland spelled it. "She has other names, but I don't know them."

Duncan wrote it down. "Interesting," he said, cocking his head. "That the same as the kid's name?"

Sutherland shrugged. "Sure, but so what?"

"The key, what's that about?"

"Beats me. Wasn't any."

Duncan turned over the paper and studied it. "This gallery, Chapultepec? You know it?"

"Sorry."

Duncan dropped the note on his desk, leaned back, and crossed his arms across his chest. He inhaled deeply, and while he exhaled, slowly shook his head. "I'll be honest, Mr. Sutherland. I just can't buy that somebody walks off the street after being shot and gives a perfect stranger a note that means nothing. You blame me?" He picked up a sheet of paper and glanced at it. "If the doorman didn't corroborate your story, we might think you shot him."

"Me? I don't even know him. I've got no idea what the note's about. Did he say anything? How bad is he?"

"Still in intensive care. We'll be talking to him when he wakes up." He smiled. "This note wasn't the only thing on him. Maybe you took off the wrong boot. Were you looking for something else? A little coke to cap off your night?"

Coke? As in cocaine? Sutherland felt his stomach lurch. " I told you. I never heard of the guy." Christ, you're sleeping off a party one minute. The next, you're in the middle of what…a drug deal?

Detective Duncan's smile turned nasty. "I see your type all the time, Mr. Sutherland. Professionals with too much money. Think drugs are cool. As long as you get your kicks, you don't care if someone gets hurt. Think the world owes you and laws don't apply. You a banker? Stockbroker? What?"

He was being accused of buying drugs. Is that what Duncan meant by the wrong boot? Javier had coke there? Is that why the poor kid got shot?

"What do you do, Mr. Sutherland?" Duncan insisted. "You don't live in places like yours on welfare."

"Ah, well…I…" This cop seemed to have it in for him. Maybe he just didn't like where Sutherland lived. Did he need to make an arrest? He'd heard of bad cops framing innocent men, but it couldn't happen to him. Could it?

"Your line of work, Mr. Sutherland. Who do you work for?"

"For myself. I'm a developer."

Duncan smirked.

"This is great," thought Sutherland. "Now he thinks I'm a drug dealer or something." This had to stop now. This cop wasn't going to roll over him.

He took a deep breath, locked on Duncan's eyes, and said, "I also know the law, so I wouldn't get ahead of yourself."

Duncan frowned, unimpressed. "You better hope that Mexican corroborates your version of things." He picked up the packing slip with the note on it. "For all I know, you wrote this. In any case, we'll talk again. Meantime, why don't you think some more, just in case something else slipped your mind. We understand each other?"

"Never clearer."

Sutherland left the room and walked down the stairs and out the front door. If he'd read the cop correctly, the kid must have had cocaine in his other boot. Lucky Sutherland knew the difference between *derecha* and *izquierda,* right and left. Otherwise, he might not be going home.

As Sutherland approached his building's parking garage, he noticed a white van with a picture of an Aztec Indian in a feather headdress on the side. It was unoccupied, partially blocking the driveway. As Sutherland squeezed the Jaguar past it, something about the Aztec's picture piqued his memory. It hit him when he handed his car keys to the attendant. The logo was the same as the one on the packing slip, the Chapultepec Gallery. Aztec chieftains were common enough in Mexico. What were the odds of coming across the identical image twice on the same day in Chicago?

He'd barely entered the lobby from the parking garage when Carl, the weekend doorman, waved and shouted from his desk, "Mr. Sutherland!" He pointed in the direction of the driveway. "Maybe you can still catch them."

Approaching the desk, Sutherland asked, "Catch who?"

Carl looked perplexed. "Your installers. I had to send them away. They were really mad. I had to threaten to call the police."

"What for?"

Carl raised his hands in a conciliatory gesture. "Sorry, you know the rules. No one admitted without written permission."

"I didn't order anything. What did they say?"

"They just waved these papers around, said something about measurements. Two Mexicans. Could barely understand them."

Sutherland hurried to the side door and stepped outside. The van was just pulling away, and he took off after them. When the van slowed at the street, he sprinted alongside the passenger window and glanced in. The sun reflected off the glass, and he could only make out a face and a cowboy hat. Sutherland slapped the window, trying to get them to stop, but the driver gunned it and the van fishtailed down the street. The rear plate was partly iced over, but he made out the numbers: 165-230.

As the van disappeared around the corner, he stood in the slush by the curb trying to get his breathing back to normal. Then, repeating the license number, he spun around and ran up the driveway. Whoever these guys were, their visit had to be related to the wounded kid. They had to be looking for something, and it wasn't some worthless note. Maybe they wanted the cocaine or whatever the police found in the boot. It was something they'd shoot a kid for.

Barging through the side door, he brushed by a woman with a baby and headed for the reception desk.

"I need some paper," he blurted to Carl.

"You catch them?" Carl asked.

"Paper," Sutherland barked. He could hardly control his voice.

Carl shrank back like a scolded dog, a hurt expression on his face. "Don't have to yell, sir." He dug beneath the desk and plopped a small pad on the counter.

Sutherland felt his shirt pocket for his pen. Dammit, must have dropped it chasing the bastards.

He plucked Carl's pen off the desk and scribbled the number. His hand was shaking so wildly the writing was barely readable. A damned stupid thing to do, he thought. It was an insane impulse to run after them. One person had already been shot. Was he trying to make it two?

# CHAPTER SIX

▼

Sutherland's hands had stopped shaking by the time he returned to his apartment. To work off the adrenaline, he began pacing the living room's hardwood floor. Visitors seeing the large space for the first time thought he hadn't finished decorating. But he had lived there since his divorce and liked it as it was. In the words of Mies, less is more. His route took him around an island of couch, chairs, and coffee table, past the stereo and two abstract oils, and ending at the north window. There, he retraced his steps to the east window and turned again, head down and focused.

"I'm involved in some drug scheme," he said to himself. "A kid gets shot, and the police suspect me of buying or dealing." He stopped. What was he concerned about? He didn't buy cocaine. No one could prove otherwise. As for the would-be intruders, the police could track them down. He had to calm himself. This would soon be over, and his only concern would be zoning approval for his townhouses.

He phoned Detective Duncan. Not finding him in, he left a message about the two men, the license number of their van, and their connection to the Chapultepec Gallery note. Feeling better for unloading a portion of his worries, he dug a beer out of the refrigerator and flicked on the television in his den. The Australian Tennis Open was on. He eased into his TV chair and propped his feet on the ottoman.

Even though he didn't play, he appreciated tennis as a game. Each player relied on his own skills. No one could win or lose it for him. As a youth, the only team sport he'd liked was baseball. As pitcher or batter, it was still one-on-one. But he'd lost his enthusiasm for it in high school when he pitched a no-hit, no-walk game, only to lose because of his teammates' fielding errors.

During a commercial, he found himself examining his old trophies on the bookshelves. He'd had a few second- and third-place finishes in local

10K races, accumulated several wins in junior sailing, and garnered two for runner-up in squash. It wasn't a great record, but it was better than any team he'd been part of. He fixed his eyes on a photo taken of him at the helm of his sailboat. At forty feet, the sloop needed six crewmen to race. As skipper, micromanaging every maneuver, he'd lost race after race and driven off his whole crew. He couldn't help himself. He had trouble depending on others.

Wasn't it the same with his careers? He'd quickly learned that law firms didn't value independence in their associates, so he quit after four months. Options trading proved to be a better match, allowing him to succeed or fail on his own. It was lucrative enough, but he wasn't producing anything tangible. Real estate brokerage had been the same. He felt like a pimp, nothing but a go-between. Now he was betting on a new venture. He would be building something, but he needed a team to do it. And the stakes were much higher than a sailing trophy.

The phone on his desk rang.

"Dammit."

He didn't want to move, but it was probably Kelly. Answering the phone, he heard Detective Duncan's brusque voice. "What's this about a van?"

Sutherland told him.

"So they didn't get in?" Duncan sounded irritated, his words clipped.

"They tried. It had the same logo as that note. The Chapultepec Gallery, remember?"

"Got it in front of me. I see your point. Don't see a thing like that everyday. We'll check it out as soon as we can. Meanwhile, you think of anything else about last night?"

"Nothing."

"Then there's nothing much we can do 'til the kid wakes up."

After Duncan disconnected, Sutherland sat and looked at the phone for a long time. It didn't seem like the Chapultepec was a priority with the police. Was the detective right? Was there nothing else to do? He couldn't clear things up until (or unless) Javier regained consciousness? Gabriela could help, but Sutherland had no idea where she lived. When he visited her, she was planning to move away from the city of Guanajuato in Mexico. She could be anywhere now. Besides, did he really want to see her?

Milwaukee Avenue was a long, diverse street. Sutherland had driven it many times, but he couldn't remember seeing the Chapultepec Gallery. It was a cold Saturday, and the tennis match was over. Why shouldn't he check into some Mexican art? Just to satisfy his curiosity. He wasn't holding his breath for the police to look into it.

The address was for a building in the middle of the block. The gallery was on the second floor. Sutherland took the elevator. When the doors opened, he thought he had returned to Mexico. He faced a mural depicting Aztec Indians battling Spanish conquistadors. It could have been painted by Diego Rivera. Copies of Frida Kahlo self-portraits hung on either side. Paintings of centuries-old cathedrals and Aztec pyramids lined the hallway. When he entered the main gallery, he saw demon masks from Michoacán, fantastic animal figures carved in Oaxaca, pottery from Chiapas, and Mayan figures from Yucatán. It was like reliving his time there. The only thing missing was the tequila.

A half-dozen people were browsing, studying a painting, handling a mask, or sizing a pot. Sutherland walked to a desk at the far end of the room. A young blonde woman sat there, writing. She looked up when he approached.

"Can I help you?" She had blue eyes, a freckled nose, and a contagious smile. Sutherland guessed she was in her twenties and unmarried, but she had a choice of interested young men.

"This is my first time here. Who does your buying?"

She put down her pencil and handed him a color brochure. "This will tell you about the shop."

He glanced at the brochure and thumbed through the eight pages of photos of Mexican artisans at their work, pueblos, and street scenes. On the last page he saw a portrait of a man and woman standing in the gallery.

"The owners?" he asked.

"Before my time. They sold it six months ago."

Sutherland read down a list of names in the brochure, the origin of the various works. One of the towns had an asterisk beside it.

"What's that mean?" he asked.

"San Miguel de Allende? An associated gallery. They ship the items to us."

The phone rang, and she answered. He wandered over to a wall where a dozen *retablos* were hung, miniatures of scenes from everyday village life. As he pretended to study one, he glanced into a room marked "Shipping" behind the young woman's desk. Inside, a teenage boy was covering a painting with plastic bubble wrap.

Sutherland moved along the wall, out of her line of sight, and stepped into the room. A copy machine sat on the left. A work table and shelves of wrapping materials were on the right. Across the room, there was a freight elevator and exit door.

"Can you help me?" Sutherland asked.

Startled, the boy looked up. He blinked and stammered in broken English, "I only working in here." He indicated the room around him.

"That's okay. Do you have your van's schedule? I'm expecting a delivery."

"Van?" the boy said.

"*Camión, camioneta?*"

"Ah." The boy nodded. "*Pero*, I pack only. Señor Sanchez, he is driver."

Just then, the freight elevator ground to a stop and the door opened. Two men stepped out. One wore a cowboy hat.

"*Señor* Sanchez," the young man said. "*Le buscaba este hombre.*" He pointed to Sutherland.

Sanchez, the man without the hat, looked Sutherland up and down. He was short and solid, and his dark eyes weren't friendly.

"*Y qué?*" was all he said.

The other man hardly glanced Sutherland's way before entering what must have been a bathroom.

Sutherland took a deep breath. He wanted information, but he didn't expect it firsthand. Then again, what could happen here?

"You were at my place earlier." He gave his address. "You talked to the doorman, right?"

Sanchez scowled and looked puzzled. "*No comprendo.*"

"Your *camioneta. Placa numero.*" He pulled out the license plate number from his pocket. "165-230? My apartment. *Ustedes vinieron a mi apartamento.*"

"*Es* mistake. And you no suppose to be here." He strode toward Sutherland with the determined look of someone prepared to use force.

Hold his ground or retreat? The Mexican was a fireplug with simian arms. Sutherland wasn't going to win a pushing contest. What would it prove if he did? The man was denying everything. With his decision made, he backed out and the door was slammed in his face.

When he turned around, the young woman was looking his way.

"Everything all right?" she asked.

"I just met Mr. Sanchez. Not very friendly."

She rolled her eyes. "I know. The warehouse and shipping guys. The people here in the shop are nice though."

"How about the new owner?"

She looked around her, as if she was afraid of being heard.

"It's kind of a mystery. I'm only here on Saturdays, and he only came in once since he bought it. He's supposed to be an archeologist, but I didn't think so. Do archeologists wear Guccis and Rolexes?"

# CHAPTER SEVEN

▼

When he returned from the gallery, Sutherland had two messages waiting for him. The first was from Kelly, reminding him that she had opera tickets for that evening.

"Damn," he thought.

After the day he'd had, it was the last thing he wanted to do. He was apparently out of the penalty box, but he could still depend on a full account of his offense at last night's ball. As he contemplated tonight's opera, *Aida*, he thought about the four hours without fidgeting. Maybe his sentence wasn't over. She instructed him to pick her up at 5:30 so they could eat first.

They had been together for five months, a record for him since his divorce six years, four months, and two days ago. They'd first met in the early nineties when both were working on a Mayan dig in Mexico near the Guatemalan border. She was on summer break from college. He had just dropped out and was on a quest to find himself. They were only casual friends then, and when the project was over, she set off for Costa Rica and he continued wandering around Mexico. Fifteen years later, they had a chance encounter in a bookstore, which ended in a lunch date. It had been the start of a good thing, but he wasn't sure how far it would go. Both of them were products of broken homes, and both were divorced. It wasn't a history conducive to snap decisions about marriage.

The second caller hadn't left a message. Sutherland just heard a pause before the click.

Sutherland leafed through the Chapultepec Gallery's pamphlet again. Colorful photos of artisans didn't explain Javier's visit or what these people were after. He threw the folder on his desk, deciding to forget it and let the police handle it.

He was in his den when the phone rang.

"Mister Sutherland?" It was a guttural male voice with a Spanish accent. "Douglas Sutherland?"

"Depends," he said. "Who's this?"

"That is not important." The gravelly tone suggested a heavy smoker. "Last night the boy gave you directions on where to find something of mine. I would like to have it, *señor* Sutherland."

Was this the man who shot Javier?

Sutherland felt himself shudder. "There's some mistake. I don't know what this is about."

"Your mother sent the boy to take something from me," the man continued. "We found the taxi driver who dropped him at your apartment. We talked to your doorman. It was you the boy came to see."

"He gave me a note, and I gave it to the Chicago Police. Talk to them."

"If it was only words, he could have called. What else did he give you?"

"No drugs, if that's what you're thinking." Sutherland wanted this to be over. If he told him everything, he figured he might go away. "The note said something about the things in the attic. Beats me what it means."

"He must have given you more than that. An address? A key?"

"He was shot, remember? Maybe you did it." Sutherland said. "He passed out after giving me the note. Anything else went on the ambulance with him."

"No, Mister Sutherland. We checked the emergency room."

"Then you're out of luck. I don't know the kid or what it's about. And I don't want to." He hung up and exhaled, as if expelling something noxious.

The phone rang again. He let the answering machine pick up. After his own voice finished its greeting, the stranger said, "I think you can hear me, *señor*."

Sutherland just stared as the machine recorded.

"You saw what happened to the boy who fucked with me," the man said.

Sutherland eyed the recorder, as if it was about to leap at him.

"If you give us everything, we'll be gone. I will call again in an hour. Be a smart man, Mister Sutherland."

He disconnected. This man wasn't giving up. He or one of his men shot Javier, tracked him, and talked to the doorman. How could Sutherland prove he didn't have what they wanted?

Sutherland tapped in Detective Duncan's number again and got his voice mail.

"Listen to this," he said after the beep. "This guy just threatened me."

He replayed the recording over the phone. When it was finished, he said, "He admitted shooting Javier Castellano, Detective. Now he's after me. You still think I'm guilty of something?"

If the stranger did call back, nothing would have changed…except Sutherland would be picking Kelly up for dinner and the opera. He was in no mood for it, but maybe a hall full of opera lovers was the safest place to be.

# CHAPTER EIGHT

▼

Sutherland pulled to the curb in front of Kelly's condominium building at 5:25. He'd forwarded his home number to his cell phone, though he hadn't decided if he'd answer if the stranger called again. How many times could he deny having what they wanted?

Kelly, in a long black coat and white scarf, came out of the building's front door and picked her way down the icy walk to the Jaguar. She slid in and closed the door. The overhead light gleamed on the chestnut hair framing her face. He saw her green eyes flick to the silver wristwatch on her left arm before she smiled at him and said, "Not bad."

"Do I detect a hint of sarcasm?" He leaned over, and she met him with a warm kiss. It was a good sign.

"A compliment. You're early." She pulled the seat belt around her. "You excited about *Aida*? I am."

"I wish I were. It hasn't been a good day."

"Don't feel well?" She smiled. "Serves you right."

"You going to tell me what particular sin pissed you off?"

It had been a charity ball, black-tie and expensive. He only agreed to go because Kelly was on the fund-raising committee. In a crowd of people he didn't know or care to meet, he was apt to say what he thought. That didn't always sit well with those who were used to platitudes.

He pulled away from the curb and headed toward the Loop.

"Don't worry," she said. "I'm over it. Anyway, my leaving gave you a chance to close the bar with Marco."

Someone must have told her. He knew Marco from law school. Sutherland had run into him after Kelly left the ball. His was a friendly face among strangers.

"We did some catching up," he said. "But let me tell you what happened. It's weird."

"Uh-oh. Where'd you go from there?"

"Home. That's when it started. After I went to bed," he said.

"Maybe you should keep it to yourself."

"You've got a dirty mind. Listen."

So much had happened that he barely believed it himself, but he summarized everything from Javier's visit to the threatening phone calls. She didn't say a word. Every time he glanced her way, she was staring back with her head slightly cocked. He finished just as they pulled into the parking garage a block away from the Civic Opera Building. As he turned off the ignition, she was looking at him as if he had just told her he could fly.

"Well?" he said after a long silence.

"You're bullshitting me."

"All true." He handed her the copy of Javier's note. "Read this."

After a year in Costa Rica and another in Spain, her Spanish was much better than his. She read it and shook her head.

"And your mother's in Mexico?"

"She was born there."

"She's Mexican?" He nodded.

"I've known you all this time, and you never mentioned that? You ashamed of her?"

"What difference does it make?"

"You are one strange guy, Doug."

"Excuse me, but drug smugglers are threatening me and trying to get into my place. Meanwhile, the police think I'm doing cocaine." He looked down at the console to make sure the phone was still on. "And this *pendejo* is supposed to call back any time."

She stared through the windshield. There was nothing to see except a concrete wall. Her lips were moving as if she was talking to herself.

Finally she said, "I know you're worried. Lots of bad stuff happening. Even so, I thought we were starting a relationship. You couldn't tell me about your own mother? I assumed she'd died, for crissakes."

He took a deep breath and exhaled slowly. "Look, I'm sorry. It's just a thing with me. I promise I'll explain, but it'll take some time. How about after the opera?"

"You're not wiggling out of it."

"I won't." He looked at his watch. "If we want to eat first, we better go."

They hurried across Wacker Drive to the Civic Opera Building's lobby. While they were waiting for the elevator, she slipped her arm under his and said, "Maybe he won't call. Maybe he believed you don't have what he's looking for."

"Let's hope so."

"At any rate, he better call soon," she said. "You'll get lynched if that phone goes off during the performance."

"Lynched? Opera buffs are too refined for that."

"Let's not test them."

They ate dinner in the Tower Club, a full floor of wood-paneled rooms at the top of the building. On opera nights, it guaranteed prompt service. The main room was nearly full, and the warm lighting and animated chatter made Sutherland forget the cold they had left outside.

Kelly was wearing a new black dress that revealed just enough cleavage to keep a man's interest. With her shoulder-length, chestnut hair, high cheekbones, thick eyebrows over green eyes, and a full, smiling mouth, she looked more like a cover girl than the brightest student in her law school class five years earlier. While they ate their salads, she told him about her progress on her latest cases as an attorney for the City of Chicago.

"I've nearly got that scumbag landlord nailed for fraud," she said. "And we're close to a settlement on that playground injury case. I spent all day in the office today. The more I get done, the more crap's in my in-box. We need two more lawyers with our load."

"Why do you put up with it? You could work for anyone. Name your price."

"Money isn't the issue. Besides, I don't want to get on the billable hours treadmill. I'm thinking maybe the public defender's office." She sipped her Chardonnay and nodded her approval. "How about you? Any news on your zoning?"

"I'm waiting for the zoning committee meeting. A week or so, max. Meantime, I can't do much." He glanced at his cell phone, hoping it wouldn't ring. "I might as well leave town. Why don't we charter a sailboat in the Virgin Islands? Balmy breezes…white sand."

"You sail all summer. Besides, if I ever cleared my schedule, I'd vote for scuba diving."

He felt a shudder, and the familiar image of being underwater with the surface far above flashed to mind.

"What's wrong?" she said "You're pale."

He gulped down a mouthful of wine. "You know about my nightmares. Nix the diving."

She shook her head. "You don't think that's odd? A sailor afraid of water?"

It wasn't the first time he'd faced the inconsistency. He didn't understand it either, even though he had a pat answer. "I'm afraid of being underwater. Sailing, when done correctly, takes place on the surface."

"It's still weird. Any idea how it started? When you got that?" She pointed to his cheekbone where he had a comma-shaped scar. An accidental jibe on his father's sloop had swept the boom around, knocking him overboard, unconscious.

"I had the nightmares long before that. It took my father years to get me on a boat. If there was a trauma earlier, I don't remember. The funny thing is, I had the dream last night. It's been a while."

"The same one? The closet? The man with the burning hair? What's that about?"

He shrugged. "Who understands dreams? Burning hair? Go figure. This time, I woke up before crashing into the water though."

She glanced over his shoulder and stiffened.

"Damn," she said. "Wouldn't you know?"

"What?"

"Lawrence Reynolds, the man you pissed off last night."

He turned to see a burly man with rusty hair and graying temples.

"Oh…him."

The ball had been for Grassroots World Wide, a nonprofit that made micro-loans for small business start-ups in developing countries. A hundred dollars would buy a sewing machine for a single mother so she could pull her family out of poverty. Kelly had spent several years in Latin America and was now a volunteer director of the organization, monitoring loans there. Last night's event, the $250 per ticket ball, was her idea.

"He has awfully thin skin. What did he say?" Sutherland asked.

"He claimed you'd insulted him and defamed our whole organization," she said. "He said it loudly and in front of my whole committee. I wanted to crawl into a hole."

"He tell you what I said?"

"I wouldn't want to guess," she said. "You didn't want to be there. You had a few drinks…"

"I was still drinking soda. The cognac came later." He hooked his thumb in Reynolds' direction. "He's a pompous ass. Besides, I thought you said strings would never be attached to your loans."

She arched her brows. "Did he say there was?"

"Not yet. He said there'd be big changes when he became chairman. Borrowers would have to give up some of their practices and change their beliefs. I didn't ask what."

"Uh-oh." She swallowed. "What did you say?"

"I simply said the Spanish tried that centuries ago. They destroyed whole civilizations and fucked up the better part of two continents."

She stared at him with her fork suspended halfway to her mouth.

"Was that an insult?" he asked.

She put her fork down, tightly drawing her lips. Sutherland inhaled, preparing for an onslaught. Instead, she blurted, "He's wrong. We're not like that. If he tries to change us, I'll fight him." She glared over his shoulder at the director's table. After breathing deeply, she said, "I think he's alone. He'll never be chairman."

He exhaled. "Does this mean we're okay?" He folded his napkin and reached for his phone.

She pointed to the phone. "Not if you're leaving that on."

"Would I do that?" He made a show of turning it off, but put it on vibrate instead.

During the overture and most of the first act, he tried pushing the events of the last twenty-four hours from his mind. Unfortunately, the call came during the chant of the priestesses in the second scene of the first act.

"Hello," he whispered and Kelly jammed her elbow into his ribs. "Just a minute."

He stood and sidestepped past grumbled epithets and scowling faces along the row. He then went up through the doors to the mezzanine vestibule.

"Hello, you there?"

"Mr. Sutherland, this is Bob at the front desk. Your guests are here."

It took him a second for it to register. His home phone was forwarded here. When it struck him, he felt a shiver as he realized someone was in the lobby of his apartment building and wanted to go up. He sat on a bench and collected his thoughts.

"Bob, listen carefully," he said. "You are not to let anyone up. Understand?"

"Just a minute." There was a few words with another person. and then Bob spoke again. "Mr. Sutherland, he wants to talk to you."

"Put him on."

A moment later, the same guttural voice from earlier said, "I come to expedite things. You can give it to me, and I'll be gone." His tone was friendlier than earlier, probably for the doorman's sake.

"Give you what? There was just the note about the attic."

"Did I mention your mother's health could suffer without your help." A hint of menace entered his tone.

"What about her?" Sutherland said.

"Why not let me come up?"

"Tell me," Sutherland snapped.

"We are watching her. She's fine for now."

"I gave you everything," he said. "As for her, I haven't seen her in years. Why do I care?"

"I find that hard to believe. She keeps your photo. She sent that boy to you from San Miguel." His tone turned icy. "Now why don't I come up?"

It wasn't a mistake. Gabriela had started this, and she was in trouble. How could Detective Duncan protect someone in Mexico? Sutherland needed time to think.

"Give me the doorman," he said.

He heard some voices and then Bob spoke again, "Should I let them up, Mr. Sutherland?"

"How many are there?"

"Two."

"Tell them to call tomorrow. And Bob, call the police."

After a pause, Bob said, "Sure, Mr. Sutherland."

The usher wouldn't let him back in until intermission. He couldn't sit through the opera now anyway. He wanted to leave, but his coat and car keys as well as Kelly were inside. Instead, he ordered a scotch at the bar and walked the lobby. While he paced, he called Detective Duncan again, leaving a message about the latest visitors to his condominium building. Sutherland had to talk to Javier before the man called again. He would go to the hospital tonight and hope for the best.

The first act finally ended, and people spilled into the lobby. He fought against the flood of bodies, rehearsing what he'd say to Kelly and how he'd escape the fat lady singing. His topcoat was on his seat, but Kelly had left the other way.

The note on his program said, "I have your car keys. If you're thinking of leaving, forget it. You still owe me that explanation, *cabrón*. I'll be at the bar."

# CHAPTER NINE

▼

Sutherland found Kelly with a glass of red wine in her hand. When he told her about the visitors to his apartment building, she swallowed slowly.

"Anxious, aren't they? This thing with your mother. Are you sure it's her?"

"My question exactly. He said she had my photograph and she sent the Mexican kid, Javier, to me."

"It still doesn't mean…"

"That's why I have to leave."

"To see Javier?" she said.

"Right."

She put down her empty wineglass and fished his car keys out of her coat pocket.

"What are we waiting for? This is a hell of a lot more critical than the fate of Radames and Aida."

They left as the audience was reentering for the second act. Back in the car, the snow was enough to make the driving interesting. The Jaguar was a fair-weather cat.

"You know," she said as she fixed her lipstick in the visor mirror, "I'm sensing a trend here. It took a month to learn you were divorced. Two more months to learn you had a daughter. From your silence about your mother, I thought she'd died. Tell."

"There isn't much to tell. She split when I was four. Back to Mexico. It fries me that she's involved me in this."

"Why'd she leave?"

"My father never said. I was too proud to ask her."

"You saw her since?" Kelly asked.

"Once. Remember the dig where we met? When you went to Costa Rica, I went north. I passed through Guanajuato where she lived. We said hello, had lunch, and I left."

"What is she like?"

"She's an artist." He pictured the woman he'd met that day. She had called him *guapito,* as if he were a boy of five, not nineteen. "I think she's a kind of amateur archeologist."

"Look like you?"

"No. She was prettier than the snapshot my father kept hidden though. Dark eyes and black hair. She had light skin and looked more European than Indian."

"What if it is your mother they're talking about?"

"I don't know. She's Gabriela, a lady in Mexico, to me. She's never been my mother." What gave her the right to drag him into this shit? Hadn't she done enough?

They turned off Dearborn, passed the Newberry Library, and headed north on Clark. Snowflakes swirled in eddies around the parked cars. There was little accumulation, just a suggestion of what might come.

His thoughts returned to Javier.

"He may be under arrest or protection," he said. "You'd think they'd let me see a kid claiming he's my cousin. Detective Duncan might have to okay it. I just tried him, and he's not in. If we have to get past a cop, what's your choice: persuasion or stealth?"

"How about pretending to be a doctor? Tell them we're his lawyers."

Sutherland laughed. "Nobody's that stupid."

"How about diversion? I show some leg and lure him away. It worked in a movie."

Glancing sideways at her, he said, "You have too much free time."

"We could get lucky. Maybe there's no police."

When they arrived at St. Joseph Hospital, it was 9:15. Two squad cars were outside the front entrance. So much for luck.

He parked in the garage, and they walked through a dusting of snow to the lobby. Four uniformed policemen milled around inside, relaxed and chatting. One of them saw Kelly open her coat and said something to the others. All heads turned. From their expressions, the only thing missing was the wolf whistles. Whatever emergency had brought them seemed to be over.

"You'd think you had donuts in that dress," Sutherland whispered as he guided her to the main reception desk. A young woman was staring at a computer screen. Behind him, Sutherland heard the cops heading out the front doors. Their good-byes were salted with a few groans when the cold hit them.

"Why all the police?" he asked the woman.

She didn't look up. "Some troublemakers. They're gone."

"Glad to hear it." With the police out of the way, maybe their luck was back. "What's Javier Castellano's room number? He's my cousin."

She flinched. He followed her quick glance outside in time to see the last squad car's taillights disappear into the street. When she turned back, she looked them over while biting her lip. He straightened his tie and considered Kelly's cocktail dress. Anyone would regard them as respectable citizens.

"Just a minute." She picked up the phone, dialed a number, and swiveled her chair so her back was to them. Then she hunched over and spoke in muffled tones into the handset. Sutherland shrugged at Kelly and she returned a doubtful smile.

"What now, Sherlock?" she asked.

"White coat and stethoscope? Search from room to room?"

"Too many rooms," she said. "Do we run?"

"Why? We haven't done anything."

When the receptionist hung up, she smiled at them and said, "Someone will help you shortly."

After a minute passed, the elevator opened and Detective Duncan strode toward them. Two men who looked like plainclothes police followed close behind.

"So it's you." Duncan grinned. "Here to see your Mexican friend? He's a popular boy."

"Popular?"

"That's why we're here." Duncan gestured to include the men behind him. "Couple guys tried to get to him. Our man stopped them."

"Probably the same guys who tried my place. You catch them?"

Duncan frowned. "Slipped out somehow."

"Try the Chapultepec Gallery yet?"

"It's on my list. Now it's time we had another talk. Who's this?" He inspected Kelly from head to toe.

"Kelly Matthews, a friend. Is he awake?"

Duncan stared at Kelly for a second longer than necessary before addressing Sutherland again. "Why are you here?"

"You get my messages? Badasses are calling, coming around, and threatening me. I thought Javier could tell me why."

"You don't know what they want?"

"That key I don't have. Now they're threatening my mother in Mexico. You heard, right?"

"Yeah, I heard." The detective scratched his cheek. "Our boy came around for a while this afternoon. We questioned him, but he couldn't—or wouldn't—talk."

"Let me try."

"You're not his attorney. He's a suspect."

"What's he accused of? Getting shot?"

"He had drugs on him."

"Let's find out why. He says he's my cousin. Whether he is, I don't know, but he may talk to me."

Detective Duncan furrowed his brow as if this was a life-or-death decision. He finally said, "I guess so. But we need a translator."

"What for? I can speak to him."

"An official one. He can be here in ten minutes."

The translator was a thin, coffee-colored man in uniform. His name was Carlos and from his accent, Sutherland pegged him as Puerto Rican. Carlos, Duncan and Sutherland took the elevator to the third floor. Kelly was left, under protest, in the lobby with the two plainclothes officers.

Javier Castellano's room was at the end of a pale green corridor. When they entered, they found a uniformed policeman in a chair watching television. Javier was propped up in his bed with his eyes closed. A tube taped to his wrist led to an IV bag hanging on a stainless steel pole. Another tube extended from his nose to an oxygen machine. When Detective Duncan turned off the television, Javier opened his eyes halfway. Two bleary pools peered out through narrow slits. After a long moment, he seemed to recognize Sutherland.

He took a deep breath and whispered, *"Primo."*

*"Qué tal?"* Sutherland said.

"Wait a minute," Duncan said. "I gotta know what's happening. Carlos?"

Carlos rolled his eyes. "The *chico* said 'cousin.' The other said 'how's it going?'"

Sutherland sat down in the bedside chair. Carlos stood behind him. Detective Duncan took out a notebook and eased into a chair near the window. Sutherland started with last night's brief conversation. *"Javier, anoche me dijiste que mi madre estaba en peligro. No?"*

The injured man took another breath, winced, and exhaled, "*Sí.*" His eyes were closed again, and his breathing was labored. Meanwhile, Carlos was telling Duncan that the kid had said Sutherland's mother was in danger.

"*Por qué?* Why my mother?"

"*Artefactos,*" he said with effort. "They rob the excavation. She find out."

"Who gives a shit about stolen artifacts?" Detective Duncan said after he heard the translation. "Ask him about the drugs."

Javier lifted his head and glanced in Duncan's direction. Maybe he understood English after all. Then he closed his eyes again and sagged into the pillow with his mouth wide open. Sutherland shook his arm. "Javier. Can you hear me? *Puedes oirme?*"

Nothing.

"He's out," Sutherland said.

"Convenient," Duncan said. "But he can't sleep forever. We'll get it out of him. What's with the artifacts?"

"Could be connected to the Chapultepec Gallery," Sutherland said. "Someone robbed them, and my mother discovered it. The connection makes sense. She supposedly lives in San Miguel, where there's also a branch of the gallery."

"You sure like that gallery angle," Duncan said. "Part of a drug ring?"

"I wish I knew because the guy's gonna call again. What do I tell him?"

"You don't know anything, so what's the problem?" Duncan stood, put his notepad in his inside pocket, and buttoned the jacket as he prepared to leave.

"I don't want to end up like him." Sutherland pointed to Javier. "You gonna give me a bodyguard?"

"You serious? Just keep a low profile and stay out of this."

Sutherland thought for a moment. Whatever was happening had its origins in Mexico. Chicago was downstream. Maybe he should get out of there. The Caribbean sounded pretty good. "Does leaving town qualify as low profile?"

"Where you thinking of going? Mexico?"

"No. Just where people aren't after me."

"If you interfere, I'll have your ass." He raised his index finger. "Don't hold anything out on me. Got that?"

"Perfectly. I'll keep you posted, and I'm sure you'll do the same." He couldn't keep the sarcasm out of his tone.

Duncan scowled and left the room. Carlos gave Sutherland a smile and a thumbs-up signal, then followed Detective Duncan into the hallway. He apparently didn't like the detective either.

Sutherland returned to the hospital lobby and found that Kelly had left. She left a message with one of the policeman saying she'd take a cab and meet him in his apartment.

He drove to his building and dropped his car with the parking valet. In the lobby, he saw Bob, the doorman he had talked to several hours earlier. When Bob saw Sutherland, he shook his head with a look that said, "I hope I don't gotta do that again."

"Any trouble getting rid of those two guys?"

"I had to call the cops."

"What did they look like?"

"Latinos. The talker was in a suit. Dark skin, black hair, mustache. The other was bigger and wearing jeans. He didn't say anything."

Probably the same guys who were at the hospital.

"You see Kelly come in?"

Bob seemed puzzled for a moment. "Sorry, been busy. I had to help Mrs. Abrams with her luggage. Then the pizza delivery guy showed. She could've gone up then."

Waiting for the elevator, Sutherland realized how tired he was. It had been a trying day after a long night. He only wanted a glass of wine and a good night's sleep. For once, he hoped Kelly wasn't in the mood for love.

Getting off the elevator on the twentieth floor, he heard the television blaring from the apartment across the hall. His neighbor was watching the fights. He dug his keys out of his pocket, but his door handle turned without the key. Kelly apparently hadn't locked it after entering.

Careless.

# CHAPTER TEN

▼

Sutherland pushed open the apartment door and listened. Kelly had preceded him by at least ten minutes, so he expected to hear music, maybe the latest CD she'd bought him. Instead, the only sound was the nasal voice of the boxing announcer coming from across the hall. He closed and locked the door, flicked on the vestibule light switch, and called, "Kelly?"

No answer. He dropped his coat on the hall table and walked into the living room. The automatic timer had turned off the floor lamp, and the room was dark. By the glow through the windows, he could see that no one was there. He started toward the rear of the apartment and called again, "Kelly?"

His senses strained for an answer. Hearing nothing, a rush of panic hit him. He took a few deep breaths, telling himself it was just paranoia from all this Javier crap. His apartment was long and narrow, and the walls were solid. Kelly wouldn't hear a cannon go off if she was in a rear room. She was just in the master bedroom.

He passed through the dining room and went into the kitchen. He pulled out two wineglasses and found a good bottle of California Merlot in the wine rack. Grabbing the corkscrew, he carried it with the bottle and glasses down the corridor.

"Kelly?"

When her answer still didn't come, icy prickles shot up his neck to his scalp. He stopped and listened. Silence. He tiptoed to the master bedroom door on his left. The light was on, and he glanced inside. No Kelly. Beyond, on the right, the den door was open halfway, allowing light into the hall. Before he could call out again, he heard a thump and a sharp crack, as if a pane of glass had broken inside. The words that followed were unintelligible, but it was a man's angry voice.

Sutherland retreated into the master bedroom and tossed the bottle and glasses on the bed. After a quick glance around, he plunged into the closet. He shoved aside the hanging clothes, knocked over the squash racquets, and found his aluminum softball bat.

He bounded down the hallway to the den. He kicked the door completely open and jumped aside. From within, a man calmly said, "No need to fuss, Mr. Sutherland. Nobody's gonna hurt anybody."

Sutherland gripped the bat with both hands and stepped into the doorway. A glance told him there were two men...and no Kelly.

"Where is she?" he demanded, threatening the closest man with the bat.

The man sat unfazed in Sutherland's desk chair. He looked to be in his late fifties with neatly cut silver hair; thick, snow-white eyebrows; and a ruddy face, like a red Irishman who had been in the sun too long. The suit under his open overcoat was a conservative navy blue. The flat stomach and muscular neck indicated he was fit. Despite his relaxed posture and easy smile, his pale blue eyes said he was a careful man.

Sutherland turned to the other man on his right. Erect as a sentry, he stood against the wall with his hands behind him. Even in suit and tie, his stance, square jaw, and buzz cut shouted military.

"What the hell is this?" Sutherland said, brandishing the bat. "Where's Kelly?"

The seated man held up both palms in a peace gesture. "She's fine. Let me explain."

"Where is she?" Sutherland took a step toward him. The standing man sprang forward, his large hands ready in front of him. They were empty, but it didn't matter. They looked like forged iron. Sutherland gripped the handle tighter.

"Let me introduce myself." The first man stood and reached into his suit pocket. He flipped open a leather wallet containing a silver-and-gold badge and a photo. "I'm Agent James Christopher with the DEA. That's Agent Bradley." The other man nodded, but remained poised for action. "We're here about the Castellano boy."

Sutherland waved the bat again. "I'm only asking once more. Where's Kelly?"

"I had her driven home after she let us in."

"Bullshit. Why would she leave?"

"This doesn't concern her."

"I want to talk to her."

"She tried calling you."

That could be true. Sutherland remembered turning his phone off after seeing Detective Duncan. But Kelly wouldn't calmly go with them. She was smarter and more stubborn than that.

Agent Christopher raised his wallet closer, like an offering. Sutherland stepped close enough to read it, but he was still ready with the bat. The photo matched the man. Agent James Christopher with the United States Drug Enforcement Agency. He stood a few inches shorter than Sutherland but, judging by how solid he looked, he weighed more.

"That mean you can just bust in here?" Sutherland said. "You got a warrant?"

"What for? Your girlfriend let us in. Have a seat, and I'll explain." Christopher gestured to the leather chair in a corner.

"I'll stand." Sutherland couldn't decide whether he was more worried, scared, or angry, but he was too jumpy to sit. Even with the bat, he doubted his chances with Bradley.

He backed against the wall and noticed several of the desk drawers were open. This was his private room. The shelves housed his trophies. The walls were covered with his photographs. Even Kelly knew not to meddle here.

On the hardwood floor was a picture of his father's sloop, the boat he learned to sail on. The glass was cracked, as if it had fallen. He faced Christopher again.

"What's with this?" He pointed with his bat to the broken photo.

"Sorry about that. An accident. Look, we're all on the same side. We just want to ask what the Mexican boy gave you."

"Just a note. Why don't you talk to Detective Duncan, the cop on this thing? I'll call him." Sutherland reached for the phone on the desk.

Christopher pulled the jack from the wall. "Hold on. Understand something." His tone was friendly but firm. "The man who called you is Enrique Arias. The Chicago Police know nothing about him. He's a drug dealer and a lot worse. He's small enough to stay out of the way of the cartels, but he's big enough that we want him. With this latest thing, we finally have the means. Because of that kid, you're in the middle of it."

"His name is Arias? Well, like I told him, I don't know anything. Nothing about the attic or the key Javier's note talked about. I just saw the kid in the hospital. He said it was about stolen artifacts. Ask Duncan. He was there."

"There's more to it than the artifacts. What else did he tell you?"

"That's it. You got a card? If I learn anything, I'll call."

Christopher took out a pen and scribbled a number on the back of an envelope laying on the desk. "It's a private line. Look, Arias mentioned your mother, right?"

"How did you know?"

"I told you. We've been after him a long time," Christopher said. "You can protect your mother and help us at the same time. We only want Arias."

Sutherland looked at his watch. "Kelly should be home by now. Let's call."

"Let's finish our business first," Christopher said, moving in front of the phone.

"Why won't he let me call?" Sutherland thought, raising the bat. Christopher backed away. Bradley inched forward.

"Hold it there," Sutherland said." Bradley stopped. His hands were at his sides, but they were ready. Sutherland said, "One last chance before I break someone's head."

"Okay, we'll call," Christopher said with his hands up. "She's all right. Believe me."

Sutherland saw Bradley reach into his coat and panicked. Was he going for a gun? With a leap, Sutherland was on him, swinging. Bradley partially deflected the blow, but it hit his ear with a whack. He dropped like an empty suit. Sutherland's momentum carried him into the wall. When he turned, Christopher was charging him. Sutherland blocked the first thrust, but a punch to the solar plexus put him on his knees. He couldn't breathe. As he gasped for air, he saw a fist flashing down on him. His last image was the object that had flown from Bradley's hand.

A cell phone.

# CHAPTER ELEVEN

▼

He was inside a coffin. It was cold, and water was flooding in. The man with the flaming hair was there, laughing in his face and making the lights go out. It was the same dream except someone was shouting his name this time.

Sutherland awoke facedown. Through his left eye, he saw a dark stain on the carpet. Lifting his head, he felt a pain in the back of his neck. He tried cursing, but his mouth was dry, and nothing came out.

"Doug." He heard a familiar female voice, smelled peach-scented hand lotion. "Are you awake? You all right?" Her voice was strained and anxious.

A shadow moved above him. He felt a smooth hand stroke his cheek.

"I'll call an ambulance." A man's voice this time.

"Wait," she said. "He's awake."

Sutherland's head was clearing. His encounter with Agents Christopher and Bradley returned in fragments. He pushed himself up on his side and peered into Kelly's face. She was in the dress she'd worn to the opera, but her hair was pulled back in a ponytail and her eye makeup was smeared. The doorman was hovering over her.

"I was so worried," she said. "You wouldn't wake up."

Sutherland nodded carefully while he inventoried his injuries, checking for broken parts. His chest and neck hurt. The metallic taste in his mouth could have been blood or fear. That was about it. He twisted into a sitting position and croaked, "S'okay. I'm all right."

"The DEA agent said you weren't hurt bad. His partner looked awful." She pointed to the bat. "You hit him with that?"

"Yep." He could still see the agent's pained face, feel the impact of the bat, and hear the metal striking bone. He'd bashed a man's head because of a fucking cell phone. This bullshit was really getting to him.

"Get me some water?" he said. She hurried from the room. Sutherland turned onto his hands and knees and the doorman helped him to the desk chair. By the time Kelly returned with a glass and a washcloth, his dizziness had cleared. He drank, and between sips, she dabbed his face with the damp cloth. For a while, they were silent, as if no one knew what to say. Finally, Sutherland said, "I was worried about you. You okay?"

"Why wouldn't I be?"

"I thought they kidnapped you. I don't know. It happened so fast. I come into my place, and two strangers are waiting. You let them in?" he asked.

"Not right away," she said. "They were in their van when the taxi dropped me off. They showed me their badges. The head guy knew all about Javier, the detective, and everything else. I didn't think this would happen."

"How did they know who you were?"

She shrugged. "Who knows about these feds? They even knew where I worked."

"I've gotta get back," the doorman said. "Want me to call the police?"

Sutherland thought about another session with Detective Duncan and said, "No. I just want to sleep."

After the doorman left, Sutherland said, "Why did you go? I'm surprised you agreed."

"They were very courteous but insistent. Said it was secret government business and all. So I went. I planned to return after I changed my clothes. We never got to my place. The driver got a call, and we turned around to take the injured guy to the hospital. The head agent said you overreacted. You went after his partner when he reached for his cell. He had to take you out so you didn't cream him, too."

"Overreacted," Sutherland said, rubbing his neck. "I was sure you were in trouble."

"I thank you for that." She leaned over and kissed his forehead. "Now you know it's about drugs."

"According to Javier, it's about stolen artifacts. Either way, why did I get sucked into it?"

The phone rang at 7:00 AM. Kelly shook Sutherland awake. She was already dressed in jeans and one of his shirts. The call was from Christopher. Before Sutherland could say a word, he said, "Sorry about putting you out, but you almost killed Bradley."

"What did you expect?" Sutherland growled. "You showed up like that, surprised me, and nearly kidnapped Kelly."

"I said I'm sorry. Next time, we'll call first."

The more Sutherland relived their ambush and his uncertainty about Kelly's safety, the angrier he became.

"There is no next time. If you want to bust this guy, be my guest. Work with the police or the FBI. Hell, for all I care, call Batman. Just leave me out of it."

"I understand, Mr. Sutherland." Christopher's tone grew more conciliatory. "But it's not that simple. As long as Enrique Arias thinks you know where his shipment is, you're involved. I know him. He won't stop. He knows all about your mother. If he gets desperate, he'll have her picked up. You can stop that."

"Why her?"

"Couple reasons. She sent the Mexican kid. She may know where he hid the shipment. If not, she can be used to coerce you. Arias thinks you're helping her."

"Sounds like you know more about her than me. Can't you warn her? Protect her?"

"She's in Mexico, and we don't know where. Just someplace around San Miguel de Allende. She doesn't have a phone listed." From the way he pronounced Allende, he didn't speak Spanish.

"What am I supposed to do?" Sutherland asked.

"Think back to what the Mexican kid said. He must have explained that note or given you a key. It's natural that you don't remember everything."

"Why would you think that?"

"The ambulance driver said you smelled like a saloon."

"I remember perfectly. Javier Castellano didn't say or give me anything else. Why don't you interrogate him?"

"So far, he won't talk. Besides, he needs another operation," Christopher said. "We don't have that kind of time."

"You'll have to make time because I can't help."

"That's too bad, Mr. Sutherland, because Arias won't quit. He'll get what he wants either from you or your mother. It doesn't matter which one of you. If you don't really know anything, he'll go for your mother. We can help you. We can put away Arias with this latest play, but the ball is in your court. You got my number."

He hung up.

Kelly set a coffee cup on the bedside table. "The same guy?" She'd been listening.

"Called to apologize."

"Is the agent all right?"

"I guess. Can you do me a favor?" he said as he got out of bed. "While I shower and change, will you make flight reservations for San Miguel? I want the fastest flight leaving today."

She followed him into the bathroom. "The hell I will. Why?"

"I'm going to find Gabriela." He lathered his face.

"How about calling? It's a lot easier. I thought you didn't care about her."

"Christopher said she doesn't have a phone, and I'm not doing this for her. If she knows what this is about, we can tell the DEA. We'll let them take care of Arias."

"You're not thinking clearly," she said. "They already shot one person."

"If I don't clear this up, they may shoot me too. Am I supposed to stay holed up in my apartment?"

"You think you're safer in Mexico?"

"They won't know I went."

# CHAPTER TWELVE

▼

Enrique Arias hung up his phone and stared at the notes he'd scribbled on the back of an envelope. Sutherland was booked on a flight to León, Mexico, later that morning. What was going on?

His office behind *El Chapulín Verde* held a desk and a few file cabinets at one end and a rectangular table, couch, and wall-mounted flat screen television at the other. Two of Arias' men, Paco and Elián, sat at the table wolfing down breakfast tacos and watching soccer on ESPN. The air was thick with the smell of onion and garlic, but a glance at the soft flesh spilling over his belt was enough to stifle Arias' hunger and make him more irritable.

"*Bajen el volumen, pendejos,*" Arias shouted. "I can't think."

While Paco, the larger of the two men, lowered the volume with the remote control, Arias lit another Marlboro and tried interpreting Sutherland's actions. León was the nearest international airport to San Miguel de Allende where Gabriela lived. However, the shipment was in the United States somewhere, presumably still in Chicago. Sutherland couldn't have found the truck yet, or Arias would have known. If he wasn't traveling south carrying something from the shipment, he was concerned about his mother after all.

Underneath Sutherland's flight information, Arias had scratched, "Detective Duncan, Chicago Police—DEA—time to get out."

He'd been careless, maybe even stupid, to show up in person at Sutherland's apartment and the Castellano kid's hospital. Sending men from his gallery wasn't smart either. It was just the kind of impetuous behavior he counseled Marcelo against. He had needlessly exposed himself. Now he could be identified and connected with the wounded *joven* and the truck. It was a matter of time before the authorities sought him out. He couldn't afford to be in the spotlight, and his American connections could only do so much. They couldn't control things as well as his friends in Mexico.

There wasn't any sense dwelling on it. He would leave until this blew over. Leaving Esmeralda now wasn't easy, but he couldn't take her with him. Long ago, he'd placed the apartment in her name and after the latest diagnosis, he'd arranged for twenty-four hour nurses. She also had two adult children, and Paco would be there if needed.

His Chicago assets would be safe while he was gone. Ownership in the Chapultepec Gallery and *El Chapulín Verde* was hidden from the feds by a web of corporations. The gallery and bar ran themselves, and his special team would handle everything else. They had an arsenal of weapons and sophisticated listening and tracking devices. They'd already learned of Sutherland's travel plans. He could count on them to find the truck. Just to make sure, Arias and Marcelo would deal with Sutherland and Gabriela in Mexico. Marcelo already had his instructions for Gabriela. Once he found Sutherland, he would arrange a "friendly" meeting. On Arias' turf, *el hijo de puta* wouldn't be able to refuse.

He consulted his airline guide, looking for a flight that day. He'd have Marcelo pick him up at the airport for the drive to his hacienda outside San Miguel. As always, his wife, ailing mother, and sister-in-law would be there, along with the cook, the maids, and the hands that took care of the grounds and watched over the family.

He'd married Marguerite fifteen years ago when she was barely eighteen. It was an arranged union. Arias paid handsomely for the privilege of marrying into such an aristocratic Mexican family. It would have never happened if her father hadn't desperately needed money.

Arias wanted Marguerite to emigrate to the United States with him. However, she'd never learned English and was accustomed to San Miguel's mild climate. She hated the weather in Chicago. After experiencing the treatment non-English speaking Mexicans, even wealthy *blancas* (whites) like her, received outside of their barrios, she vowed to never return. In Mexico, she was at home, surrounded by family and the comforts she'd grown up with.

His two sons would be away at military school, out of reach of Marguerite's influence. Years of her pampering and zealous Catholicism had already turned them into effeminate weaklings. Without Arias' intervention, exposing them to the masculine discipline of a macho school, they'd been destined for the priesthood or worse. He had more than enough justification to despise the Church and he couldn't bear anyone thinking he'd sired a pair of *maricones*.

Although his hacienda outside of San Miguel held every comfort, for Arias, life there was tolerable at best. Marguerite was a beautiful woman, but since she began going to church every morning, their rare and mechanical couplings gave him little pleasure. While her family never accepted him, their venerable name helped San Miguel's society close their eyes to Arias' lowly beginnings and questionable reputation. So while there, he put up with Marguerite's disapproving looks and comments along with her occasional rages over his mistresses. Despite her belief that Arias was destined for hell, she was too comfortable to leave or openly defy him. Arias suspected that fear of what he might be capable of also kept her there.

"*Oiga, jefe*!" Paco yelled from the other end of the room. "When are we going back to the apartment of Sutherland?"

"We're not. You're staying here, and I'm going to Mexico," Arias said. "I'll send instructions."

Paco flicked off the television and lumbered over to Arias' desk. He was tall and bulky with dark skin and shaggy, black hair. "You want I go to the hospital? Maybe the *policía* are gone now?" He smiled, exposing a silver front tooth.

"Just stay here and wait."

"You want I take care of the *Chapulín*? Maybe one of your *señoritas* while you are gone? You do not want them out of practice." Paco leered as he grabbed his crotch and pumped his hips.

"The place will be fine. The only woman you help is Esmeralda. See she has whatever she needs. Otherwise, you and Elián stay out of sight until I call."

Whenever Arias thought about his *amigo* Paco and others like him, he felt depressed. They shared the same background, small villages where the *ancianos* still spoke the old languages. Through a policy of suppression and neglect, the government and *los ricos* kept them ignorant and illiterate. If Arias hadn't taken care of them and needed them for some of the unpleasant aspects of his operation, they'd be in a slum *cantina* or picking fruit. That was the disheartening and maddening part. Downtrodden immigrants like these gave the whole nation its reputation. So, men like Arias, men who were luckier and had escaped from poverty and illiteracy, still found it difficult to gain respect in white society. Despite education, money, and property, Arias was a second-class American citizen. Not that things were better in Mexico. His operations afforded him comfort and protection there, but he knew that, what disguised itself as respect, was really fear and venality. Behind his back, they still thought of him as a dirty *indio*.

Padre Teodor had been Arias' lifeline, his angel. He had also been his tormentor. When Arias was five, the white priest from Spain had singled him out, just as he had done every year with other Indian boys from the mountain villages. He was taken to Guanajuato to live with the other youngsters in an annex to the convent. The sisters tutored them until, one by one, at the age of ten or eleven, they were sent to live in the village in a large house with the padre. At any one time, a half-dozen boys lived there, along with the padre and two laymen who cooked and maintained the house and garden. Sister Katrina would come during the day to teach and then leave.

Arias was twelve when he learned the price of his special treatment. From the beginning, the private sessions with Padre Teodor were cloaked in religious mystery. The touching, disrobing, and submitting were acts of faith and contrition. The weekly visits continued through his teens until, like those before him, he went to the University of Guanajuato. Theirs was an unwritten code. Silence was the quid pro quo for entrance to the university. But Arias' education was cut short in his third year when Padre Teodor came to justice. It had taken place during a break in the school year, and Arias had witnessed it. Two of the other boys beat the priest, dragged him up the church's bell tower, and pushed him into the courtyard fifty feet below. Rather than risk being arrested as an accomplice, Arias fled across the border.

After he made his plane reservations, Arias looked around the office, wondering when he'd see it again. It shouldn't be long. He'd been in the crosshairs before and survived. Gabriela was a witness to his first scrape with American law. She and her husband were the losers that time. She should have known better.

# CHAPTER THIRTEEN

▼

San Miguel de Allende is in Mexico's state of Guanajuato. One can arrive there by landing in León and driving sixty-five miles east or flying into Mexico City and driving four hours northwest. After some Internet research, Kelly booked Sutherland into León.

After his plane touched down, it took twenty minutes to pick up his bag and make it through the *extranjero* customs line. It was mid-afternoon, and the day was too warm for the leather jacket and sweater he'd needed in Chicago. Stripping them off, he stuffed them into his bag. Dressed in a polo shirt and jeans, he looked like an average *gringo* tourist.

A group of men were talking by the curb at the head of a line of taxis. When he told the first driver that he wanted to go to San Miguel, three more overheard the conversation and jumped forward. They argued among themselves until one took off his baseball cap, drew a handful of pea-sized objects from his pocket, and dropped them into the hat. Each driver reached in and retrieved one.

The smallest of the group whooped, "*El negro!*"

He showed his pick to the group. As his fellow drivers grumbled, he walked toward Sutherland while holding a black corn kernel for him to see.

"My name Roberto." He was maybe five-foot-four with Indian features, toffee skin, and a drooping mustache. His T-shirt was stretched over a beer belly and a grimy New York Yankees baseball cap was pulled down to his ears.

"To San Miguel is hundred American, okay?"

A bus or *colectivo* would have been much cheaper, but Sutherland was in a hurry. Still, he had learned years ago that you never agree to the first offer.

"Seventy-five, *no más*," he said.

Roberto frowned, chewed on his lower lip a moment, then said, "Okay."

He led the way to a green-and-white Nissan with a broken front headlight and dented fender. Sutherland slid into the back and was searching for the seat belt when the car lurched from the curb with a roar and grinding of gears. Considering the bad clutch, muffler, and driver, he could only hope the brakes worked.

He tapped Roberto's shoulder. "No seat belt? *Cinturón de seguridad?*"

Roberto turned halfway around in his seat. "I drive safe, *señor*. No worry."

Just then, a tourist bus crossed the road in front of them.

"*Mire!*" Sutherland yelled, pointing.

Roberto spun around in time to hit the brakes, sending Sutherland against the front seat. The tires squealed, the car skidded to a stop, and Roberto honked the horn. Then he turned around and smiled.

"You see? No problem."

Sutherland settled into his seat, grateful for functioning brakes, but questioning whether he'd make it to his hotel.

"*Se llama Roberto, verdad?*" he asked. He might as well practice his Spanish.

"*Sí.* I speak good English, no?" He was still looking at Sutherland.

"Perfect. I'll make you a deal, Roberto. If you watch the road and drive slowly, I'll give you a good tip. *Una propina grande. Comprende?* Slow and safe."

"*De acuerdo.* No problem." He set off again with the same grinding but slower. "First time to San Miguel, *señor?*"

"A long time ago."

"I live there many years. Have many friends. But now are many *Americanos. Todo es costoso.*"

"Higher prices. The influx of foreigners will do that," Sutherland thought.

Before heading to the airport that morning, Sutherland had printed a few pages on San Miguel from the Internet. As they left the airport behind, he leafed through the information to refresh his memory. According to the Web site, some 70,000 people lived within the town and Approximately 130,000 in a ten-mile radius. Located in a valley with an elevation of more than 6,000 feet, it claimed a year-round springtime climate. Founded in 1542 by Fray Juan de San Miguel, it was renamed San Miguel de Allende in honor of General Ignacio de Allende for his heroic efforts in the revolution of 1810. The article went on to say it was a popular tourist destination and was home to thousands of expatriates from North America and Europe.

Following Roberto's comment about living in San Miguel, Sutherland decided to test his usefulness. Artifacts might be the best path to Gabriela.

"With all your friends in San Miguel," he said, "you probably know who sells artifacts. You know, carvings, pottery, and masks. Stuff like that? From ruins."

"*Hay muchos*," Roberto said. "I get them for you cheap."

"Old ones. Olmec or Aztec. Authentic."

"*Por supuesto, sí.*"

"You sure?" Sutherland said. "Selling copies is an old trick, Roberto."

In the rearview mirror, he saw Roberto wrinkle his brow and shake his head. "You are right, *señor*. Authentic is for the government only."

Sutherland had read that anything uncovered at excavation sites had to be turned over to government museums. Any genuine pieces for sale would not only be illegal, but rare and valuable. That's why someone would steal them.

On the highway, Roberto's commitment to safe driving gradually gave way to old habits. With every mile, the countryside rushed by faster. Sutherland's fatigue caught up to him, and he drifted off. He woke to the rumble of tires over San Miguel's cobblestones. They drove down a main street lined with buildings that could have dated from the Spanish colonial era. The ground floors housed shops selling art, antiques, and crafts. As the narrow street opened onto the central plaza, the rose-colored spires of the cathedral, *La Parroquia,* towered over them. He hadn't seen this church for years. The sight of its exaggerated gothic design, accentuated by the afternoon shadows, jolted him. He'd read a native man had built it by learning architecture via a study of postcards of the great French cathedrals.

"Where you go, *señor?*" Roberto said.

"Across *el Jardín.* The Hotel Posada de San Francisco."

Roberto circled the town's central plaza, the *Jardín,* and stopped in front of the hotel. Sutherland paid his fare and was about to enter the hotel when Roberto said, "*Señor*, I will see about *artifactos.*" He glanced around him, as if to assure they were alone. "*Auténticos.*"

Sutherland told him to call if he found any, though he doubted he would hear from him.

The hotel hadn't changed much since his last visit. More than fifteen years earlier, Sutherland had stopped there on the way to see Gabriela. He didn't stay. The Posada was too expensive for a backpacker living off what he'd made as a mate on sailboats and a worker on archeological digs. However, he did sit in the hotel's central patio while nursing a beer and wondering what Gabriela would be like when he met her.

At the time, she lived in Guanajuato, a nearby city and her birthplace. When they met in her small studio, it had been a tense reunion. She had run away years before. He was running away then. She seemed less joyful at seeing her grown son than guilty for having left him. On the bus leaving Guanajuato, he had felt more of an orphan than before.

Sutherland hadn't slept well since Thursday, three nights ago. After he checked in and unpacked, the lure of the double bed overcame him. It was 7:00 PM when the split notes of a mariachi trumpet from the patio below woke him. It took a few seconds to remember he was in Mexico, another moment to realize it was Sunday night.

He only had a couple pieces to this puzzle. One was Gabriela; another was the Chapultepec Gallery. Finding a gallery had to be easier than locating a person, so he'd start there. The hotel receptionist's directions were easy to follow. Sutherland found the gallery three blocks away. It was next to a nightclub advertising flamenco guitar and Spanish dancers.

The public portion of the shop was small, no more than twenty by thirty feet, a fraction of the size of its Chicago counterpart. But the contents— masks, carved animals, sculptures, and paintings by Mexican artists—looked similar. A young woman in a white blouse and black hair sat behind a desk, reading. Sutherland wasn't sure where to begin, so he picked up a stone carving, a chieftain's head with exaggerated facial features and a headdress of feathers. He held it up so the woman could see it. "*Auténtico*? Authentic?"

She looked up and smiled. "No, *señor. Una reproducción.* Is beautiful, no?"

"I'm looking for *auténticos.* Do you have any?"

"*No, señor. Sólo aquellos.*" She pointed to the shelf of reproductions, more stone heads and statues made to look old and eroded.

What did he expect? Even if there were real Indian artifacts, they would have to be sold secretly or smuggled out of the country to be sold. A store clerk wouldn't be privy to that kind of business He pulled out his only photograph of his mother, the shot he'd taken that time in Guanajuato. He held it out.. "Know her? *Conoce a esta mujer?*"

She took the photo, studied it for a moment, and shook her head. Her long hair swung with the movement and a faint scent of perfume wafted his way, reminding him of desert flowers. For the first time, he noticed she wasn't young after all. She was as petite as a teenager, but the tiny lines around her eyes and mouth suggested she was a woman of at least thirty-five.

"*Una artista. Su nombre es Castellano.*"

He saw a flicker of recognition with the name, but she shook her head. "No."

"It's an old photo," he said. "You sure? *Está usted cierta?*"

*"Estoy cierta."* She turned away and refocused on her reading, a gesture that indicated the interview was over. He noticed her magazine was a Spanish version of an entertainment rag. Hollywood had come to San Miguel.

He left the store with the lingering memory of her perfume. As he crossed the street, a new smell, corn tortillas, struck him. He hadn't eaten since his airplane sandwich and the thought of a taco or enchilada made his mouth water. He entered the small restaurant and sat at a table facing the Chapultepec Gallery. While he waited for his beer and chicken enchiladas, he leafed through a local paper. There was an article on the Instituto Allende, a school for artists and language students not far from the hotel. He'd stop there tomorrow to see if they knew Gabriela.

On the second-last page of the weekly, he read an article about a recently discovered ruin a short distance from San Miguel. It quoted a professor Hidalgo, the archeologist in charge of the dig, as saying it had been recently looted, probably by the local men who found it. A search for them had been futile. Sutherland was about to turn the page when a name stopped him. A separate item mentioned a local patron of the arts, one Enrique Arias, was offering a reward for the looters and stolen items.

It was the name Agent Christopher used for the man harassing Sutherland. Why not test it on the woman in the gallery and see how she reacts? He paid his bill, left ten pesos for a tip, and looked up in time to see the lights go out in the gallery.

Damn.

By the time he reached the sidewalk, she had locked the door and was stepping into a dark Jeep Grand Cherokee. He couldn't see the driver, but the letters on the license plate were clear enough.

ARIAS.

# CHAPTER FOURTEEN

▼

When Sutherland returned to the hotel, the receptionist gave him a message from Kelly. He called from his room and reached her in her condominium. She told him a cold front with ten-degree temperatures was moving into Chicago. Under different circumstances, San Miguel's weather would be a welcome reprieve. However, this trip wasn't for pleasure. He'd readily trade the hours in airports, airplanes, and taxis for Chicago's cruel wind.

"But you didn't call with a weather report…" he said.

"Detective Duncan asked where you were. I said I didn't know. To be precise, that's true. I don't know what room you're in."

"Then I won't make a liar out of you."

"Anyway, he wanted you to stand by in case Javier came around. I got the feeling he's not doing well."

"If I'd been alone with him last night, I might have learned more. He doesn't trust the police."

"Any luck on your mother?"

"I'll need time to find her. She's not in the phone book, so I'll have to dig around."

"Don't be long. I worry."

"No one knows I'm here, remember? Can you do a couple more things? Will you call my secretary and tell her I won't be in? If anything comes up on the zoning, she can leave a message at home."

"No problem. What else?"

"Will you tell Duncan about the DEA's visit?" Sutherland had no way to judge the police's abilities, but it was Chicago's finest or the DEA. He'd rather forget his encounter with Christopher. "Tell him to check out Enrique Arias. He definitely has a connection with the Chapultepec Gallery."

"As if he'll do what I ask," she said.

"Use your charm. I saw the way he looked at you."

After agreeing to talk with her again the following night, Sutherland went downstairs to the bar in the courtyard. The half-dozen tables were empty, but the small candles centered on each flickered hopefully. He ordered a *Herradura Reposado* from the young woman in a blue uniform. While he sipped the tequila, sitting with his back to the garden, he pondered what more he could do to find Gabriela.

"*Señor…*" He heard a whisper from behind.

He looked over his shoulder and saw Roberto, his taxi driver. He stood next to a palm tree in the courtyard. Roberto beckoned and started toward the door to the street. Sutherland downed his tequila, left a fifty-peso note on the table for the drink and a tip, and followed.

He caught up to Roberto on the sidewalk and together they walked around the corner and into the shadows. "*Señor*, good news. I find you a stone figure. *Auténtico.*"

"*De veras*? I thought they were illegal."

Roberto tilted his head, shrugged, and held his palms up. "My *primo*, he hears things. There is someone who sells a *máscara* of a jaguar. The price will be very good. He is hiding and very afraid."

"Of the *policía*?"

"More dangerous than the *policía, señor. Contrabandistas.*"

"Smugglers? Was one of them Enrique Arias?"

"Better not to know names, *señor.*"

One thing was clear. These artifacts reeked of trouble. Some men got shot. Others disappeared. Now some guy had to hide. He'd better take it slowly.

"Good work? No, *señor*?" Roberto said. "You want to buy it? Only 10,000 pesos. Nine hundred American."

Sutherland put a friendly hand on Roberto's shoulder. "We have a little misunderstanding, a *malentendido, amigo*. I don't want to buy, I wanted to know who is stealing them. *Comprende*? I have other reasons."

Roberto retreated a step. "*Es usted policía?*"

"Me? Police? Hell no." Sutherland had to make a decision about Roberto. First, he was picked by chance at the airport. Second, brokering stolen merchandise was probably as common among taxi drivers as knowing where the whorehouses were. It didn't connect him to Arias. The risk was minimal, and Roberto and his cousin "who hears things" could be helpful.

Sutherland waved him closer. "These people are threatening a woman I'm looking for. Come here."

He led Roberto back into the light near the hotel entrance and showed him Gabriela's old photo.

"You ever seen her? She's an artist. Her name is Gabriela Castellano."

*"Muy bonita,"* he said as he held the picture to the light. "But I never see her."

"Want to make a little money? Help me find her?"

He smiled. "This woman? *No problema.* Thousand pesos each day."

*"Váyase!* That's ninety bucks. I'll pay seventy, *no más.* One day only."

Roberto chewed his lower lip again, frowning.

*"Bueno,"* he said finally.

Sutherland remembered the hotel had a copy machine in the office. When the office opened in the morning, he'd copy Gabriela's photo.

"Meet me here at nine o'clock tomorrow," he said. "You can start by showing her picture around town."

Roberto hurried away down the street and Sutherland returned to the hotel. As he picked up his room key at the desk, the clerk gave him another message. He assumed it came from Kelly again. Who else knew he was there?

Minutes later, when he sat on his bed and opened the envelope, he was surprised to find a note containing only a local telephone number.

He sat and stared at it. Then he looked at the envelope. According to the time scribbled on the back, it had arrived when he was talking to Roberto, so it wouldn't be his number. On the front was his name in block letters: *SENOR SUTHERLAND.* It couldn't be a mistake. In this small town? Creepy.

He thought about the threatening calls he'd received in Chicago and decided he wasn't biting. He called Kelly.

"You mention to anybody where I was?" he asked as soon as she picked up.

"Why? What's the matter?"

"Did you?"

"Course not. Doug, what's wrong?" She sounded worried.

"Take it easy. I'm just making sure. Nothing's wrong."

He heard her exhale. "Jeez, don't scare me like that."

"Sorry. Look, I'll call you tomorrow."

For twenty minutes he lay in bed while staring at the ceiling. He finally switched on the bedside light and dialed the number on the note.

"Someone already knows I'm here," he thought. "What could I lose?"

*"Hola, Señor* Sutherland." The man said over a hiss of static. "Thank you for your kind response. *Qué tal?"* It was a man with an accent, but his pitch was higher than Arias' raspy voice.

"Who's this?"

"My name is Vicente Hidalgo. I'm a friend of your mother."

"How did you find me?"

"It was not difficult. For lunch, you had a chicken burrito. Compliments of the airlines, no? You did not finish."

Sutherland's scalp tingled. He'd been followed all the way from Chicago. Even the walls were watching him.

"Why are you following me? What do you want?"

"To help you...zzzzz...your mother." The static crackled and came in spurts, drowning out some words.

"What? You're breaking up. It's a bad line. What do you know about Gabriela?"

"*Disculpe.* I use a *teléfono celular.* The batteries they...zzzzz...Be in *el Jardín* across the street from the church, the *Parroquia*...zzzzz...at seven. Then I tell you everything you...zzzzz...to know."

"Seven in the morning?"

"*Sí.* Good night, *señor* Sutherland."

"Wait!"

But the man hung up. Was this Vicente Hidalgo really a friend of Gabriela? Or of Arias?

The next morning, Sutherland awoke with one of those dream-inspired revelations. Last night's caller could be the Professor Hidalgo who was quoted in the local newspaper. He was the archeologist whose dig was looted. It made sense. He looked at his watch. Six o'clock. There was still time to get breakfast and meet the professor.

An hour later, with a paper cup of black coffee from the corner restaurant, he sat on a bench in the main square. It was called *el Jardín*, garden in English. The *Parroquia*, its rosy façade radiant in the morning sun, looked on silently as worshipers trickled in. In front of the *Parroquia*, the statue of Fray Juan de San Miguel, his hand on a kneeling sufferer, watched the town come alive. Locals scurried by. A man whisked litter into the street with a palm frond. A taxi waited by the curb. A delivery truck bounced past.

Then the bells started. Churches from all over the town took up the chorus, as if they were making up for their forbearance during the night. It was an aspect of San Miguel that took some getting used to and it only made Sutherland more anxious. It was fifteen minutes after seven o'clock already. Was Hidalgo playing games? Was he having him followed, like he had yesterday?

"*Señor* Sutherland?"

He started, then turned. Standing there was a tall woman. She had black hair, was in her early thirties, and was gorgeous. Even in her weathered jeans, denim shirt, and boots, she looked like a fashion model. He swallowed and cleared his throat.

"*Sí.*"

"Is something wrong?" She had large, dark eyes and the full mouth only seen in lipstick ads.

"I…ah…wasn't expecting…a woman. I talked to a man last night."

"My father. We will meet him shortly." She looked him over, checking his clothes, including his jeans, tennis shirt, leather jacket, and boat shoes. "Do you have boots?"

He looked at his Top-Siders, then at her dusty, scuffed Western boots. "No."

She shrugged. "Never mind. Are you ready?"

"For what?"

"A drive, if you're agreeable."

"Where? To see Gabriela?"

"An hour's drive, *más o menos.* But she's not there."

"Then why go? I'm supposed to meet someone."

Roberto would be waiting for him at nine o'clock. Besides, why would he drive off with a stranger? A pretty face wasn't a guarantee.

"You want to know about your mother?" she asked.

"Sure. Can't you tell me here?"

"You don't trust me?" she said, smiling.

"I don't know you or your father. You blame me?"

"Under the circumstances, no. But your mother trusted my father. That's how we learned about the stolen artifacts and you. If you want us to help, you will have to trust as well. We can help each other." She planted her hands on her hips and stared at him. "Well?"

He shrugged. It wasn't a yes or no. He still wasn't sure.

"*Bueno,*" she said, as if he'd agreed. "We'll take my Jeep." She set off across *el Jardín* and motioned him to follow.

He watched her long, confident strides as her hair swayed with her hips. He could be walking into a trap, but he might lose his only link to Gabriela if he didn't go with her.

Her Jeep had a canvas top and open side windows and offered little shelter from the morning chill. Her name was Mercedes. Over the noise of wind, rattles, and engine, she told him they were heading to a sacred place.

# CHAPTER FIFTEEN

▼

"If Gabriela's not there," Sutherland said, "why go? What's with this sacred place?"

They were on the outskirts of San Miguel, the Jeep bouncing along in light morning traffic. Mercedes downshifted as they approached a traffic signal, looked both ways, and accelerated through a solid red. Shifting into third, she glanced at him.

"Everything started there. Your mother, your cousin, and the artifacts. My father will explain."

"Your father's a professor?"

"An archeologist. He specializes in pre-Columbian civilizations."

"Can't you give me a preview?"

"We'll be there in less than an hour."

She seemed determined not to tell him more about their trip, so he leaned back and watched the countryside fall behind. It was a dry land of cactus, tumbleweed and scraggly trees. In the distance, he saw brown hills and mountains. He kept telling himself that he was doing the right thing. Otherwise, his imagination wandered back to images of Javier. That could be him.

Out of the corner of his eye, he studied Mercedes' profile. Was she American or Mexican? The thin nose, sharp chin, and tall stature weren't indigenous. Her speech suggested she had learned English in American schools.

"You study in the States?" he asked.

"Which states?"

"United States."

"Yes, I was born in Mexico."

"I meant America."

"We're in America." She turned and smiled. She had a feline look that said, "Let's play! But watch out for the claws." He liked it. "I'm kidding with you. This is America, too. The United States of Mexico."

He laughed. "One more time. Did you study in the United States of America?"

"Stanford and Columbia. I work in New York."

"Let me guess. A model?"

She frowned, keeping her eyes on the road. "Because I'm tall? I'm also from Mexico, but I don't pick crops or cut grass."

"It was meant as a compliment. What do you do?"

"I work in a museum. I'm taking some time off." She gave him a sideways glance. "Your turn. What do you do?"

"I'm a developer. Town houses."

"Does your wife work or take care of the kids?" Mercedes certainly wasn't bashful.

"My ex-wife hasn't done a day's work in years. She takes care of our daughter."

"Ah." She nodded as if that answered a critical question.

They turned off the highway onto open country and a trail that was almost nonexistent. He only saw dirt tracks and trodden brush. Alongside a dry arroyo, coming over a rise, she pointed ahead. "See anything?"

Before them, the terrain continued all the way to the distant mountains. It was mainly flat with some rolling hills, all covered with cactus, brush, and the odd solitary tree. No crops, no cows or animals except the hawk soaring high overhead.

"No sacred place…if that's what you mean."

"That's why it wasn't discovered earlier."

She had to veer sharply to miss a hole, and Sutherland was thrown against the door. "*Disculpe*," she said as she wrestled the wheel. "We're getting close. Keep looking."

Sutherland watched through the dusty windshield as he clung to the bucking Jeep's door. Ahead were more low hills. Some had short scraggly trees, but he didn't see anything of note. The sky overhead was getting bluer as the sun burnt off the morning clouds. A few more birds, hawks or vultures, glided effortlessly high above. The Jeep hit a rut, then a rock and his weight strained against the seat belt.

"Can't you slow down? I just ate."

"Almost there."

Minutes later, the Jeep rounded a small stand of scrubby trees and slowed. Ahead, an olive-colored truck with a canvas canopy over the cargo bed blocked the path. On one side of the path were trees. The other side was a steep grade leading up to a small mesa. Sitting on the hood of the truck was a boy in green fatigues holding a rifle. He didn't look more than sixteen.

"Watch out," Sutherland cried, bracing himself.

"Relax. He's on our side. They posted soldiers here to stop the looting." She geared down and approached the truck.

The soldier jumped off the hood. "*Buenos,*" he shouted, waving.

"*Buenos días,*" she answered. "*Está mi padre?*"

"*Sí. Dentro.*" He gestured at Sutherland. "Who is he?"

"*Arqueólogo.* He's here to consult with my father. *Todo está bien.*"

"*Bueno. Pase. Muevo el camión.*" The soldier climbed in the truck's cab, backed twenty feet, and turned into the grove in order to allow the Jeep to pass. After another quarter-mile, they came to a gully, a dry arroyo. She stopped next to an old Range Rover.

"My father's car. We have to walk from here." Mercedes jumped from the Jeep and pulled a small backpack from behind the seat. While she put on the pack, Sutherland tried to find signs of a path, but there was nothing except sandy dirt, rocks, and the deep gully ahead.

"We're nowhere," he thought. "What's with the kid with a gun? Jesus, what am I doing here?"

"There was once a large stream in that arroyo," she said, pointing. "That's why they built here."

"What? Who?"

"Just follow me closely," she said. "There are snakes sometimes." She started for the arroyo. He looked at her boots, then at his exposed ankles, and hurried after, stepping where she had.

They picked their way down the rocky slope of the gully, stopped for a drink from her water bottle, and climbed the other side. After another five minutes, they came to a gradual descent and then a mound that was twenty feet high and one hundred across. Covered with the same cacti and brush as the surrounding rugged landscape, it didn't stand out as anything special. As they approached, a soldier in the shade of a canvas lean-to stood and picked up his rifle. After recognizing Mercedes though, he waved and sat again.

Behind the lean-to and next to a pile of earth and loose rock, a hole was crudely dug into the side of the mound. To the right and ten yards from the hole sat the remnants of a small camping trailer. Its window was broken, its door hung by one hinge, and its paint was scorched black-gray by fire. The smell of burned plastic and rubber was unmistakable.

"What happened?" Sutherland asked.

"My father," she said, shaking her head. "He'll kill himself some day. His gas stove exploded. He wasn't hurt and fortunately, he hadn't brought his research files yet. He's living in his old trailer a half hour away until they can move it here."

"Where is he now?" Sutherland asked, checking out the hole in the mound.

Earth had been shoveled away to reveal a five-foot by three-foot passage. Completely dark inside, it reminded him of a Mayan dig he'd worked on years before in Chiapas. He'd stayed a month, sifting through outdoor trenches with a trowel and brush. He never once ventured inside the burial chambers. When the supervisor assigned him underground work one day, he had to quit. He didn't last a minute in those close quarters before bolting for daylight, stifling the desire to scream.

Mercedes rummaged in her pack and pulled out two flashlights, handing one to him. "Watch your step. The tunnel has a sharp descent."

Suddenly he felt cold, and his knees wobbled. "There?" He pointed to the entrance.

"My father's working here. There was a worker's funeral this morning, so he's alone."

"Can't he come out?" This was crazy. She was a stranger. They were in the wilderness. Did she think he would climb down a small hole in the ground, especially when the roof could cave in? "I'm not going down there."

She faced him with her hands on her hips, her eyes narrowed. "What's the matter?"

Nightmares flashed before him. Enclosed in the dark, water was seeping in. He knew he'd die in there. "Just a thing I have. Some people don't like heights. Me, it's this."

"Well, if you want to know what's going on, get over it. It's not just my father. You've got to see inside. Come on." She held out her hand. "If you hang on to me, we'll be there in a minute."

"Really, I..." he stammered. "It's too small...and dark." And there was always the worry of who—or what—might be waiting.

"It gets larger, and there are lights inside." She pointed to a gas-powered electric generator next to the burned-out camper. A cable ran along the ground from the generator into the opening.

She stepped forward and took his hand. Hers was warm and soothing, his was cold and clammy. She turned toward the entrance and gently tugged. He sucked in his breath and took his first step, hoping his legs held out. Looking over her shoulder into his eyes, she urged him on. At the entrance, she flicked on her flashlight and pulled him inside. He held his breath and stood there for a moment, frozen. When he exhaled and breathed in again, he smelled dank earth.

"Like a grave," he thought. "For crissakes, we could be buried here."

She grabbed his flashlight and turned it on. With both lights cutting the darkness, the space didn't seem quite as menacing. He could lift his legs again.

The tunnel narrowed and sloped downward. Then it was level for another twenty feet before descending steeply. His rapid breathing and heartbeat were all he heard. It was slow going, bent over and edging forward over uneven ground. He squeezed her hand as if it was the only thing holding him up. He told himself the roof wouldn't fall and he wouldn't be trapped. "It won't cave in" became his mantra. At least there was no water. After inching forward, stooped down with only their lights to see by, he saw a glow ahead.

They entered a stone-lined room about 400 square feet in area. The generator outside powered an electric lantern in the center. He straightened and breathed deeply, thankful for more space. Then, taking in the room, he felt as if he'd awakened into a dream world. The walls were of cut stone, perfectly stacked and fitted. From shoulder height up, rows of images were carved into the rock. He saw Indian warriors with headdresses, lizards, skulls, a feathered serpent, and jaguars. All were arranged in a seemingly meaningful way. The light followed the patterns up to where the ceiling began, a roof of two enormous stones coming together in a peak fifteen feet up. He slowly turned and tried taking it in.

"Amazing." He almost forgot his fear.

"Only the beginning," she said. "Come on. Through here."

She bent down and entered another passageway. The next room, bathed in the light of another lantern, was circular, larger, and higher. It had elaborately carved walls with an empty shelf at eye level where one would expect to see stone or pottery objects. The smell of dank earth was so strong that he could taste it. Six doorways leading to smaller cavities, all dark, led off from the room. A bearded man with a miner's light on his head came out of one doorway. A camera hung around his neck. He was a few inches shorter than Sutherland and thinner. His face was lined and leathery. He smiled when he saw them, spreading his arms in welcome.

"*Señor Sutherland. Bienvenido.*" He offered his hand, and Sutherland shook it. His grip was strong, the skin callused. "*Me llamo Vicente Hidalgo.*" He then remembered he was speaking to an American. "Thank you for coming. Welcome to the tomb of the virgins." He had a slight accent.

Sutherland barely heard him. He couldn't take his eyes off the carvings, especially the serpents and skulls covering the walls. He had seen dozens of pictures of other tombs, but nothing like this.

"You are impressed, señor Sutherland? Sit down. I'll tell you why I asked you here." He gestured to a half-dozen wooden crates on the floor.

Hidalgo and Mercedes sat, but Sutherland was too antsy. His emotions teetered between panic and fascination. He was underground and surrounded by images meant to instill dread. The combination was working. Mercedes passed him her canteen. As he drank, he noticed the image over her head. It was a carved face—half-human/half-monster—of what must have been one angry god. He had seen similar faces in photos of Olmec and Aztec ruins.

"I wasn't expecting this," he said. "On the phone, you said this was about Gabriela."

"*Bueno*, Gabriela," Hidalgo said, as if the subject had just occurred to him. "I didn't know she had a son."

"How does she fit into this?" Sutherland asked, finally sitting on the nearest crate to take the weight off his unsteady legs.

"Two months ago, a man came to Gabriela with a statue of a Chacmool." Hidalgo pointed to the carving of the angry god. "A day later, they found the man with a bullet through his heart. Apropos, no? The heart was what the Toltecs sacrificed to Chacmool to bring rain."

The three of them sat facing each other on the scattered crates inside the underground chamber. Light from the electric lantern threw their silhouettes against the wall and highlighted the carving. The air was still and heavy with a musty smell.

"They only found the one looter," Professor Hidalgo continued. "We assume the others met the same fate. They thought they could be rich. Instead? Well…" He shrugged.

"Slow down, professor. What is this?" Sutherland swept his arm around to include the whole room. The walls, crates, and table were piled with pottery and photos.

"A tomb," Hidalgo said. "For virgins sacrificed to Chacmool or Tláloc, the rain god."

"How do you know?" Sutherland couldn't take his eyes from the row of carved skulls along one wall.

"The looters didn't break into the burial chambers." He pointed to the dark doorways that led off the room. "From their *esqueletos*, espically *la pelvis*, we know the women never bore children. We learned from knife scrapes on the ribs that they were killed for their hearts. That they were virgins?" A thin smile peeked through his graying beard. "An educated guess."

High on one wall, another image caught Sutherland's eye. A two-headed bird was clutching what looked to be a heart in its talons. He shook his head. It wasn't even noon, and he was seeing dark tunnels, skulls, and heart-eating birds. But its allure was seductive, checking his fear of being underground and holding him from bolting back to the open air.

Hidalgo placed his hand on a foot-high urn on the table. "The Toltecs preceded the Maya and the Aztecs. Their capital was Tula, a few hours from here. They conducted human sacrifices and passed the practice to the Maya in the Yucatán. With the contents of these tombs and their symbols…" he pointed to a row of glyphs along one wall, "we may decode pre-Mayan and pre-Aztec history. It's a find of a lifetime."

"Is it worth a lot of money?" Sutherland asked. "In the States?"

Hidalgo grimaced. "You can't put a price on them."

"It's enough to kill some of your countrymen and threaten me. How was it found?"

"There are many *montículos* or mounds in Mexico. All are not lost pyramids or tombs, so they are not noticed. An earthquake could have uncovered the entrance. Some *campesinos* were curious and dug."

"They looted it and tried selling the stuff?" Sutherland asked.

"To the wrong people."

"And Gabriela?" Sutherland asked.

"For some reason, she suspected a San Miguel gallery of something illegal. Her nephew, Javier, got a job there to spy for her. One of the *campesinos* showed him a Chacmool, one of the statues. It holds the *cántaro,* a type of bowl where they placed the sacrificed heart. When Gabriela saw it, she thought it was authentic. She showed it to me, and I agreed. By then, the others…" He paused and looked to Mercedes for help. *"Contrabandistas?"*

"Smugglers," she said. "But they are much worse."

"These men," he continued, "stole the artifacts from the *campesinos.* Gabriela discovered this when she found the dead man."

"Where is she?" Sutherland asked.

Hidalgo took a deep breath and looked at Mercedes. She averted her eyes and studied her hands. Hidalgo finally said, "She was supposed to meet me last night. She didn't."

"You call the police?"

"You're in Mexico, *señor,"* Hidalgo said.

"So what? Why her?"

"When she learned of this, she told the federal police. That's why the soldiers are outside. But by then, the *contrabandistas* had shipped the artifacts to Chicago, so she had her nephew go there. He was to follow it and inform the authorities. He did more. He stole the truck with the shipment."

"And got shot in the process," Sutherland added. "What happened to it?"

The question seemed to annoy Hidalgo. He crossed his arms and glared at Sutherland, brooding. What was his problem? What was he waiting for? It was so quiet in the tomb that Sutherland could hear his own heart pumping.

His fascination was wearing thin. The room felt smaller, and the walls were closing in. After an awkward silence in which the professor's face grew darker, he finally exploded.

"Don't pretend you don't know," he blurted. "*Mentiroso!* The boy told you where it is, *pendejo.*"

Sutherland was more shocked by the professor's vehemence than being called a lying asshole. "The boy didn't say where anything was," he said with equal intensity. "So back off."

"Give him the telegram," the professor hissed at Mercedes. "Translate it for him."

She cast her father a warning look, then pulled a Western Union envelope from her pocket. "My father didn't mean that," she said, handing Sutherland the telegram.

The message was addressed to Gabriela Castellano.

"*Todo salió según lo previsto. Está escondido. Entrego la llave al primo esta tarde. Javier*"

He handed it back to Mercedes. "He says it went as planned and he hid the shipment. But, despite what he said, he didn't give me a key. He also didn't tell me where anything was. I said the same thing to the man who called me. Do you know an Enrique Arias?"

"*Claro.* What about him?"

"The shipment was sent to the Chapultepec Gallery in Chicago. Does he own it?"

Hidalgo shrugged. "We think a gallery by that name shipped it. But *señor* Arias? He is an influential man…"

"Who threatened me and Gabriela," Sutherland said.

"You must be mistaken," Hidalgo said. "He has offered a reward for the shipment and information about the missing *campesinos.*"

"Mistaken my ass!" Sutherland was through being polite. He wasn't lying and inventing things. He definitely didn't like being called a *pendejo.* "He threatened me, you hear? Gabriela, too. Besides Javier, she's the only one who could know where your precious artifacts are. So let's quit screwing around and find her before it's too late."

"Too late?" Hidalgo said. "No one would hurt her. Maybe someone scares you because you intend to sell the artifacts yourself. Is that your plan, *señor?*"

"Bullshit!" Sutherland banged his flashlight on a crate, breaking the lens. His voice echoed off the stone walls. Hidalgo stared at him, looking stunned. Sutherland waited a moment, collecting himself. When he spoke, he strained to be calm, as if he could shut out the reality of where he was by controlling his voice. "Only scaring me? They killed the men who found this place. Does that mean anything? They shot Javier. That's more than a scare."

"We don't know who is responsible," Hidalgo said. "And only one *campesino* was found."

"Are you naïve or just don't care?" Sutherland's anger was the only thing staving off his fear. Objects around him were dimming. The professor's face took on the angry features of the god overhead. "Does nothing matter but the fucking artifacts? The best thing to happen is to destroy them before anyone else is killed."

Hidalgo's face reddened, and he stood.

"What do you know about these things?" he rasped. "This treasure has waited for 1,000 years. You would stand in our way? Again, you are mistaken, *señor*." He raised his right arm and pointed. "All of that was lost…" As his arm swept to take in the empty shelf, he hit the electric lantern, knocking it off the crate onto the stone floor. With flying sparks, the light flashed and went out, leaving the chamber in darkness.

Sutherland was doused in cold panic. Too far away to reach a wall, he squatted down and placed his hands on the floor to steady himself. Mercedes flicked on her flashlight, and the professor turned on his mining lamp. But the ceiling seemed lower now. Everything blurred. Sutherland inhaled deeply, knowing he'd scream if he waited another second.

"I gotta go," he blurted and lurched toward the tunnel. But in the face of the blackness beyond the door, he spun around.

"Mercedes," he said. "Help me out of here. Or this'll be my tomb, too."

# CHAPTER SIXTEEN

▼

The Jeep rose over the rocky lip and down into the gully, throwing Sutherland hard against his seat belt. At the bottom, his knees slammed into the dashboard, and his head smacked the windshield. Mercedes gunned the engine, and the Jeep lurched forward and up the far bank of the arroyo. Sutherland tightened the seat belt and hooked the door with his elbow. He still wasn't over his panic. His mouth was dry, and his breathing shallow. As his pulse rate slowed, anger, frustration, and a painful embarrassment replaced the paralyzing helplessness he experienced in the tomb. How could he let this thing control him?

They hit another bump. Over the wind and engine, he yelled, "Are you trying to kill me?"

"*Disculpe*," she shouted back as she power skidded around a sandy bend in what passed for a road. It was as if she was punishing him. What for? Not knowing where the shipment was? Getting pissed at her father? Why? Besides calling Sutherland a liar, the asshole couldn't care less about the deaths of the *campesinos* or Gabriela's whereabouts. Who was in the wrong here?

Maybe it wasn't punishment, but merely contempt for turning into jelly inside the tomb. He shouldn't have gone in. He knew better.

Ten minutes into the ride back to San Miguel, they had barely spoken a word. Mercedes negotiated around the ruts, her eyes fixed forward, while Sutherland hung on and thought. The professor had filled in a few blanks, but the essentials, including the key and the shipment's whereabouts, were still a mystery. Which brought his thoughts back to Gabriela. She had missed the appointment with Hidalgo. That didn't have to mean something terrible happened. She could be sick or hiding. If Sutherland knew where she lived, he could check. He studied Mercedes' profile. Her face was smeared with dirt, and a blue bandana bound her black hair. It was time to make peace.

"That didn't go very well, did it?" he shouted. "Sorry."

She glanced sideways at him. "You understood what he said?"

Hidalgo had followed them out of the tomb with a string of invective. "Not all of it, but it wasn't flattering. Lying, stealing son of a whore close enough? He thinks I want to sell the shipment for myself. Do you agree with him?"

She furrowed her brow and said, "I haven't made up my mind."

"I don't give a damn about the artifacts!"

The Jeep slowed enough to hear without yelling. "In Javier's telegram, he said he gave you the key."

"He sent the telegram before he saw me," he said. "Before he got shot. There's a difference between what he planned to do and what he did."

"But you talked to him."

"He was hurt and scared. He just mentioned stolen artifacts"

"How did you know about the Chapultepec Gallery?"

"His note was written on paper from there. I checked on it in Chicago and then here. But you know that."

She turned to him. "What do you mean?"

"You followed me from Chicago, right? Didn't you see me go into the gallery here?"

She shrugged as if to say yes.

He now asked the question that had been bothering him since Hidalgo called him the night before. "How did you find me in Chicago? And why?"

"Gabriela told us about you. She thought you could help Javier with the Chicago police and take them to the shipment."

"Why didn't she warn me? Why the surprise?"

"It was last minute. Javier needed help. She thought of you."

"I wish she hadn't," he said. "I'd be doing fine without her or men like Arias and your father in my life."

She braked hard, and the Jeep slid to a stop. Glaring at him, she said, "Despite what you think, my father's a good man. He only wants the artifacts returned. They are important to Mexico. I don't know Arias, only of him. My father would have nothing to do with him."

"You hope so. But people choose strange bedfellows when they're after the same thing."

"You can go to hell," she said, slamming the gearshift into first and gunning the engine. When they reached the highway, she downshifted and the Jeep bounced onto the asphalt and headed west toward San Miguel. The road was smoother, and Sutherland eased his grip on the seat and door, settled back and tried relaxing.

He glanced sideways at her and said, "You know where she lives?"

She shook her head. The silent treatment.

"Do you know how I can find out?" he asked.

The rush of air across the open Jeep made the silence less awkward. After another mile passed, she said, "We don't know where Gabriela lives. Anyway, my father says she's not home."

"How is he so certain she's not at home if he doesn't know where she lives? She doesn't have a phone. So he either does know where she lives or the reason she didn't meet him. Which is it?"

She didn't look at him, but he could tell by her perplexed expression, the question or its implications bothered her.

"I don't know," she said.

He hunched down into his seat, out of the wind, and closed his eyes. The morning had brought him no closer to extricating himself from this mess. If Arias was responsible for one or more of the *campesinos'* deaths, he was as dangerous as Christopher claimed. Sutherland wished he could just disappear until the artifacts were found and this all blew over. The problem was that he couldn't hide for long. Once zoning was approved on his project, he was committed to close on the land or forfeit serious money. Then he'd have all sorts of decisions to make, designs to approve, materials to select, and contracts to let. He couldn't run his development from a bunker. This, his first project, was too important to risk screwing up. It was his future.

His course still seemed disturbingly clear. Because he couldn't hide, he'd have to locate the artifacts or find someone who could. As San Miguel came into view, the fact that Hidalgo knew Gabriela wasn't home pestered him like a stone in his shoe.

# CHAPTER SEVENTEEN

It was late morning when Mercedes dropped off Sutherland at his hotel. He had hardly closed the door before she drove off without a good-bye.

"To hell with her," he thought. "And her father, too."

The streets around *el Jardín* were busy with weekday traffic. Sunshine had warmed away the morning's chill and the plaza itself was a picture of lazy contentment, with men, women, and children strolling or sitting on the tree-sheltered benches. Approaching the hotel entrance, he heard, "*Señor!*" He turned to see Roberto hurrying toward him.

"I look for you all over." He slowed to walk beside Sutherland. "We going to meet this morning, no?"

"Sorry, Roberto, something came up."

Roberto nodded and pointed in the direction the Jeep had gone. "I don't blame you, *señor*." He smiled knowingly. "You can't say no to a woman like that."

"*Qué pasa?*" Sutherland said, wanting to change the subject.

"When you don't come this morning, I look for the place of the woman in the photo. I take *toda la mañana,* but I find it. Maybe she no want people know where she live."

"How'd you find it?"

"You give me her name. Say she is *artista*. I ask other *artista*."

"Is it close?"

"*Sí, señor.* But she is not home."

"Where's your taxi? *Vámonos!*"

Roberto drove his Nissan down narrow one-way streets, climbing higher to a barrio that overlooked the city center. He stopped the car and said they had to walk the rest of the way. They left the taxi and entered an alley of uneven cobblestones. They turned and ascended a steep grade with a row of houses on either side. Their façades were crumbling and brick and adobe showed underneath the eroded stucco. The aroma of chocolate floated from an open window. At the top, Roberto pointed to the last house on the dead-end alley.

"*Allá!*"

It was so unlike the dark structures they'd passed, Sutherland might have guessed it to be an artist's home. It was a block of whitewashed stucco with a door on the right. The only break in the sheer façade was a horizontal band of windows near the flat roof. It was no larger than the other houses, maybe twenty-five feet in width. Yet, its pale simplicity made it stand out like a pearl in the sand.

A locked iron bar gate protected the front door. Just inside the bars, in the center of the bright blue door, hung a sign: "CUIDADO—PERRO. He pushed the button in the doorframe under the brass nameplate reading "G. Castellano" and heard the bell ringing inside. No one answered. If there was a dog, it was deaf, dead, or gone.

"Can we get in?" He looked at Roberto, who shook his head and shrugged.

A gap separated Gabriela's house from her neighbor's. Roberto followed Sutherland around the back of her house, where they faced an eight-foot wall. There was probably a courtyard or garden behind the wall, because the house was set back some thirty feet and rose to a wide balcony on the second floor. Red flowers hung over the railing like spilled paint. Set in the courtyard wall was another gate, rusty and locked.

For years, thousands of miles had been between them. Now he was just outside her world. He wasn't sure what he hoped to find, but he had to enter. There might be clues to her whereabouts, but he couldn't deny another motive. He wanted an answer to a decades-old question. Why had she left? If she wasn't there, he would walk in her space, see how she lived and worked, breathe the air she breathed. Only a wall and a lock stood in his way.

The yard behind the house sloped down to a steep ravine and was covered with tall grass, bushes, and the litter of decades, including a bathtub, couch, chair, tires, cans, and plastic bottles. A goat was tethered to a stake, but no one was in sight. A light breeze carried the smell of foul water from the stagnant pool below.

He studied the courtyard wall. It wasn't too high, but a row of broken glass was set into the mortar along the top.

"You don't have a ladder hidden in your taxi, do you Roberto? *Una escalera?*"

"*No, señor. Lo siento.*" Roberto looked more relieved than sorry.

Sutherland took off his leather jacket, picked up a rock, and motioned Roberto over to the wall. "Give me a boost."

"*Mande?* What you mean, *señor?*"

"Lift me. I'm climbing the wall."

Roberto retreated several steps, waving his arms in disagreement. "*Está usted loco?*" he said. "*La policía.* Big problems."

"It's my mother's house, for Christ's sake. Now give me boost. *Ayúdame.*" Sutherland knitted his fingers together and held them out as a foothold to show Roberto what he wanted.

Roberto shook his head, as if he wondered how he ever got into this. He exhaled, crossed himself, and trudged to the wall.

The extra three feet from Roberto's boost was enough for Sutherland to reach. With the rock, he was able to break away the largest glass shards from the wall. Then he spread his leather coat over the top, and with a foot on Roberto's shoulder, he shinnied up and swung one leg over. The area below was mostly flower garden. A table and chairs under an awning stretched from the house. Two large bowls sat side by side in the shade.

"One for water and one for food?" he thought. "Thank God, there's no sign of the dog."

He told Roberto to wait in the taxi and jumped to the soft earth below.

The patio door was unlocked and Sutherland found himself in a small kitchen that opened into the dining and living room. The ceiling was high and beamed, the tile and furniture were brightly colored and Mexican. Large oil paintings hung from the whitewashed brick. Nothing seemed out of place. On the table by the front hall, he found a note. "*Hola, Gabriela. Frida estaba ladrando. Así que, la llevé conmigo para darle de comer. Abrazos, Carlota.*"

So Carlota heard the dog barking, had a key, and knew Gabriela well enough to come in and take the dog away to feed it. No doubt Frida was named after Frida Kahlo. She told him that she once met her in Mexico City.

A bedroom was on the first floor. When he opened the door, he gasped. It was torn apart. A mattress was half on the floor. Dresser drawers were open, and clothes were scattered. He tiptoed around the garments to the center of the room and surveyed the scene. Whoever did this wasn't your common burglar. The radio, stereo, and television were still here. The intruder had been looking for a particular something. Sutherland retrieved a silk scarf hanging from an open drawer. He held it to his nose and inhaled. The peach fragrance brought back a dull memory of a bright room and a soft pillow. He dropped the scarf in the drawer and returned to the living room.

The paintings hanging around the room all bore Spanish signatures. The small Toledo and Morales were probably very valuable. There were also several large abstracts, a landscape, and some brightly colored street scenes. On the way to the stairs, he glanced again at the canvas over the fireplace and stopped. The face in the portrait looked like Gabriela, but something was strange about it. Moving closer, he saw the black letters scrawled across the eyes, making her portrait less recognizable.

He touched the printed letters. They lacked the texture of thick paint, felt and looked like ink drawn over the hardened oil. When he saw the magic marker on the mantel, he nodded. He spelled out the letters: *ENTROMETIDA PUTA*. Evidently a meddling whore is what you labeled one who interfered with your smuggling scheme.

A staircase spiraled up to a high, open space with a skylight and a balcony at the rear. Canvases were stacked against the walls, several easels held partially finished abstracts, brushes were lined up on a table, paint-stained rags and smocks hung from hooks. The smell of oil paint and turpentine pervaded the room.

He crossed the studio to her desk. After the mess downstairs, he wasn't surprised to find drawers opened and papers strewn on the floor. On hands and knees, he sorted through the pile of paper. He found old clippings and reviews of her shows, business correspondence with her agents, and bank statements that showed she was doing well. Discovering Gabriela was a well-regarded artist wouldn't help him find her.

Stuck under the blotter, he found several newspaper articles, one about Enrique Arias' purchase of a the Chapultepec Gallery in San Miguel. Another was about his association with a gallery in Chicago. A third mentioned his business exporting local crafts to the United States. Why was she interested in his activities? What made her suspect something?

The drawers had been emptied. On the desk, he saw a few bills and three picture frames, two with photos of people he didn't recognize. The glass on the third was smashed, the frame empty. Then he saw Gabriela's picture hanging on the bulletin board. It was a torn half of a snapshot. A red thumbtack was jammed between her eyes, an angry message from the intruder.

In the photo, she was as young as when he had seen her last. He recognized the setting. It was the picture he'd sent years ago. They had stood side by side in front of her gallery in Guanajuato. Now, the half with his image was gone. Someone had broken the frame and taken it. Probably not an admirer.

When he removed the torn snapshot from the board, he noticed something wedged between the desk and wall. He pulled the desk away, and a thick album fell to the floor. A picture of his father stared out at him. His hands shook as he picked up the album and set it on the blotter. He had to sit down.

He took a deep breath and opened it again. Pasted on the last page was a newspaper clipping with the headline: "Distinguished Attorney Faces Two Years For Bribery."

He didn't need to read the text. In the years up to that crushing news, his father had seemed the pillar of moral rectitude. When the words appeared in print, they launched a bewildered Sutherland on a long journey. Feeling betrayed by his father's hypocrisy, he dropped out of college. He crewed on sailboats in the Caribbean and worked on digs in Mexico. His father died two years later, a few months before Sutherland returned to Chicago. In all that time, they had not spoken. Now the words were just as painful as the first time he'd seen them.

When he flipped to another page, he felt his breath catch. One photo was of him in a cap and gown with the caption: "High School Graduation, 17 *años.*" Next to it, he found his picture in his baseball uniform. He was with his father, and his father looked so proud standing there with his arm around him. Sutherland, puffed up and beaming, couldn't be happier for having pleased his idol. He felt his eyes well up.

The first part of the album held photos of his baptism, early birthdays, and holidays. Gabriela was in some of them, his father in others. But the snapshot of his fifth birthday stopped him like a punch in the stomach. He was sitting in a cowboy outfit in front of a cake with five burning candles. His wide-brimmed hat was tipped back, revealing sad, hungry eyes. Gabriela would have left them not long before. He swallowed hard and turned the page.

Later photos showed him in Little League, on his father's boat, and in a Sea Scout uniform. He was caught eating cake on his sixteenth birthday, holding a trophy, or posing with a prom date. Memories flooded over him. He remembered events he'd forgotten and milestones long past. Were these happy days, living alone with a kind but strict father? He'd thought so, but one doesn't know what one has missed.

What did this album mean to Gabriela? She had maintained a pictorial history of his life, and judging from the worn cover, she had turned these pages many times.

He went to the back of the book, skipping past his father's picture. Inside the rear cover was a pocket holding a large manila envelope. He opened it and spilled out a half-dozen, yellowed newspaper clippings onto the desk.

At first glance, the photos and articles seemed disconnected to Gabriela or Sutherland. The first article, dated February 1980, was about a Latino man found shot to death in a cottage in Beverly Shores, Indiana. The sheriff was investigating the stranger's death. There was nothing more. The following clipping, also thirty years old, described the apprehension of one Enrique Arias for a robbery-murder in a Chicago pawnshop. Two men had been seen leaving, but the accomplice was still at-large. He then saw an article with his father's name. It said Assistant State's Attorney Sutherland was dropping charges against Enrique Arias.

What was that about? It meant Gabriela's involvement in artifacts was not a coincidence. She and his father had crossed paths with Arias thirty years earlier. That's why she was suspicious and had her nephew work in the gallery to spy on him.

The next clipping was just a photo with a caption that didn't seem to belong. The picture showed a tow truck hauling a car from an icy body of water. Underneath, it said, "Fishermen Rescue Mother and Toddler From Icy Depths."

He stared at the photo, trying to steady the hands that held it. There was no date, no way to tell which paper it was printed in. It was a dark VW Beetle. A moment ago, he'd seen a similar car in a snapshot with his father holding him as a baby. Slowly, the panic seeped over him. He felt closed in and cold. He had been there. He felt it.

There was scribbling across the picture. He read it three times, but he still couldn't make any sense of it.

*"Que vayas con Dios, mi hijita."*

Sorting through the brittle clippings, he tried to find a thread. A stranger killed. A robbery-murder. Arias arrested and released. Then the car driven into the water. He had come to find a stranger named Gabriela. Not out of love for a mother, but in the hope that she could clear up the mess she put him in. Instead, he found a woman who had never forgotten him. A woman whose past posed more questions than answers. Not just related to artifacts or keys, but the events of thirty years earlier that caused her to desert his father and him. An act, like his father's crimes, that made trust an empty word.

He reread her scribbled words on the photo of the car and tow truck, focusing on the final word.

*"Que vayas con Dios mi hijita."*

He translated it aloud. "May you go with God, my little daughter." Or was it a carelessly written *hijito*? As in son?

# CHAPTER EIGHTEEN

▼

When he returned from Gabriela's house, Sutherland found Roberto waiting in the car. Fifteen minutes had passed since he discovered the photos and news clippings, a half hour since he climbed the wall. The car was running, and Roberto seemed nervous. He drove off as Sutherland closed the door. It was good to know where his trusted driver drew the legal or ethical line. It was okay to deal in stolen artifacts, but breaking and entering was wrong, or at least more dangerous. Maybe he had a history with the police.

"*Todo bien?*" Roberto asked.

"*Más o menos.*" He handed Roberto the torn photo of Gabriela. "Show it around. See if anyone knows where she is. Ask your *primo* who knows things."

On the way to the center of town, he reflected on what he'd found. Gabriela had systematically recorded and revisited the events of his early life. For some other reason, she saved news clippings that initially seemed unrelated to him. But they weren't. That picture of the car in the water had shaken him as much as his nightmares.

He wondered why she didn't mention the scrapbook when they met years before. It might have changed things. As it was, their meeting had been brief and superficial. He had a chip on his shoulder. She only spoke of the present and of Mexico, as if she never had a life in Chicago.

He asked Roberto to drop him at the hotel. Parked in front, he gave him 500 pesos to begin his research. "Stop by this evening. If I'm not in, leave me a note."

"*Sí.* At the desk. Like the other lady."

"You mean the one in the Jeep?"

Roberto smiled mischievously. "The other one, *señor*. I saw her leave a note with the *recepcionista* in the hotel when I wait for you this morning. Already you have two *mujeres* here, no?"

"What did she look like?"

"*Muy bonita. Pero* with more years than the one with the Jeep."

Not Gabriela?

"The one in the picture?" Sutherland asked.

"*No, señor.*" The only other woman Sutherland had met in San Miguel was in the Chapultepec Gallery. Could she know who he was and where he was staying?

Sutherland gave Roberto the address of the gallery and told him to drive there and double-park outside. Sutherland peeked in, careful not to be seen. The same woman as the night before was seated behind the counter.

"Is that her?" he asked.

Roberto stepped out of the car, went to the door, nodded, and returned. "*Sí*, the same one," he said. "She ask about you in the hotel."

If Arias knew where he was staying, he couldn't go back to the hotel. Roberto dropped him on the street north of *el Jardín*. From there, he walked block after block, dodging the sunburned tourists and brown-faced venders looking for the first hotel that was secluded and inconspicuous. *El Colibrí* was a smaller, run-down version of the San Francisco. He checked in.

Sitting on the bed, he called his old hotel for his messages. Kelly was the only caller. He asked the receptionist to have his belongings packed up and left at the desk and emphasized that he wasn't checking out. Anyone wanting to reach him would call him there.

He dialed Kelly's number at the corporation counsel's office in Chicago's city hall.

"Doug." She sounded relieved. "You okay?"

"Busy, but no closer to Gabriela. You?"

"You tell me. Someone broke into my building's basement yesterday. A neighbor saw him. The police found electronic bugging equipment in the central phone box. My line was tapped."

Arias couldn't know about Kelly or where she lived. How could he?

"Did you give the DEA guys your address the other night?"

"They were driving me home. The police said it was high-tech stuff, so it could've been the DEA's."

"Better them than Arias. Is that legal?"

"Everything's national security these days. Meantime, I had my assistant get the bio on that agent. The details will take a while, but do you want what we got so far?"

"Shoot." He leaned back against the headboard with his feet on the bed.

"James 'Rusty' Christopher. Born in Muncie, Indiana in 1952. Junior college. Then the Marines. Vietnam vet with decorations. Honorable discharge in 1976. Family trucking business. Bachelor's degree in law enforcement. Joined the DEA in 1986. Assigned to Minneapolis, Detroit, Indianapolis, and finally the Chicago division, working out of Hammond since 2005. That's all so far."

"How do you do that?" he asked.

"I work for the city. People have to be nice to me."

"I hope I can be so lucky. I'm going to an Internet café and do some of my own research." He pulled out Gabriela's envelope with the clippings and spread them on the bed. "I'm looking into a 1980 murder in Beverly Shores and a pawnshop murder in Chicago around the same time."

"Really? What for?"

"When I know, I'll tell you."

"Why don't I pull the case histories?" she said. "I doubt you can."

"You're too busy. Besides, you don't know what I'm looking for."

"Dammit, Doug, let me help. You're not the Lone Ranger. I'll have my assistant do it. Now what do you want?"

"All right! All right!" When she assumed her hard-nosed lawyer's attitude, he was better off giving in. Besides, she was probably right about the case files. There was a limit to what you can get on the Internet without special subscriptions. "First, a man was shot in a cottage in Beverly Shores around 1980. I've got a Gary paper with a short item on it. I'd like to know who he was and who killed him."

"Jeez, that's strange. Okay, next?"

"Enrique Arias was arrested around that time for a pawnshop murder in Chicago."

"That'll be easier. What else?"

He glanced at the tow truck clipping. "This one may be tough. Can you do a search on cars falling through the ice? A lake or pond? Something like that?"

"Where? When? Help me."

"I don't know." He studied the picture for clues, but it didn't help. "Start with Chicago. Anytime after 1978."

"Where are you getting this stuff? You been smoking some of that gold?"

"Don't even go there. After Duncan's accusation, it's not funny. Which reminds me, how's Javier?"

"No change."

"I hope he's under guard. The more I think about it, you shouldn't stay in your place. Why don't you go to your aunt's house until this is over? No one will find you there."

"I hate the suburbs. And I have a job, remember?"

"Somebody got into your condo's basement, for crissakes."

"Why should I worry about the DEA? Now tell me what you found out."

He recounted the activities of the day, including his discoveries at Gabriela's house.

"That explains the research assignment," she said. "This isn't the first time she's crossed paths with Arias."

"But what happened the first time? And what's it have to do with the other clippings?"

"I've got a court date, but I'll do my best," she said. "Now, what's this Mercedes like?"

He hesitated before answering. "Typical. Short and dumpy. But smart." No sense giving her anything else to worry about. Which brought him back to his own concerns. "When did they tap your phone?"

"Yesterday afternoon."

"When did the police find it?"

"Oh…oh." Her tone said it all. "After I called you. Whoever it was may know where you're staying."

"I'm not there anymore." But it might answer a question that had been nagging him. "I've got an alternate theory about that phone tap, and it's a scary one. What if it was Arias, not the DEA? It would explain how that woman from the Chapultepec Gallery found my hotel. The only other people who knew were Mercedes and her father."

# CHAPTER NINETEEN

▼

The sound of the phone ringing startled him from a deep sleep. His watch said 5:00 PM. He sipped from his water bottle while he cleared his mind. The phone kept ringing.

"Who in hell knows I'm here?" he thought. "I didn't even give Kelly the name."

He lifted the receiver. "*Hola?*"

"*Señor* Sutherland. It's Mercedes."

He exhaled. It could have been worse. "How did you know I where I was?"

"I had your taxi driver watched. Why did you move?"

"Still spying on me? God dammit, leave me alone. Unless you know where Gabriela is, we've got nothing to talk about."

"That's why I called. But I need you to promise something first. If I help you find her, will you do your best to retrieve the artifacts?"

"Where is she?"

"I don't know yet."

"All I'll say is, if we find her, and if she knows where the shipment's hidden, I'll ask the police in Chicago to sort it out. After that, I'm through. Arias won't need to bother us anymore."

"My father will never agree to that."

"So he knows where she is?" He bolted to his feet. "I thought there was something funny. I should've squeezed it out of him."

"He doesn't know yet," she said. "But he has a friend."

"Until then, it's moot. I told you what I'll do." He hung up.

He had to be more careful. This time he was lucky. The person who had followed him there worked for Mercedes. Someone who wasn't dangerous, or so he hoped. Yet she or her father might have told someone he was staying at the San Francisco.

He took a shower, got dressed, and walked the two blocks to *el Jardín*, stopping now and then to look behind him. He found a bench in the shadows under the trees. *El Jardín* was filled with children, strollers, and hawkers selling hats, balloons, and dolls. As the town life drifted around him, he imagined a conversation with Arias in which he promised to deliver the shipment if Gabriela was released. But it would never work. He wouldn't be that gullible.

His best chance was if Mercedes or Roberto located her. She would be guarded, so he would need some help, either from the police or *federales*.

With nothing he could do at the moment, a good dinner was in order. He headed across *el Jardín*, went down *Calle Correo*, and walked toward *El Pegaso*, a restaurant he'd seen advertised. The street was well-lit and crowded. Striding along, he thought about how his life had changed since Friday. One day, he was carefree. The next, he was pursued and paranoid. He glanced over his shoulder just in time to see a big man wheeling around to look into a store window. He wore a blue blazer and looked American. After a second, he peeked back at Sutherland. When their eyes met, he hustled away.

Sutherland started after him. Whether Arias' or Christopher's man, it was better to meet him in a public place. After a few steps, he stopped. If the man had wanted to talk, nothing was in his way. Evidently he had something else in mind.

He circled the block, watching to assure he wasn't followed, and entered the restaurant. The room was warm, the air filled with the aroma of garlic and coriander. After ordering *vino tinto y chiles en nogada*, he examined the paintings and *artesanía* hanging on the walls behind him. When he turned around, Agent Christopher was standing on the other side of the table. He wore a jacket and tie, looking more like a middle-aged banker than a tourist. Except Sutherland knew better. Silver hair and a conservative suit didn't mean he wasn't lightning-fast and strong. Two nights ago, he'd put Sutherland's lights out.

Reflexively, Sutherland rubbed his solar plexus. It was still sore. He felt his hair raise on his neck. When he balled his fists and started to rise, Christopher held up his hand in peace.

"Mind if I sit?" he asked.

For a moment Sutherland didn't move. He was half-standing, poised to defend himself. He finally eased back into his chair and gestured at the chair across the table.

"That your man following me?" He sipped his wine, trying to keep his hand from shaking.

Christopher nodded and sat. "I'm afraid he's a little green. You put Agent Bradley out of commission for a few days."

"What can I do for the DEA?"

"Arias has your mother. We can help you."

Sutherland slowly set his wineglass down. He felt a trapdoor sagging beneath him, and it was on the verge of tripping. Despite his suspicions, he wanted Christopher to be wrong or lying. This whole thing was her fault, and he didn't want to be responsible for what happened to her.

"Why should I believe you?" he said. "How would you know?"

"We have some of Arias' phones monitored. Her men picked her up last night."

If Christopher was right, Sutherland's suspicions about Hidalgo were, too. The professor knew why she missed their meeting.

"What's he going to do with her?"

"He thinks she knows where her nephew hid the stuff. She had the kid watching that gallery ever since Arias got involved. If she won't tell or doesn't know, Arias thinks by holding her you'll cooperate. He's convinced you're working together."

"Why can't I just talk to him? Tell him the truth. I can't give him what I don't have."

"You can't trust him. Believe me. Besides, he'd never believe you."

"And I can trust you? Didn't you bug Kelly's place?"

Christopher opened his mouth to answer when the waiter came and set the plate of *chiles* in front of Sutherland. He spoke to Christopher. "*Algo que tomar?*"

"*No gracias,*" Sutherland said. "He's not staying."

The waiter left and Christopher said, "That's true about her line. Like Arias', we monitored it. He knows you're here. You met with Hidalgo this morning and stopped into the Chapultepec Gallery last evening. He's counting on you to lead him to the shipment. So are we."

"But I told you…"

"Right. You don't know where it is. But as long he thinks you do, he'll be after you. As long as he's after you, we'll be there. You're our key to nailing him."

"You're after him for drugs, right? I mean, the DEA and all?" Sutherland took a bite of stuffed *chile.*

"Right. He's a small fish compared to the cartels, but he's my fish."

"Why not just arrest him? Why do you need me?"

"I have no authority here. Anyway, he's nearly untouchable in Mexico. His money's bought all the locals. Now that he knows we're on to him, he'll avoid the United States and do business long distance. The artifacts will lure him back, and only you can do it. He'd suspect anyone else."

"Do you know where he's keeping her?"

"Not yet."

"If you have his lines tapped and can't find her, how do you expect me to?"

Christopher smiled amiably. "You remind me of guys I played cards with in the Marines. They'd say, 'I'm just a dumb ol' country boy. You slickers gon' take advantage of me.' Then they'd strip me clean. I figure, if you don't know where she or that shipment is, you'll find out. You've already found the tomb and Arias' girlfriend at the gallery. I still think Javier gave you more than that note."

"He didn't," Sutherland said, feeling his face grow hot. "Like I told the waiter, you're leaving. When I find Gabriela, if she knows anything, I'll help you. Otherwise…"

Christopher leaned forward. The cords of his neck strained against his collar. "Don't be stupid. Forget freeing your mother. Arias will kill you."

"That's what I don't understand," Sutherland said. "What's that stuff worth? Fifty or a hundred thousand on the black market? What's that to a drug trafficker?"

Christopher leaned back and chuckled. "Hidalgo didn't tell you?"

"If you ask him, it's priceless, but not in dollars."

Christopher grinned like a man with an ace-high flush. "You know what a stele is?"

Sutherland thought for a moment. "A slab of stone carved with pictures. Hieroglyphics."

"You're a better archeologist than Arias. The greedy bastard didn't know what those farmers stole. He shipped all that crap from the dig to Chicago, including the stele. It's worth serious money, but that stele's the thing. It had a lizard on it. Professor Hidalgo calls it the *lagarto* stone. By the time Arias found out, the shipment was gone, and that kid hijacked it."

"What's the big deal with the stone?"

"If the legend is true, it means tens of millions."

Sutherland almost choked on his *chile*. "Legend?"

"Toltec or Mayan, I don't know. Ask the professor. The legend says that the stone, the *lagarto*, is the key to a horde of precious metal mined before the Spanish arrived."

"How'd Gabriela know about this *lagarto* stone?"

"She didn't. She's just trying to stop Arias from selling Mexican treasures."

"So you bust him for drugs, even though this is about gold?"

"If we connect him to this shipment, he'll go down for murder as well."

"The *campesinos* who robbed the tomb?"

Christopher nodded, then paused "And Chicago."

Sutherland stopped with his fork halfway to his mouth. Kelly's image flashed before him. If they went after Gabriela, why not Kelly?

"Couldn't be," he thought. "For God's sake, I just talked to her a couple hours ago."

Christopher stood up. "Finish your meal, Mr. Sutherland. I'll be in the square. Or call me." He handed Sutherland a card.

Sutherland was out of his chair. "Who in Chicago?"

Christopher looked surprised and then a little pleased.

"You didn't hear? They slipped into Javier Castellano's hospital room. If he'd been conscious, he might have told them where he put the truck. You'd be off the hook. So I doubt he said anything before he died."

# CHAPTER TWENTY

▼

"How did you know?" Detective Duncan said over the phone. Even with the bad connection, the detective was obviously in a cranky mood. "Javier Castellano died last night. Where are you?"

"Mexico," Sutherland replied. He didn't waste any time after learning about Javier. He paid his bill and left the restaurant. Making certain he wasn't followed, he turned often and went a street beyond the Hotel Colibrí, circling the block to arrive from the other direction. He called the detective from his room. "How did he die?"

"Complications. Who told you?"

"Agent Christopher, the DEA guy Kelly told you about. Did someone get past your guard?"

Several seconds elapsed before Duncan answered. "No one got past no one. What makes you think that?"

"Your 'complications' were guys looking for a shipment. They were questioning him. Maybe they pushed a little far."

"Who said he was killed? We don't know."

"Look, he hid a shipment of valuable artifacts somewhere. I don't think he told them where. Otherwise, they wouldn't have kidnapped Gabriela."

"Who's Gabriela?"

"My mother. She lives down here."

"What would someone want with her? You making this up?"

"I wish I was. Now I'm worried about Kelly. Can you protect her?"

"Mr. Sutherland, we don't know that the boy was killed. He was in critical condition from a gunshot wound. As far as the department is concerned, we got a dead illegal, probably shot in a drug deal. You know how many of those we see? And as for someone being kidnapped in Mexico? We can't go around guarding people on those grounds. You got more to tell me, I'm all ears."

Duncan knew nothing of what Sutherland had learned since yesterday. He probably didn't want to either. He just wanted to close the book on a dead illegal and be done with it. If he expected any help, he had to tell the policeman everything. His summary took ten minutes.

"You're saying there's a shipment with gold or silver?"

"No. Statues, masks, and pottery. Stuff like that. It must be in crates. One piece is supposed to lead to a tomb worth millions."

"This kid knew where it is?"

"He hid it. They think I know where it is." Sutherland was becoming impatient. It was very confusing, but aren't cops supposed to be used to this stuff?

After a few seconds of silence, Duncan said, "Look, Sutherland. The best I can do is talk to my lieutenant. I can't promise anything. Most of this is out of our jurisdiction. Smuggling…kidnapping…Mexico. Call me tomorrow morning."

Sutherland hung up, muttering. "Jurisdiction. Talk to my lieutenant. It's another way of saying no. Serve and protect? Bullshit."

Sutherland didn't waste any time calling Kelly's office. The woman answering said she had just left. He tried her cell phone number and found her in her car.

"Glad I caught you," he said. "Where you going?"

"Home. Then I'm having dinner at Maggiano's with my aunt. You convinced me. I'm spending the night at her house. What's new there?"

He told her about his meeting with Christopher and Javier's death.

"Why do you have to go to your place at all?"

"My laptop's there. And I need some clothes. Just in and out. Don't worry."

"Be careful. Any progress on the Beverly Shores thing or Arias' arrest?"

"I'm working on it. I also did a quick search on your friend Mercedes. Why didn't you tell me she was famous?"

"She said she works in a museum."

"Not *a* museum. New York's Museum of Natural History. She has a PhD in archeology and has published all kinds of articles on Mayan and Olmec civilizations."

"She didn't tell me."

"Then she's humble, too. Another thing. Vicente Hidalgo, her father, has had some problems. They think artifacts from one of his digs were taken from another location and he fabricated his findings. He lost a big grant as a result."

"Interesting."

"Anyway, I gotta go. I'm in the garage. Love ya."

He hung up the phone, relieved that she took his advice about going to her aunt's house, but annoyed at himself for not asking for the phone number. Then her last words registered. It was the first time the word "love" had intruded into their relationship. It complicated matters. But, from where he sat, feeling lost and alone in a strange hotel, it sounded pretty damn good.

He splashed water on his face. Javier's death added urgency to finding Gabriela. He hadn't known Javier. He didn't know if he really was a cousin. He'd seen him twice in his life, once lying in his lobby and once in his hospital bed. The image of those frightened eyes haunted him. Gabriela sent him on what she naïvely believed was a simple matter of following the smuggled shipment. She didn't know about the stone or gold, didn't know more was at stake than artifacts. So he'd died in the effort.

*Que en paz descances, Javier.* Rest in peace.

When he called the Hotel Posada de San Francisco, he learned that Roberto had left a number, which he dialed immediately. He heard loud music and voices in the background when Roberto answered.

"*Buenas noches, señor.* I have news," he said. "*Buenas noticias.*"

"I can hardly hear you. What good news?"

"*Bueno.* I find some things. Your mother, two men take her. To a mine."

Sutherland's stomach heaved, like he was falling. Christopher had been right. "That's your good news? Where's the mine?"

"One hour. Near."

"We'll get the police. Can you take us there?"

"Only *mi amigo* knows the mine. No police."

"They're kidnappers, Roberto. That's against the law, isn't it?"

"*Sí, señor.* But *mi amigo* no like *la policía.* They no like him."

He thought about Christopher and the man he had with him. DEA guys were trained for this type of thing. Maybe not kidnappings, but dealing with bad guys in general. He just wouldn't tell Roberto's *amigo* who they were.

"I'll bring some friends. We may need help."

"He no trust people he don't know. I had to promise you okay."

Sutherland wasn't sure it was smart, but what else did he have?

"When can he take me?"

"This night. He wants 3,000 pesos."

Sutherland calculated quickly. That was $270 or $280. "Give me a half hour. Meet me at…" He thought a moment. "In front of the library."

"*Sí, señor. Hasta pronto.*"

"Oh, Roberto?"

"*Sí?*"

"Can you bring some weapons?"

"*No problema. Mi amigo* is a very cautious man, *señor. Por si acaso.*" Just in case.

After hanging up with Roberto, Sutherland tried Kelly's number, hoping to catch her in her apartment. He got her machine. Even though the police had removed the tap, he was careful to leave a message that wouldn't jeopardize either one of them.

"Leave the phone number of where you're staying with Detective Duncan."

There was no answer on her cell phone either, but she usually turned it off after work.

Before going out, he called his old hotel one more time and asked if his bag was at the desk. The receptionist told him yes, then noticed another note for him from earlier that day. In heavily accented English, he read it to Sutherland, "I would like to meet on the subject of your visit and the reward I am offering. Tomorrow morning at the southwest entrance to the botanical garden. Eight o'clock."

It had to be from Arias. Roberto had seen the woman from the Chapultepec Gallery in the hotel lobby. Sutherland had been stupid to visit the gallery. Even if Arias hadn't tapped Kelly's line, once he suspected it was Sutherland asking questions, he could have had every hotel checked.

As Sutherland headed for the cash machine across from *el Jardín*, he hoped he wouldn't need to go to the botanical garden. If they found Gabriela tonight, the police would be greeting Arias tomorrow. If they didn't free her, he just didn't want to think about it.

# CHAPTER TWENTY-ONE

▼

Kelly passed up the building elevator and took the six flights two stairs at a time. It was her way of burning off a few calories and some of the day's tension. She had to cut her run short that morning because of an early meeting with her boss at city hall. She strode down the corridor to her condo apartment, unlocked the door, and entered. Seeing the bouquet on her hall table made her smile. After Doug had arrived with flowers the first time, she started bringing them home herself. It was a small but pleasing touch to her otherwise perfect apartment. She couldn't name a single flower in the latest bunch, but she loved the way the purple and blue complemented the white and yellow.

Her loft was part of a converted warehouse. She loved the spaciousness, the high ceilings and exposed brick walls, and the south-facing view of the city. It was a practical size for a neat person who disliked maintenance and cleaning. It contained a master bedroom, bath, and walk-in closet. It also had a modern kitchen with adjacent dining area, a den with a second bathroom, and a living room with a large balcony and fire escape.

She threw her coat over a chair, opened the refrigerator, pulled out a bottle of water, cracked open the top, and drank it in one long chug. Work had been nothing but meetings, combative discussions, and "cover your ass" positioning. Lunch was an apple and yogurt at her desk with no time to finish preparing for court the next morning. She'd have to do that at her aunt's place after dinner.

She checked her phone messages and found there'd been a call fifteen minutes earlier. There was no message, and the caller's number wasn't familiar. Holding that phone, knowing someone had been listening on a wiretap only hours earlier, gave her a chill.

In her bedroom, she pulled an overnight bag from under the bed. Besides her laptop, she'd need toiletries, running gear, and at least one change of clothes. Tomorrow was a big day and she planned to wear her power suit, the Burberry navy blue pinstripe.

Half-packed, she sat on her bed and stared into the dresser mirror. The circles under the eyes weren't becoming. She had to get more sleep. The last few days had been hectic, and between work and worry, she was drained. Going to her aunt's place in the suburbs wasn't helping either. Was Doug being paranoid by insisting she go?

No, she thought, standing again with a sigh. He was right. Her phone had already been bugged and this Arias character was threatening a woman in Mexico. Why wouldn't he target someone closer to Doug in Chicago?

Was she close to Doug? She sometimes wondered. After all these months, she was still learning consequential details about him. He told her nothing about his failed marriage except he adored his daughter and had loved Margo but she was very insecure and needy. As a result, she compensated by spending money on everything and everybody. Kelly tried to imagine Doug with a needy person and gave up. Just as he had.

He'd been secretive about his father as well. She only knew that he had died some years ago. Now it comes out that his mother—his Mexican mother—was still living. His Mexican heritage would never have occurred to Kelly. When they first met, years ago at that dig in Chiapas, the first thing she noticed was those startling blue eyes shining from that deeply tanned face. She'd been attracted to his quiet manner, good looks, and the special feeling she got when they were together, digging side by side or practicing Spanish over *cerveza fría* with Arturo, the head of the excavation. Their relationship never had time to develop beyond friendship. They both had too many plans, which sent them in different directions.

Ex-wife...father...mother. What other surprises awaited? On his behalf, Kelly had her assistant looking into an old murder in Indiana, another in a Chicago pawnshop, and a car accident. All were supposedly tied into this mess with the boy who was shot. DEA agents...Mexican hoodlums...archeologists. She thought her life as a lawyer for the city was complicated.

Where was all of it going? Not just with the Arias business. Where was it going with Doug and her? Not long ago, she thought they were getting closer. With a little more time, they'd both feel comfortable enough to take the plunge. Now things felt out of kilter. She wasn't calling it quits, but she had to make a serious assessment of where they stood. She, like Doug, had married once. Hers lasted two years before mutual apathy set in. She didn't feel compelled to get married again. Having children wasn't a priority. She was a successful lawyer and could be as independent as Doug.

He was certainly that. He wanted neither to need nor be needed. Could she live with that?

Nearly packed and changed into slacks and a sweater, she went to retrieve her suit from the walk-in closet. She was removing the plastic cleaner's bag when she heard a crash followed by tinkling glass. Startled, she dropped the suit and cocked her head to listen.

There was another crash and then another. Before she could move, she heard voices and footsteps crunching on broken glass.

# CHAPTER TWENTY-TWO

▼

The heat of the Mexican day had died with the sun. Sutherland zipped up his leather jacket as he watched San Miguel's library from the doorway of the *farmacia* across the street. It was 8:30 PM when the green-and-white taxi pulled up. Roberto was alone, hunched over the wheel with his baseball cap pulled low over his eyes. Sutherland looked up and down *Calle Insurgentes*, looking for anything out of place, like a pedestrian or car that didn't fit. Nothing seemed suspicious. Horns sounded at double-parked shoppers. Buses rattled by spewing fumes. Street venders went about their business. Who could tell?

Dodging a VW Beetle, he jogged across the street and slipped in the passenger side of Roberto's car.

"Where's your *amigo*?"

"Angel no like *el centro*."

"Something to do with the police?"

Roberto shrugged. "He very careful."

"What did he do? Why does he avoid the police? I've got to know that I can trust him."

"No worry, *señor*. Was a *malentendido*. You can trust Angel."

A *misunderstanding*. Sutherland would bet the 3,000 pesos in his pocket that Angel didn't live up to his name. But he couldn't be picky. The police didn't know where Gabriela was. Then a scary thought struck him. What if this was a trap? Were Roberto and Angel working for Arias? Since arranging this meeting a half hour ago and running to get the cash, he hadn't had time to think about that.

"Where are we going, Roberto? After we meet your *amigo*?"

"Toward Guanajuato. Many old silver mines there. Angel knows the one."

"How did he find where she was?"

"A man who was there drank too much *mescal*." He laughed. "There are no secrets in *las cantinas*."

"Does Angel have a plan to rescue her?"

Roberto jerked his head to indicate the backseat. "I have it."

Sutherland turned around and saw a cardboard box with a half-dozen bottles inside. "*Mescal?*"

Roberto nodded.

"It doesn't seem like much of plan. How many guards are there?"

"No worry, *señor*. It is strong."

Fifteen minutes from the center of San Miguel, they turned into *Refaccionaría Raúl*, an auto repair shop, on a dark side street. No one was in sight and there were no lights showing from within. It was a perfect place for a trap. Roberto got out, rapped on the overhead door, and disappeared inside as it opened. The ignition keys were gone, so Sutherland would have to depend on his worn deck shoes if he needed an escape. He opened the door and planted one foot on the ground, keeping his eyes on the shop. The ground was oily black, and the smell of spray paint made him want to hold his breath. What were they doing in there? Meeting with Arias? Loading their machine guns? He'd wait another minute. Then he was splitting.

The front door opened. A man with a Western-style hat, jeans, boots, and a Dallas Cowboys jacket walked out in front of Roberto. Angel was six inches taller and twenty pounds lighter than his squat *amigo*, but he sported the same droopy mustache. As he approached the taxi, he waved Sutherland to follow and said, "Bring the bottles." He continued around the side of the building.

Sutherland was retrieving the *mescal* when Roberto started the car.

"*Hasta luego, señor.* Good luck."

"Wait a minute." Sutherland nearly dropped the box. "Where you going?"

"Home. I pick you up tomorrow."

"But…" Sutherland couldn't speak. "You aren't coming with us?"

He held up his hands. "I am only a taxi driver, *señor*. I have three little ones. Angel no have a family."

Sitting next to Angel in a new Ford SUV with Texas plates, Sutherland wondered what he was in for. He knew it was a snap judgment, but men in Angel's apparent social circle don't buy expensive autos on what they legally earn. And why the foreign plates? He cast a sideways look at Angel, who was chewing on a toothpick as he wheeled the car onto the highway.

"Nice car. Looks brand new," Sutherland said before correcting himself. *"Es nuevo, no?"*

*"Sí."* He pointed to the odometer. *"Tiene pocos kilómetros."* He smiled at Sutherland, showing a gap where an incisor should have been.

"You speak English?"

Angel puffed out his chest. *"Sí, señor.* I learn from *un Americano.* He brings cars. I fix and sell. We talk *inglés,* okay?"

Judging by the way he pronounced cars, Angel's friend was from New Jersey.

"Okay. How far are we going?"

"Eighty kilometers, *no más."*

"You're sure Gabriela Castellano is there?"

He shrugged. "A woman. In a mine."

It was a stupid question. How many women from San Miguel are being held in a mine?

"How many guards?"

"One or two. I meet one of them in jail. He trust me."

"You plan to get them drunk?"

*"Sí, señor."*

"What if they don't want to drink?"

"Like my *Americano amigo* say, plan B."

"Which is?"

"We shoot them."

Sutherland didn't think Angel was kidding. He cinched his seatbelt tighter, as if that would protect him from guards and guns.

After a gradual climb into the mountains, Angel stopped in a tiny pueblo consisting of a dusty strip of tumbledown shacks. He disappeared through the open doorway of the village's *taberna* for a few minutes and returned with a scrap of paper in his hands.

"The old mines they are difficult to find," he said as he started the car.

Ten minutes out of town, they left the main highway and bounced over back roads until finally rising to a wide mesa bordered on one side by the mountain. In the center of the mesa stood a cluster of crumbling brick buildings, pale in the three-quarter moon. A few trees overhung the fallen walls. A dim light glowed from behind the largest of the buildings.

"We arrive," Angel said.

"Where's the mine?"

"There are many. I find the one. Stay here." He pulled a gym bag from behind the seat. From inside, he withdrew a small revolver and checked the cylinder for bullets. Satisfied, he put it back in the bag with his car keys and one of the mescal bottles.

"*Hasta pronto.*" He took the bag and walked toward the buildings forty yards away.

They must have been a couple thousand feet higher than San Miguel, which was already around 6,000 feet. It was getting cold, and Sutherland started to shiver. He zipped his leather coat up to his neck while he tried to picture what Angel was doing. He hadn't heard any shots. It was a good sign, but it didn't mean his plan was working. The more he thought about it, the lamer it seemed. Angel could be a prisoner himself. On the other hand, he and the guards could be passing the bottle around while planning his fate. Had there been any other way, he would have seized it. Now there was no turning back.

He got out of the car and stamped his feet, trying to warm and calm himself. On his second lap around the car, Angel returned.

"*No problema,*" he said. "This *guardia,* he remember me. He has a gun, but he is a pig and drink too much." He grabbed another bottle from the backseat. "Fifteen minutes."

"Have you seen her?"

Angel looked at him as if he was crazy. "I no go in the mine."

"What?"

Angel walked away without answering, leaving Sutherland stunned. It wasn't so much what Angel had said, but how he said it. As if going into a mine was the last thing he would do. Who would bring Gabriela out if Angel wouldn't do it? Sutherland remembered the paralysis he felt at the entrance of the tomb, when Mercedes had to almost drag him in. He knew it was illogical, but situations like that conjured all the panic of his dreams, the terror of being trapped inside the dark space. From nowhere, the image of the VW being hauled from the water flashed through his mind. He felt his heart race, a cold sweat forming on his brow.

Angel returned twenty minutes later, he was showing his gap-toothed smile.

"We find the mine. Come."

Sutherland followed him around the wall to an overhead tarp stretched from the wall to several trees. Underneath was a mattress, a crude table cluttered with bottles, two wooden stools, and a dying fire. A bare light bulb swung from a wire in the center of the tarp, casting moving shadows over the man on the mattress.

"Is he?" Sutherland asked.

"He drink *mucho.*" Angel held up a pistol. "I have his gun."

"Where's the electricity come from?"

"They bring a *generador* and *baterías* for the mine." From the top of a pile of clothes and blankets by the wall, Angel grabbed a hard hat with a miner's light and put it on.

"Take one for you and one for the woman," he said.

Sutherland tried on a hat and tied a second to his belt.

"And *guantes* for the rope," Angel said, pointing to the pile.

"Gloves? Rope?"

Sutherland's hands trembled as he pulled on the worn work gloves. Did he have the nerve to do this?

Angel took a long pull from the *mescal* bottle and offered it to Sutherland, who sipped tentatively. It tasted like kerosene, just as he remembered. After a deep breath, he took a large swig and let the slow burn settle him.

They found the mine by following the wire from the lean-to where the guard slept. It was a hundred yards from the buildings and nothing like Sutherland expected. It was only a gaping hole with a fifteen-foot diameter cut into the rocky ground. On one edge sat the rusted frame of a winch or crane. The stone remains of a small building sat on the other rim. Peering down into the darkness, Sutherland could barely breathe. He reminded himself that Gabriela was down there. At least he hoped so.

"You sure she's there?"

"Why have a *guardia* if no one there?"

Sutherland looked down into the black hole. "You said there were lights."

"*Un momento.*" Angel flicked on his helmet light and searched around the derelict crane. "The *guardia* say it was...*aquí.*" He bent down and Sutherland watched as he connected two wires to the pair coming from the generator. A glow shone from a bare bulb twenty feet down. Sutherland felt as if he was looking into the mouth of hell. It was almost vertical and sheer rock.

"How?"

Just then, Angel heaved a coil of rope down the hole. He gestured an invitation to go.

"Aren't you coming?"

Sutherland already knew the answer. Looking into the dark hole, he breathed deeply, trying to quiet the pounding in his temples. Despite the cold, sweat trickled down his sides. He took the rope in his hands and pulled.

"What's this tied to?"

Angel followed the rope to where it was knotted around the winch.

*"Es seguro. Está listo?"*

He would never be ready. For the first time in memory, he didn't trust himself. He'd gladly put his faith in someone else. It was ironic that it concerned something as important as his mother's life. He wasn't here for her. She was the only one who could pull him from the quagmire she'd thrown him in.

"*Momento.*" Angel held out his hand. "You have the money, no?"

That wasn't a good sign. "Afraid I won't come back?"

Angel shrugged, still with his hand out.

Sutherland looked at Angel and then peered into the chasm below. "I'll pay you double if you go instead," he said.

Angel shook his head and spit to the side. "*De ninguna manera,*" he said. "These mines they are *hechizadas. Hay fantasmas.* They take your body."

A haunted mine with body-snatching ghosts? There was no telling how that superstition got started. Sutherland removed his glove and counted out 1,500 pesos.

"The rest when I return."

Angel shrugged once more and stuffed the money into his jeans. Sutherland peered over the edge again. The first light on the string was almost straight down, maybe ten degrees off vertical. He kicked a rock into the hole and listened. It chunked once against the wall and hit twice again. It then disappeared into the silence below. This was crazy. One slip and his next stop would be hell.

With his first step backward over the lip, he felt his stomach revolt and had to swallow bile. The strain on his arms and shoulders as he paid out rope stopped the shaking, but his legs felt wobbly. His feet skidded down the rock to the first hold. His whole body was rebelling. Before he reached the first light, he could no longer make out Angel above. As the walls closed around him, he had to stifle the urge to scream.

"I have to do this," he repeated to himself. "No one else will."

Hand over hand with one foot below the other, he blindly felt his way. His head lamp only illuminated the rock face in front and above. The lights along the wire were thirty feet apart and too dim for anything except a ghostly glow. Thirty feet…fifty feet…seventy feet. It was excruciating labor. His forearms, biceps, and shoulders were already aching. He cursed Angel repeatedly for refusing to go.

Eighty feet from the top, the shaft was sloped twenty degrees from vertical. The only sound was his heavy breathing and the scuffling of his shoes against the rock. Then suddenly as he shifted his weight onto his right leg, his foot slipped. His body slammed against the rock, elbows first, forcing him to ease his hold on the rope. He scraped down the rock face, his feet scrambling for purchase, hands trying to regain their grip on the rope. His knee finally hit a protrusion, slowing him enough to get the rope around his wrist. After a few more feet, he slid to a stop. He hung until he found a toehold with his left foot. Pressing against the wall, he breathed deeply and took inventory. He'd lost his hard hat and headlamp. His knees were banged up and probably bleeding, but his leather jacket had protected his elbows and chest. He felt a trickle of blood from his eyebrow and his left hand had been rope-burned after he'd lost one glove. His right foot felt strange and he thought his shoe was gone.

He slowly moved his foot and realized the deck shoe was there, but only barely. The heel had pulled out and the shoe hung on his toes, dangling like a hat on a hook. Another inch…*adiós*.

He knew what he had to do. He just hoped he had the strength. First, he double-wrapped the rope around his left wrist. Then he inched his right foot up as he reached down with his right hand. His toes cramped twice, and he had to stop, holding the shoe on by pushing it against the wall. With a last effort, ignoring painful cramps, he grabbed the heel and forced it back on.

Hanging there, he wondered how much farther he had to go. Too far, he'd never make it up again.

"What a place to keep someone!" he thought. "Without this rope or wings, no one could escape. Hell, even with this rope, it wasn't very likely."

It didn't matter. He had to keep moving. It was work to just hang on and by focusing on the descent, he kept the fear at bay.

After he passed another light, the shaft began leveling out, making his descent easier. It was like walking down steep stairs backward. Soon after, the string of lights took a sharp left turn, leading into another tunnel, leaving the vertical shaft below in total darkness. He released the rope and scrambled into the branch tunnel. It was six feet in diameter and inclined upward. A shallow rivulet ran down its center and cascaded into the shaft. He leaned against the wall and flexed his fingers and arms to loosen the knots.

The tunnel had barely enough room on either side of the water to avoid getting wet. The electric wire was draped over rusted hooks in the wall. After passing three lights, he entered a twenty-foot by thirty-foot chamber with a ceiling barely visible in the darkness. On the left, water ran down the rock face and streamed into the tunnel. In a far corner, he could see a mattress and blanket. Glints of reflected light shone from crystals in the black rock surrounding him. The only sounds were gurgling water and his own breathing.

Where was she? Had this been a trick?

He heard a soft shuffle behind him, and he spun around.

The rock the woman held was as large as a cantaloupe, and she was ready to throw it.

*"Quién es usted?"*

He didn't recognize the face. Just then, the string of lights blinked and went out.

# CHAPTER TWENTY-THREE

▼

The darkness was suffocating. The lights had blinked once and vanished, engulfing him in black. He wanted to cry out, but the sound caught in his throat.

"*Caray!*" The woman's voice jolted him. Remembering she had a rock, he leaped sideways. He listened. The only sounds were the streaming water and his racing heartbeat. What happened with the lights? Who was the woman?

"*Quién es usted?*" Her voice echoed in the chamber.

"*Soy* Douglas Sutherland."

She gasped. "*No puede ser. Imposible.*"

He remembered the other hard hat on his belt and fumbled with the strap, finally untying it. Retreating a few precautionary steps, he switched on the light and focused on her. She was ten feet away, the rock now resting on her hip. She wore jeans, running shoes, and a jacket over a heavy sweater. Her hair was matted, her face swollen and dirty. In the stark light, she was shocking. He barely recognized her.

"Gabriela?" he said, "It's you?"

She squinted at him. He turned the light on his face. Banged up as he felt, she might not recognize him either.

After a moment's hesitation, she said, "*Sí*, my son. But how?"

She dropped the rock and stepped toward him, her eyes wide with disbelief. She touched his cheek and nodded. Tears spilled down her cheeks. She lay her head against his chest and sobbed. Slowly, as if he might burn himself, he wrapped his free arm around her shoulder. For an instant, he was elated he had found her. But the triumph quickly disappeared. The darkness, the sound of water, and her voice, his nightmare was real. He let go and staggered backward, dropping the headlamp.

She picked it up and shined it at him. "*Qué te pasa?* Are you sick?"

He heard her words and saw the concern in her eyes, but he couldn't answer. The gurgling water resonated in his head until it was a deluge. They were trapped…together. He dropped to the cold floor and hugged his knees, trying to stop the trembling. A moment later, he felt a blanket around him.

She knelt in front of him. "Douglas. *Tranquilizate.* Calm yourself." She grabbed him by the shoulders and shook him. "You must be calm. It is all right."

Her words soothed him. She lit a candle and set it on the rock floor between them. His mouth was dry and tasted of copper. He found himself staring into her worried eyes. Then she slapped him.

The sting jarred him back to the present. As he looked around the dim chamber, the dire reality of their situation replaced irrational fear. Had someone pulled up the rope when they cut the lights? He struggled to his feet and grabbed the miner's lamp.

"We have to go. *Rápido,*" he said. "Are you ready?"

"*Sí. Vámonos.*"

They started down the tunnel toward the main shaft. Sutherland went first with the hard hat on. She carried a candle.

"*Cabrones!*" she said. "Pigs and murderers."

"How long have you been here?"

"They took me Saturday night. How do we get out? Is there a rope?"

"If they didn't take it…" That was only the first of his concerns. If the rope was there, they had to manage a difficult climb. Who knew what awaited them at the top?

When he saw the rope, he felt the weight of the mine off him.

Tugging hard, it held. "It's a long way," he said, pointing his light up the shaft. "Tie this around you and I can help."

"Who was going to help me?" he thought.

She snuffed the candle with her fingers and put it in her back pocket. Then she pulled out her shirttail and tore off three strips of cloth. She handed him one.

"Put it around your hand," she said. "It bleeds."

He wrapped his rope-burned hand while she tied the cloth around her own palms, using her teeth and free hand to tie the knot.

"I go first," she said.

The first part sloped gradually with good footholds, but the ache in his arms immediately returned. She climbed easily, picking her path ahead of him in the cone of his headlamp. After glancing back at him several times, she said, "Don't climb only with your arms. Use your legs."

He was breathing hard, but he managed to say, "Can you see enough?"

"The lamp is bright."

As they continued up the forty-five-degree incline, he took her advice and found the climbing less tiring. He tried conserving his energy, knowing the steepest part of the shaft was ahead. And one worrisome question remained. What was waiting at the top?

"*Dios mío.*" Her cry echoed around the rock walls.

"*Que pasó?*"

She didn't have to answer. In the beam of his light, he saw it, a body lying head down above them. The torso was wedged in a crevice where the shaft took a slight bend. In the dim light, the face was unrecognizable, a black mass. But the jacket was Angel's. He swallowed hard, fighting the reflex to vomit.

"Don't look. Climb past it."

She hurried by the body while he breathed deeply, directing the light beam away from the dead man.

Poor Angel. He'd never see the balance of his fee.

Had he been pushed in? Sutherland took another breath and followed Gabriela, concentrating on the rope while avoiding another glimpse of the bloodied face. He had no stomach to retrieve his 1,500 pesos. After climbing a few more feet, he noticed Angel's fall had torn away one of the bulb sockets, leaving bare copper wires touching. A short circuit could explain the loss of lights. Maybe Angel's fall and the blackout weren't intentional.

They stopped on a stretch of the shaft where they could lean against the wall and rest.

"Where'd you learn to climb?" he asked. It was one of a thousand things he didn't know about her.

"In the Sierra Madres. *Descánsate.* Rest."

There was no time to rest. He couldn't stop imagining someone at the top cutting the rope.

"I'm ready. Let's go," he said.

They finally saw a glow from above. He put out his light, not wanting to alert anyone. They continued a few more feet in near darkness until she stopped at a small ledge, a three-inch outcropping, just wide enough for them to stand side by side.

"I remember this place from when I go down," she said. "Above us, there are *grietas,* cracks and small places for the hands and feet. Here one can climb without the rope. I thought I could escape then, but it is too hard below."

"Let's use the handholds," he said. "If anyone's waiting, they'll see the rope moving when we get closer."

He followed her, feeling for cracks and toeholds, pressing against the sloping rock face, pulling himself up a few inches at a time. His fingers weren't used to the strain, and he was tempted to grab the rope again. Then the night sky and rim were visible overhead. When he caught up, she was waiting just below the lip.

He peered over the top. No one was around. The only sound was the wind. They eased over the edge and crawled behind the crumbled brick wall beside the mine. Three feet high, the walls were all that remained of an old shed. On the ground by the door lay Angel's hat alongside an empty *mescal* bottle. If he'd finished that bottle, he could have stumbled into the mine, which would mean no one was waiting for them.

"Let's get to the car," he said while getting his bearings.

The buildings were barely visible in the distance. They kept low and took a circular route around them. As he led the way, all his questions for her swirled in his mind. Not only about Javier and the shipment. Why did she keep those photos and news clippings? He forced himself to focus on the present, the dangers they still might face. The answers would have to wait.

The SUV was still there. The area behind the wall and the camp was dark and silent. He remembered that Angel had thrown the car keys in his gym bag, which he'd left near the sleeping guard. His choice was to go in after the keys or walk.

"Wait behind the car," he said to Gabriela. "If I'm not right back, run that way. Stay off the road until you get to the highway." He started toward the buildings.

Light from the moon helped as he picked his way over the dry ground. He slowed as he reached the wall, placing each foot softly until he peeked into the camp. In the darkness, everything seemed the same—the tarp, cluttered table, pile of clothes, and snoring hulk on the mattress. Angel's bag was next to the table.

He inched to the edge of the tarp and stopped. Something was wrong. Two plastic grocery bags lay on the dirt beside Angel's bag. They weren't there before.

Just then, from behind, a man's voice spat out, *"No se mueva, hombre."*

# CHAPTER TWENTY-FOUR

▼

Sutherland stood rigid, his back to the voice. An image of Angel's battered face flashed in his mind. Was that to be Sutherland's fate now? A light went on behind him, projecting his silhouette across the mattress and the sleeping guard. By the table, he could clearly see Angel's bag. He imagined the gun and the car keys inside.

*"Vuélvase, amigo. Tengo una pistola."*

When a guy with a gun gives you an order, you obey. Sutherland turned and was blinded by the flashlight. "If I was your *amigo*, you wouldn't need a gun." He couldn't see the other's face.

"Ahhh, a *gringo*. Who the fuck are you?" The accent suggested he had lived in the United States.

"I'm lost. How do I get out of here?"

The man moved closer, keeping the light in Sutherland's eyes.

"Your wallet," he said. "Throw it here."

"Don't have one."

"Empty your pockets on the ground." Sutherland heard a click and assumed the gun was cocked. Sutherland's credit cards and passport were in the hotel. He only had a wad of pesos, the card with Christopher's phone number, and the stub of his airline boarding pass. As he laid them on the ground, he realized his name was on the stub. Too late now.

"Back away, and lay down on your stomach," the man said.

Sutherland did what he was told. When the man bent to collect the pocket's contents, Sutherland could see he wore a leather jacket and a gold watch. Was he alone? If so, there was a chance. He watched the man shove his gun into his waistband and shine the flashlight on the boarding pass. Was this Sutherland's opportunity? Should he rush him before he could grab the gun again?

Before he could act, the man stuffed the money, card, and stub into his pocket and retrieved the gun.

"*Señor* Sutherland," he said with satisfaction. "We've been looking for you, *pendejo.*"

Sutherland slowly exhaled, as if the air was lost hope. "Who are you? You work for Arias?"

"*Sí.* Arias." He said the name as if it was sacred. "I am Marcelo Arias. My Uncle Enrique will be happy I found you."

Marcelo's footsteps crunched closer on the ground until Sutherland was staring at a pair of Italian loafers a foot away.

"Where is the woman? Your mother, no?"

"In the mine. Where you bastards put her." Sutherland squinted into the light, wondering whether the gun was pointed at him. He had to do something.

"I am not stupid," Marcelo said. "You were down there."

"She couldn't climb it. I had to leave her."

Marcelo didn't say anything for a few seconds. He was probably debating whether to believe him. A few feet away on the mattress, the guard grunted something and continued snoring.

"Get up. We take a walk."

Sutherland pushed himself to his feet, but was still unable to see anything of the man's face.

"That way." He flashed the light in the direction of the mine.

He followed the electric wire again, Marcelo Arias a few steps behind.

"There's still some *mescal* in the car." Sutherland needed to know if Marcelo was alone. "Your *amigo* left plenty for the rest of you."

"*Imbécil.* Lucky I came with his supplies."

He'd said "Lucky I came." So he was alone. That meant Gabriela could slip away for help.

"What now?"

"You tell us where the shipment is."

Sutherland saved his denials. They were convinced he knew. At the mouth of the mine, Marcelo began a ground search with his flashlight, probably looking for evidence of a woman's footprints on the stony ground. He was maybe five-foot-eight and well-built. From the look of his expensive clothes, he was high in his uncle's circle. Sutherland casually edged his way to the door of the ruin where he had seen Angel's hat and the empty *mescal* bottle. It would be a good weapon in a pinch, and that's what this was. Before he could pick it up, Marcelo walked over and shined the light on the hat.

Sutherland said, "Did you push Angel in?"

"I didn't get his name."

"Bastard."

Marcelo smiled. His teeth were white against a dark, round face. "You'll also go, if you don't cooperate. Come here." He motioned toward the edge of the mine.

Sutherland took a step and stopped. "Sorry. Been there. Didn't like it."

"I could kill you right here."

"And piss off your uncle? He'll never see his stuff."

Marcelo shifted his weight and looked around, as if to find a rebuttal. It had to be true, his uncle wouldn't want Sutherland killed yet.

"Okay," he said. "You will either climb down yourself, or we lower you unconscious. Either way, you're there until he comes."

Sutherland glanced at the mine entrance. The image of the chamber and the thought of being in that darkness, alone this time, knotted his stomach. It would take hours for help to arrive. He'd die of panic first. His mouth was so dry he could hardly utter the words, "You might as well kill me. I'm not going down there."

He turned to Marcelo with the fatalism of a man facing the firing squad. That's when he saw the two figures walking toward them. Gabriela was alongside a man. For an instant, he thought he'd been saved, that she'd brought help. But her hands were behind her, as if bound. From the disappointment in her face, he knew the help was for Marcelo.

Sutherland watched them approach in the light of the three-quarter moon. The man beside Gabriela looked like a fireplug, short and bowlegged. He shoved her forward. Hands bound behind her, she stumbled, barely managing to keep her feet. When she regained her balance, she turned and spit at him.

"*Cabrón.*"

Marcelo laughed. "*Aquí está.* Good going, Juan." he said, obviously pleased.

Juan's hands were empty. Marcelo's back was turned to Sutherland. This was his chance. Sutherland hit Marcelo with all his weight, pinning his arms as he tackled him. They pitched forward and Sutherland straddled him, yanking back his gun arm. The gun flew out of his hand, but Sutherland kept pulling until he heard a sickening crack. Marcelo shrieked, a blood-chilling scream that tapered to pathetic groan.

Sutherland scrambled to his feet. Frantically turning, he searched the ground for the gun. He couldn't find it.

Fuck! Did it go down the shaft?

He heard a yell, but it was Gabriela this time. He spun to see Juan holding a knife to her throat. She struggled, but her wrists were still tied.

"*Voy a matarla* I kill her. I cut her throat."

Juan pushed her forward and Sutherland got a close look at him. His nose was bleeding, and his cheekbone was scratched. Back at the car, she'd put up a fight. Now the jagged blade of the knife was pressing against her neck. From the menace in Juan's eyes, he'd enjoy killing her.

"Okay, *bueno*." Sutherland raised his hands.

Juan dragged her to where Marcelo lay, still holding the knife on her. Marcelo was groaning, his right arm limp by his side. Could they escape? If Juan released her to help Marcelo, they could run to the camp, grab the keys, and take the car.

Marcelo slowly got to his feet alone, holding his arm by the elbow. His eyes were wet and glaring at Sutherland.

"*Hijo de chingada.* You're going to die." He looked at Juan. "*Dónde?* Where's my gun?"

The man shook his head, confused. It was dark, and no gun in sight.

"*No sé.* Did it fall in the mine?"

"*Carajo!*"

Marcelo took a step toward Sutherland and stopped, maybe thinking twice about attacking. His face was even darker now, contorted with pain and anger.

"Down there…" he hissed, pointing to the shaft, "or Juan cuts her throat. Now."

Sutherland could run. It would be easy. Marcelo was injured, and Juan didn't look fast. Neither one could catch him.

"You hear me, *pendejo*?" Marcelo screamed. "In the mine."

Sutherland could find Angel's gun at the camp, come back, and free Gabriela. He saw the moonlight glint off the blade at her throat.

"If they didn't kill her first," he thought.

"Juan, show this *pendejo* the color of her *sangre*," Marcelo said.

"*Cabrón*," Gabriela screamed. She squirmed, and Juan tightened his grip. He drew his knife edge along her jawline, leaving a thin, dark line.

"*Vete al diablo*," she shouted. She wriggled and must have grabbed him by the testicles. He howled and threw her to the ground. He landed on her with both knees, grabbed her by the hair, and held the knife at her jugular.

"You want to see more blood?" Marcelo asked.

Sutherland backed toward the hole and peered into the darkness. He couldn't return to that subterranean chamber. He wouldn't. The first time had been terrifying. This time, it meant certain death. Arias would have him killed eventually.

Then he remembered the ledge he and Gabriela found on their ascent, the three-inch outcropping just out of view of the mine's mouth. He could wait there until Marcelo left and then pick his way up using the handholds they'd used before. But he couldn't leave Gabriela with them.

"She has to come with me," he said. "If she's harmed, I tell your uncle nothing."

Marcelo glanced at her, and she glared back. "*La puta* goes after you. Now go."

Sutherland grabbed the rope and prepared to descend for the second time that night. This time, his fear was rational. If his plan didn't work, he was a dead man. He lowered himself over the lip and into the shaft. When he was five feet down, Marcelo peered over the rim, looking like an Olmec god considering Sutherland's fate.

"I change my mind."

He held up a knife. It might have been Juan's. He ran its edge lightly across the rope, as if to say, "One slice and you tumble into the *nada*."

"We don't wait for my uncle. You tell me now, or I cut the rope. Then the woman."

He might be bluffing, but Sutherland couldn't risk it. If he fell from here, he'd drop right over the ledge and all the way down. While he felt around for handholds and footholds, he tried inventing something, anything remotely believable. He found a small toehold and then a thin crack for the fingers of his left hand. But he needed a better grip.

"I'll count to ten," Marcelo said. "You tell me where it is, or I cut. *One.*"

"Tell him anything," Sutherland thought. "They knew Javier's note mentioned a key and an attic. Right now, any place and any key would do. Think."

"*Two.*"

"A house…an attic in a house…in Chicago," Sutherland thought.

"*Three.* Where's the shipment?"

"Say it was Pilson. Maybe a relative of Javier's. Eighteenth Street. What number?" he thought.

"*Four.*"

"You can't remember the number. You have to show them. They have to need you," he thought, finding another crack for his fingers, deeper and more secure.

"*Five.*"

"The key to the attic door was in his office desk. That's it," he thought, looking up, ready to shout it out.

"*Six.* Running out of…"

Marcelo didn't finish. He dropped the knife. It bounced off the rock and flashed past Sutherland's face. Then he tilted forward. His mouth was wide open as he grabbed air with his good arm. His loafers scuffed at the ground as he tried to get his balance. Stones skittered down the shaft and pelted Sutherland's head. When he saw him fall, Sutherland pressed against the wall and tightened his grip. Marcelo hit him on the shoulder, tearing his left hand from the crack and dislodging his foothold. He hung from the rope, his right hand straining to hang on. Marcelo had him around the ankle with his good arm.

"Help me!" he cried.

Sutherland had been spun around, his back to the rock wall. He looked down into Marcelo's terrified eyes. Sutherland's hand was slipping. There wasn't any choice. He kicked. His heel smashed into Marcelo's teeth and then nose. Marcelo hung on with desperate strength. Sutherland kicked again and again. When the kick crushed his eye, Marcelo let go. He scraped and bounced down the rock face, screaming. Sutherland squeezed his eyes closed, wishing against reason that it could shut out the cries. Then it stopped. Marcelo had joined Angel.

Sutherland got both hands on the rope and, as he explored for a foothold, he realized Marcelo had pulled off his shoe. With one bare foot, he climbed to the lip and peered over, preparing to face Juan again. Instead, he saw him sprawled on the ground. Mercedes Hidalgo stood over him, a broken bottle in one hand. With her other arm she pulled Gabriela to her feet.

"I presume this is your mother," she said.

"That's her," he gasped. "Gabriela Castellano. Thank her for getting us into this."

# CHAPTER TWENTY-FIVE

▼

Sutherland lay on the rocky ground, his legs still dangling over the edge. His heart was racing, his breath came in gulps. He'd just sent a man to his death. Did he have a choice? No. But that didn't make it less repugnant. Killing was to be confined to news and movies. Criminals, terrorists, cops, and soldiers killed, not ordinary citizens. It wasn't to be viewed firsthand, much less participated in. Seeing Angel's corpse was bad enough, but, seconds ago, he'd personally added to the body count. What did that make him?

"You all right?" Mercedes was untying Gabriela's hands.

He pulled himself up and flexed his shoulder. His arm felt as if it had been yanked from its socket. His hand was skinned and bleeding. As he hobbled toward the two women, he stepped on a sharp stone with his bare foot.

"Dammit!" He half-hopped and half-stumbled the rest of the way. "Where'd you come from?" he asked Mercedes.

Mercedes finished freeing Gabriela and said, "I had your hotel watched. I lost you for a while, but luckily your driver stopped for directions. When I arrived, that animal was hitting her." She pointed to Juan, the unconscious hulk on the ground.

"*Hijo de puta.*" Gabriela rubbed her wrists. Her knife wound was only a scratch, but her lower lip was swollen around a fresh cut.

"I was too far away to help," Mercedes continued. "I followed them and ducked behind that wall until their backs were turned. They'd have killed you both. Why didn't you tell him what he wanted?"

"We've covered that. I don't know anything."

"You don't?" Gabriela looked at him, dumbfounded. "But Javier said he gave you…"

"He was wrong. And now he's dead." He wanted to add "because of your naïve plan," but he stopped himself. "So now you're the only one who knows where your precious shipment is."

The news shocked her. Her shoulders sagged, and she leaned into Mercedes.

"Javier is dead?" she asked. "How?"

"Arias or one of his men killed him."

"*Que en paz descanse*," she said and crossed herself. "It is my fault." She breathed deeply. Her lips were tight, as if she was fighting back tears. "He wasn't supposed to steal it. He was only supposed to follow it and tell the police. He never told me what he did with it."

"Great," he said. "Arias is after us, and neither of us knows anything. Right now, let's get out of here before someone else comes."

"What do we do with him?" Mercedes pointed to Juan.

He was tired and shaken, his thinking confused. These men had killed Javier and the *campesinos*. They had also thrown Angel into the mine. Juan deserved the same. But the memory of Marcelo's terror-filled face and his bloodcurdling scream made Sutherland queasy. He didn't have it in him. Not again.

"We'll tie him up," he managed to say, "but I'll take his shoes if I can get them on."

The shoes were worn black oxfords and too small. They pinched like hell, but it was better than bare feet. After tying up Juan hand and foot, they hurried back to the camp and bound the sleeping guard. They left Angel's car where it was. Who knew who would be the next illegal owner? Mercedes' Jeep was parked behind Marcelo's SUV in a grove of trees.

On the way back to San Miguel, the three of them were quiet, as if absorbed in their own thoughts. Mercedes and Gabriela sat in front while Sutherland curled up against the cold in the tiny backseat. Despite all the bad things that had happened, there were several bright spots. Gabriela was safe. Kelly would be at her aunt's place by now and out of harm's way. If they could now find an uncorrupted policeman in San Miguel, they could have Arias arrested. It was at least something to hope for. He felt his fatigue weigh on him and after a few minutes, he was asleep.

He dreamed he was in the cockpit of his sailboat. The Chicago skyline was in the far distance, and the wind was bone chilling. Steep waves battered the boat, tossing him from side to side. Suddenly the boat hit a trough, and he was thrown off the seat.

He awoke with a start, shouting. "Ahhh.!"

"Sorry. *Un tope.* Speed bump," Mercedes yelled to him.

The street was riddled with ruts throwing the Jeep around. Ahead, he saw a familiar *abarrotes* store and, soon after, Gabriela's house at the top of the narrow street. As Mercedes parked and turned off the headlights, he glanced at his watch. It was 3:30 AM.

"You still have those *pesadillas,* the nightmares," Gabriela said, stepping down from the Jeep.

"I dreamt I was sailing."

"The other dreams. The closet…the burning man…the car."

It was usually a dark space and water. The man with flaming hair sometimes appeared. But she'd added the car. The VW in the newspaper clipping? They walked side by side toward her front door. Mercedes lagged behind.

"How do you know about my dreams?" he asked.

"Your father told me. And of the phobia. I thought you would get over it. But in the mine you…"

"So I have a problem," he said, as angry at his weakness as with her. "I didn't ask to be dragged into this. If you want a hero, call someone else next time."

He sped up to walk ahead of her, wanting to put the mine behind him. He wondered about his father staying in touch with her. He could understand sending photos, but why would he give particulars about nightmares? They must have had something to do with her.

Gabriela had lost her house keys, so Sutherland repeated his journey over the back wall. This time, Mercedes boosted him. After he let them in the front door, Gabriela directed Sutherland to a guest bathroom and disappeared into her bedroom.

The full-length mirror said it all. His jeans were torn and bloody. His jacket was shredded to the lining, and his face was caked with dirt and bloodied from a cut over the eyebrow. He stripped and stepped into the shower. The soap stung his cuts and rope-burned hand, but the hot water soothed the aches in his back and shoulders.

When he returned to the living room, clean but wearing the same tattered clothes, Mercedes had started a fire in the large fireplace. The room smelled of wood smoke and coffee. She sat on the sofa facing the hearth and the vandalized portrait of Gabriela. Three steaming mugs waited on the table. He eased himself down next to her, picked up a mug, and inhaled the cinnamon-rich *café de olla.*

Mercedes inspected his face. "That happen in the mine? You were very brave to go after her, considering your fear."

"But it was you who saved our asses. Thanks." He sipped the coffee and found it too hot. "Why'd you follow me?"

"My little spy told me you went to the bank. It was late, so I thought you were up to something. I waited and followed the taxi out of town."

"I had to go alone. Angel, the man who took me, insisted. He should have let me bring Christopher's men. He'd still be alive."

"Who's Christopher?"

"He's an American drug agency guy who's after Arias."

She wrinkled her brow, perplexed. "What do drugs have to do with this?"

"He smuggles them. But this isn't about drugs. Why didn't you tell me about the *lagarto* stone?"

Her face reddened. She stared at him like a guilty child who had just been found out.

Just then, Gabriela entered the living room. She wore a clean pair of jeans and shirt. Her hair was wrapped in a towel and she had a bandage over the cut on her jaw. Approaching the fireplace, she noticed her portrait with the words scribbled across her face.

"In my life, I never like that picture." Sitting down, she smiled at him for the first time that night. It was amazing what soap and a smile can do. She was a pretty woman. "They made a mess here, but, *gracias a Dios,* it is behind," she said. "*Ahora,* what do we do about the artifacts?"

"They'll eventually turn up," he said. "For now, let's try to get Arias arrested and get on with our lives."

She arched her eyebrows, alarmed. "What do you mean? We must find them. They belong to our country, our people."

"Not to mention the *plata,*" he said.

"*Sí,* the artifacts are valuable," she said. "But they are not to be sold. They are part of our history."

So she didn't know about the stone. Sutherland's comment about *plata*—slang for money, but literally silver, as in the legend—had gone over her head.

"Do you think the shipment is just a research bonanza for archeologists and anthropologists?" he asked.

She shrugged her shoulders. "*Sí.* We can learn much from it. The Toltec were writing in logograms before the Mayans. Is that not important?"

"Professor Hidalgo forgot to tell you the rest of it, especially what Arias is really interested in." He exchanged a frosty glance with Mercedes. "Drink your coffee. I'll tell you."

It only took a few minutes to relate what Agent Christopher had told him about the legend, the tomb, and the treasure the Toltecs supposedly left.

"I don't know if it's true, but the professor and Arias believe it. What do you think?"

Gabriela took her time. She finished her coffee and nodded. "It's possible. They mined silver and gold here long before the Spanish came. It was for jewelry and ornaments for the ruling classes. Much of it was buried with them. This *lagarto* stone could give the directions to such a tomb."

"Where did you learn about this stuff?" he asked, again conscious of how little he knew about her.

"In the university. Much of my painting has archeological themes. For that, one of the looters came to me with the Chacmool figure. If I had acted sooner or the others did not go to Arias, he and Javier might still be alive."

"And I'd be in bed in Chicago," he said. "Meanwhile, what do we do about Arias? You know anyone in the police?"

"*Sí*, but they will not touch him," Gabriela said. "I watch Arias for a year. He is like family with the *jefe de policía*."

"He's not going to leave us alone," he said. "I killed his nephew. Do you have a place to go?"

"I have friends in Guanajuato," Gabriela said.

"You should stay with them," he said.

"I'm not hiding," Mercedes said. "I'm going to find the shipment before he does."

"Its location died with Javier," he said. "Our only hope is that someone stumbles over it and calls the police."

"We don't have to wait," Gabriela said. "I gave Javier two other names in Chicago. These people can help you."

"They can help the police," he said. "I'm not a detective."

"Have you no pride?" Gabriela said. "It is your heritage, too."

"My heritage?" he said. "Why is that?"

"*Soy mexicana,*" she said proudly. "I am Mexican and I am your mother."

He jumped up, knocking the table and spilling the remnants of his *café*.

"I didn't ask to be involved," he said, spitting the words. "You didn't ask me either. As for heritage, tell me. What part of me is Mexican? I live and went to school in the United States. I look Anglo, and my name is as *gringo* as they come. As for a mother? I've never known one, Mexican or otherwise."

She faced him with a look of profound sadness. Just as quickly, she turned defiant again. "You don't see it, but it is there. It is in your blood."

"If it is, I can't see why I'd risk it for an old stone and a dubious legend," he said. "You have no reason to ask me to. You relinquished those rights thirty years ago."

He felt better for saying it, but it didn't change things. Arias wouldn't be deterred by petulant words.

# Chapter Twenty-Six

Gabriela came into the living room with a suitcase and dropped it by the front door.

"I turned off the gas and wrote a note to my neighbor. I'm ready."

She walked to the fireplace and traced her hand over the graffiti on her portrait: *ENTROMETIDA PUTA*.

"They were angry," she said. "They made a mess of my desk and files. What were they looking for?"

"They got my picture and my name," he said.

They faced a warm fire with logs sputtering and flames throwing shadows on the floor. Mercedes was cleaning up in the bathroom, so the two of them were alone. Was this the time to ask about the album?

"Ah," she said, nodding. "That's why they took the photo."

"They saw your album, too. With my pictures. My father sent them, right?"

"It was my only way to see you grow."

"And the newspaper clippings?" he asked. "What are they about?"

She stared at him for a long time, until her eyes were on the verge of tears. "I shouldn't have saved them."

"You knew Arias back then, didn't you?"

"I knew of him."

"What about that thing with the car?"

"If your father didn't tell you, it's best to forget."

He was about to press the matter, but Mercedes returned. She'd washed the road dust and dirt from her face and tied her hair in a ponytail.

"It's 5:30. We should leave before it's light," she said. "We can be there by seven."

They had decided that Gabriela would go to Guanajuato, where she would be safe with friends. He would go along while they tried reaching the other two Chicago contacts she'd given Javier. If they could help locate the shipment, Sutherland might resume a normal life. The flaw in that fantasy was that Arias might have other plans.

"Wait a minute," Sutherland said. "I'm not thinking straight. Arias left me a message at the Posada de San Francisco just before I went to the mine. He wants to meet at the botanical garden this morning. It was some bullshit about the reward."

"He must think you're stupid," Mercedes said.

"I know, but he might be there if he doesn't know Gabriela escaped. If the police won't do anything, maybe Christopher can at least watch my back while I talk to him." He sank his hand into his jeans pocket. It was empty. "Damn. I lost Christopher's phone number. Arias' nephew took it."

"You think you can reason with him?" Gabriela said.

"Not reason. Trick him. I can tell him I know where it is. Later, when he comes to get it, the DEA is waiting. I won't talk to him unless he's alone and unarmed. And I'd need backup."

"I know where I can borrow a rifle," Mercedes said. "My friend doesn't live far."

"You know how to use it?" he said.

"I shot elk and deer in the Rockies. If Arias comes alone, I can keep him in my sights."

"Do we know what he looks like?" Sutherland turned to Gabriela. "You've seen him, haven't you?"

"He has dark skin, with black hair, moustache, and glasses." Gabriela said. "He wears expensive clothes."

"Now or thirty years ago?"

"Today. I saw him once when he arrived here," Gabriela said. "He did not recognize me. In Chicago, the papers were filled with stories about him, but we never met."

"What did dropping the charges against him have to do with you? It must be something. Otherwise, why have Javier spy on him?"

She sat a moment, her gaze lowered. When she looked up, she seemed to be staring into the past. "Your father was a brave man, but he had no choice," she said. "Enrique Arias is *el diablo*. He stops at nothing. Last year, when he comes here, I know it is only a matter of time."

"What did he do?" he asked.

"Isn't it time we go?" She stood and walked to her suitcase.

★        ★        ★        ★

Mercedes parked the Jeep by the *Parroquia* and ran across *el Jardín* to the Posada de San Francisco. She picked up Sutherland's bag at the desk. When she returned, she dropped Sutherland and Gabriela at the Hotel Colibrí and went to collect her camera and borrow her friend's rifle.

In his room, Sutherland shaved and changed into clean slacks, a sweater, and sandals, the only other shoes he had with him. He packed his carry-on and tossed his torn jeans, jacket, and borrowed shoes in the wastebasket. Gabriela was waiting in the hotel café, which was just opening. They took a table by the window overlooking a patio that had a fountain centered in a garden. The waiter came with coffee and menus.

Gabriela rested her elbows on the table and stared at him. "You look more like your father now."

"So I've been told."

"He was lighter though."

"It's the sun. Sailing."

"I remember. You came to Guanajuato after being on a boat. And some Mayan digs in Chiapas, no?"

"Until they wanted me to go into the tombs." His visit had been during his two-year escape from the shock of his father's conviction.

"After he died, I heard less, only from his *abogado*, I mean lawyer," she said. "You are happy? Successful?"

"I'm doing fine." He remembered their awkward hug on his departure the last time they met. After those years of separation, he couldn't warm to her. She had deserted them. Did it change anything knowing that she hadn't forgotten?

The waiter returned and they ordered fruit, yogurt, and eggs. Then they sat in awkward silence and sipped their coffee.

She finally said, "You resent this, and I don't blame you. I'm sorry."

He shrugged.

"You don't owe me," she said. "I left you."

He hadn't asked before. He'd said it didn't matter. Maybe he didn't want to know then. "Why did you?"

She leaned back and looked at the ceiling for a moment. "You deserve an answer, *pero*…Could you just accept that I made some mistakes?"

"It has something to do with Arias and the photo of the car, doesn't it?"

She took her time again. She finally sighed and said, "It has everything to do with that. So do your nightmares. And your fear."

He felt light-headed. The lack of sleep, the rush of caffeine, and now this. Did he really want to hear more?

"Tell me," he said, gripping the armrests.

The fruit and yogurt arrived. She ate what was probably the first real food since her kidnapping. He couldn't tell if she intended to answer, but he was hungry, too. He finished the fruit by the time the eggs and tortillas arrived.

After a few minutes, she put down her fork and said, "The car in that picture was ours. You and I were in it. It went through the ice one night. We nearly drowned."

As if that was the end of it, she picked up her fork and continued eating. He waited as long as he could stand it.

"And? You left because of that? That doesn't make sense."

She stopped eating and said, "Your father told me the nightmares began after that. You slept with the lights on and were afraid of dark places. It was because of that night. First, it was the closet. Then it was that car in the water under the ice."

"That doesn't answer my question."

"I left a month later. For good. For everyone's good."

"Why?"

A waiter refilled their coffee. When Sutherland looked at Gabriela again, she had a handkerchief to her eyes and had begun to sob.

Mercedes walked over to their table, holding a Nikon camera with a telescopic lens.

"The Jeep is outside. I got the rifle. You ready?"

Sutherland wouldn't learn more from Gabriela for a while.

# CHAPTER TWENTY-SEVEN

▼

Sutherland watched as Mercedes focused the scope of the rifle, aiming at the gate where Arias had suggested they meet. They were high above San Miguel de Allende, outside the hundreds of open acres known as *el jardín botánico*, the botanical garden. It stretched for miles, a plant and wildlife preserve surrounding a dammed reservoir. A narrow canyon below the dam descended to the city below. Isolated from traffic and anyone but the occasional hiker, it was a perfect place to meet privately in the open.

A hundred yards away, they had found a partially constructed house on a slope overlooking the meeting place. The brick wall was completed to the second floor, and they peered through an open window behind a waist-high sill. With the dark interior behind them, they wouldn't be seen from below. Sutherland crouched next to Mercedes, who was holding a pair of high-powered binoculars. It was seven o'clock, an hour early.

"If he comes, he'll be on this road that climbs from the center." She pointed to the street that rose from the city and passed by their hiding place. It was new, paved in anticipation of more construction. To avoid being seen, they had come from the opposite direction.

"He can't have heard about the mine," he said. "It's only been a couple hours." It was light enough to make out the gate in the fence. No one was around, the only sounds the chirping and cooing birds and a distant church bell. He sat on the concrete with his back against the wall, dead tired. The events of the night raced past him like a fast-forward movie. He saw faces of Angel, dead, and Marcelo forcing him into the mine. The man they were waiting for would kill him for what he wanted. If he came and they shot him, would it be justified?

"Would you ever shoot a man?" Sutherland asked. He thought he knew the answer. Hadn't she pushed Marcelo into the mine a few hours earlier?

He heard her boots scuff across the ground as she shifted position. "You mean Arias?" she said.

"For example."

"I couldn't just shoot him standing out there. It would have to be self-defense or to protect someone. Is that what you're thinking? You want the rifle?"

"I couldn't hit a barn. I've never hunted."

"A cop-out," she said. "If you knew how to shoot, would you?"

He pictured himself aiming down a rifle barrel, the head of a man with glasses and a mustache in his sights. He imagined what the trigger would feel like as he pulled and the stock belted his shoulder, what the man's head would look like when it exploded.

"No," he said finally.

"I didn't think so," she said. "What's this between Arias and Gabriela?"

"I'm trying to find out. Something to do with his arrest and release." He closed his eyes. "Let me know if you see anything."

It didn't seem like he'd been asleep long when a sharp nudge awakened him.

"Huh?"

"They're here."

He peeked over the windowsill at the road.

"They? Where?" he whispered.

She pointed to the right of the gate. "Inside *el Jardín*. The other side of the fence."

They were 150 yards away. Through the binoculars, they seemed too close. Two men were running, low to the ground. They stopped behind some bushes, crouched with their rifles ready.

"There…on the roof." She pointed at a house on the road to the left and seventy yards away. A man on a ladder slid his rifle onto the flat roof and climbed up after it. They hadn't come to talk.

"Let's get out of here," she said. "We didn't count on this."

"Let's see if Arias comes."

"Are you *loco*?"

"I want to see this bastard. Wait in your Jeep if you want."

"I'm staying," she said.

At eight o'clock sharp, a Grand Cherokee came up the road and pulled up to the gate. It sat on a line between the man on the roof and the two inside the botanical garden. The rear license plate identified its owner: ARIAS.

They waited a minute, but nothing happened. Then Sutherland noticed the man on the roof talking into a two-way radio. Whoever was in that car wouldn't have to move. He had a lookout with a 360-degree view.

"We've got to get him out of the car. I can't see him," he said.

"Just stay out of sight," she hissed.

"We're out of range," he said.

They watched as one of the men in the bushes talked into his two-way radio. The man on the roof was also talking, but no one left the car.

Tired of squinting through the lenses, Sutherland glanced down and saw a broken piece of brick, the size of a baseball. He picked it up, weighed it, and tossed it from hand to hand. He judged the distance to Arias' car. A hundred yards downhill. Like center field to home plate. It was a throw he'd made dozens of times in school. He rolled his shoulder to loosen up, careful to stay behind the wall.

"Get your camera ready and be ready to run," he said

"Are you crazy? They've got guns."

"Ready?"

She focused the camera on the Grand Cherokee. Springing to his feet, he hurled the rock. The direction was perfect. It bounced down the hard ground toward the car and struck the back window with a loud clunk.

A few seconds passed. Through the binoculars, Sutherland watched the man on the roof talk into his two-way radio while looking up the hill to where they hid. Then the car door banged open and a man jumped out and stared in their direction. He was short and compact with a mustache and dark, graying hair. He wore glasses, a suit, and a tie.

Click, click, click. Mercedes snapped the pictures. They backed away from the window, staying low, until they were on the other side of the house. Then they ran up the road to her Jeep.

As she wheeled away, Sutherland glanced back. The two men were running toward the Grand Cherokee. The man on the roof was aiming at the Jeep. They hadn't traveled twenty feet when a bullet clanged into the roll bar. Another hit the rim of the spare tire. A third shattered a hole through the windshield.

"Holy shit!" he yelled.

Mercedes shifted into second gear and swerved off the road. They bounced into a drainage ditch and up the other side. She was in third as she zigzagged between the scrub trees and bushes, an erratic target. A few seconds later, they were out of sight.

She pulled onto a side road and headed for the *Gigante*, a huge retail mall on the road to Querétaro. At the corner, she turned into the parking lot and around to the back of the sprawling one-story building. Out of sight of the highway, she parked between a van and a small mobile home.

"That was stupid," she said, slumping down into her seat.

"How did they hit us?" His heart was racing so fast that he felt like he'd run all the way. "They were miles off."

"They had high-powered rifles," she said. "Couldn't you tell?"

"What do I know?" he said. "I'm not a hunter."

"That's obvious. Why didn't you tell me you were *loco*?"

"I wanted a picture. They weren't supposed to see us."

"Really? You threw a rock. What did you think?" After rummaging around behind her seat, she pulled out a screwdriver and handed it to him. "They'll be looking for this car. Take off the license plates while I pack up."

As he removed the plates, his adrenaline still had him on edge. He mentally replayed the escape scene, flinching at each ricocheted bullet.

"She's right," he thought. "I was stupid."

He was lucky she was around. Not only did she save his ass twice, she drove like an Indy driver and didn't miss a trick. The rifle, the camera, and now the plates, she was a female Indiana Jones.

By the time he finished, she had the rifle and camera back in their cases and on the hood.

"Grab the camera. We'll find a taxi," she said.

He jogged after her through the mall. They passed dozens of closed shops and went to the front of the building and the taxi stand. Arias' Grand Cherokee was nowhere to be seen. After a five-minute drive down the narrow back streets, the driver dropped them two blocks from the Hotel Colibrí.

Gabriela was waiting in an alcove off the lobby. Her hair was braided with strips of yellow and green ribbon, the Frida Kahlo look. They didn't tell her about the shooting, only that Arias hadn't been alone, so they didn't talk.

"*Bien*," she said. "We go to Guanajuato?"

"Not in the Jeep," Mercedes said. "I'll drop off this rifle and make other arrangements. It will take a couple minutes."

Sutherland and Gabriela settled into the couch after Mercedes left.

"Can you stay?" Gabriela said. "Until it is safe?"

"I have a life in Chicago and a girlfriend." He planned to call Kelly as soon as Mercedes returned.

"I wondered when you would marry again."

"You know all about me." His father's attorney must have kept her informed about his marriage and divorce. "What about you?" At their last meeting, she was still married to his father. They had been estranged for fifteen years, but good Catholics didn't divorce. Her painting career was just taking off, and she was taking graduate courses at the university. He wondered how much could he tactfully ask? "You married again?"

"No."

"You have no one?"

"I have many friends…and a son." Her hand went out to his. "If it's not too late."

He wasn't ready for that. He reached into his bag and pulled out the envelope with the clippings. He held it up.

"You haven't told me why you left or about these."

She glanced at the envelope and frowned. "I should have burned them. You should, too." Then she looked down at her hands, as if to say she was through talking.

"Nobody keeps stuff like this without a reason," he said. "What could you tell me that's worse than being deserted?"

Mercedes entered the alcove and said, "I talked to my father. The police are sending men to the mine. As for the other thing…" She was apparently alluding to the shots. "Forget about an arrest."

"It figures." They kidnap Gabriela and nearly kill him and the police play with their *huevos*. "Don't tell me," he growled. "This is Mexico."

He went to the lobby phone and called the Hotel Posada de San Francisco. No messages. Then he called his apartment. There was a message from eleven o'clock the night before.

"Doug, this is Julia Waterman, Kelly's aunt. I was to meet Kelly for dinner this evening. She didn't show, and it's not like her. I was hoping she was with you. Please call."

He wrote down her number and called it immediately. His hand shook as he punched the buttons.

"Hello?" a woman with an anxious voice answered.

Sutherland blurted, "Is Kelly there?"

"Doug? No. She's not with you?"

# CHAPTER TWENTY-EIGHT

▼

Enrique Arias removed his glasses and wiped away an impudent tear with his handkerchief. He stared through his library window at the cascading fountain and purple bougainvillea in his *hacienda's* garden. In the last few days, all of this—the acres of land, the sprawling house, and the imported furnishings—seemed to be losing its beauty and the significance he had once attached to it.

What good was it compared to the lives of Esmeralda and Marcelo?

On his deathbed, his older brother had begged Arias to take care of Marcelo, and he promised to raise him as a son. What else could he do? The car crash that had ended his brother's life was Arias' fault. He had been drunk and speeding. His brother had hung on for an hour before the internal injuries overcame him. His sister-in-law never walked again. Now their precious boy had been killed following Arias' orders.

*Marcelo está muerto.* Gabriela was freed, and Marcelo was dead. His men, once awakened and untied, confirmed it. They hadn't found the body yet, but it had to be so. One does not fall down a mine shaft and live. Sutherland, Gabriela's son, did it. With the help of some woman. Yesterday, Sutherland had only been an obstacle in his path. Today, his destruction had become as important as finding the stone.

He heard a knock on the library door and a woman's voice. "Enrique, can I come in?" It was his sister-in-law, Marcelo's mother. She must have heard.

*"Sí, pasa."* He wiped his eyes again and replaced his glasses. This was a time for strength.

The tall, oak door opened and a dark woman in a black dress rolled into the room in a wheelchair. Her eyes were reddened and wide with hysteria. Strands of graying hair stuck to her tear-streaked face.

*"Es la verdad?* He's dead? Tell me no," she wailed.

Arias stood, walked to her wheelchair, knelt in front of her, and took her hands in his.

"*Cálmate, Lupita*. Calm down."

What else could he say? His words were useless.

"So it is true? He is dead?" she cried. "How could you let it happen, Enrique? You promised." She wrenched her callused hands from his and tore at her hair. "*Mi hijo*," she shrieked.

"*Lo siento.* I'm sorry, but I wasn't here. He…"

"You promised. My only son is gone. You promised."

"I know. I know. I have failed you. I failed my brother."

"Now I have no one. Marcelo…" She let her hands fall to her lap and she slumped in her chair, sobbing.

The two remained like that for almost a minute, she sobbing, Arias on his knees holding back his own tears. When he looked up, he saw his wife standing at the door. Slender and erect in a long, white dress with her hair in a tight knot and her calm hands holding a Bible to her breast, she stared at Arias with disapproving eyes. She didn't say a word, but he knew her thoughts.

"Marguerite, can you help her?" he asked. "Maybe a sedative or something?"

She entered the room and handed him the Bible.

"I can help her," she said, grabbing the handles and turning the wheelchair toward the door. She stopped on the other side of the threshold and glared at him. "But there is no help for you."

Arias had to control, or at least postpone, his seething impulses. As much as he wanted vengeance, killing Sutherland had to wait. The *cabrón* was surprisingly resourceful. Following him could be the best route to the stone. It was uncanny the way he found Gabriela. That mine was a perfect place, and only Arias' men knew about it. That woman must have helped him. Despite the depth of the mine, Marcelo, and the armed guards, they had freed Gabriela. This morning, the *hijo de puta* outmaneuvered them again, escaping their trap at the botanical garden. Again with this woman, driving like a *loca*. Who was she? She couldn't remain a mystery for long. They'd find her car, and they'd find her.

Sutherland's father had been smart, but Arias had defeated him thirty years ago. Gabriela Castellano had made her husband vulnerable, and Arias' plan had worked perfectly. In the end, Sutherland's father disowned her and let Arias go free, saving him from prosecution and certain conviction. He hadn't pulled the trigger, but he'd been there. They'd only wanted to rob that pawnshop, but the owner pulled a gun. Arias' accomplice didn't have a choice. It was the first time since seeing Padre Teodor die that Arias had witnessed a murder. This time, there were no screams, just an earsplitting bang.

He never divulged the real killer's identity. Diego left town right after Arias was freed. When he returned years later, he and Arias renewed their partnership. Theirs was nothing like Arias' one-time association with Alfonso Rivera, a war which ended with the murder of Rivera's brother. Having Alejandro Rivera killed had been the final stroke that established Arias' control over the business.

Arias glanced at the silver-framed photo on his desk and pulled it closer, bringing it into the focus of his bifocals. In the faded picture, the two Arias brothers flanked Marcelo on his eighth birthday. Despite the happy occasion, the three stared into the camera with identical solemn expressions, as if they knew what was coming. A week later, Marcelo's father was dead and his mother was crippled.

At the time, Arias was not a stranger to death. He'd watched his father, a poor peasant protesting the expropriation of his only cow, being run down and shot by an army captain. At the university, a student standing with him in a crowd was downed by a stray police bullet. He'd witnessed Padre Teodor's murder and seen the pawnbroker take a thirty-eight-caliber slug in the eye. His brother's death was different. Arias hadn't pulled a trigger or plunged a knife, but he was the murderer nonetheless.

Despite what his enemies were allowed to believe, it was ironic he had never intentionally killed anyone. More than once, he'd issued the orders, but he'd never felt the gun's recoil, the scrape of blade on ribs, or hot blood on his hands. He often fantasized about being the executioner, but he'd resisted the temptation. It wasn't out of fear of earthly or divine punishment. It was fear of himself. His operation relied on addictions, and he knew how seductively they began and how irresistible they became. He also knew himself. Once started, he wouldn't be able to control it.

That precaution no longer concerned him. Marcelo's death changed things forever.

He lit a cigarette and stared at two names scrawled on the desk notepad. The first was Kelly Matthews. The second was Margo Sutherland. The *cabrón* had said his mother meant nothing to him, yet he came to San Miguel for her. Arias wanted to see how Sutherland would react when someone he really did care about was being held.

He looked at his watch. He should be receiving news of *Señorita* Matthews' new whereabouts anytime now.

# CHAPTER TWENTY-NINE

▼

Sutherland changed their plans after making a phone call to Kelly's office. She hadn't shown up in court. When her assistant called her home, no one answered. Her boss was smoothing things with the judge, but he was almost as worried as Sutherland. Kelly wouldn't miss a court appearance unless something was terribly wrong.

Sutherland and Mercedes made a deal. He promised to search for the shipment as soon as he ensured Kelly was safe. Meanwhile, Mercedes would accompany Gabriela to Guanajuato on the bus. She could watch out for Gabriela as well as he could. Maybe she would be even better.

He didn't create this mess, but Kelly's trouble was his fault. Coming to Mexico had seemed to be the only thing to do. Who knew it would put her in jeopardy? As he waited by the curb for Roberto, the knot in his stomach wouldn't go away. He imagined Kelly's face, her large eyes teary, and her lips trembling. He couldn't bear anything happening to her.

Fifteen minutes after being called, Roberto pulled up to the hotel in his taxi. He tipped up his baseball cap and then winced when he saw Sutherland's banged-up face.

"What happened to you, *señor?*"

"*Mucho, amigo.*" Sutherland threw his carry-on bag into the backseat and slid in beside it. "We found the woman, my mother, but Angel didn't make it. *Está muerto.*"

Roberto slammed the steering wheel with his palm. "*Ay, caray.* Bad luck."

"Sorry. Was he close?"

"*No, señor.* He was a bad one, but he owes me money." He jammed the shift into first. The car lurched forward, skidding over the cobblestones. "*Hijo de puta.* You could never trust Angel."

"You told me I could." He remembered how shaken he'd been when Angel refused to go into the mine shaft. "Did he owe you for me?"

Roberto squirmed and glanced back with a sheepish look. "*Sí, señor.*"

He couldn't help picturing the dead Angel, his broken body caught in the bend of the mine shaft. They'd find Sutherland's 1,500 pesos on him.

"How much was he paying you?"

Roberto turned around. "One thousand pesos."

"Get me to the airport on time, I'll give you 500." He had to catch the next flight out of León or wait three hours, an eternity when it came to Kelly's safety.

The speedometer crept past 130 kilometers, about eighty miles per hour, but Sutherland's mind was in Chicago. He wondered what the police would do. Her aunt and Kelly's office should have reached Detective Duncan by now. He could be tracking Kelly down. Would he? Sutherland could almost hear the detective's questions. Was she really missing? How long had it been? Was there a ransom note?

The DEA there might be able to do what the police could not or would not. They had tapped Kelly's line. He wished he hadn't lost Christopher's direct number. If the police didn't act, he'd call the DEA's Chicago office.

He wanted to think positively, imagining alternative explanations for her disappearance. She was in bed nursing a case of twenty-four hour flu with her phone jack unplugged and her cell phone off. She'd been in a minor accident, unhurt, but lying sedated in a hospital. He knew that was bullshit. By his churning stomach, he knew she was in trouble. If he was right and if getting her back meant finding the shipment and handing it over to Arias, that is what he would do. He'd locate the men Gabriela told Javier to call, a boy named Pedro and a man named Rivera.

He wondered if he was deluding himself. Could he find the *lagarto* stone, save Kelly, and have Arias put away? Could he make everyone happy? Gabriela? Mercedes? Her father?

Where were the superheroes when you needed them?

On the airplane, Sutherland found himself pinched between two women from Kansas. Before takeoff, they prattled on about the charming Mexican people, the wonderful food, and the resort where they stayed outside of San Miguel.

"How did you like the city?" he asked. "Spend much time in *el Jardín* or the market? Visit the *Parroquia?*"

They laughed, thinking he was kidding. They didn't feel comfortable in town.

"You know how they are." The woman on his right leaned over and whispered, "I don't think they ever bathe. You'd think they'd speak English by now."

"You have to excuse them," he said while trying to keep the sarcasm out of his voice. "There's a water shortage there. And you don't have to be as smart to speak Spanish."

"I know," the woman said. "We're fluent after a week."

"I'll bet." He was tempted to test her with something caustic in Spanish, but decided he needed some good karma.

He suggested they could continue their conversation better if he wasn't between them and they let him take the window seat. After they took off, he used his credit card to call Kelly's aunt from the cell phone on the seatback in front of him.

"You talk to her yet?" he asked when she picked up.

"Not a thing." Her tone was anxious. "Do you have a key to her apartment?"

"It's at home. Why?"

"That detective said there aren't enough grounds to break the door down. Her building doesn't have a super."

"Duncan hasn't checked her place?"

"He said he couldn't. I'm worried."

"Shit." He calmed himself with a deep breath. "Sorry. I'll call him. We'll find her." He wished he was as confident as he sounded.

He tried Detective Duncan and left a message with the detective who answered. Then he closed his eyes to avoid talking to his neighbors. Unless worry counted, there was nothing to do until landing. It was Tuesday, and he hadn't really slept since Friday night. Adrenaline and fear had kept him going. The drone of the plane's engines pulled him under.

He dreamed he was in the front seat of a car with Kelly. Gabriela and Mercedes were in the back, waist deep in water. Using wide-brimmed sombreros, they were bailing water, throwing it through the windows into the blackness.

He slept fitfully again after changing planes in Houston. Three hours later, when they landed in Chicago, snowflakes were in the air. After clearing customs, he waited in the taxi line, freezing. He wished he hadn't thrown away his coat. Inside the car, he borrowed the driver's cell phone. Duncan answered on the first ring.

"Nothing?" Sutherland said. "You've done nothing?"

"Look, we checked the hospitals. We tried her neighbors. We can't just break in."

"Is her car there?"

"Ah, I don't know."

"Listen, detective. Kelly was stopping by her place before seeing her aunt. I have a key. If I have to, I'll go in alone. Considering what happened to Javier, I'd rather have you there."

Duncan took a second before answering. "All right," he huffed. "Bring the key. I'll meet you there."

When Sutherland arrived at Kelly's loft building in River North, Detective Duncan was waiting outside in an unmarked car with a blue-and-white squad car behind. Two uniformed cops got out. One was a light-skinned black man. The other was a blonde white woman. The elevator took them to the sixth and top floor. Judging from their bored looks, they might have been going out for coffee. As they walked down the corridor toward the apartment, Sutherland asked if he should knock.

Duncan shook his head. "Just open it."

The police hung back, relaxed, as Sutherland fumbled with the key ring. There were two keys for the door. He inserted the first and threw the deadbolt. It made a loud clack. He slid the second key into the door handle, but before he could turn it, he heard a man's voice inside. He backed away. The policewoman's two-way radio squawked in the background.

"What's the matter?" Duncan must have not heard the voice.

"A man inside," he whispered. "There shouldn't be anyone in there."

"You sure?" Duncan appeared more alert.

"Positive." The other two came closer to listen.

"There's a fire escape, right?" Duncan turned to the policeman. "Swanson, call for more cars. Get around to the alley."

The male cop jogged to the emergency stairway. Duncan motioned Sutherland away and took a position to the side of the door. The policewoman took the other side. They drew their guns.

They waited a moment and listened. Nothing. Had he imagined the voice? Staying behind the frame, Duncan reached for the door handle. As he turned the knob, the policewoman's two-way radio squawked again.

"18, 24 going on that assist."

"Turn that down," Duncan growled.

Too late. The steel door exploded with holes. A machine gun roared from inside. It was deafening as bullets rained in the corridor, ricocheting off pipes and pounding the opposite concrete wall into powder. Sutherland dove and rolled away from the door. Dust and noise was everywhere. The overhead light went out. A pipe ruptured, spewing steam. The shooting lasted ten seconds, but each was like a minute. Then silence. He heard the policewoman shouting and the two-way crackling back. Another blast hit the door, the machine gun coughing off bullets from somewhere in the loft, but farther away. More silence. Sirens screamed in the distance.

"Jesus. What was that?" Sutherland shouted.

"A fucking lunatic. That's what." Duncan pushed the door open, then retreated behind the frame. No more shots. A moment passed and Duncan charged in with the policewoman following.

Sutherland waited a moment before he sat up and stared into the darkness and hanging dust, listening to the sirens draw nearer and wind down. He jumped up and started for the door when shots echoed from inside. It wasn't the staccato of an automatic. Instead, it was single pops. Twenty feet down the corridor, the stairway door burst open, and lights appeared. He threw himself to the floor again. Footfalls approached and he saw figures running toward him. He lay still.

"Hands behind your head," someone shouted.

Sutherland obeyed. Flashlights blinded him while someone patted him down.

He wasn't the bad guy, for crissakes.

But there was too much noise and confusion to argue. Someone cuffed his hands behind his back.

"Jesus H. Christ," someone said. "Look at this shit."

"Goddamn war zone," answered another.

Sutherland lay on the floor while police raced by and shouts rang back and forth inside the condo. He could only see shadows and the legs of the policeman standing over him. He finally heard Detective Duncan's voice.

"He's okay. Let him up."

Someone helped him up and removed the handcuffs. He looked at the damage around him. The steam had abated to a drip, but the dust and acrid smell still hung in the air. The concrete wall across from the door was chewed with holes. A ceiling light dangled from its wires. The floor was strewn with concrete chips.

"You get him? Them?" Sutherland asked.

"They used the fire escape. Two of them. They got out before Swanson got all the way around."

Duncan didn't look happy.

"Lucky you were here," Sutherland said. He almost had to beg Duncan, but he wouldn't remind him. Then the main question. "Kelly?"

"Nothing. Take a look. Tell me what's different. But don't touch anything."

Entering the apartment, he was surprised by how normal it was. The furniture was in its usual place. A few lights were on. Even a vase of flowers was on the hall table. Everything in its place, just like how fastidious Kelly liked it. The holes in the door and the spent shell casings scattered over the carpet told a different story. The acrid smell of gunpowder drowned out any scent of flowers.

He walked through the living room and glanced into the den and television room. Cushions were on the floor and empty cans strewn around. Plastic shopping bags contained fast-food wrappers, chips, and soda bottles. The wastebasket overflowed with garbage. He wondered how long they had been there.

The kitchen was spotless, probably because anyone would see it immediately after opening the front door. Her bedroom also seemed normal. The bed was made, the shades were open, the top of the dresser was uncluttered. A sweater lay on the bed and her running shoes were at the foot. Then he saw the suitcase on the chair.

It was an overnight bag, the one she brought to his place and the one she would take to her aunt's house. He opened it and found her favorite nightshirt, toiletries, makeup kit, and some underwear. Before meeting her aunt after work, she had come here to pack. Then what?

"Find anything?" Duncan entered the room and looked around. "I told you not to touch anything."

"She wasn't with them, was she?" Sutherland asked.

"Just the two of them."

"You search the place?"

"The uniforms did. Why?"

Sutherland crossed the room to the closet and opened the door. Inside was a row of clothes hanging on one side, a mirrored wall at the end, a built-in cabinet, shelves and drawers on the left, and a bench down the middle. It was a large space, doubling as a dressing room.

"I told you they looked," Duncan said.

Except for the large pile of sheets in the far corner, everything seemed normal. He inched toward it, holding his breath. In the mirror, he could see Duncan several steps behind him, looking over his shoulder. Reaching the pile, Sutherland grabbed the top sheet and heaved it away. Nothing. Just more sheets and clothing. He picked up her windbreaker and running shirt. It was still damp from her run the morning before.

He wondered why the laundry was in a heap like that. Knowing Kelly, it seemed unusual. She'd never stand for it. Dirty laundry belonged in the hamper, in the cabinet to his left. He opened it. The hamper was the size of a large grocery cart and full. He slowly lifted the corners of the towels piled on top.

"Jesus!" Duncan shouted.

# CHAPTER THIRTY

▼

Sutherland stared at Kelly's face inside the laundry hamper. Her hair was in tangles, her eyes wide and staring. The way she was crammed into that small space, she could have been dead. Sutherland felt his stomach turn over.

"Nooo," he moaned.

She blinked, and her mouth shot open. "Doug!"

Startled, he backed into Detective Duncan. "You're okay?"

"Hell no," she rasped. "Help me outta here."

Sutherland and Duncan each grabbed an arm and pulled her out. She wore slacks and a white sweater. The smell of stale sweat and urine was unmistakable.

"I thought you were them." She sobbed as her eyes filled with tears. "All that shooting. I thought I'd had it."

She could barely stand. Sutherland grabbed her around the waist. "How long you been in there?" he asked.

"Forever," She threw her arms around him, still sobbing. "How'd you find me? What happened?"

"Take it easy. You're safe now. They're gone." He held her tightly and felt her tremble as she held on to him. "Should we call a doctor? Are you hurt?"

He felt her take deep breaths as her tremors subsided. "No," she said. "Just help me to the bathroom. Bring me some clean clothes."

"We gotta get prints. You can't touch anything." Duncan was blocking the closet door.

"I can't?" she said, pushing by him. "Try and stop me."

★   ★   ★   ★

A half hour later, Sutherland, Kelly, and Detective Duncan sat at her neighbor's kitchen table. The technicians were still taking fingerprints in Kelly's place. After her shower, Kelly had thrown on a sweatshirt and jeans. Her hair was still wet. Between sips of red wine, she attacked half a pizza left by the intruders. Sutherland drank coffee while he explained what had happened in San Miguel.

"So, your mother is safe with some woman named Mercedes." Duncan made notes in his book while he spoke. "Two men are dead. This guy Arias shot at you. You didn't notify the police because it was Mexico?"

"Arias has the top police honcho in his pocket. Besides, when I heard about Kelly, I had to come back. Which brings us here." He turned to Kelly to change the subject. "How'd you end up in the hamper?"

"Not much to tell," she said. "I'd only been home a couple minutes. I was throwing some things into the suitcase when I heard a crash and then voices."

"So you hid." Duncan said.

"What else could I do? I didn't have time."

"Did you hear anything else? Names? Anything?" Duncan asked.

"Not much. What I heard was in Spanish," she said. "It was clear they were looking for me. One wanted to leave, but the other kept saying that *El jefe* told them to wait."

"You understood them?" Duncan asked. "In Spanish?"

"Sure. But only what I could hear." After a year in Costa Rica and months in Spain, Kelly's Spanish was almost perfect.

Sutherland rested his elbows on the table while he sipped his coffee. He felt drained. The anxiety, fear, and then relief of the last hour had sucked out whatever energy he had left.

"Waiting here. They had balls." Duncan scribbled in his notebook, then looked up. "Sorry."

"*Cojones grandes.* Big ones," she said. "Judging by my door, they also had plenty of ammunition. Who were they?"

Sutherland poured himself another cup. "They had to be Arias' men."

"But he had your mother." She took another bite of pizza. "What did they want me for?"

"Maybe he thought I was too removed from her. What now, detective?"

Duncan closed his notebook. "We're getting a search warrant for the Chapultepec Gallery. So far, we've got nothing on this Arias."

"You should. He was indicted for a murder here thirty years ago." Sutherland remembered the shots Mercedes had taken in San Miguel. He handed Duncan the undeveloped roll of film from her Nikon. "These are current pictures of him. Are you going to work with the DEA on this?"

"The feds are all alike. They don't tell us squat. We've got zip on what they're doing. I have a call into this guy. What's his name?"

"Agent Christopher," Sutherland said. "We could have used his help this morning when Arias' men shot at us. Local police can't be trusted."

Duncan dropped the film in his jacket pocket. "Cops down there make a lot less than we do." He stood and put on his overcoat. "Is your place okay? Nobody waiting for you?"

"I was there just long enough to pick up Kelly's keys, put on warm clothes, and split. I'm going back now."

"I'll go with you," Duncan said. "Just to make sure. I'll try to get a squad posted outside for the night. Then you're on your own."

"I'm coming, too," Kelly said. "I've had enough of this place for a lifetime."

If anyone had entered Sutherland's apartment, he couldn't tell. Duncan stayed a few minutes and left. He said he would call the next morning and promised to search for the two names Gabriela had given Javier if he needed help. The first name was Alfonso Rivera. He was a man Gabriela knew from her school days in Guanajuato. She wasn't sure he was still living in Chicago or even alive. The second person was Pedro Guzmán, the young son of a friend. She had given him Pedro's cell phone number and a restaurant name, *La Olla*, where Javier was to look for him. When Sutherland tried the cell phone number, no one answered.

"You look dead," Kelly said.

He scratched his beard, a two-day's growth. "I am. How about you? Did you sleep in that hamper?"

"I must have. Now I'm just one big kink."

It was nearly nine o'clock. He went to his den and picked up his messages from the answering machine. Julie, his secretary, called late that afternoon to say the City Council zoning committee had moved his hearing up to the coming Friday afternoon. Larry Adams, his architect, wanted to know if he wanted to be there. The meeting was a week early, which normally would have been great news. However, today was Wednesday. He wasn't sure Arias would give him time off for business.

Sutherland couldn't miss the meeting. Larry was a competent architect, but Sutherland wasn't going to trust anyone else with the fate of his project. If it wasn't done right, he might not get the exceptions he needed. The committee's ruling could also be pushed off to next month. That was too late. His purchase contract provided for a 180-day zoning contingency. It was nearly over. If he didn't have his approvals this month, he'd either have to close on the property without them (a financial risk he couldn't take) or forfeit his deposit (a loss he couldn't afford). Besides the money, he had too much time and ego invested. This project was his future. He decided to call his architect tomorrow and review their presentation to the board.

He poured himself a Scotch and checked the refrigerator. He only saw Chinese takeout that had been there for a week.

"I'm going downstairs to get my mail and maybe a snack from the vending machines."

The lobby was empty except for the doorman at his desk.

"How's Jimmy doing?" Sutherland asked. He'd last seen the night doorman after he collapsed seeing Javier's bloody stomach.

"He's fine. Back on duty already."

He went to the mailroom and emptied his box, collecting the magazines and notices without sorting through them. Then he went to the vending alcove and bought two bags of potato chips and a ham sandwich. On his way to the elevators, he passed the cleaners and saw the owner locking up. The old woman's real name was Korean, but everyone called her Angie.

"You're working late," he said.

She turned and then smiled. "Ah, Mr. Sutherland. I look for you. What happen your face? You take my advice. Slow down."

"I intend to. Why were you looking for me?"

"Your tuxedo. Was something in your pocket."

"You already gave it to me."

"Ah, yes. Same pocket. Just minute. I get for you."

He waited outside the door while she went back into the shop, turned on the lights, and disappeared behind the racks of clothes. In the same pocket as Javier's useless note? Was there another piece to it? An address for where he hid the artifacts? That was too much to hope for.

When Angie reappeared, she was examining an object in her hand. "Is strange one. Not like mine," she said, holding it up for him. "Key."

He wasn't missing one. His condo keys were in his pocket. The office and car keys were on the entryway table. This key hung on a rawhide loop crusted with a dark brown stain.

"Is blood?" she asked, looking into his face. "From you cut?"

He held Javier's key in his palm, staring at it as if it was something poisonous.

"Men had died for this damn thing," he thought, "and I had it the whole time."

Now Sutherland wasn't sure he wanted it. On one hand, it might be the way out for him. On the other, it could be like chum to sharks. There was already enough blood on it.

# CHAPTER THIRTY-ONE

The key was brass on a strip of stained rawhide. Sutherland turned it over while Kelly looked on. The number twenty-three was stamped into the metal.

"He had that in his boot?" she said. They were at his kitchen table. His mail was piled to the side. The bags of chips and sandwich remained unopened.

"With the note," he said. "But I don't remember seeing it."

"Is that blood?"

"Probably. Like the paper."

"You had it from the start."

"Yep. But it's no good unless you know what it opens. And I don't. Arias apparently doesn't either. One thing for sure, it isn't a normal key. Look at it. Teeth on both sides."

"Are you going to give it to him?"

"If I thought he'd go away, I would. But his nephew is dead because of me. Plus, he still thinks I know more." He put the key down and tore open the wrapper on the sandwich. Looking between the bread at the slice of ham, he said, "Besides…" He got up and opened the refrigerator door.

"What?"

He held up a jar. "Mustard."

"No, besides what?"

"I want the bastard caught."

★   ★   ★   ★

Fifteen minutes later, when the sandwich and chips were consumed, Sutherland looked at his stack of mail. He was tempted to ignore it, but he shuffled through it, tossing junk into the garbage and magazines to the side to be read at some future date when things were normal. "The Economist" and "Sailing" weren't going to help with his current problems. He threw away a utility bill without opening it. He then stared at a tuition notice for his daughter's private school.

"Oh shit," he groaned.

Kelly rushed in from down the corridor. "What happened?"

"Jenny and Margo. It never occurred to me. They could be in trouble."

"They're in Los Angeles."

"Yeah, but who knows? If he found out I'd been married, he could track her down. Margo didn't change her name. After he came after you, nothing would surprise me. I have to warn her." He reached for the phone and dialed the long-distance number.

"What do you want her to do? Will she listen?" Kelly asked.

"She better."

"Hello?" A young woman's voice answered.

"Jenny? Is that you, honey?" Sutherland asked.

"Dad? Where are you?"

His daughter was twelve years old, pretty, blond, and gangly, but that would change soon—at least the part about being twelve and gangly.

"In Chicago. Is your mom there? I need to talk to her, sweetheart."

"She's out. You could call her cell phone. Are you coming to Los Angeles?"

"Not now," he said. "But you can meet me in Vail during spring break."

"Cool. But you'll have to work on mom. She wants to go to Hawaii."

"We'll see if we can work something out, but I really have to talk to her now. Give me her number again."

Sutherland took down the number, said good-bye, and dialed the digits.

It rang three times before his ex-wife answered.

"Hello?" He would never forget her soft voice. It was like she was whispering, but louder.

"Margo, it's Doug. Can you talk?"

"Doug? Just a second. I'm at the cash register."

Of course, she was shopping. It was what she did best. He heard voices in the background and after a full minute, she came back.

"There. Sorry, the help in these stores is dreadful. Are you in LA? You decide to get out of the cold?"

"No. We need to talk. It's important. You may be in trouble."

He heard more background noise, wind, and a car honking.

"What? Trouble?" she said, forcing her whispery tone.

"It's a long story…" He heard a door slam and then a warning alarm from the seat belt. "You and Jenny have to get out of your house, and you can't waste time."

"Are you drinking, Doug? Why would we leave our house?" He heard traffic sounds. She was probably in her convertible with the top down.

"Margo, are you driving?"

"I'm going to the club. Now what about leaving?"

Images of their former lives together flashed through his mind. He thought of the hyper Margo, attention-deficit Margo, Prozac (or whatever drug was fashionable) Margo. She was always beautiful, always had the perfect outfit, and was always on top of the latest craze.

"Margo, I need your absolute attention. Will you please pull over so we can talk?"

"I'm late. Armani was so darn busy…"

"Margo, will you listen? Pull the fucking car off the road."

"If you're going to be that way…"

"Just do it, Margo. You and Jenny are in danger."

He heard screeching tires, a horn blast, and angry shouting. There was silence for a moment before she came back on. "I hope you're happy now. That Jaguar gave me the finger and called me a…Never mind…What danger? What's so goddamn important?"

"Are you stopped? Are you listening?"

"Go ahead. You've already made me late."

"Some bad people are after me. They've already kidnapped my mother…"

"Jeez, Doug. You are drunk. I thought your mother died a long time ago."

"Completely sober. After my mother, they tried kidnapping Kelly and nearly killed me. I'm afraid they might come after you and Jenny."

"What for? Who are these people? Why don't you just go to the police?"

"They're not going to guard you there. They couldn't help me. You've got to get out of your house for a few days. Just a few. That means no club for you and no school for Jenny. Don't tell anyone where you've gone."

"Doug, Jenny can't. I have all sorts of…"

"I know. But could you forgive yourself if something happened to her?"

"This is ridiculous. Who cares about us?"

"They might want you to get at me."

"What have you done? How'd you get into this mess? And now you drag us…"

"It wasn't my fault, but here I am. I'm sorry to say it, but you may be caught up in it now."

"I don't know, Doug, this sounds…"

"Would it help if you talked to a Chicago detective? He can tell you that I'm not making this up."

"Well…"

"Okay. Go to an ATM. Get enough cash for a few days. Then go home and pack. I'll have a Detective Duncan call you on your cell phone. He's from the Chicago Police Department, and he will call, though I have to reach him first. After you've packed, disappear. Go to a friend's place or hotel. Don't use your credit cards and don't tell anyone where you are. Call Duncan every day to see when it's safe. Is that clear?"

"Jeez, Doug. This is creepy. Now you got me scared."

"Good. You should be."

He hung up the phone, hopeful she would do what he asked. Maybe he was being overly cautious, but he couldn't bear to see them hurt. Then he found himself smiling. Despite the seriousness of the situation, the image of Margo unable to use a credit card was hilarious.

Sutherland called Detective Duncan and left him a message requesting—in what he hoped were convincing terms—that he call his ex-wife and corroborate what he'd told her. Duncan wouldn't be happy, but he'd probably do it. Sutherland turned out the lights and went into the bathroom. After brushing his teeth, he contemplated his face. With his two day's growth, a cut eyebrow, and bruises, he looked more like the loser than the winner of the fight. The usual retort of "you should see the other guy" seemed in bad taste.

He turned to see Kelly emptying her overnight bag into a bureau drawer. He fastened a towel around his waist and walked into the bedroom.

"Remember Javier's note?" he said. "About the *ático*? If he hid the shipment in an attic, what's the key for? It isn't a normal key, especially for a house. We really need to find one of those men and hope they can tell us. Unless…"

"A locksmith?" she said. "I read your mind."

"That's scary." He followed her movements as she took off her bra and pulled on her T-shirt. "What am I thinking now?"

She chuckled. "You said you were tired. You better take a shower."

"A cold one? Thanks."

"Oh no, *muchacho*." She spun her bra around her index finger like a stripper. "The hotter the better. Don't shave. I have this fantasy about a Mexican bandito."

# CHAPTER THIRTY-TWO

▼

Sutherland woke at 8:00 AM to the radio news. They announced that the temperature was thirty-three degrees and there was a fifty-minute commute from the airport to downtown and twenty from Hollywood to Monroe. Rolling over, he groaned. He was still sore everywhere. He smelled coffee.

"Thank you, Kelly," he thought.

"The morning news had sixty seconds on the break-in and shooting at my place," she said when she handed him his cup. "My boss was speechless. He said the mayor called and asked how I was. I didn't know he cared."

"Who? Your boss or the mayor?"

"I knew my boss cared. But Hizzoner? Anyway, I'm supposed to take a couple days off and go somewhere safe. They'll fill in or get a postponement on my cases if they have to."

"Nothing like friends in high places," he said.

Dressed and working on his second cup, he went to his den and called Larry Adams, his architect. They spent the next half hour discussing Friday's presentation to the zoning board, agreeing on the changes Sutherland was willing to concede to get the approval. At the end of the call, Larry said, "Doug, I saw the news on Kelly this morning. You should take her somewhere. I've done a dozen of these presentations. You don't have to be there. That's what you pay me for."

"I know." Though he said it, Sutherland wasn't convinced. When it came to important things, he believed in doing it yourself. "You do the talking. I'll be a fly on the wall."

Adams laughed. "Like the last time. I didn't get a chance to say boo. All right. I'll see you on Friday."

"I'll be there," Sutherland said. The *lagarto* stone would have to wait. With Kelly safely in the other room, his confidence was returning.

While drinking his third coffee, he pulled the yellow pages from the stack of books on his desk and turned to locksmiths. There was a security store on Clark, ten or so blocks away. He called its number and a recording informed him that they opened at nine. Then he tried Pedro's cell phone number again. He still didn't get an answer. Sutherland didn't place much faith in Duncan finding him. Sutherland guessed he was in the country illegally and wasn't likely to have a permanent phone or a driver's license. As for the other name, Rivera, he didn't know where to start. He could be a ghost by now. Gabriela hadn't seen him since her school years.

"You were going to show me what you found at your mother's place," Kelly said from the den door.

"In my bag. Take a look."

She was back in a few minutes and laid the clippings and the photo on the end of his desk.

"Wow. Talk about a mystery. Who's the dead guy in Beverly Shores?"

"Gabriela wasn't saying. You said you'd look into it."

"I would have. Remember where I spent yesterday?" she said.

"Goofing off in a hamper."

"Thanks to you. Anyway, my assistant probably has something. I'll get it today. Meanwhile, you haven't told me everything about your trip." Kelly pulled herself up and sat on the edge of the desk.

"I gave you and Duncan the whole story."

"Not about your mother," she said. "You haven't seen her for years, and there's nothing to say?" She folded her arms across her chest, waiting.

"She's a nice woman. Smart, creative, and successful. What else?"

"Come on, Doug. That's it? You're a hard case."

Whenever she stared at him with her large, green eyes, like now, there was no escape. He might as well start with the photo of the car being towed from the drink.

"I learned a few things," he said finally. "Like a hint at why I freak out in certain situations."

"Say it. Your phobia?"

"You have one, too," he said, defensively. "That's why we're not going skiing."

"If I didn't have to take chair lifts. Don't change the subject. She say it was about the car accident?"

"It seems she drove off the road one night when I was four. The car went into a lake or something with ice. There was also something about a closet, but she wouldn't elaborate."

"How awful. You don't remember?"

"No, but it explains my nightmares." Although it didn't explain the one where the burning man grabbed him. But why go into that with Kelly? She must think he was fucked up enough.

"Repressed memories. What else? Did she explain why she left?"

"She said that was the reason, but I don't believe her. It doesn't make sense."

"What about your father? You never told me he was a prosecutor. I'd have thought you'd be proud."

"He was a state's attorney and then went into private practice. I thought he was the greatest...until he went to jail." He took a deep breath and slumped in his chair. "Between a felon and a deserter, my parents didn't leave me much to be proud of. Why talk about them?"

She slid off the desk and circled behind him. Leaning over the back of his chair, she wrapped her arms around his neck and pressed her cheek against his. "But it's not your fault. You turned out okay."

"Yeah, well." Her hair tickled his face and smelled like peach.

"When did it happen?" she asked "Your father's jail thing."

"It was just before I met you in Mexico. I was running away from it. When I came back to Chicago, he'd died already. He left me his mortgaged income property in a trust. It was years before I touched the money, and even then I paid it back because I didn't know how clean it was. It's like this thing with Arias. The charges on him were dropped about the time Gabriela left. Some coincidence, huh?"

★    ★    ★    ★

Sutherland left his apartment at 8:45, allowing enough time to walk the eight blocks to the security shop. He entered the store a few minutes after nine. The space was crowded with cardboard displays for car alarms, wheel locks, and burglarproof doors. Merchandise hung from hooks on the wall or lay on dusty shelves. There were door locks, bike locks, chains, alarms, steel bars, pepper spray, and padlocks of all types. It was everything one needed for life in the big city.

The man behind the counter wore jeans and a blue shirt with "Jim" over the breast pocket. He had a brush cut and bushy mustache.

"What do you need?" he asked.

Sutherland handed over Javier's key. Before he could say anything, Jim glanced at it and said, "I can't help you."

"It doesn't say 'Do Not Duplicate.'"

"I don't have a blank like that. What's it for?"

"I thought you could tell me."

Jim scratched his chin. "Beats me. See those teeth? I saw something like it once. Let me ask Tito. Mind?"

"Who's Tito?"

"He installs alarms for me. He's Mexican. Just a second. He's in the back." Jim disappeared into the rear of the store and returned a minute later. "Yep, it's from Mexico. You might try a locksmith down there."

"Mexico?"

"No. Tito used to work in Pilsen, a neighborhood on Eighteenth Street. He remembers working with some keys just like that."

By the time Sutherland returned to his apartment, Kelly had finally given in to her boss. The city's top attorney insisted she take a few days off considering she'd nearly been abducted or worse. She planned to catch the train to her aunt's house, well away from her apartment and would-be kidnappers.

Sutherland volunteered to drive her to Union Station and as they headed south on Halsted, she said, "Don't you think you should tell Duncan about the key?"

He checked the rearview mirror for the tenth time. Their route had taken many turns down side streets and alleys. Wasn't that what you were supposed to do to avoid being tailed? He never thought he'd be taking lessons from Hollywood.

No one was behind them.

"I'll give him the key," Sutherland said. "But I want a copy. Anyway, it can't hurt if I follow on this. The sooner we find out, the sooner we're back to normal."

After dropping her by the station, he waited to see that no one was following. Then he went to Halsted and headed south to the Pilsen neighborhood. While cruising Eighteenth Street and reading the signs, he felt like he'd returned to San Miguel. Everything was in Spanish. He saw a *carnicería, panadería, zapatería,* and *librería.* In one block he could buy meat, bread, shoes or books, but he didn't see a locksmith anywhere. Parking near Racine, he walked east and stopped in a small taco restaurant. A woman told him the hardware store made keys.

"Ask for Carlos, the father of the owner," she said.

Carlos was an old man with graying hair and skin like a coffee bean. He sat alone in the back of *Ferretería Azteca.*

"Do you have this type? *Este tipo?*" Sutherland asked, handing him the key.

Carlos held it in gnarled fingers close to his eyes. "*Sí, señor.* From Zacatecas. Very strong locks."

"Can you make a copy?"

"*No, señor*," he said. "I no have the blanks."

"Do you know anyone who has them?"

"*Sí. Don Alfonso. Es importador,*" he said. "These are his special locks."

Sutherland got don Alfonso's address, thanked Carlos, and started for the door. Halfway there, he stopped and walked back. Maybe he could do Detective Duncan's job for him.

"Another question, *señor*. Do you know a man named Arias? Enrique Arias?"

Carlos stared back for a moment through cloudy eyes. "Is a common name."

"He's an importer, too. He has something to do with the Chapultepec Gallery."

Carlos seemed to be thinking, scratching his thinning hair and studying Sutherland's face. After a moment he asked, "He is a friend?"

Sutherland had the feeling that Carlos' response depended on how he answered.

"I've just heard of him. That's all."

Carlos nodded. His eyes were wary. "I know of him, too. He used to have business in the *barrio*."

"Does he still live near here?"

Carlos shook his head. "He would not live long."

"Has enemies?"

"Ask don Alfonso Rivera, *señor*. They were *socios* once. Partners."

# CHAPTER THIRTY-THREE

▼

Alfonso Rivera's warehouse sat between vacant lots along a side street south of Eighteenth Street. A sign on the steel door said "GUADALAJARA IMPORTS—TOQUE EL TIMBRE." High above and on the side, a closed-circuit camera pointed down at Sutherland. He pushed the doorbell next to the frame. A few seconds later, the latch clicked open, and he entered. Inside, a young Mexican woman sat behind a reception desk. She wore a red sweater and jeans. Despite her overdone eye makeup, she was pretty. In front of her was a television monitor with images that changed every several seconds. One flashed to the sidewalk where he had just been waiting. While she admired her long, acrylic fingernails, she informed Sutherland that *don* Alfonso was out and might be back tomorrow.

"Damn." He was cold from the walk from the hardware store and anxious to learn about the key. This had to be the same Alfonso Rivera that Gabriela knew from school. Javier must have contacted him. "Can someone tell me what this belongs to?"

She glanced at the outstretched key. "Maybe Mr. Rivera."

"I'll settle for a copy. Can you do that?"

She led him through a door into the warehouse, the size of a high school gymnasium, lined with metal shelving racks. Half of the shelves were empty. The other half held cardboard cartons, woven rugs, pottery, decorative ironwork, and painted wood carvings. She called to a young man working a hand forklift. In rapid and slangy Spanish lost on Sutherland, she must have told the boy to make a duplicate because he took it to a bench and began working on it.

"Do you keep records of who buys the locks and keys?" Sutherland asked.

"Me?" She giggled. "The records are in *el jefe's* head." She left him to watch the boy copy the key. It was more complicated than normal because the key had teeth on both sides. In less than five minutes, he was done.

On the way out, Sutherland stopped by the receptionist's desk with the original and his freshly cut duplicate.

"How much?"

She shrugged. "Five dollars?"

He fished a bill from his pocket. "I might be back...when Mr. Rivera returns."

She took the ten-dollar bill he handed her and opened a metal cashbox. Suddenly, the front door rattled behind him. Someone was trying to get in. Then the doorbell buzzed with an insistent drone. She looked at him and scowled.

"A friend of yours?" She reached for a button on her desk.

Sutherland glanced at the television monitor. The screen showed a man in a Western hat rattling the door while he leaned on the buzzer. His face was familiar. He was the man from the Chapultepec Gallery.

"Don't open it!" Sutherland shouted. He grabbed her wrist before she pushed the button.

"What's the matter?" Her eyes were wide with fright.

The man began banging his fists on the metal door. Sutherland let go of the receptionist and ran toward the warehouse.

"Just call the police!" he yelled over his shoulder. "Don't open that door."

He ran into the warehouse, spotted the exit sign, and ran. Barging through the doorway, he found himself in an alley.

Great. His car was blocks away in a strange neighborhood, and a man was chasing him. Maybe more than one. The man in the gallery had a side-kick.

He jogged down the alley, crossed a street, and continued down the alley three more blocks. Alleys were the last stretches the city plowed and his progress was slowed by ruts and heavy slush. He was breathing hard when he turned north and ran toward Eighteenth Street. He slowed to a walk, not wanting to appear more obvious than a *gringo* in this part of town already did. Glancing back, he saw the man with the Western hat. He was well behind, but he was slogging after him. Sutherland started jogging again.

Eighteenth Street was a busy retail street, and he felt safer when he reached it. He saw his car from half a block away and stopped. Two men were standing on the sidewalk by the passenger door.

"Shit," Sutherland said, startling a woman coming out of a bakery. Then he saw a policeman a few storefronts away from him, writing a ticket for a pickup truck parked at a hydrant. Sutherland trotted over to him.

"Officer?" He was breathing hard.

"This yours?" The policeman, a solid Hispanic, pointed at the pickup.

"No. Mine's over there." He pointed to his Jaguar on the other side of the street, five doors down. The two men standing by it were looking in his direction. "Those men are trying to break in."

The cop lowered his pen and followed Sutherland's finger. The men stared back and seemed to be talking to one another.

"You sure?" the cop said.

"Go with me. I'll show you." Sutherland stole a glance behind him and saw his pursuer at the corner, watching.

The cop tore the ticket out of his book and stuck it onto the pickup's side window. "Okay, let's go."

As they crossed the street, the two men eased away from the car, turned, and quickly walked in the other direction. Every few steps they glanced over their shoulder until they disappeared around the corner.

"What did I tell you?" Sutherland said.

"In this neighborhood, it means nothing."

When they reached the car, the cop looked it over and frowned. "You putting me on?"

Sutherland looked around for the man who had followed him, but he'd disappeared as well. He took a deep breath, relieved. "I guess we got here in time."

The cop looked at the parking meter. "Afraid not, sir. The meter's expired." He pulled out his ticket book.

When Sutherland opened his apartment door, the phone was ringing. He picked it up before his voice mail kicked in.

"Finally," a voice said.

"Who's this?"

"Agent Christopher. In San Miguel. What happened? I expected to hear from you."

"Something came up," Sutherland said. "We found my mother. She's safe now."

"Jesus, why didn't you tell me?"

"I had to go alone. That was the deal."

"I don't know how you did it, but congratulations. Does it have anything to do with a couple bodies found in a mine?"

"No comment."

"I'll take that as an affirmative. That means you're in worse danger. Did you know one of them was Arias' nephew? He was like a son to him. It's a good thing you got out of here."

"It's no better in Chicago. They were after my girlfriend."

"Arias isn't going to quit. Now he'll be on you like a dog on a meat truck. I'm flying back today. Do you have my number?"

"I lost it."

Christopher gave him his cell phone number again. "Hang tight," he said. "Running around today could've got you killed."

"How do you know about that?"

"Arias' men followed you when you went to that neighborhood. My men were there, too. They would have stepped in if the cop hadn't been there."

"How did they know I was there? For that matter, how did you know?" Sutherland asked. He had taken every precaution driving to Eighteenth Street. He had driven a circuitous route with turns and double-backs, watching the rearview mirror half the time. It was uncanny.

"Arias' men? I don't know," Christopher said. "I told you. We have a couple of his lines tapped. Not the whole picture, but it helps. That's how we knew they followed you."

"Do you know about last night?"

"Your girl's place? She's all right, isn't she?"

"Yes, but it was a close call. You're telling me knowing all this, you can't arrest him?" Sutherland said.

"In the United States, sure. We don't have jurisdiction in Mexico. Anyway, we couldn't get around his local protection. We're working on getting their *federales* to help. Until then, the stone is the only reason he'll leave Mexico again."

"What makes you think he'd come here?"

"We heard. He may not trust some of his men in Chicago. He hasn't told them about the stone. He's just mentioned the shipment. If that legend's true, it's megabucks."

"The lost tomb," Sutherland said. "His and Professor Hidalgo's wet dream."

"We just want Arias. Mexico can do whatever they want with the artifacts. It will be fun to watch because I don't think the professor's motives are purely academic."

That was interesting. Christopher just corroborated Sutherland's suspicions about Mercedes' father.

"It may be moot. We're a long way from finding it."

"You have the key, right? That's why you went to Guadalajara Imports?"

"Are you guessing, or do you know something?" Sutherland asked.

"A little of both. We overheard Arias' men saying you went to a hardware store trying to get a key copied. I'm guessing that's why you went to Rivera's place. It's weird."

"Why?"

"Alfonso Rivera and Arias hate each other. It's a turf thing."

"That's not why I went. They're the only ones who could duplicate the key and Gabriela told Javier to contact that same Alfonso Rivera. It makes sense, doesn't it? I still don't know what the key fits. Let the police figure it out. I have to give it to them."

"Keep your copy," Christopher said. "We'll work on it when I get back. In the meantime, stay put. Now that he's sure you have the key, he'll assume you know where the shipment is."

"So I can expect another visit?"

"I don't think so. I'm guessing they want you to lead them to it. We'll keep monitoring things and move in if we need to."

"What if the police find it first?" Sutherland said.

"It will be more complicated, but Arias will win in the end. If the police find it, it gets sent back to Mexico. He'd use his contacts there to get his hands on the *lagarto* stone or at least a copy. He doesn't have to worry about someone beating him to the treasure. Professor Hidalgo has the other piece. And anyone will need both pieces to find that tomb."

# CHAPTER THIRTY-FOUR

▼

After Sutherland hung up from Christopher's call, he thought about Mercedes and her father. Hidalgo had been secretive about the stone and not particularly concerned with Gabriela or the fate of the *campesinos*. If he was working with Arias and was only interested in the silver and gold, where would that leave Mercedes? She was supposed to be protecting Gabriela.

He called Detective Duncan and told him the dry-cleaning lady had found the mystery key. "Javier gave it to me after all. Maybe your guys can figure out what it fits."

"I'll send a uniform over to pick it up."

"There's something else," Sutherland said. "Arias knows I have it."

"How?"

Sutherland had been afraid of that question. Duncan didn't appreciate amateur ingenuity. "I was doing a little research," he said finally. "I found out the key came from the Pilsen neighborhood. I was followed there."

"Because you're a smart-ass," Duncan growled. "If you'd let us handle it, they wouldn't know."

"That didn't stop them before. They keep coming no matter what."

"We don't have the bodies to guard you. Stay put, and lock your doors. Your building has a security guard."

"And Arias' guys have guns," Sutherland said.

"Look," Duncan said, sounding frustrated. "We're doing what we can. That shit storm at your girlfriend's last night got a lot of attention downtown."

"Did you find out anything about them?"

"We identified their car. It's registered to Chapultepec Gallery."

"Figures."

"We'll get a warrant. Meantime, write what you know about the key and give it the copper when he comes. One other thing, I called your ex and got an earful. She acted like everything was my fault."

"Thanks. She believes you at least?"

"Yeah, but she's not happy. She told me you're going to owe her big time."

"I always do."

A half hour later, the doorman called and said a policeman was downstairs. He went to the lobby and met a uniformed cop. He looked authentic, but Sutherland asked for identification. After seeing it and signing a form, he handed over the key and the address of Guadalajara Imports.

"Weird," the policeman said, turning the key over in his hands. "What's it to?"

"That's for your guys to figure out."

Back in his apartment, Sutherland opened the stack of mail that had accumulated in the last week. As he set aside bills and tossed the junk, his thoughts went back to how he was followed. He'd heard of tracking devices in cars. Radio signals or GPS devices were small and accurate to within feet. The only way to find out was to search his whole car. It was probably underneath. Crawling under a car dripping with road salt and ice wasn't appealing.

"I'll leave it to Christopher and the experts," he thought and drifted off.

The phone awakened him.

"Doug?" It was Kelly.

"Are you at your aunt's place?"

"No. I found Pedro Guzmán."

"How? Where?" The news left him glad and angry at the same time. "You shouldn't be..."

She interrupted. "Listen to me. Breaking into my place makes this personal. You're not the Lone Ranger, so just accept it."

"All right," he said, not liking it at all. She should've been out of the way by now, safe at her aunt's house. "Did Pedro finally answer his phone?"

"No. After you dropped me off, I did a little checking."

"Oh?" he said. "Finding an alien with a common name takes more than a little checking."

She chuckled, seemingly enjoying the chase. If she'd seen Javier holding his belly soaked with blood or Angel's blackened, lifeless face, she might not be so enthusiastic. "Remember the restaurant where Javier was to meet him, *la Olla?*" she said. "I asked around there. It took all day, but I'm in Pedro's room. He's very nervous."

"Does he know where the shipment is?"

"He won't talk. I'm sure he's illegal and afraid I'll turn him in. But you're Javier's cousin."

"How can I convince him of that?" Sutherland said. "What if I showed him the key?"

"Try anything, but you have to hurry," she said. "I don't know how long I can hold him here."

Sutherland left his building by the back door. He slipped down the alley onto Clark Street and hailed a taxi. Five minutes later, he entered the Borders bookstore on Clark, left by the Broadway exit, and waved down another cab.

No one was going to follow him this time.

The address was five blocks west of Logan Square in the middle of a residential neighborhood. Two and three-story dwellings that once housed Hispanic families in crowded conditions were being gradually converted to tidy, single-family homes. Sutherland got out of the taxi a block away and waited. Nobody was following him.

He found the house, two stories and in need of paint, between a restored Victorian on one side and a remodeled brick two-flat on the other. He passed down a walkway and entered by the side door, locking it behind him with a deadbolt. A narrow staircase led him to the attic floor and three doors. The center one opened to a bathroom. He knocked on the one on the right.

"Who is it?" It was Kelly.

"Doug."

The door opened, revealing an attic room barely large enough for a bed, chair, and dresser. On the bed, back to the wall like a cornered animal, sat a small Mexican who couldn't be more than eighteen years old. He wore jeans and a denim jacket and held a red bandana to his mouth, as if it was injured. There was a red lump under his left eye. His breath misted the cold air.

Kelly closed the door. "Finally."

She had on the corduroy pants and leather jacket she'd worn when he dropped her at the station that morning. Her thick hair was in a ponytail. A trickle of blood had clotted under her nose. Evidently Pedro Guzmán wasn't tamed by her good looks alone.

"He give you a hard time?"

She held up a six-inch switchblade. "He wanted to use this. Thought I was from the INS. I calmed him down."

"And I thought martial arts classes were a waste." Sutherland took a step closer to the bed, grazing his head on the ceiling. From its peak, it slanted down to a dormer window covered by a towel. Pedro pulled his legs up, shrinking against the wall.

"Does he speak English?"

"I don't think so."

"Javier's note said the things were in the attic. Could the shipment be here?"

"Not in this tiny place. There's another room across the hall."

"Take a look while I talk to him."

"Okay. Watch out. He's slippery."

Kelly left the room and Sutherland pulled out a photo and the duplicate key from his jacket pocket. He held up the old picture of Gabriela and him together, taken fifteen years earlier.

"It's my mother and me, *mi madre y yo. Se llama Gabriela Castellano.*"

Pedro looked at the photo, at Sutherland, and then the photo again. He took the bandana away from his mouth, revealing a swollen lip.

"*Y qué?*"

Sutherland pointed to his mother in the picture. He said she was Javier's aunt and then confirmed that Pedro was Javier's friend.

Pedro shrugged, then nodded. "*Mi amigo, sí.*"

Sutherland held up the key, turning it over in front of Pedro's eyes. "Javier gave me this."

Kelly came back into the room. "Nothing," she said. "How are you doing?"

"We'll see." He turned back to Pedro and asked if he recognized the key.

Pedro nodded again.

Sutherland explained that Javier came to him for help, but he couldn't because he didn't know where the shipment was. He asked if Pedro knew where Javier hid it.

Pedro studied the key and the photo again. He shivered and wrapped his arms around his thin torso, his fingers clenching the threadbare jacket. He finally looked up and spewed something in rapid Spanish.

Sutherland turned to Kelly. "Did you catch all that?"

"He said it's in an *almacén*, a warehouse. He asked about Javier," she said.

"He probably doesn't know he's dead. What warehouse? Where? *Dónde?*"

He shook his head and rattled off more Spanish.

"I think I got that," Sutherland said. "The warehouse was like a garage. Then he said something about Chicago."

"He gets lost here," she said. "It's too big, he says."

"There's hundreds of warehouses," Sutherland said. "What about Javier's *ático*? Is he lying to us?"

Pedro's eyes widened. *"Ático?"* he said. *"Eso es el nombre."*

"All right," Sutherland said. "A warehouse called the Attic. Something we can get our arms around."

They suddenly heard banging. Someone was pounding with heavy fists on the outside door. It was like thunder rumbling up the stairway. Then they heard angry shouts, *"Pendejos, hijos de putas."*

Sutherland turned to Kelly. "Did they follow you?"

"I don't think so." She turned to Pedro and asked if he knew who it was or whether he was expecting someone.

Pedro, his eyes electric with fear, shook his head. A crash echoed in the hallway.

Sutherland tore the towel curtain from the window and looked outside. The roof of the neighboring house was ten feet away. It was steeply pitched and covered with ice. "Shit. What's in the other room?"

"It's the same as this one," Kelly said, looking over his shoulder at the treacherous roof. "But it's flat."

He opened the window.

"Maybe they'd think they left that way," he thought. Then he turned to Pedro. *"Vámonos."* The boy was pressed against the pillow, terrified. Sutherland grabbed him and hauled him toward the door. Kelly was already in the other room, opening the window. Sutherland pushed Pedro inside and locked the door behind him. Shouts and pounding filled the passageway.

The neighboring building was no more than five feet away, its snow-covered roof slightly below them. It would take a standing leap to get there and the center frame of the double-hung window was in the way. Sutherland pointed to the small dresser in the corner. He and Kelly immediately went for it. It was empty. With a running start, they heaved it through the window. It smashed through the glass and wood, taking the center frame with it. After hitting the parapet of the adjacent house, the dresser toppled back and fell into the walkway below.

Sutherland grabbed the chair and cleared away the loose glass and wood, making room to stand stooped over on the windowsill.

"You first," he said to Kelly.

Without hesitation, she climbed up and jumped. She landed, tumbled forward, and rolled to her feet. Sutherland pushed Pedro up on the sill.

"Jump. They're going to kill us. *Salta*."

Pedro hesitated, frozen, his hands gripping the frame. Sutherland thought he would have to throw him.

"Now. Hurry. *Ten prisa*."

Finally, just as loud footfalls echoed up the stairs, Pedro released his hold and jumped.

Sutherland watched him land and pitch forward. The voices were right outside. He climbed up and leaped. When he hit, he skidded on some ice and landed on his butt. Scrambling to his feet, he saw Kelly at the rooftop door, waving him to follow. Pedro had taken off toward her. A burglar alarm started to yelp in the walkway. He was halfway to the door, stumbling through the snow, when the first shot whizzed by his ear.

Shots cracked behind Sutherland as he ran. He followed Kelly and Pedro's tracks through ankle-deep snow across the roof. They had disappeared through the door of a small penthouse perched on the rear of the house. As he approached the door, he glanced over his shoulder. A man was charging from twenty yards behind. Another pointed a gun from the window they had jumped from. Just as Sutherland grabbed the door handle, a bullet splintered the wooden frame over his head.

He ripped the door open and charged in, locking it behind him. The room was small with a few stacked chairs and a wet bar. Snow that had been tracked in led to the top of a spiral staircase. He wound down the stairs in near darkness, stumbling into a hallway. The burglar alarm was louder inside, echoing down the passageway.

"Kelly?"

Light shone through the door ahead of him. He ran for it. As he passed into a bedroom, something banged his shins. and he flew sprawling onto a hardwood floor. He rolled over and looked into the angry eyes of a man holding a large gun.

"Move and you're dead."

Sutherland didn't move. The man had a bushy mustache and a wild shock of silver hair. Kelly and Pedro were on their stomachs a few feet away.

"You okay?" Sutherland asked.

"Okay," Kelly said. "He lives here. I told him we're being chased."

"Shut up." The man held up his free hand and tilted his head, listening. Between the yelps of the alarm, they heard pounding from the roof and then more shots. "In there." The man pointed to a walk-in closet. "All of you. Now."

Sutherland jumped to his feet. Kelly pulled Pedro up by the arm. They hurried into the closet with the man behind. "Face down on the floor." In ten seconds, he had them cuffed together. He left them there and a moment later, the alarm stopped wailing.

They waited and listened. There was a crash from the roof, sounding like the locked door breaking. Seconds crept like minutes. They heard distant sirens. Suddenly, shouts were followed by more shots—louder this time—from the hallway. Then there was a cry of pain and then a loud thump, as if someone fell. Sutherland's heart raced. The sirens wound down on the street below. He wondered who had won.

It was too familiar. The second time in as many days. He sat and waited while the police and the technicians did their thing. This time, the mood was better. There was more banter and joking among them. The homeowner, their captor, knew many of the cops.

Sutherland, Kelly, and Pedro sat on a couch in a TV room. Thirty minutes had passed since the last shot was fired and he still didn't know what happened. Sanchez, the owner, barely said a word to them when he removed the cuffs and led them down the hall. He only grunted when Sutherland told him to call Detective Duncan.

After another fifteen minutes, Duncan arrived. Sutherland filled him in while the detective took notes, grumbled, and shook his head.

"Now we've got an idea where the shipment is," Sutherland said.

"When are you gonna learn?" Duncan said, jabbing his pen at Sutherland. "Lucky you weren't killed."

"What happened?"

Duncan slid his notebook into his jacket pocket. "Sanchez shot the one in the hall. DOA." He stood up, as if to go, then glared at Sutherland. "One's dead. Another was arrested on the street. But not before they wounded a cop. Happy?"

"Look, I didn't ask for this. Besides, you wouldn't have found Pedro." He nodded toward the boy. "Even if you did, he wouldn't have said squat to you."

Duncan laughed. "Yeah, he looks real tough." He started for the door. "I gotta get back to the gallery's warehouse."

"Did you find anything there?"

"The drug dogs are having a field day," Duncan said. "No Arias. But we've got three of his men. We'll get him."

"Not if he stays in Mexico," Sutherland said. "Did you talk to the DEA?"

"They'll be advised. It's our bust."

"Turf battles, huh? Who gets the credit and all that?" Sutherland stood. "Are we through here?"

"Not up to me," Duncan said. "There's a matter of breaking and entering."

"You can't be serious."

"Sanchez can press charges."

"That's ridiculous. Just explain it to him."

Duncan smiled. "Don't worry. You're in luck. He's a retired cop. He hasn't had this much fun since he left the job. You just made his day."

# CHAPTER THIRTY-FIVE

▼

"Okay, Mr. Sutherland. You can go on one condition," Detective Duncan said. They were with Detective Parisi of the Fourteenth District Station, the unit having jurisdiction over the shootings at Sanchez' house. Detective Parisi had called the station Shakespeare, presumably because it was at Shakespeare and California. The interview room was barely large enough for a scuffed table and three uncomfortable chairs. Sutherland had just signed his statement explaining what had happened. Kelly and Pedro were somewhere else in the building, presumably doing the same thing. It was past eight o'clock, and Sutherland's stomach was growling.

"Let me guess," Sutherland said.

"No guesses. I'm telling you." Duncan stood and placed his large hands on the table. He leaned over Sutherland. "Stay the fuck out. Got that?"

Sutherland stared back. "I'd love to. But is it up to me?" He held up the fingers of his left hand. "Let's count. First, they killed the four *campesinos*, the peasants." He shot out his thumb. "Then, there was my guide, who was pushed down the mine. That's five." He started on his right hand. "Six is Javier, who died while he was in the hospital. My mother, me, Kelly, and Mercedes would bring it to an even ten. What's stopping them? You're not."

Duncan stood over him, looking as if he was about to turn purple. "You'll fuck it up."

"Fuck up what? We've got the key. We have to find the artifacts and put Arias away. Otherwise, he won't stop at finding the shipment. He'll come after me. He's lost his nephew and two more guys today. The DEA knows all this. Why don't you work with them?"

"We'll do fine without those dickheads," Duncan said through clenched teeth. "Assholes don't even return my calls."

"Great. You guys fight over who gets the credit while I get my ass shot." Sutherland took a deep breath. He felt as if he was talking to himself.

"Do you think Arias is gonna walk in the front door with his hands up?"

"Hell no. He won't leave Mexico without a good reason. That stone's our one chance." Sutherland stood up. "He has men here. And since I'm the one they're interested in, I've got the most incentive. So, with you or the DEA, I plan to find it."

Duncan's eyes were bulging. He banged his fist on the table. "Don't interfere. I'll find the damn warehouse. You go home and stay there."

"Hurry. Christopher will be back from Mexico tonight." Sutherland turned and walked out, not daring to look behind him.

Kelly was waiting for him downstairs by the front door. Her face was flushed, her eyes moist. In the six months Sutherland had known her, he had rarely seen this softer side. He put his arms around her.

"Two close calls in a row," he said.

"It's not that," she said. "They're holding Pedro. I think it's for the INS. Can't you talk to them?"

"My stock's not worth *mierda* right now." He released her and looked into her eyes. "We'll see what we can do after we're out of this ourselves." He pulled on his jacket.

"It's my fault Arias' men found us," she said. "I talked to a dozen people to find Pedro." She dried her eyes with a handkerchief. "I just called a lawyer friend. There's nothing he can do."

"Right now, he's better off with the INS than out where Arias can get to him." Sutherland looked through the window at snow swirling around the streetlight. "Why don't we get you to Union Station? You can still pick up your suitcase and take the train to your aunt's house."

Kelly's eyes hardened. "No fucking way, Doug. I'm staying with you. You can use my help. My aunt and suitcase can wait."

Sutherland was taken aback by Kelly's determination. Despite the obvious danger and without being asked, she'd tracked down Pedro. After hiding from would-be kidnappers and dodging bullets, she still seemed up for whatever came their way. Tests under fire might bring out character, but these could be fatal. It was no way to discover a lover's virtues. Nevertheless, her hard stare and set jaw told him that arguing would be futile.

They caught a cab outside the district station. On the way to his apartment, they picked up pad thai and curried noodles at a restaurant on Diversey. As he and Kelly entered the lobby, the doorman motioned them over to his desk.

"Mr. Sutherland, you got a guest. She insisted on staying." He pointed to the waiting area, an alcove to the side and behind the desk.

"She? How long?" Sutherland asked.

"Couple hours," the doorman said.

Sutherland walked to the waiting room with Kelly following. The alcove was dimly lit, but they could see a carry-on bag on the floor and someone lying on the leather couch. When they approached, he saw she was on her back, sound asleep. She wore jeans, a leather jacket, and Western boots. Her hair was loose, cascading over the edge of the couch.

"Do you know her?" Kelly was right behind him.

"It's Mercedes. The woman I told you about."

Kelly stepped around him for a closer look. "Really? I had the impression she was short and dumpy." She turned and grinned. "Has she been kissed by a prince since you saw her?"

"Compared to you, everyone's dumpy," he said.

She chuckled. "Not bad, but you don't get off that easy. You owe me."

"She saved my life, remember?"

He shook Mercedes' shoulder. She opened her eyes and blinked several times. When she finally focused on him, she said, "*Señor* Doug. What time is it?"

"About nine. Is Gabriela okay?"

"She's safe. She's at her friend's place." She sat up and pushed her hair out of her face. "I was so tired. But I had to come. Have you found him? Pedro?"

"Him and the key," he said. "But not the shipment."

She frowned. "You haven't given up, have you?"

Sutherland felt the heat rise in his face.

Give up? What the hell was she talking about? You'd think he'd spent the day at the beach. He was about to tell her to take a flying leap back to Mexico when Kelly saved him.

"Hi, I'm Kelly," she said, stepping forward. "You must be Mercedes. Doug told me all about you. Thanks for helping him."

Mercedes hesitated, as if noticing Kelly for the first time. Her eyes swept from Kelly's head to her feet. She nodded in approval. "*Encantada.*"

Sutherland said, "Let's get upstairs, we have to talk."

An older couple joined them on the elevator, making the ride to the twentieth floor a quiet one. Inside his apartment, Sutherland put on the lights. Kelly took the Thai food into the kitchen. Mercedes wandered into the living room, looking first at the evening cityscape and then glancing around the room. "Nice place," she said. "Just move in?"

"Why do you say that?" Sutherland said.

"It's not crammed with things."

"It's his aesthetic side," Kelly said, joining them. "Less is more. Besides, he needs the room. He paces."

"It helps me think," he said. "If you weren't here, that's what I'd do to figure out what to do next."

"That's not complicated," Mercedes said. "Find the shipment."

He sighed, forcing back his irritation.

"We're trying." He turned to Kelly. "I'm getting cranky. I have to eat. Are you hungry, Mercedes?"

"Starving."

"We all could use the blood sugar," Kelly said. "I'll dish. You get the beer."

They ate in the breakfast nook. Sutherland filled Mercedes in on his activities since leaving Mexico.

"So we've got a key, but nothing to open with it."

"We can't let Arias find it," Mercedes said.

"I agree." He dished hot sauce on his pad thai. "Which brings us to your father."

She stiffened, holding her fork in midair. "Why?"

"I wonder if he's as idealistic as he pretends." He forked in a mouthful of noodles and watched her.

Mercedes' eyes narrowed. "What's that supposed to mean?"

He took his time and swallowed. "Is he after the money, like Arias? Christopher thinks he is."

She put her fork down. "You believe that?"

"I'm asking you."

"My father has no interest in money. Just the artifacts."

"Why didn't he mention the *lagarto* stone to Gabriela or me?"

"It's not important to him. Besides, it may only be a legend."

"You never mentioned it either."

She threw her napkin on the table. "*Pendejo*. After all I've done?"

"That's not the point. Gabriela discovered the looting. She sent Javier after the shipment. She told your father, and he found the broken piece. But he never told Gabriela he found it. Nor did he tell her about the legend or another tomb. Why?"

She paused, as if thinking it through, her lips a tight line. "Maybe he doubts there's anything to it." She pushed her noodles around the plate with her fork.

"I have another question you won't like," Sutherland said. "How did Arias learn about the *lagarto* stone in the first place? He knew about the artifacts because he sent them. Who told him about the stone and the legend?"

She seemed stunned, swallowing hard. She looked past him as if the answer was in the living room.

"Was it common knowledge?" he continued. "Who else knew?"

"That point never occurred to me," she said finally. "Mexico is filled with legends. The piece of the stone the looters left behind had the head of a lizard, like the Toltec legend. No one else knew."

"Your father must have told Arias," he said.

"He wouldn't deal with a man like that."

"If you have another explanation, I'd like to hear it."

She glanced away. Her jaw was clenched, and her chest rose and fell with deep breaths. She finally said, "If he told Arias, it was because he worried he would unwittingly sell the stone in the United States. It would be lost forever."

"Then we agree. It's about money."

"It's about another tomb," Mercedes insisted, slapping the table with her open hand. "A new discovery."

"Is your father the only one who can decode it?" he asked.

"No. But he has the broken piece. Another cryptography expert would need it, too." She frowned, apparently thinking. "To tell Arias…"

"Can I say something?" Kelly said, breaking in. "It seems to me that your father doesn't realize the danger he's in. Whether he's naïve or in league…"

"He's not," Mercedes blurted. She stood up. Sutherland thought she was going to leap across the table at Kelly. "He would never…"

"Hold on," Sutherland said, waving his hands for calm. "Kelly's right. We're sure Arias is a killer. Look at the *campesinos*. Your father knows all about it and hasn't been harmed. It's because now Arias needs him for the piece of the stone and his knowledge. But what are the odds of Arias letting him live after it's been deciphered?"

Mercedes slowly sat down and stared straight ahead. She looked drained, as if picturing her father's bloodied corpse.

"He'd be better off if the shipment was never found," Kelly said.

"Eventually it will be," Sutherland said. "How long can a truck stay hidden?"

"If the police find it, couldn't they lure him here?" Kelly asked. "Like the DEA?"

"The police don't have a clue about Arias," he said. "The shipment would be tied up in red tape. It would eventually be sent to Mexico, where Arias has influence. I'd never have another night's sleep and Mercedes' father would find out what a mistake he made."

"He must have told him." Mercedes spoke slowly, as if she was still reasoning it out. "One of his published articles on the Maya was discredited. Since then, he's lost some major grants. He's taken it badly, but I've never had a reason to doubt him."

"He might value his reputation as much as the money," Sutherland said. "That gives me two reasons not to trust him."

# CHAPTER THIRTY-SIX

▼

While they finished eating, Kelly called her office. A message said her assistant had e-mailed the information Sutherland requested. Five minutes later, she had printed the reports and was leaning against the desk in the den while reading it aloud to Mercedes and Sutherland.

"Enrique Arias was arrested for the murder of a pawnshop owner on Chicago's south side in June 1979. He'd been picked out of a lineup by two witnesses who saw Arias and an accomplice, a white man with reddish hair, run from the shop. The accomplice or the murder weapon was never found. In February 1980, Assistant State's Attorney Bernard Sutherland announced the charges against Arias had been dropped."

"Not much new there," Sutherland said. "Just the part about the accomplice."

"Here's something though," Kelly said. "Your father resigned a week after that. He went into private practice."

"That's strange," he said. "What would make him do that? Any reason given on why the charges were dropped?"

"No. My assistant is probably the city's best paralegal. She doesn't miss anything," Kelly said.

"Your father released Arias in 1980?" Mercedes said. "And you think my father's bad?"

"He's been dead for fifteen years," he said. "There's not much he could do now. What else, Kelly?"

"Next, the murder victim in Beverly Shores," Kelly said. "This comes from the sheriff's file. His name was Emiliano Valdez. He was on parole for grand larceny. Born in Morelia, Mexico, in 1943. Does the name mean anything to you?"

"Not to me." He had a bad feeling about it though. He wondered why Gabriela would keep news of a murder if it didn't have something to do with her.

"You, Mercedes?"

"No. What's he got to do with this?"

"Maybe nothing," he said. "It's a clipping I found in my mother's place. Did they find the killer?"

"Wait." Kelly skimmed down the page. "He was killed in January 1980. An old couple owned the cabin where he was found. They only used it in the summer. He must have broken in. Two unidentified sets of fingerprints, one of them on the murder weapon, a 38 caliber Saturday-night special, couldn't be connected to anyone. They also couldn't connect the blood that wasn't the victim's. The deceased's alcohol level was way over the legal limit. There was no car or evidence of how he got there. In addition to the victim's clothes and suitcase, they found a woman's scarf and a child's glove that didn't belong to the cabin owners. The case was never solved." She looked up. "That's it."

He blew out a breath. A child's glove. Why were those words so ominous? A glove left behind with a dead Mexican who Gabriela knew. Did he remember anything? He would have been four, but memories are vague and unreliable from that age. Yet he'd been there. He was almost sure of it.

"How about the VW in the water?"

"Nothing yet. She's checked the Chicago papers, and she's working on Wisconsin and Indiana." Kelly tilted her head and looked at him. "Are you okay? You've turned pale."

"Yeah," he said. "This thing's got me confused."

"Why are we even wasting time with it?" Mercedes said. "It won't help us find the warehouse."

"You're right." He couldn't think about it anymore. If he was to learn the truth, Gabriela would have to tell him. "Let's find this Attic warehouse. I'll try the Internet. Mercedes can check the yellow pages while Kelly tries the people she talked to in Pilsen today."

He logged onto the Internet. Mercedes sank into the corner chair with the phone book on her lap. Kelly sat on the desk and phoned the bartender who'd told her how to find Pedro.

After a few minutes, Mercedes closed the yellow pages. "Nothing with 'Attic' under warehouses or storage." She got up and watched Sutherland's screen over his shoulder.

"Odds are that it's near Eighteenth Street," Sutherland said. "Close to Guadalajara Imports. If Rivera had been there today, he might have told me. I have a feeling he pointed Javier to it."

"What's his full name?" Kelly asked, holding her hand over the phone's mouthpiece.

"Alfonso Rivera. Everybody calls him don Alfonso."

Kelly went back to her Spanish conversation on the phone. She had apparently made a friend earlier that day.

"Struck out," Sutherland said to no one in particular. There wasn't an "Attic" for a Chicago warehouse on the Internet. Next, he tried Rivera and found hundreds of names, but there wasn't an Alfonso. It was after ten. They might have to wait until tomorrow and hope Rivera returned to his office. He was about to log off when he thought to check his e-mail. It had been four days since he last looked.

He had twenty messages and quickly deleted the spam. That only left questions from his architect, which he'd answered earlier that day. The reminder about Friday's zoning meeting made him uneasy. Was he going to be rid of this *lagarto* albatross by then? He had to be.

"Kelly," Sutherland said, poking her leg. "Are you getting anywhere?"

She held up her hand. "Wait." Then she spoke into the phone, *"Mande?"* She scribbled on a scratch pad and said, *"Muy amable, Julio. Buenas noches."* She hung up and smiled at Sutherland and Mercedes. "Julio just told me about Rivera. He seems a little shady, some kind of neighborhood Robin Hood." She tore off her scribbled note and held it up. "I couldn't get his private number, but I have his address. It's a converted warehouse on the southwest side. Kind of a fortress."

"Like his warehouse." He snatched the note from Kelly's fingers. "If he's shady, he's not likely to cooperate with the police. If he's the same guy who knew Gabriela and helped Javier, why wouldn't he talk to me?" He switched off his computer and stood up. "I guess I have to go to Fort Rivera."

"Not alone. No way," Kelly said.

"I'm not staying here," Mercedes said. "We're finding that stone."

He sighed. They were serious. Then he recalled Mercedes' bravery at the mine and Kelly's nerve dealing with Pedro. They were like two of Charlie's Angels. Was Rivera ready for them?

Sutherland was convinced that Arias' men had hidden a tracking device in his Jaguar. How else could he have been followed?

It took some persuasion, but Sutherland talked Aziz, one of his apartment parking valets, into lending him his '94 Buick. It was a return of a favor. Sutherland had lent him the Jaguar for his wedding the summer before. Aziz returned it in spotless condition, except for the odd kernel of rice.

Kelly drove out of the overhead door with Sutherland and Mercedes slumped down in the backseat. It was after 10:00 PM, and traffic was light on Lake Shore Drive. Heading south, the Drake Hotel loomed brightly before them. On the left, the lake was a black void. Mercedes stared into that darkness, seemingly in thought. With her father's relationship to Arias in question, she had plenty to think about.

"It won't take long to get there," Kelly said. "Do you really think he'll see us?"

"Maybe not. The more I think about it, I'm sure he helped Javier. He imports that kind of key," Sutherland said.

"Can we trust him?" Kelly said. "He's a neighborhood hero, partly for what he gives back and partly by beating the Man."

"He probably wouldn't talk to the police. According to Agent Christopher and the old man in the hardware store, he's Arias' enemy. We have to count on that and him knowing Gabriela. We can't tell him everything. We don't mention any lost tombs, silver, or gold, okay?"

It took another fifteen minutes to find Rivera's renovated warehouse. It was a five-story brick structure with balconies on the upper floors. The neighborhood looked deserted. There were a few abandoned warehouses along the street, some vacant lots and a closed wire factory with a faded "Help Wanted" sign on the front gate. Except for the entrance door, Rivera's building was surrounded by a high fence with razor wire along the top. On one side was a parking lot for a half-dozen cars. Two German shepherds growled from behind the fence. Kelly parked in front of the entrance, the only car on the dark street. He didn't need to ask if they wanted to wait in the car. The neighborhood was too spooky.

The front door was heavy glass. A television camera pointed at them from the vestibule inside. He rang a bell and a man's voice from overhead startled him. "Can I help you?"

"We're looking for Mr. Rivera," Mercedes said.

"He expect you?"

"No, but he'll want to talk to us," Sutherland said. "Tell him we're friends of Gabriela Castellano. We're trying to put Enrique Arias in jail. But we need *señor* Rivera's help."

"Wait." They heard a click.

Standing in the cold on that desolate street made the minute seem like an hour.

"Come in."

The door buzzed, and they went through the vestibule and waited until a heavy metal door slid open with a clang. They passed into a small lobby facing a guard behind a desk in the glow of a console filled with television screens. He held out the phone to them.

"He wants to talk."

Sutherland took the receiver.

"Who are you?" a man's voice asked. "What about the *hijo de puta* Arias? The bastard of the Chapultepec Gallery?" He had a heavy Mexican accent, but his words were clear.

"That's right. My name is Sutherland. My mother is Gabriela Castellano. With help, we can put Arias in jail, but we need information about a key you imported."

"Were you the one in my office today?" Rivera must have learned of his visit and escape through the alley.

"Your man duplicated the key. I need to know what it's for."

There was silence for a moment.

"Wait there." He hung up.

A moment later, a muscular young man with slicked-back hair and a black T-shirt got off the elevator. He was Sutherland's height, but he was built like a bodybuilder. "I got to pat you down," he said.

Sutherland raised his arms. The man frisked him and then looked at Kelly and Mercedes.

"You going up?"

Kelly put up her hands and smiled. "What? No female guards?"

The man searched both women. The fact they were female didn't seem to bother him.

"Follow me," he said.

In the elevator, Kelly said, "You've done that before. Didn't miss a thing." He didn't return her smile.

They got off on the fifth floor, the penthouse. There was only one apartment, and its door was stainless steel. It opened and a tall, handsome Latino with graying black hair and a thick mustache greeted them. Sutherland guessed he was in his mid-fifties. He wore slacks and a loose, white sweater. He glanced at Sutherland and then took in Kelly and Mercedes.

"*Bellísimas.* You go in beautiful company, *señor.* I want your secret."

"Meet my friends, Kelly and Mercedes," Sutherland said.

"And you," Rivera said. "You are not like Gabriela Castellano. You are Anglo. How do I know you are who you say?"

Sutherland pulled out the old photo of him and Gabriela and gave it to him.

Rivera studied it a moment and shrugged. "*Pasen.* I give you five minutes."

The apartment foyer opened into a wide-open living area. It had twelve-foot ceilings with three quarter-height partitions separating the rooms. High-tech lighting, exposed air ducts, and concrete columns completed a sophisticated loft effect. A decorator had spent a lot of Rivera's money. The place was a live-in art gallery. Canvases covered every white partition and wall. Sutherland recognized some of the larger pieces. There was a Frankenthaler, a Tamayo, and a Gorky. Each cost more than the average house.

They followed Rivera across thick carpeting to a seating area in one corner of the huge living room. Rivera sat in a leather couch and motioned for them to sit facing him in three designer chairs.

"You say you put Arias in *la cárcel*. Jail? *Cómo?*" Rivera said, struggling with his English.

"He'll be arrested if we can get him to return to Chicago," Sutherland said. "He'll only come if we find the artifacts he stole. We think they're in a warehouse called the Attic, which uses the locks you imported. You may have directed a young man, Javier Castellano, there."

Rivera studied him a moment. "Do I understand your English? Arrest Arias? Why aren't I talking to *la policía*? Why you?" His expression suggested he hadn't believed a word.

"Let me tell you, *señor*," Kelly said, moving her chair closer to Rivera. She leaned forward, almost nose to nose with him. *"Empezó con cuatro campesinos en San Miguel de Allende."* Using her courtroom clarity and fluent Spanish, she told him about the artifacts robbed from a tomb. She also told him about Arias killing and robbing the peasants and then sending the artifacts to Chicago.

Mercedes slid her chair beside Kelly's and picked up the story in her native tongue. "Gabriela Castellano is his mother." She pointed to Sutherland, "and my father is an archeologist."

Sutherland could barely follow her rapid Spanish, but he knew the story well. She explained how Gabriela sent Javier to find the shipment and that he hijacked and hid it.

"Then," Kelly broke in, speaking as fast as Mercedes. "Arias kidnapped his mother." She nodded toward Sutherland and continued with the events of Gabriela's rescue.

Sutherland kept his eyes on Rivera. He seemed transfixed. His gaze moved back and forth as Kelly or Mercedes picked up the story in turn. He wore a look of lecherous curiosity, which gave Sutherland the feeling that he might have been more taken with the women than their words. What was the harm in his fantasizing, as long as he helped?

"*El maldito Arias*," Mercedes continued, explaining how they'd been chased by Arias' men and the only way to be free of them was to help the authorities arrest him. Sutherland had the key. "*Pero…*"

Their account had come so rapidly that Rivera had merely watched and listened. He finally held up his hands.

"Enough. Is too complicated," he said.

He walked over to a wet bar and poured himself a short tequila from a bottle of *Herradura*. The three of them waited. When he sat down again, he said, "You only want this warehouse, no?"

"*Claro*," the women said in unison.

"I think you are maybe playing with me," Rivera said. "Fucking with Arias is *loco*. You have met him?"

"Only from a distance," Sutherland said. "We've seen his men. A few are dead. Others in jail, but they keep coming."

Rivera thought a minute. "Have you seen an Anglo?" He seemed hopeful. "With blue eyes?"

"Just *mexicanos*. Why?"

"I name him *el biche cobarde*. It is personal." He shrugged, as if to say, "too bad." After downing his tequila with a gulp, he said, "The information you want cannot harm me. So I tell you for the sake of Gabriela. This boy, Javier, did not mention Arias. He just said he was the nephew of Gabriela and needed to store something *grande*. So I help him. The place you want was called the Attic when I bought it. A market for junk. Now it is only a warehouse."

"It has an address," Sutherland said.

"*Sí*." He gave him an address on the other side of Midway Airport. As Sutherland wrote it down, the phone rang. Rivera picked it up, listened, and turned to Sutherland. "You expect someone else? In a BMW? It is parked in front of your car."

Sutherland bolted upright. "I don't believe it. How does he do it?" He looked around, but he didn't know where they could go.

"Arias, again? *Entonces*, how will you leave?" Rivera asked.

"Good question," Sutherland said. "We'll have to call the police."

Rivera held up his hand. "*No necesitamos policía*." Rivera said a few words into the phone and hung up. He walked behind a wall partition and returned, carrying an assault rifle.

"What are you doing?" Sutherland said. "You can't just…"

"*No problema*," Rivera said, walking toward the windows. "I own this building," he said with a mischievous grin. "Only my people live here. The neighborhood is deserted. We often celebrate *así*." He opened a sliding door and disappeared onto the balcony looking over the street. They heard two short bursts of shots and the screech of tires. A few seconds later, Rivera returned with the devilish grin of a boy who had played a prank. He held up a green ammunition clip.

"Only blanks," he said, chuckling and shaking his head in amusement. "But they didn't know. They are gone."

He led them to the door. *"Adiós mis bellísimas,"* he said and kissed Mercedes and then Kelly on the cheek. When he shook Sutherland's hand, he said, "Your *amigas* are very beautiful and convincing, *señor*. You may or may not be the son of Gabriela, and your story may or may not be true. *Pero*, if you do see that *hijo de chingada* Arias, you can piss on him for me. If he is with a blue-eyed Anglo, *el biche cobarde*, do not turn your back. Just shoot him."

# CHAPTER THIRTY-SEVEN

▼

A few minutes after leaving Rivera's building, the three of them were in the Buick following the directions to the warehouse. Sutherland said, "A machine gun with blanks. It made his day. I'm glad he's on our side."

"Very handsome," Mercedes said. "He sees right through you."

"Macho without overdoing it," Kelly added.

"You two…" he said. "If I hadn't been there, you'd forget all about the stone. He had you both undressed with his eyes."

"Try it sometime," Kelly said. "It felt good."

"Whatever." Sutherland drove in silence for a while, replaying their conversation with Rivera. "What was that stuff about a *bicho*? Isn't that an insect?"

"*Biche* with an 'e,'" Mercedes said. "Blue-eyed. He means blue-eyed coward."

"How did those men find us?" Kelly said. "Driving this old beater should have fooled them."

"Who knows?" Sutherland said. "They might have tapped my line and heard your conversation. They knew we were going to Rivera's place."

"How could they do that?" Mercedes asked. "Did they break in?"

"It's probably the same as with Kelly's apartment," he said. "In big buildings, all lines come through a central panel someplace."

They stopped for gas on Cicero. While Sutherland filled the tank, Kelly bought two flashlights in the all-night convenience store. When they left the station, they took extra care not to be followed. Sutherland turned often while Kelly and Mercedes watched for a following car.

It was after 11:00 PM when they found the warehouse. It was off of Fifty-First and Central, in a neighborhood of bungalows at the edge of an older industrial district. The single-story building sat on a large corner lot with an alley on its south side. Along the street, there was a stretch of side-by-side overhead doors, each large enough for a small truck. Sutherland counted fifteen doors facing the street and guessed the alley behind would have the same. A faded sign across the top of the building read: "ANTIQUE MARKET—THE ATTIC."

"That's why Javier called it *el ático*," he said, pointing. He imagined times past with each opening as a business selling old furniture and junk. A newer sign on the roof simply read, "Storage," followed by a phone number.

It was snowing lightly, but it wasn't settling. No one was on the streets. They parked a half-block from the alley, hiding the car behind a van. While Kelly held a flashlight, he dug out a jack handle from the trunk. If the shipment was there, they might need it to open boxes.

Door 23, the number on the key, sat on the alley side of the building. Sutherland kicked away the crusted snow at the bottom of the door and found the lock. It secured the door to an iron hasp set in the concrete. The duplicate key fit, and it turned after a few jiggles. He removed the lock. When Kelly heaved up on the door, it grated metal against metal on its rails, sending a shiver right through him. She pulled it up waist high and the three of them slipped underneath. He lowered the door and he and Kelly flicked on their flashlights. They were staring at the rear cargo doors of a delivery truck. The license plate was from Texas.

There were no windows or skylights in the garage. Their breaths floated eerily in the flashlight beams. He tried the switch on the wall, but the overhead fluorescent lamp didn't blink. He turned the handle on the truck's rear door and opened one of the two sides. With a sweep of the flashlight, they counted dozens of wooden crates stacked inside. They climbed into the hold and looked closer. The largest box was about two feet by four feet. The smallest was two by three feet. The label on the nearest crate read, "Chapultepec Gallery—*Cerámica*."

"Javier hijacked this whole thing," he said. "Quite a feat."

He handed Mercedes his flashlight and knelt beside the nearest crate. Using the jack handle, he pried open the lid. Inside, packed in wood chips and newspaper, were reddish-brown vases, urns, and plates with painted designs. Some were chipped or had small cracks. All were dusty. The strong smell of earth brought back the memory of the tomb and Mercedes' father.

"What exactly am I looking for?" he asked.

"It'll be stone about a meter long," Mercedes said.

"This could take all night," Kelly said. "It's freezing. Why don't we just take the truck?"

"Because Arias' men would recognize it," he said. "We'd be pretty obvious. Where would we hide it? No one except us knows where it is now. Let's find the stone. Everything else stays here."

Mercedes swept the light over the crates. "There," she said. The beam pointed to a crate with a similar label. It read *"Piedra,"* or stone instead of ceramics.

They opened that crate and found a face of a jaguar carved in stone. Mercedes traced her fingers over the sculpted features. *"Qué bonito,"* she said. "This could be over 1,000 years old. They were going to sell it."

"There must be more boxes with carvings," he said. "Help me."

The crates were heavy. After a few minutes, he was sweating despite the bitter cold. They pulled each *"piedra"* crate to the back of the truck bed, then cracked open the lid and hovered over it, like expectant children on Christmas. Inside, they found figures of birds, frogs, and dogs. They also found masks and urns with faces of wild creatures that could be gods. These were glyphs that must have been pried from the walls of the tomb. With each discovery, Mercedes examined the object in her gloved hands, caressing it, as if transporting herself back in time to its making. She was lingering over a carving when Kelly called for her help with another crate.

"What's your hurry?" She held up a mask of a bat-like creature. "Look at this."

"It's nice," Sutherland said. "But Arias' men followed me three times today. Let's not press our luck."

"You're paranoid." Mercedes replaced the mask and helped Sutherland and Kelly move crates, dragging them aside to get at a large one at the bottom.

They opened it and found a heavy slab wrapped in straw matting and packed in newspaper. As he removed the wrapping, he heard the sharp intake of Mercedes' breath with the first glimpse of rough gray stone.

*"Aquí está."* Her tone was filled with awe. She bent to touch it, *"Qué maravilla."*

It was three feet long with raised symbols around the edges of its face. In relief, like a spine along the slab's center, stretched the body, legs, and tail of a lizard. More glyphs were chiseled into its back. At the top of the slab, where the lizard's head would have been, the stone was broken off.

"The *lagarto* stone." He touched it, feeling one of the symbols through his glove. Its age alone was impressive. If Mercedes' father was right, centuries ago, an indigenous craftsman had chiseled this as a guide to another tomb and a cache of silver and gold. It was a great discovery, but "great" wasn't powerful enough. Fantastic or phenomenal was more like it.

"Incredible." It was the only thing he could say.

Their heads were together, their breaths forming a single cloud of mist. Mercedes turned and kissed him on the cheek. "*Gracias.*"

He looked into Mercedes' dark eyes and had an impulse to return the kiss, but Kelly nudged him.

"Ahem," she said. "Remember Arias? People chasing us?"

"Don't thank me yet," he said to Mercedes. "We have to get out of here." He edged her aside and lifted the bottom end of the stone. Its weight surprised him. "Whoa. Give me a hand."

Mercedes stood up. "Not yet," she said. "I want to see what else is here."

"You can stay," he said. "But Kelly and I are going."

"*Estúpido.*" Mercedes faced him, one hand holding the flashlight, the other on her hip. "You're going tell the police where this is, right?"

"At some point. Along with the Mexican Consulate."

She pulled out a small camera from her jacket pocket. "I want to record it to make sure all of it gets back to Mexico. Give me twenty minutes."

He sighed. Even twenty minutes was too long with Arias on your mind.

"Ten minutes. We'll get this to the car and wait for you. Lock the door when you're through."

Kelly helped him haul the stone out of the crate to the edge of the truck bed.

"Why not bring the car here? It'll be easier," she said.

"It'll draw too much attention. I can carry it," he said. As soon as he lifted it off the truck, he almost changed his mind. The stone weighed close to seventy pounds, and its size made it unwieldy.

The nearest streetlight was out, leaving the alley in shadow. Nothing moved. He adjusted his hold on the stone, pressing it to his chest, and started for the street. Kelly followed after she closed the garage door. When he reached the car, Kelly opened the trunk, and he lowered the slab into it. They got in, and he started it, relieved to get into the relative warm.

"Now what?" Kelly said, holding her hands in front of the heater vent.

"If Arias did tap my phone, it might be easier than we thought. We can inadvertently let him know we have the stone. If Christopher was right about him, Arias won't trust his men and will come after it personally."

"So you're the bait?" she asked.

"With the DEA and the police waiting. You and Mercedes will be somewhere out of danger."

"No way. I'm not leaving you alone," she said. "Mercedes won't want to be separated from that stone." She waited a second and then added, "Or from you."

He looked at her. "Give me a break."

"Where there's smoke…"

"Come on," he said. "She saved my life. We've been through a lot, that's all. She deserves some slack."

"She'll get more than slack if she doesn't watch out," she said.

"You have nothing to worry about." He looked at his watch. "She should be coming soon."

Just then, a set of headlights rounded the corner from the street side of the warehouse. The van in front of him blocked his view, so he couldn't make out the type of car. It stopped by the alley, and the lights went out. Sutherland opened his window, straining to see better. A car door slammed. Then a man stepped into view and walked around the corner toward the street side of the warehouse. Judging by the minute it took, he must have reached the far end of the row of doors and returned. He yelled something at the driver and turned into the alley.

Kelly gasped. "He's going to hear her or see the light under the door."

Sutherland dialed 9-1-1 on his cell phone.

He waited while it rang, feeling his heart speed up and his breathing quicken. As soon as the operator answered, he said, "A woman's being attacked." He gave them the address. "Hurry. She's in the alley behind the warehouse."

"What's your name, sir?"

He didn't have a chance to answer. The man jogged out of the alley toward the car he came in and was out of sight again. Sutherland slipped out of the Buick and peered around the van. It was just as he feared. It was the BMW. By the inside light, he could see two men talking. He sneaked back to the Buick and put it in gear. Pulling out, he drove right past the BMW, giving them a chance to see both of them clearly. Then he turned right, slowly passing the street side garage doors, hoping Arias' men would follow. When he reached the next intersection, he cut his lights and waited. Just as he saw the BMW coming, he turned right, gunned it, and turned right again into the other end of the alley.

Crashing through potholes and over speed bumps, they raced back toward number 23. They skidded to a stop in front of the door, and he jumped out. After heaving the door open, he was face-to-face with Mercedes. The tire iron was raised and ready in her hand.

"Get in fast!" he shouted. "They're here."

He slammed the overhead door down, and she locked it. They scrambled into the Buick just as headlights appeared behind them in the alley. The BMW pounded along the alley toward them, engine roaring and tires hammering over potholes. As Sutherland jammed the Buick into gear, a man jumped out twenty feet ahead.

"Doug," Kelly yelled. "He's got a gun."

Sutherland stomped on the gas. The Buick's tires screeched. The car lurched forward.

"Duck!" he yelled, slouching down.

He saw the gun flash and heard a shot. Then he saw the man's shocked face and felt the crunch as they hit him. The man catapulted over the windshield and disappeared behind. At the end of the alley, they turned and raced north. No one was following, but he could hear sirens.

# CHAPTER THIRTY-EIGHT

▼

Sutherland's heart pounded, and his breath came in shallow gasps. He may have just killed a man. The image kept replaying in his mind. He remembered the surprise and fear on the man's face and the thump when they struck him. Sutherland imagined bones snapping along with flesh and organs turning to jelly. Then the broken body sailing over the windshield. He felt sick.

He couldn't hear the sirens anymore. The warehouse, shipment, and Arias' men were behind them. The overpass for the Stevenson loomed ahead. They'd gotten away, but he'd run down Arias' man to do it. The light-headedness and nausea was the same as after he'd sent Marcelo Arias to his death. That had also been self-preservation, but he wondered if that mattered.

Kelly sat beside him, staring straight ahead. She was rigid, as if in shock as well. Mercedes was in the backseat. In the rearview mirror, he saw the back of her head as she watched for a following car.

Kelly finally spoke. "Do you think he's dead?"

"I don't know," he said. "I was going maybe thirty-five or forty."

"You have to report it," she said.

He didn't answer. He was looking at the bullet hole in the windshield. Dead center. They'd been lucky.

"They look down on hit-and-runs," Kelly said. "Even if it is in self-defense." She spoke in a distant, monotone voice, as if she was still reliving the collision.

The ramp for the Stevenson Expressway was just ahead.

Should he turn around and go back? Report it to the police who answered the 9-1-1 call? Arias' man, the BMW driver, wouldn't stick around. Maybe he'd pick the other man up or just split, leaving him in the alley. What's another casualty in Arias' world?

"What if he dies?" she persisted.

"I don't know, dammit," he said. "I don't know what to do." But he'd made up his mind. He turned onto the ramp for the Stevenson. "What I do know is that thing in our trunk is the only hope we'll escape Arias for good. If we report this now and the police take the stone, it won't be over."

"Another death," Kelly continued, still staring straight ahead. "All the others things–the break-in at my place, the man shot in that ex-cop's house–they were different. We did this. A man was..."

"I know." He felt the same way. Even though no amount of justification would eliminate the feeling, he had to try. He pointed to the bullet hole. "They would've killed us for that shipment. It's nothing to them."

"We still have to tell the police," Kelly said. "You just ran over a man."

"I'll tell Duncan. But not about the stone. Not yet."

"I wish we could just let Arias have it," Kelly said. "What's a piece of stone compared to lives?"

"Here's my cell phone," he said. "Call Duncan's number."

They drove in silence while Kelly dialed the numbers. Chicago's Loop, a gray mass of office towers, rose before them through a light snowfall, a saw-toothed silhouette with thousands of lights. It was approaching midnight and as expected, Duncan wasn't at his station. Sutherland left a message telling him about finding the shipment and the 9-1-1 call he'd made. He said they hit a man who shot at them, but the police who answered the call might not find anything.

"They might just find some broken glass," he said as he noticed that one of the Buick's headlights wasn't working.

"How did they find us this time? It couldn't be your condo phone," Kelly said after he hung up. She seemed to be feeling better after reporting the event. It was the honest lawyer in her.

"I'll bet they put something on this car when we were at Rivera's," he said.

"James Bond stuff," Kelly said

He'd thought Arias was just a thug heading up a smuggling ring. Merely a killer without any compunctions, running more thugs. Sutherland hadn't given him enough credit. Arias' methods were sophisticated and included his technology as well as force. That made him more dangerous. Who was he? Sutherland had heard his raspy voice on the phone and had seen him from a distance in San Miguel. He was more ghost than real. *Un fantasma* who was trying to kill them.

"It might not be all spy stuff," he said. "The security shop owner could've told them I was headed to Pilsen. My Jaguar would stand out there. Anyway you slice it; we're barely a step ahead of them."

He turned off Lake Shore Drive onto North Avenue. There wasn't any traffic, but he drove slowly on the slippery asphalt.

Passing the zoo in Lincoln Park, he said, "He's paying a price in people. The police shot two and arrested one this afternoon. They arrested two more at the gallery warehouse for drugs."

"He lost another one tonight," Kelly said.

"The problem is…" Mercedes said, "that men like him can always buy more."

Aziz wasn't happy to see the damage to his car. He stared at the broken headlight and the bullet hole in the windshield as if he'd lost a loved one. He slowly shook his head. Sutherland thought he was going to break into a Turkish tirade, but he merely mumbled as he paced around the old car.

It wasn't as if this Buick was cherry. Its rocker panels and wheel wells were rusted through. The new rear fender was a different color, the result of a previous clash with something hard. The patches of filler on the passenger side weren't even sanded, much less painted. When Sutherland told him he'd pay for any repairs, he expected Aziz to calm down.

"I bring back your car good. Why you no do the same?" he asked with tears in his eyes.

"Aziz, I'm sorry. Tell you what. You get it fixed. I'll pay, and you can drive my car while you're waiting. Okay?"

That seemed to do it, which was a relief. If it hadn't, Sutherland was ready to pay an extra couple hundred dollars for a newer wreck, just to get it behind him. He took off his jacket and wrapped it around the stone in the trunk. He didn't want Aziz or the doorman to see him carrying it.

In his apartment, two calls were waiting on his voice mail. The first was from Christopher, recorded right after they'd left for Rivera's place. He said he was back in the country and wanted Sutherland to call him. The second must have arrived within minutes before their return.

"Mr. Sutherland, this is Detective Duncan. We gotta talk. Call me."

"He sounded pissed," Kelly said. "Do we have to go back to that station?"

"Let's hope not. I'll have to find a safe phone. I shouldn't even trust my cell." He pointed at the stone. It was on the kitchen table, still wrapped in his jacket. "First, let's look at this thing." With Kelly's help, he removed the jacket from the stone and replaced the heavy *lagarto* on the table. For him, there wasn't a single identifiable character on the lizard's back. At least on the border of the stone's face, he recognized animals and men, as if a story was being told.

"Can your father decipher this?" he asked Mercedes.

"He's one of the best." She moved beside him to have a closer look.

"Will photos be good enough?" he asked.

Mercedes thought a moment and nodded. "Maybe. Why?"

"Just asking. Why don't you two get some pictures? I'm going next door and make my calls. I doubt they bugged my neighbor."

There were three other apartments on his floor. Sutherland knew two of the other owners by sight only. The third, a retired bachelor named Jeff, rented the apartment next door. Months ago, in their only conversation, he had learned that Jeff didn't have any living family, hated liberals, foreigners, and "coloreds" as he called them, and spent all his time watching television. Sutherland vowed never to talk to him again, but this was an emergency. He knocked on his door. He heard voices inside. It was probably the television because Jeff never had visitors. He knocked again, louder. He saw a shadow on the other side of the peephole. The door opened, and Jeff stood there in his underwear with a beer can in his hand. He was in his sixties, short, pink, and bald. He squinted, as if he had been sleeping.

"Sorry to bother you," Sutherland said. "I know it's late, but my phone's busted and I need to make a couple calls."

Jeff looked skeptical. "There's a pay phone in the lobby."

"It's broken, too. They're local calls. It will only take a minute."

Jeff stuck his head out of the door and looked both ways down the hallway. "You alone?"

"Yeah."

He turned his back and walked into the apartment, leaving the door open.

"Knock yourself out. Phone's in the kitchen." Jeff walked into the living room and sank into the couch. There was a chase scene on the television, the volume blaring. Sutherland found the wall phone and dialed.

Christopher answered immediately. "Sutherland? Where you calling from?"

"It doesn't matter. We found the shipment."

"So that's it," Christopher said. "Arias' phones have been on fire the last half hour. They don't know if you found the stone. Did somebody get shot?"

"Almost," Sutherland said. "Now that we have it, I'll try to convince the police to work with you."

"They know you found it?"

"Not yet."

There was a long silence before Christopher spoke again. "Don't even bother."

"The fucking turf thing again?" Sutherland said. "Who gets the credit? What do you call it, the collar or the bust?"

"Listen, They closed the Chapultepec Gallery and Arias' warehouse. As far as they're concerned, his operation is finished. As long as he stays in Mexico, who cares? If you tell them, they'll make you give it up. They're not going after Arias anytime soon."

"But you are," Sutherland said. "He's your white whale."

"It's my job."

"Well, it's not mine. Now that I've found it, can you get him without me?"

Christopher took his time before answering. "If his men found the stone in your apartment or office, he probably wouldn't suspect a trap. Because he wouldn't trust his men with the stone, he'd probably risk coming himself. In any event, you wouldn't have to be around."

Finally, there was a safe way to end this. The scenario Christopher described might entail actually relinquishing the stone, possibly losing it for good. Sutherland reminded himself of everything Mercedes had done to help him, not the least of which was saving his life. Didn't he owe her anything? Giving up the stone was a decision he didn't want to make alone.

"Let me think about it," he said. "I'll call you back."

"Where are you? I don't recognize the number." It figured Christopher would have caller ID.

"A neighbor's place. Arias might have tapped my phone. Where did he learn this stuff?"

"These guys can buy anything. In the meantime, do you know where Professor Hidalgo is?"

"How would I? Why?"

"Arias is looking for him. He hasn't been at the tomb for days."

Sutherland was about to return Duncan's call as well, but he changed his mind. It could wait. If Arias was looking for Hidalgo, the professor might be in danger. Even though Sutherland didn't trust the man, he was Mercedes' father. Sutherland owed her. As he hung up, Jeff shuffled into the kitchen. He threw his can into a nearly full bag of empties on the floor and retrieved another from the refrigerator.

"Want one?"

"No. Thanks for the phone."

He shrugged. "No biggie. We gotta stick together. What with everything." He rolled his eyes and hooked his thumb in the direction of the outside hallway.

Sutherland didn't have a clue. "What do you mean?"

"Our new neighbors. In Mrs. Gardner's place. Short-term renters."

"What about them?"

"Bunch of wetbacks. That's what we need, spics on the same floor."

Sutherland didn't waste any time. Back in his apartment, he found Kelly taking pictures while Mercedes held a flashlight to give the chiseled features more relief. They were working on the underside of the stone. It was flat with row after row of glyphs.

He leaned between them and whispered, "Get your stuff. We're leaving."

They both looked at him, their eyes wide.

He grabbed the notepad and wrote, "They're right next door. They could be listening."

# CHAPTER THIRTY-NINE

▼

They were out of the apartment in five minutes. Sutherland packed a change of clothes into a gym bag and dug out a large backpack from his closet. With Kelly's help he stuffed the *lagarto* stone inside. It barely fit, and the zipper wouldn't close. He muscled his way into the backpack. Mercedes grabbed her carry-on, and they slipped out the door.

They took the stairs to the floor below, the elevator to the lobby, and eased out the back. As they hurried along the alley, the stone seemed to grow heavier. The straps dug into his shoulders. He was sweating by the time they reached Clark. It was late, and they had to wait in the shadow of a storefront until an empty cab finally approached. Sutherland hadn't decided where they were going, so he gave the driver the address of the Hilton Hotel on South Michigan. They needed to stay out of sight while they thought through what to do next. By the time the cab dropped them off, he'd opted for his office. They caught another cab to Madison and Clark.

The building security guard glanced at Sutherland's ID and asked him to sign in. Sutherland took off the backpack and laid it on the desk.

"What's in there?" the guard said.

"Cornerstone for my new building. Want to see it?"

The guard shrugged and ushered Sutherland, Mercedes, and Kelly through the metal detector. As soon as Sutherland picked up the backpack, the guard went back to his magazine.

They went directly to the fifteenth floor and the Sutherland and Associates suite. He didn't want to turn on the lights in case someone was watching outside. The glow from the neighboring high-rises was enough to find his way. When they entered his corner office, Mercedes was attracted to the renderings of his town house project that covered one wall. She studied them in the dim light.

"Are these yours or your associates'?"

"I don't have associates." He circled his desk and sat in the leather chair.

"It sounds better than 'Doug Sutherland, Loner,'" Kelly said. "After Friday, assuming he gets his approvals, he'll have to hire some. That should be interesting."

He thought about Friday's meeting. Could he do what he had to do before then? Barely, but he thought he could make it.

Kelly fell onto the couch with a groan. "I feel like I've run two marathons. How do you know it was Arias' men next door?"

"A Latino and his pals happen to move in during all this shit?" he said. "Want me to knock on his door and ask?"

"Funny," Kelly said. "Now that we've got the thing, why not give it to Agent Christopher and let him set his trap? You don't have to be involved anymore."

"I've been thinking about that," he said.

"*De ninguna manera!*" Mercedes faced him in front of the desk, fists on her hips. "We don't give it to anyone—not even the Pope—until my father sees it. He's in charge of that dig. After he has a chance to study it, the *federales* can have it. You stay here if you want. I'll take it to him myself."

"Hand him the stone? I don't think so," he said. "For one thing, it won't get through customs."

"I have this." She held up a roll of film. It surprised him that that her small camera wasn't digital, but then, either was her fancy Nikon in San Miguel.

"Okay," Sutherland said. "Let's talk reality. Arias has been searching for your father. Do you know where he is?"

"If he's not at the tomb, he'll be at his trailer," Mercedes said. "If I know him, he's studying the code on the broken piece. He has a virtual research library in that trailer."

"Can you reach him?"

"He has a cell phone, but he hardly uses it. I tried it from your place while you were calling Agent Christopher. No luck."

"Who else knows where he is?" Sutherland asked.

"Just a widow who cooks for him," Mercedes said. "The trailer is near an old ruin, almost impossible to find."

"Good," Sutherland said. He got out of his chair and walked around the desk toward her. "He's temporarily safe if he stays there. Give me that film." He held out his hand.

She took a step back from him. "I'm taking it to him. Tomorrow on the six o'clock flight." She thrust her hand with the film into her pocket.

"I can't let you do that," he said.

The silence was as charged as air before a lightning strike. After glaring at him for several seconds, she said, "Are you going to stop me?"

"I'm going with you. Was that six o'clock in the morning?"

Kelly bolted upright on the couch. "No way!"

"Chill," he said, waving Kelly to calm down. "Let me explain. Arias can't know we have the stone for sure. We were interrupted at the warehouse. We can warn Mercedes' father and get him and the other piece out of Arias' reach. Arias will eventually find the trailer."

"My father will never leave it," Mercedes said.

"Which proves how naïve he is about Arias. But what if we only give him the photos if he agrees to leave with us? That's why I want to hold on to them." He held out his hand again. "I can say no to him."

"Don't you trust me?" Mercedes said, stiffening.

"Absolutely. But you're his daughter. Now give me the film."

She didn't move. She just stared back at him. He hoped he wouldn't have to take it forcefully. It wouldn't be easy, and he'd hate doing it. Then she nodded and handed him the film.

"You promise you'll give him the photos?"

"Scout's honor," he said. "Now let's get some sleep."

"Is there a restroom around here?" Mercedes asked.

Sutherland directed her down the hall and gave her the key to the women's room. When he looked at Kelly again, she was shaking her head.

"I sometimes think you have the brains of an ass. No, you're dumber than that. You're going to risk your life traipsing around Mexico with *la señorita caliente?*"

"You're jealous?"

"No, you idiot. Worried."

He sat on the couch and put his arm around her.

"So am I. For both of us. That's why I was hoping you'd go to your aunt's house, where you'll be safe. From there, you could explain it all to Duncan."

"And bail us out of a hit-and-run."

"You're a smart attorney," he said.

"Smart enough to know you're not telling me everything. You expect me to believe you're going down there to give her father the photos and protect him? You don't trust him. You don't even like him. You probably think he deserves what he gets."

"That's true, except he doesn't deserve to die. I don't know if he's after the stone for intellectual reasons or money. In either case, he stupidly involved Arias. He probably told him he had the broken piece of the stone. Giving the professor the photos would be like handing everything to Arias. The DEA would have no way to suck him in, and I'd still be on his hit list. Until Arias is put away and we're sure the professor's motives are legitimate, he shouldn't be trustee of either part of the *lagarto* stone. So I plan to separate him from his piece."

# CHAPTER FORTY

▼

It had been a stressful several days for Enrique Arias. He felt helpless hanging around his *hacienda* knowing that events shaping his destiny were out of his control 1,000 miles away. The reports he received only made him more anxious because any input he had was already too late. First he'd learned that his men failed to abduct Sutherland's girlfriend. Then he was told that Sutherland found the key and had gone to Alfonso Rivera's office.

"How did that *hijo de puta* find out about Alfonso?" he thought. His old partner was a formidable enemy and didn't need an excuse to bring Arias down.

The worst news, adding to the weight of his nephew's death, was that Paco and Elián had been killed while chasing Sutherland. They were his oldest, most loyal amigos, the two he'd trusted to watch over poor Esmeralda. It seemed that death was creeping up all around him, stalking him. Marcelo's death had made his *hacienda* into a mortuary. Arias' wife, mother, and sister-in-law were dressed in black. The servants tiptoed around, afraid to make a sound. Friends and neighbors wore long faces.

Arias chose to grieve alone, deadening his feelings with cognac-laced coffee. When not distracted by events in Chicago, a stream of images involving Marcelo haunted him. It was a disjointed loop, a lifetime of memories. He'd known him since his birth and watched him grow into a younger version of himself. It was this resemblance, as much as his guilt-ridden responsibility to his brother, which prompted Arias to invest so much of himself in the boy. Now he was gone, just as Esmeralda would be soon. Arias had no one he cared about to share what the *lagarto* stone could bring. All he had left was the sweet prospect of revenge.

In the garden, the wind swayed the laurel and palm trees and misted the spray from the fountain. A warm breeze through the window rustled the papers on his desk. The moon peeked from behind the clouds just above the stone wall. San Miguel was known as the city of eternal spring, so the weather was one thing he'd never miss about Chicago. He was missing some good news though.

The phone rang. Arias picked it up and listened.

"He found it?" He bound out of his desk chair, spilling his spiked coffee over the blotter. "The shipment? The stone?"

"That's right," his caller said. "The miracle of electronics led us right to them."

"You have it? You bring it here?" Arias' hand trembled as he shook a cigarette out of his pack and lit it.

"There are complications."

Arias couldn't take any more Sutherland-caused complications. "You don't have it? What is the problem now?"

"We lost him. Temporarily anyway. I think he found out about the men next door and split."

"He has the truck?"

"They only took the stone."

Arias sucked hard on his cigarette, nearly biting off the filter. "Who are they? Is that woman with him?"

"Two of them. His girlfriend and Mercedes, your professor's daughter."

Arias coughed out a mouthful of smoke. "Hidalgo's daughter? She is helping that *pinche* Sutherland?" So that was who was driving the Jeep the other morning. Now Arias had a name to go on his growing list. If Hidalgo did send his daughter to work with Sutherland, there would be yet another.

"That's her. They went to Rivera's place. That must be how they found the truck."

"The great Diego did nothing?"

"I wasn't there. They split as soon as our guys showed up. One of the men was run down trying to stop them. He's dead."

"*Chingado*," Arias spat. Another death, another debt to repay. "You only have the truck?" Arias said, crushing his cigarette butt as if it was Sutherland himself.

"They couldn't get it before the police came."

Arias took off his glasses and pinched the bridge of his nose. When this began, the whole shipment had been important. It meant money from collectors and recognition for his planned museum. Now all that mattered was Sutherland and Mercedes along with the celebrity the stone and the new treasure tomb could bring. All Mexico would recognize him for his discovery as well as his contribution to archaeology and anthropology. It was right and just that a true Mexican made this discovery. He was a pure blooded native, not one of those *mestizos* of corrupted blood like Gabriela or white exploiters like Professor Hidalgo. He must have that stone.

"How long before you find them?" Arias said finally.

"They can't hide for long. We located the girlfriend at her aunt's place and tracking down Sutherland's ex-wife. We're watching the flights in case they try to leave."

"Would they come here?" Arias saw another ray of hope.

"They might take the stone to the professor."

Arias lit another cigarette, his mind racing. He looked out over the garden, cast blue by the rising moon. Its light caught the strands of a spiderweb spanning the corner of the window outside. A brown moth struggled to free its wings, shaking the delicate network. Arias watched as the spider waited for the right moment and then attacked in a fury of legs and wings. If only Sutherland and the professor's daughter were *locos* enough to return.

# CHAPTER FORTY-ONE

They got up fifteen minutes after four o'clock. The two women were bleary-eyed and Sutherland felt like he hadn't slept at all. They agreed that after he and Mercedes left for the airport, Kelly would wait in the office and take the seven o'clock train to her aunt's house. At four-thirty, as Sutherland shrugged into the backpack containing the stone, Kelly said, "I thought you were just taking the photos."

"We can't leave the stone here. I've got a safer place." He kissed her and gave her a hug.

"No heroics. Do you hear me?" she said, her lip trembling.

"Me? Don't worry. We'll get the professor safe and get out of the way. We'll let the pros take over. I'm going to be on the first plane back tomorrow. I can't miss that zoning meeting."

"Do you have time?"

"The plane lands at about one. The meeting is at four. I'll be there."

Before leaving the building, Sutherland stopped the elevator on the twelfth floor. He and Mercedes walked to a door without a sign or number. He opened it with his key. It was a small windowless room filled with filing cabinets and shelves.

"My storage space," he said. "Cheap. We'll leave the stone here." He placed the backpack in one of the standing cabinets and locked the door behind him. "You and I are the only ones who know where it is."

The six o'clock flight to León wasn't full and they managed to get two seats together. Sutherland slept most of the way to Houston. He woke Mercedes when they were about to land. When they caught the plane to

León, Sutherland felt awake enough to pose a question that had been nagging him.

"There's something I don't understand, Mercedes," he said after they took off. "You told your father everything that's going on, right? The deaths in the mine…Javier…the men shooting at us at the botanical gardens?"

"Of course. But not about yesterday. He doesn't answer his phone."

"He knows the risks you're taking?"

She looked at him quizzically. "Yes. Why?"

"Two things. Why you do it for him? Why does he encourage you? You could be killed."

"That's not so strange. If he was younger, he would do it himself. He's a very brave man."

"Brave men don't have their daughters risking their lives for them. They also don't sit by while people get killed and kidnapped."

She twisted in her seat to look him in the eye. "Look at what you're doing for your mother. I do the same for him."

"Whoa there," he said. "I'm not doing this for her. I'm doing it because of her. I'm trying to free my ass from the fix she dumped me in."

"You saved her."

"I thought she knew how to get Arias off my back. What you've been doing and what he encourages you to do, let's just say it's not normal."

"We don't have a normal relationship." She sank back into her seat and crossed her arms, staring straight ahead. After a minute, she said, "Gabriela told me about how she left you and your father. That's why you don't understand. My situation was different."

"Explain it to me."

"What difference would it make?"

"Maybe none. We may be heading into a dicey situation. I'd feel better knowing that I'm not hooked up with a blind fool. It might run in the family."

"It couldn't. He's not my father."

Sutherland flinched. "Huh?"

"That's right," she said. "My real father was a missionary."

"And?" He tried imagining the directions this could take.

She stared at the seat back a few moments. When she faced him again, she said, "Is it really important?"

"Damn right. I'm in the middle of it."

"Have it your way." She took a deep breath. "My parents were missionaries in Guatemala during the civil war. When I was seven, they were hauled out of bed and taken away. Guerrillas or government troops? Who knew? My parents were never seen again. A peasant woman helped me, and we escaped to the highlands. We were hiding in the forest when my father—Professor Hidalgo—found us."

"Was he at some dig?"

"He was working on a Mayan ruin with his wife and a small team. We were together there for a few more weeks before the guerrillas began appearing. When their demands for food and money became more threatening, my father took me to a village where there were international observers."

"No wonder you're grateful."

"There's more. When he went back to the dig to close it down, he found his wife and two of the team dead. He never gave me the details. He returned to the village and took me out of Guatemala. He sent me to schools in Mexico City and then to college in California and New York. I owe him everything."

Sutherland wondered what it would be like to see your parents hauled away to a probable death. It was a lot worse than waking up one morning and being told your mother had gone home to Mexico. Mercedes' story didn't explain it all though.

"Maybe I see why you're doing this," he said. "How does it explain his attitude? He doesn't seem concerned at all about your safety."

She just shrugged. "He has faith in me. He always did."

It might be that simple. Or maybe Hidalgo was just an uncaring asshole who was desperate for money or reputation. Because she could have died without his help or because he saved and raised her, he could rationalize using her, regardless of the risk. He'd already gifted her with more than twenty years of life. She owed him.

Sutherland kept that thought to himself.

From the León airport, they hired a taxi to take them to San Miguel de Allende. A few days earlier, he had traveled the same road in the opposite direction. The faded signs and dilapidated buildings seemed like old friends. As the cab accelerated, he groped under the backseat for a seat belt. There wasn't one. He was thrown forward as the driver braked for a man and his pack mule.

"Welcome back to Mexico," he thought.

They drove in silence for miles, the countryside sliding by in the afternoon sun. It was just cool enough for him to be thankful for his winter jacket. He took out his cell phone and called Kelly at her aunt's house.

Mrs. Waterman answered the phone. She lived in Arlington Heights, a suburb ten miles northwest of O'Hare Airport. Her different last name and unlisted number made it unlikely for anyone to find Kelly there. She put Kelly on.

"I've been here an hour, and I'm already bored," she said. "I'm not made for suburban living."

"What about Duncan?"

"You were right. They didn't find anyone in the alley or the hospitals. So hit-and-run isn't an issue. But he's still pissed and wants to talk to you. I didn't tell him where you were."

"We're halfway to San Miguel. We should be at the professor's trailer in a couple hours. I'll call you later."

"Say hello to the...how did you describe her? The short and dumpy one?"

"I didn't want you to be jealous."

"Right. Well, I love you, even though you are an ass."

"Me too," he said and disconnected. There it was again. The "L" word. Did danger bring it out in people? Or in their case, was it just time?

Mercedes gave him a quizzical look. "She's not jealous of me, is she?"

"Not really. She worries. That's all."

"She's nice. Are you going to marry her?"

"You think I should?"

"That's not for me to say."

Mercedes didn't wear a ring, and the subject never came up.

"Have you ever been married?" he asked.

"Never had time for that kind of thing. School, graduate studies, field trips with *papá*, now the museum..."

The way she said it left him with the impression she'd never even had a relationship. It was sad that her devotion to the professor precluded anyone else in her life.

"I already tried it once," he said.

"One thing's for sure. Kelly won't put up for any macho bullshit."

"Me? Macho?"

She smiled. "No. But I wonder what you would have done if I didn't give you the photos."

He'd wondered the same thing. "You knew I was right."

"That I can't be trusted?"

"Not exactly. What I ask myself is, if it comes down between me and your father, where will your loyalty be?"

# CHAPTER FORTY-TWO

▼

The cab dropped them in the center of San Miguel. They found a camera store a block off *el Jardín* and offered the manager double if they developed the film immediately. Sutherland insisted on waiting there, partly to ensure that the attendant hurried, and partly to keep his eyes on the negatives. While he waited, Mercedes reclaimed her Jeep from the *Gigante* parking lot where they had left it after running from Arias two days earlier. She wasn't surprised that the police hadn't looked at it. Arias' influence on the local police would have made the Jeep's bullet holes invisible anyway.

Hidalgo's trailer was located at an old dig halfway between San Miguel de Allende and the tomb from which the artifacts had been stolen. A year earlier, he had moved it there from a former research center in Chiapas near the Guatemalan border. He had planned to move into the small camper near the looted tomb, but it had been destroyed in the explosion, leaving that charred, gutted shell Sutherland had seen during his first morning in San Miguel. Previously, the professor had spent his time in the looted tomb. Lately, Mercedes thought his obsession with the *lagarto* stone kept him at the trailer with his files.

As they drove in the open-sided Jeep, Sutherland shuffled through the photos. There were shots of the entire *lagarto* stone as well as close-ups accentuating the details from different light angles. He held one of them out to her.

"Are they good enough to decipher?"

"He'll complain," she said, "but I think so."

The sun was just above the low hills and the evening chill was setting in. Mercedes slowed the Jeep and turned off the road onto parched ground with only a hint of a trail. They wound past scrubby bushes and cactus for a quarter-mile until they came to a small grove of junipers sheltering a rust-stained, white trailer. Professor Hidalgo was reading at a table under a faded gray awning attached to the trailer. As the Jeep approached, he jumped up and rushed toward them. Mercedes parked next to a beat-up Range Rover.

"*La tienes?*" His eyes were bright with excitement. "You brought the stone?" He looked into the back of the Jeep.

She stepped down from the Jeep and brushed the dust from her jeans. Sutherland did the same as he watched the other two. He expected to see them exchange a hug or kiss, but they seemed to share a strained formality.

"Where is it?" Hidalgo hadn't even acknowledged Sutherland's presence. He seemed to know that they'd found the stone. How? Mercedes said she couldn't reach him.

"It wasn't easy, but we recovered it. Him really," she said, pointing at Sutherland. "At great risk, I might add."

Hidalgo didn't seem to care. He reached into the Jeep and rummaged around in their carry-on bags. "Where is it?" he repeated.

"In Chicago. We brought pictures," Mercedes said.

"That's no good. I need the stone itself."

"We were in a hurry," Sutherland said. "How could we bring it through security and customs?" He walked around the Jeep and held out the envelope. "Just look at the pictures."

Hidalgo snatched the envelope from Sutherland's hand and stomped toward the trailer, leaving them standing by the Jeep.

"You're welcome, professor," Sutherland said to Mercedes while rolling his eyes. "Anytime."

She frowned and shook her head. "It won't be easy."

"How did he know we had the stone?" he asked.

"I told you. I called him. He didn't answer, so I left a message."

"You didn't!" He felt as if he'd been punched in the stomach.

"What's wrong?"

"You know damn well what's wrong. He could've told Arias."

Her eyes hardened. "He wouldn't do that."

"I was counting on having a big head start. Arias wouldn't know for sure we took the stone last night. Now I don't know."

"We have plenty of time." Her eyes bore into him. "He didn't tell Arias."

"Why don't we ask him?"

Hidalgo was at his table, shuffling through the photos. It was getting dark fast and he lit a gas lantern that hung from the awning. When they approached, he was inspecting a photo with a magnifying glass. He pulled at his beard and mumbled. The table was cluttered with papers. Prominent in the table's center, acting as a paper weight, was the missing piece of the *lagarto* stone—the head of the lizard.

"What do you think?" Mercedes said.

He looked up, his eyes brilliant with reflected light. *"Magnífico."*

"Can you decipher it?" Sutherland said.

Hidalgo waved his hand, as if he was shooing away a fly. "What does it matter to you?"

His dismissive words touched a nerve. For an instant, Sutherland had to force himself not to smash the professor's sneer into his teeth. Hidalgo's overt hostility, combined with continued suspicions about him, was like gasoline on a fire. Sutherland stepped forward and scooped up the photos and stuffed them into his jacket pocket. Then he grabbed Hidalgo's forearm and wrenched the last picture from his hand. Hidalgo, eyes wild, jumped out of his chair, knocking it against the trailer. He raised his fists. It wouldn't be much of a fight. Sutherland had the advantage of forty pounds and twenty years.

Mercedes stepped between them. "Don't be stupid, *papá.*"

"Look, asshole," Sutherland said to Hidalgo. "You don't deserve those photos. Maybe you can look at them later. Right now, we have to get out of here."

Hidalgo didn't move.

"You called Arias. Didn't you?" Sutherland said. "Don't you know he'll kill all of us?"

"I didn't call him," Hidalgo said.

"It doesn't matter," Sutherland said. "Tell him, Mercedes. He'll be coming."

"We have to go." She clasped her hands, pleading. "Arias will find us, *papá.*"

Hidalgo glared at Sutherland. "I'm staying here."

"Then forget the photos." Sutherland grabbed the broken piece of the stone. Hidalgo reached to stop him, but he wasn't in time. Sutherland held it to his chest and said to Mercedes. "Let's go. Someone else can decipher the damn thing."

She looked at him, surprised, her mouth open. "We can't…"

"The hell we can't." Sutherland took her arm and led her toward the Jeep.

After walking ten feet together, she freed herself and turned to her father. "He's serious."

Hidalgo's shoulders slumped. *"De acuerdo,"* he said. "I will go."

Sutherland stopped and faced him. "I'll take the Jeep. Mercedes can go with you. We need a place where Arias won't find us. First, let's get out of here. He's been looking for you."

"*Por favor*! Not yet!" Hidalgo pleaded. "I need my things. My papers."

"It's true," Mercedes said. "He needs all his notes and research to translate."

"Get going then," Sutherland said.

Hidalgo walked to the trailer and climbed in. Outside, Mercedes collected the papers from the table, shoving them into a leather briefcase.

"You didn't have to do that," she said to Sutherland.

"Yes, I did."

"That's just the way he is."

"It's the same with me," he said. After she cleared the table of Hidalgo's notes, Sutherland slid the broken piece of the stone into the briefcase beside them. "Let's help him pack."

The old trailer was less than twenty feet long with the door on the right side. At the front end, there was a galley and a living/dining area. A bed and bathroom were in the rear. When Sutherland climbed in, he was overwhelmed. Cardboard boxes were stacked everywhere. Books and piles of papers covered the table and desk. It looked as if the library was run by nuthouse inmates.

"How did Hidalgo find anything?" he wondered.

The inside was lit by gas lanterns, one on the table, another hanging over the desk. Cheap curtains covered the windows. The only other exit was a roof hatch in the rear. Hidalgo was standing under the hatch, talking into a cell phone. He put it away when he saw Sutherland and began pulling folders out of a cabinet.

"Who were you talking to?" Sutherland said. "What are you doing?"

"I had to tell my cook that I leave," Hidalgo said. "She brought those enchiladas." He pointed to the galley. "Enough for all of us. We have time to eat, no?"

A pan of enchiladas sat on a propane stove. The aroma of *mole* reminded Sutherland that they hadn't eaten since the snack on the plane. He glanced back and saw Hidalgo emptying the contents of a filing cabinet into a cardboard box. Mercedes was pulling files from a desk drawer. They weren't going anywhere soon.

"How much of this stuff do you need?" Sutherland said. "Why not just take the trailer?"

"The tires are flat," Hidalgo said. "I can't leave all this. We will hurry. Heat the enchiladas while we pack."

The propane stove was similar to the one on Sutherland's boat. He struck a match and squatted. He was about to light the oven when he jumped up again. Two propane tanks were under the sink beside the stove. One was connected to the stove by a frayed hose. The other was a spare. Standing there with a lit match in his hand, next to two propane tanks with questionable connections, made him want to run, screaming. Adding to it, sitting next to the tanks was a five-gallon can of white gas for the lanterns. He blew out the match.

"Is this thing safe?" Sutherland yelled to the professor. "The stove? When was the last time you used it?"

"Of course. *No problema*," he said.

"Crazy bastard," Sutherland thought. "No wonder his camper burned up."

Propane was odorless and highly volatile. The tanks should be outside. He knew of more than one boat exploding when a leaky system blew up. This wasn't the time to educate the professor on safety. Holding his breath and mentally crossing his fingers, he struck another match, lit the oven, and slid the enchiladas inside.

While the others sorted through files and packed, Sutherland carried a box of papers and the briefcase with the broken stone to Mercedes' Jeep. On his way back, he retrieved the lantern from outside for more light. He found a cooler and dug out three cans of *Tecate*. The enchiladas were warm when they finished packing. Chicken in a dark *mole*.

When they sat down at the small table, still cluttered with paper, Hidalgo was still scowling.

"What is your plan now, *señor*? We can't find the tomb by hiding."

"It's temporary," Sutherland said. "Don't you know you're in danger?"

Hidalgo scoffed. "*En peligro*? No. I am too necessary, *señor*."

"Until you decode it. You know how many people are dead because of that stone?"

"I'm not worried." Hidalgo chewed a mouthful of enchilada and swallowed.

"You told Arias about the stone, didn't you?" Sutherland said.

Hidalgo shrugged. "He was going to sell it without knowing what it was. It would have been lost. I found the piece with the head of the *lagarto* and realized what a treasure it was. Then Gabriela's nephew stole it."

"Recover would be a better word." Sutherland stuffed another bite into his mouth. He had been right. Hidalgo hadn't cared who found the stone—so long as it got back to him to decipher. He didn't believe he'd be another of Arias' victims afterward.

"You never mentioned the stone to Gabriela or me, professor," Sutherland said. "Why? Do you have a deal with Arias?"

Hidalgo was calm while sipping his beer. He speared his last bite of enchilada and pointed his fork at Sutherland. "Why I told no one about the *lagarto?* I didn't want it known about another site. The historical significance is incalculable."

"Very noble," Sutherland said. "I'm all for that...as long as nothing of value gets into the wrong hands. I can't believe Arias wants anything except the money more gold or artifacts will bring. What did he offer you?"

"That's not fair," Mercedes cried, jumping out of her chair. "My father..."

"Told Arias," Sutherland said. "He's as clueless as you, Mercedes. You think your father's motives are idealistic. He thinks he can make a deal with the devil."

Hidalgo finished his beer and wiped drops from his beard with a paper towel. He pushed back his chair and stood.

"There are things, Mexican things, you do not know, *señor.*" He looked at his watch. "May I have the photos now?"

"When we're out of here and safe. Are you ready?"

"I changed my mind. I'm not going."

Sutherland stood and pulled Mercedes up by the arm. "Well, we are. I'm not waiting for Arias' men." He started for the door just as headlights swept past the window and tires skidded on the dirt outside. One...two...three doors slammed. A man spoke gruffly, as if he was giving orders.

"Too late, *señor.*" Hidalgo smiled. "You haven't met *el señor* Arias in person, *verdad?*"

# CHAPTER FORTY-THREE

▼

Kelly pulled on her stretch pants and tucked her turtleneck into the waistband. She knelt and tied her running shoes, careful to tug the double knots tight. She put on her windbreaker, grabbed her hat and gloves, and went to the door. She paused. Even though she'd stayed in her Aunt Julia's guest bedroom many times before, she took it all in. She saw flower-adorned purple-and-rose wallpaper, a Victorian dresser, rocking chair and bed, hand-sewn quilt and lace skirt, imitation Tiffany lamp, and faux Oriental rug. She was a long way from her loft.

She loved her Aunt Julia, who was a widow. It wasn't because they were the only family within 500 miles of each other. However, she preferred spending their time together sharing what Chicago had to offer, not what her neighborhood lacked. In Chicago, they went to the opera, the Art Institute, the Field Museum, plays, galleries, concerts, and restaurants. Here, she felt like she'd traveled to a cultural desert. There was nothing except sanitized residential islands surrounded by highways connecting shopping malls and office centers. The only redeeming features of her aunt's location was its proximity to the trains to Chicago and the nearby forest preserve.

She put on her gloves and hat and popped her head into the kitchen. Her aunt sat at the table, doing a crossword puzzle.

"I'm going for a run, Aunt Julia. Be back in an hour."

Kelly's aunt looked up. "It'll be dark soon. I think they close the park."

"It never stopped me before," Kelly said.

"You shouldn't run by yourself at night."

"It's too cold for muggers."

"After what just happened, are you sure?"

"No one knows I'm here. I'll be careful."

It was more than a mile to the entrance of the preserve, time Kelly used to warm up at an easy pace. Some streetlights were already on along the side streets and half of the cars had their headlights on. Kelly didn't mind running in the dark. The trail wasn't lit, but it was easy to follow. It was a clear path between the dark woods on either side. It offered a change from the flat, lakefront paths she was used to. There were miles of wooded pathways and once inside, one could lose oneself, insulated from noise and traffic and oblivious to the sight of the development all around.

After the last few days, Kelly needed quiet time to let her mind wander. Solutions to her most troubling problems had been unintentional by-products of long runs. She'd start with a question and relegate it to the unconscious. After eight or so miles of endorphin-induced mindlessness and purifying sweat, *voilà*, her course was clear. It also worked for Doug, though squash and sailing served him just as well. She'd stick with running. She had too poor hand-eye coordination for racquet games and, as she'd opined to Doug, sailing was an unappealing choice between boredom and seasickness. He hadn't appreciated the comment.

Mercedes and he had left early that morning. Kelly had taken the train to Arlington Heights a few hours later. After a long chat with her aunt over homemade French toast and sausage, followed by a nap, she was already feeling bored, trapped, and useless. There was no way she could help Doug, so she'd thought she could do some good elsewhere. That afternoon, after futile attempts to reach anyone of authority via telephone, she'd taken the train back to the city and went to the INS office, intending to help Pedro with his immigration problem. Attorney for the city or not, she wasn't a match for the wall of bureaucracy she encountered. After an hour of batting zero, she left and stopped into her office long enough to pick up a few files. Fifteen minutes later, she was back on the train.

Ten minutes into her run, Kelly still felt uneasy and adrift. Flashbacks of the last few days were mixed with questions about the future. Much of what happened would be forgotten in time, consigned to the fast-growing trash heap of the past. But there were other events she didn't want to forget; they'd produced emotions and reactions she'd never felt before and required skills she hadn't realized she possessed. Finding and confronting Pedro was an experience totally outside of her normal routine, yet she managed it successfully. She still couldn't believe she jumped from a window and dashed across a roof while being shot at. Later, the meeting with Rivera, the discovery of the warehouse, and their narrow escape had been a roller coaster of adrenaline and endorphins. She'd been scared and even terrified at times. Now she felt like she was coming down from a five-day buzz.

When she reached the entrance to the forest preserve, a dusting of light snow was on the path and only a few visible footprints. She set off and ran faster now that she was warmed up and away from street traffic. The path was wide enough for a car, but public motor vehicles were prohibited. On both sides of the winding trail was the still darkness of leafless trees and thick undergrowth.

Now Doug was off to Mexico again. Even though she viewed his plan as risky, even reckless, she had a slight itch to be with him. Through all of this, she'd seen a new side of him. Had she missed it before, or had events changed him as well as her? She didn't want to think about what he'd already been through in Mexico. He'd had to overcome his phobia and narrowly escaped his own demise before witnessing the horrible deaths of two men in the mine. It wasn't only the way he was standing up to all this. For the first time, he'd been willing to work together as a team, as equals. They'd needed and counted on one another.

Then the darker thoughts returned. What was awaiting him in Mexico? Mercedes was with him. She was a strong, clever person, but they were no match for this Arias if they ran into him again. How do you survive against someone who uses sophisticated methods together with brute force? Despite the risks and as unlike her former self as it seemed, Kelly would rather have been with him.

She was twenty minutes into her run when she heard a car overtaking her. Glancing over her shoulder, she saw it was an SUV with its lights off. Thinking it must be an official park vehicle, she moved to the side and stopped to let it pass.

The SUV slowed to within twenty feet and stopped. The headlights came on, and the passenger door opened. A man stepped down and said, "How you doing?"

She shielded her eyes from the headlight glare, able only to see the man was tall and bulky.

"Terrific. What's up?" She had a funny feeling about this and she glanced sideways, seeking a clear path into the woods.

"We had a report of a man acting wild out here. To be safe, you better come with us."

"Who are you?" she asked, eyeing a break in the underbrush a few feet further away.

"Park service. Come along, miss."

"I'll be all right. Thanks anyway." She noticed the open door was solid black. There wasn't an insignia or official emblem.

The man moved forward. The SUV crept by his side. "No, really. You're not safe here."

"I'll be fine. I've got a gun." She patted her pocket, as if a pistol was there.

The bluff stopped him. He looked inside the car and said something to the driver. Then the driver's side opened. Another big man stepped onto the path. "We're not kidding. Keep your hands where we can see them. Get into the car."

Squinting into the headlights, Kelly thought the first man was reaching into his jacket. She edged backward, parallel with the opening, ready to flee.

"Show me your badges," she said. "Some ID."

The two men looked at one another, and if they agreed by mental telepathy, they both started toward her.

They hadn't taken two steps before she was in the woods. The snow was four inches deep and crusty and the underbrush was thick in places. She had to weave around trees, dodge bushes and stumps, and jump fallen trunks, but she made good progress. If she could just maintain her head start, they'd never catch her. Their car was useless here.

Behind her, she heard curses, the crack of branches snapping, along with the thud and crunch of footfalls. They were falling behind. She was light on her feet and quick over the hurdles. She'd outrun those big guys easily. When she reached the entrance, she could disappear down a side street and head to the police station.

She climbed an incline covered with fir trees, jumped a rotting tree branch, and skidded down the other side of the hill. Lights were ahead in the distance, probably the main road. In another few hundred yards, she'd be safe. Without slowing, she glanced over her shoulder and couldn't see any movement. In that instant, she fell forward and slammed into the ground hard.

"Ufff."

The impact knocked the wind from her. Before she could breathe again, a bolt of pain shot up her leg. Tears flooded her eyes. She thought she might pass out. Gritting her teeth, she tried standing and had to stifle a scream as she fell again. It was no use. Her ankle must be broken. Pulling herself up on her good leg, she hopped, fell, got up once more, and hobbled over to a cluster of bushes. Lying there in the snow, she listened, watched, and waited.

# CHAPTER FORTY-FOUR

▼

Sutherland listened to the approaching voices outside the trailer. The executioners were coming. The heavy footfalls were sounding out his last minutes. Flashlight beams swept across the curtains as Arias' men drew near. Hidalgo grinned, a thin slit in his graying beard.

"You're the naïve one, *señor*," he said.

The bastard had called Arias. Even if it was Sutherland's last act, he wouldn't suffer that maddening grin. He threw all his weight into a left hook that crushed the smile. A sharp pain flared from hand to elbow, but he followed with a straight right. The professor crashed against the wall, his nose bloody, his eyelids drooping.

A voice right outside shouted orders in Spanish. Sutherland leaped for the door and slammed the deadbolt closed. It was just in time. The door shook as someone tried opening it.

"*Abran la puerta*! Open the door!"

A moment later, the rattling stopped and a voice called out, calm and reasonable.

"*Señor* Sutherland." It was the coarse voice on the phone, Enrique Arias. "You cannot escape this time."

Mercedes crouched by her father with a towel. Sutherland pulled the photos and negatives from his pocket and threw them in a pile on the carpet. Then he grabbed the nearest lantern, unscrewed the cap to the tank, and spilled gas over the photos, soaking them. His left hand throbbed with every movement. He must have broken something on Hidalgo's jaw.

Gas fumes filled the air.

"What are you doing?" Mercedes was wiping blood from her father's face.

"Another thing, *señor*," Arias said. "We have your *novia, la señorita* Matthews. We found her at the house of her aunt, *la señora* Waterman."

It was like being slammed in the chest. Kelly was in the hands of these killers. He stood there, matchbox in his broken hand, match in his right, unable to strike it.

"Give us the photos. We'll let you and your *novia* go."

Did Arias expect to be believed? He would actually let them go? Like he let the *campesinos* and Javier go? After losing one man after another, including his own nephew?

Sutherland struck the match and dropped it.

"What in hell are you doing?" Mercedes shouted.

With a whoosh, fire from the pile flared up to his waist. Hidalgo struggled to his feet and lunged at the flames, trying to stamp them out. Sutherland grabbed the lantern and swung it, catching Hidalgo across the side of the head. Gas sprayed everywhere. and he fell across the table onto the floor.

"Are you crazy?" Mercedes shrieked.

She rushed toward the door and reached for the deadbolt. Shots rang out. Bullets clanged against the metal lock. Mercedes fell back, holding her stomach. When she turned toward Sutherland, her white sweater was dark with blood. Her eyes were wild, her mouth wide. He ran to catch her.

The door burst open and three men climbed in. The first two were young and coarse, wearing sweat-stained shirts and dusty jeans. The last was Arias, dressed in a black suit, white shirt and tie. He looked just as he had at the botanical garden.

Sutherland fell back, Mercedes' dead weight pushing him against the galley table. He held on to her, hoping for signs of life. When he looked into her lifeless eyes, he wanted to scream.

"Why her?" he thought. "Why not Arias and his gunmen?"

He was vaguely aware of someone stamping on the fire. Only ashes remained, but the gas-soaked carpet still smoldered. The man finally smothered it with a jacket.

Sutherland eased Mercedes' body to the floor. The only sounds were Hidalgo's groans and the hiss of the gas lanterns. On his knees, he looked up to see Arias, his dark eyes glaring. He was short and compact with a flat nose and large lips, like an ancient Mayan wearing glasses. He sneered and lunged forward, his foot arching upward. Sutherland flinched backward, but the kick landed hard.

★        ★        ★        ★

He didn't want to open his eyes. His right temple throbbed. Someone was going through his pockets, patting him down. He heard voices in Spanish, arguing around him. His face rested on something wet and he smelled gas. Slowly the image of Mercedes' lifeless face came back to him. She was dead, and he was next. What about Kelly? A sharp pain, a kick, stabbed his ribs.

"*Cabrón.*" It was Arias' voice. "Wake the fuck up."

Sutherland rolled over on his back and struggled up to his elbows. Arias was crouched over him. His filtered cigarette was pinched between his thumb and forefinger. His men stood behind him, one pointing a stubby assault rifle his way. A moan caught Sutherland's attention and he glanced toward it. Hidalgo sat in a chair holding Mercedes' hand, crying. It was surprising, considering his previous attitude and indifference toward her welfare.

"*Por qué?*" Hidalgo said, between sobs.

"I already said to you," Arias snapped at him. "It was an accident." He turned to Sutherland again and took a long drag on his cigarette. "Where are the negatives?"

Sutherland pushed himself up to sit, leaning against the galley counter. He pointed to the ashes on the carpet.

"*Hijo de puta.*" Arias kicked him in the thigh.

"Then the stone. Where is it?"

"It's in Chicago," Hidalgo said through gritted teeth. "I hope you never find it."

"Shut up. Or I kill you, too," Arias said.

The threat silenced Hidalgo for the moment.

"Where in Chicago?" Arias kicked Sutherland again. This time, it was in the left shoulder. "We already searched your apartment."

"You won't find it." His arm, thigh, and temple throbbed, but Sutherland fought to stay focused. He had to find a way out.

"Your *puta madre* had to interfere," Arias said. "Instead of screwing her, *el pelirrojo* should have killed her along with Valdez." He turned to his men and said, "Hold him." The two jumped forward, grabbed Sutherland's arms, and yanked his head back by the hair. A moment later, Arias' full weight was on his legs, straddling him. Arias took a deep drag from his cigarette and held the glowing tip in front of Sutherland's face.

"How much of this can you stand?"

At first, he felt a poke, only a pressing on his neck. Then he heard the hiss and smelled the flesh burning. Suddenly, like a volcano, the nerves erupted. He gritted his teeth and heard himself groan. After interminable seconds, the smoke tailed away. The hissing stopped. The cigarette was out, but the pain continued.

"The next will be in your eye," Arias said as he stood. "I can wait. They search your office any minute now." The men released their grip and stepped away. Sutherland touched the burn and winced, pulling his hand away. Through tears, he saw a dark smear on his finger.

Hidalgo stood up, teetering. His face was bloody, his eye swollen. He lurched forward and grabbed Arias' arm. "Are you going to kill everybody?"

"Shut up." Arias jerked his arm away and slapped him hard across the face. Hidalgo fell against the table, knocking it over.

Sutherland's heart raced and his adrenaline was dulling the worst of the pain. The propane tanks were next to him by the stove. They were out of everyone's line of sight, behind the upset table. Hidalgo rushed at Arias again, grabbed him, and wrestled him to the floor. In a frenzy of elbows and knees, Hidalgo struggled astride the heavier man and began swinging. Arias could do nothing except cover his face.

The diversion gave Sutherland his chance. He twisted the nut holding the hose to the first tank. It should have been very tight, but it came loose. He yanked the hose off and opened the valve completely. Then he turned the knob on the backup tank. The sharp hiss of escaping gas impelled him to his feet. There was no turning back. He had to get out now.

The henchmen dragged Hidalgo off Arias and threw him against the wall. Arias, dazed and holding a bleeding nose, pulled himself to one knee and watched as his men pummeled the professor. For the moment, no one seemed concerned with Sutherland, but they were between him and the door, blocking his escape. The only other exit was the roof hatch in the rear.

With an effort, Hidalgo lifted his head, spat out blood, and said, "I'll never translate the stone for you. Never."

Arias got to his feet and stumbled to within a foot of the professor, now pinned to the wall by his men.

"I never planned for you to translate it," he growled in Spanish.

As he slipped behind them, Sutherland thought he saw the glint of a blade in Arias' hand.

He made it to the rear of the trailer before he was noticed. But the roof hatch was closed, and Arias' men were rushing him. Without time to escape through the hatch, he piled into the bathroom and slammed the door. He fell with his back to the bulkhead and feet jammed against the door, wedging it closed. Arias' men pounded and pushed, but Sutherland's leverage held.

Then Arias said, "Leave him inside. *No puede escapar.*" He was right. Sutherland couldn't go anywhere. The only opening in the bathroom was a four-inch vent, but the rooftop hatch just outside was large enough. He had to depend on that and what the next few minutes brought.

He imagined the heavy propane gas flooding the trailer floor like invisible fog. With the valves wide open, he wondered how long it would take to build up and how long it would be before Arias lit another cigarette. He felt the bulkhead and hoped it was strong enough. He grabbed a towel, wet it, and stuffed it along the bottom of the door. There was silence outside, mixed with an occasional voice. Minutes passed. A cell phone rang.

"Should that have triggered the gas?" he thought. "Wasn't there enough?"

Arias' voice grew louder, angry. He was speaking English. He finally shouted, "Search it again, Diego. It must be there." He must have been talking to the men ransacking Sutherland's office. But the stone was safely hidden in the storage room.

More silence. Over and over, Sutherland imagined Arias tapping a cigarette from his pack, putting it in his mouth. He willed him to pull out his lighter and flick it. As seconds ticked by, he almost gave up, thinking the propane tanks had been almost empty. His hopes would die, like Mercedes and her father.

Then the trailer shook. The bulkhead ruptured, and he was thrown against the outside wall. A deafening roar was followed by a whoosh of air, a flash of light, and a blast of heat. The bulkhead was pushed in, nearly crushing him. The door was buckled and wedged partially open. He grabbed the edge with both hands, put one foot against the toilet, and heaved. When the door finally inched open, the light from the flames revealed Arias' man, lying prone on the floor outside. Dark smoke rushed in. He put the towel over his nose and mouth. Another explosion shook the trailer, the fire reaching a lantern or maybe the other tank. He had to get to the roof hatch.

The heat was stifling, the smoke thick. He squeezed through the door and looked up at the hatch. The blast had blown it open. He grabbed the top of the door, got a foot on the handle, jumped, and gripped the rim of the opening. With a last glance inside, he knew no one would have survived that inferno. He hoisted himself to the roof, jumped to the ground, and ran. Where, he didn't know.

# CHAPTER FORTY-FIVE

▼

Sutherland stumbled over the rough ground behind the burning trailer. Light from the fire flickered through the junipers, casting eerie shadows along the path. He circled through the grove to the cars. On the way, he passed the twisted trailer door, thrown halfway to Mercedes' Jeep. He patted his pockets, but his cell phone was gone.

"Shit," he said to himself. It was inside the trailer, a melted lump of plastic. He checked Arias' Grand Cherokee and then the professor's Range Rover and didn't find a phone.

Mercedes had left the keys in her Jeep. From the driver's seat, he watched the flames die. The trailer was blackened and smoldering. Its sides were blown out, and the roof was caved in. Arias and his men were dead. Sutherland wanted to feel relieved. He had survived, somehow killing by deceit, a man who killed and deceived. He'd even salvaged the other piece of the *lagarto* stone, having taken it to the Jeep before they ate. It sat in the back with a few of the professor's notes. But the cost had been high.

How could you explain men like Arias? Did you just accept that some people were bad? One had less difficulty understanding the professor. He wanted to regain his reputation as much as profit financially. He was a liar and a fool, but he wasn't a killer. Nevertheless, his deceit killed Mercedes, whose only fault was blind loyalty. It was her face Sutherland saw. For her, he felt so empty. The smoke could have caused his tears to well up. Then again, they could have been for her.

As the fire's heat gave way to the night's chill, he started the engine. With the thought of leaving the trailer behind, Mercedes' image morphed into Kelly's. Sutherland had talked to her only a few hours earlier. Arias could have been bluffing. If she was taken, what then? Who was in charge now?

Shifting into gear, he turned the Jeep toward San Miguel. As he passed the Grand Cherokee, a last flare-up from the fire illuminated the license plate and the letters. ARIAS.

On the outskirts of San Miguel, Sutherland found a public phone outside a closed gas station. Using his debit card he'd bought in San Miguel, he called Kelly's aunt. Mrs. Waterman answered immediately.

"Is she there?" He held his breath.

"Doug?" Her voice was strained. "She's not with you? She went running in the forest preserve right after returning from downtown. She hasn't come back."

"What was she doing downtown? She's supposed to stay out of sight."

"She had a meeting and then went to see the INS about helping the boy you met yesterday. Pedro?"

"Damnit," he thought. "Kelly couldn't sit still for twenty-four hours?" If she had, they'd never have found her. If she stopped in her office, Arias' men could have spotted and followed her. He hadn't been bluffing.

"Doug?" Mrs. Waterman's voice edged even higher.

"I'm here," he stammered. With Arias dead, what would they do to her? "Did you talk to the police?"

"The sheriff's checking the hospitals, but nothing yet."

"I'm going to call a cop named Duncan in Chicago. He'll call you. Don't worry. We'll find her." When he hung up, he hoped he hadn't lied.

Detective Duncan answered his cell phone right away. "Where the hell are you?" he growled. "You're getting to be a pain in the ass. We've got the shipment but not the man you hit. You can't just..."

Sutherland cut him off. "Listen. Arias' men have Kelly."

A moment passed. "Ah, Christ," he said. "That bastard had some operation. We grabbed fifty kilos from his warehouse...but not him."

"He's dead. An hour ago."

"Dead? Jesus, Sutherland."

"Tell me about it. Let's focus on Kelly. Will you call the FBI?"

"You sure it's kidnapping? FBI won't get involved unless..."

"Arias told me he had her. Kelly's aunt verified she's missing. Talk to her and the sheriff for yourself." He gave Duncan the phone number for Kelly's aunt. "Another thing. Arias' men broke into my apartment and the one next door. Could you have someone check? Maybe someone knows or heard something."

"Anything else?" Duncan said. "You're worse than my wife." He hung up.

Sutherland then called Christopher who answered with a terse, "Yes?"

"Doug Sutherland here."

There was a long silence.

"Is this Agent Christopher?" Sutherland said. "What's the matter?"

"We've been looking all over for you, that's all," he finally said. "You never called me back. Arias has gone to war."

Christopher couldn't know Arias was dead. It happened less than an hour ago in the middle of nowhere. "There's a complication. Arias took Kelly, my girlfriend."

"Yeah, we know." He sounded frustrated. "We tried to stop it. She was jogging in the forest preserve when they snatched her. Does she know where you left the stone? You didn't take it to Mexico, right?"

"She doesn't know. Can you find her?"

"We might have to neutralize Arias first."

"It's already done. He's dead."

There was another long silence. With an awe-filled voice, he said, "You are one unbelievable son of a bitch, Sutherland. If that's true, you've just ended an operation we've been trying to close down for over a year. What happened?"

"When I get back. Let's talk about Kelly now."

"Okay. We can pick up one of Arias' men. Call me as soon as you get here. Did you call the police?"

"And the sheriff and the FBI."

"Oh, well. We'll manage anyway." Sutherland heard the click of the phone.

With forty pesos left on his calling card, he called Gabriela in Guanajuato. He told her about Mercedes, Hidalgo, Arias, and Kelly. They arranged to meet in the León airport before he returned to Chicago. She would take a taxi there and drive Mercedes' Jeep back. She would also take custody of Hidalgo's piece of the *lagarto* stone.

The night was getting colder. The heater barely helped in the open Jeep. His jacket and wallet were lost in the burned trailer. He rummaged through Mercedes' carry-on and found a sweater. He put it on under the one he'd brought in his own case. Thankfully, his passport and a spare credit card were there as well.

An hour later when he parked in the airport, he was stiff with cold. Inside, he went to the men's room to clean up. He barely recognized his reflection. He was blackened with soot, had an egg-sized lump on his temple, a cigarette burn on his neck, and scabs from his fall in the mine. There wasn't much he could do with his clothes or injuries, but he washed the grime from his face and hands.

Continental was the only ticket counter open. When the agent glanced up at Sutherland, his jaw dropped.

"*Está usted bien?*" he said, squinting suspiciously. "You look hurt."

Forcing his best smile, Sutherland said, "I'm okay. An accident in my car, *nada más.*" Relieved the agent didn't report the suspicious *gringo* to the police, he booked the next flight to Houston that connected to Chicago. It left in two hours. When he signed the credit card receipt, he could barely hold down the paper with his swollen left hand.

He was sitting in the airport cradling a cup of coffee when Gabriela arrived. She wore her hair in braids with red-and-green ribbon woven through. The bruises on her face had turned yellow. He stood up to greet her. When she looked at him, she gasped. "You should go to a doctor. You are injured, *mi hijo.*"

As if afraid she might hurt him, she gently touched his cheek. She still seemed a stranger to him, but the tenderness in her eyes drew him like a warm fire. Battered from a nightmare of killing, he needed comfort. When she hugged him and lay her head against his chest, he slowly encircled her shoulders. The smell of cinnamon and chocolate seemed right.

"I can't keep this up." He squeezed his eyes shut, fighting back tears.

"*Es terrible.* All these deaths. You were almost killed. I only wanted the return of the artifacts. Who knew of the *lagarto* or that Javier acts the hero? If I knew…"

"But you couldn't have." He let go of her and took a deep breath.

"And now your girlfriend. What will you do?"

"I don't know yet." They sat down at the table, and he opened Mercedes' case. "I may have to trade the stone."

"I understand. Do what you must do," she said. "What's important is your girlfriend."

"If I give it up, it won't do them any good."

"*Por qué?*"

From the case, he retrieved the broken part of the stone, which he'd wrapped in a torn shirt. He laid it in front of her. "Open it."

She unfolded the cloth and stared at the head of the lizard. "You bring it from Chicago?"

"Most of it is still there," he said. "This was the professor's part, but it can't be deciphered without it. If Arias' men ever find out you have it…"

She shrugged. "Arias is dead. Besides, what more could he do to me? I waited thirty years for justice."

"What do you mean?" He leaned forward, feeling as if he was looking down a tunnel into their past. "It has something to do with you leaving and my father dropping the charges, right?"

She stared at him until tears flowed and she looked away. After dabbing her eyes, she seemed to make a decision.

"It is a long story. Very complicated."

He looked at his watch. "I have an hour before my flight."

She started slowly, looking off into the distance as if pulling memories from dusty archives. "I was sixteen. We lived in Guanajuato when Emiliano Valdez asked permission of my mother to marry me."

Valdez was the name of the murdered man in the newspaper. It was the name Arias used in the trailer. He couldn't believe he was hearing this.

"He was older, but my mother agreed," she went on. "She was a widow, and we were poor. I had no choice." While she paused, Sutherland calculated that this would have occurred about seven years before she married his father. "He was a bad one. He found trouble and disappeared. We thought he was dead."

"He obviously wasn't."

"No. After I married your father and we moved to Chicago, Emiliano called. He came from a California jail and wanted money. He threatened and insisted I meet him in Indiana where he was hiding."

"In a cabin," Sutherland said. "Beverly Shores."

"I don't remember the name. *Una casita*. Your father was in Washington. You were only four. I could not leave you alone, so I took you. I wanted to give him the money and leave quickly. But Emiliano was drunk. He wanted me to take tequila with him and make love. We argued. He waved a gun, saying he was going to kill you and your father. Then he hit me."

It seemed somehow familiar. He remembered a cabin and shouting. "Where was I?"

She choked on a sob. "At first, you were in another room. When I woke up, you were locked in a closet, screaming."

Sutherland had another flash of memory that included darkness and angry voices. He then recalled the smell of mothballs and urine. The burning man bellowed at him, and he wet himself. "Was Emiliano a redhead?" he asked.

"No, *mi hijo*," she said. "He had dark hair."

"Was there a fire or someone else there? I dream of a man with fiery hair."

"It was all so hazy. I think I was drugged. I only remember candles and Emiliano. When I woke up, he was dead. My clothes were off. Blood was all over him. Then there was the gun."

"Shots," Sutherland thought. Were there three of them? Could he remember, or was he imagining it?

She balled her fists. Determination was written on her face, as if she had to get through this.

"I don't remember much. It is like a nightmare. I must have dressed, grabbed you, and run. In the hospital, they said I drove onto the ice and into the lake."

As if dreaming, he remembered struggling in her arms. It was too dark to see, but he could feel her warm breath and the strength of her while the freezing water rushed over them. He shuddered violently. After several deep breaths, he managed to speak. "Were you arrested?"

"They never learned it was me, but a package arrived at our house. There were pictures of Emiliano—dead. The note said the gun was covered with my fingerprints. It demanded that your father drop the charges against Arias."

"How did Arias get involved?"

"He learned of Emiliano and me being married and that he was still alive. I don't know how. He told him to call me and threaten bigamy and deportation to pressure your father. After I shot Emiliano, your father had little choice."

He didn't buy it. "What about pleading self-defense? My father must have thought of that."

She sighed and closed her eyes. After a long pause, she continued. "I told you. It was very *complicado*. They found drugs in my blood and the police wanted to arrest me. Emilianio must have put something in my drink. I couldn't tell them that the man I shot in Indiana drugged me. They would never believe me and I would have been arrested for murder. Your father got me out of the drug charge, but then he turned his back on me."

Sutherland could see it now. In his father's eyes, she was a bigamist, a murderer, and a drug user who nearly killed his son. So he gave up on her. A lot of men would have. Making matters worse, that was a time when his father might still have stood on the highest moral ground. Gabriela's sins would have been made more intolerable because they forced him to release a guilty man.

"So Arias started it all," he said.

"He murdered that man in the pawnshop. He would stop at nothing to be free." Tears were rolling down her cheeks. She didn't try to wipe them. She just stared at him. "Your father rented an apartment for me alone. He wouldn't trust me with you after that. Arias cost me two children and my husband. What did I have to stay for?"

"I don't understand. Two children?"

"*Sí*. The child I was carrying died that night. Your sister."

# CHAPTER FORTY-SIX

▼

"Can I help you, sir?" the cabin assistant asked, jogging Sutherland from his daze. He was blocking the aisle of the plane, fragments of images still whirling in his mind. Arias and Mercedes were dead. Kelly was missing. Gabriela's latest revelation piling confusion onto shock. He stared at his boarding pass. It meant something, but he couldn't think what.

The hostess took the pass. "Sixteen A," she said. "Follow me please."

He followed her and fell into his seat. When had he slept last? He was spent. Kelly was in the hands of leaderless thugs and he was in a plane about to climb to 30,000 feet. He felt powerless. His thoughts wouldn't stop skittering. He saw Mercedes' dead eyes as she slumped into his arms. He saw her father, beaten bloody and grunting out his last breath before the blade finished him. If there was anything positive in this nightmarish whorl, it was picturing Arias and his men frying in that inferno. Justifiable as it was, it didn't make it less horrible.

Gabriela's face appeared as he left her in the airport, asking his forgiveness. He tried to push it out of his mind, telling himself that what happened thirty years ago was no longer important. The thoughts kept creeping back. She had shot Emiliano Valdez, her first husband, probably in self-defense. She had lost her unborn child in an accident. Her second husband had let a suspected killer off. Then, out of bitterness or anger, he gave up on his wife. Something was still missing. In the chaos of the trailer, Arias had said the *pelirrojo* should have killed Gabriela when he killed Valdez. Gabriela knew nothing about a redhead. She said only Valdez was in the cabin that night. If she was wrong, it changed everything.

He drifted into a fitful sleep. In a dream, he descended into the mine. There was no rope. He merely floated downward, passing faces as he went. Their lips were moving as if they were speaking to him: Javier, Angel, Marcelo,

Mercedes, Hidalgo, and Arias. He couldn't understand what they were saying.

The connecting flight in Houston was delayed. It was two o'clock in the afternoon when he finally landed in Chicago. In the cab from Midway Airport, he borrowed the driver's cell phone to call Kelly's aunt. All she could report was that the sheriff had called the FBI after talking to Detective Duncan. Sutherland then called Duncan, who said there was no progress on finding Kelly. Knowing who was behind the kidnapping didn't help. Arias was dead and his men at the Chapultepec Gallery were in jail. Who had her?

"Agent Christopher may know by now," Sutherland said.

"Kidnapping isn't the DEA's business," Duncan said.

"Is the FBI supposed to run things?"

"Arrogant assholes. But we'll work together."

"What about the guy in my neighbor's apartment? And my place? Did you check them out?"

"You were right," the detective said. "Someone was in your neighbor's place, but they split. Yours was ransacked. Were they looking for that stone?"

"Wasn't it in the shipment?" Sutherland hoped he sounded convincing.

"All those boxes? We don't know. All junk to me."

"A lot of people died for that junk," Sutherland said and hung up.

The taxi was crawling along the Stevenson Expressway. It was another Friday in the big city. When Sutherland reached him, Christopher sounded as if he was high on caffeine.

"Partner, you are one helluva soldier." He spoke so loudly that Sutherland pulled the phone from his ear. "I just saw a picture of that trailer in my e-mail. What the hell did you use?"

"Is Kelly all right?" Sutherland blurted.

"We're finding out. Jesus, buddy. I've never seen anything like it. Five bodies and you got three of them. You're lucky you got out of Mexico."

"Look, I'm not a soldier. I just want Kelly. What's going on?"

"My team grabbed one of them. A little worse for wear, but we learned they're scattering like rats because Arias is dead."

"Don't they want the stone? They can have the damn thing."

"We'll have to convince them it's worth waiting for. They're scared and disorganized."

"Where is she? How can I reach them?"

"We have a cell phone number, but you'll have to call them. They know you're not a fed."

"Are you working with the FBI?"

"No time now. Here's the phone number." He gave it to him. "Try to arrange a swap. My team will back you. I want the rest of the bastards."

Sutherland tried the number immediately and got the standard phone company recording to leave a message. Damn. He imagined the phone thrown into a dumpster as Arias' men split for parts unknown.

He left a message anyway, saying he would trade the stone and he'd call again soon. He could only hope that Duncan, Christopher or the FBI made better progress.

He settled back and watched the traffic creep along. It was a line of cars without end, just like this ordeal seemed to be. Now he faced a bunch of panicked criminals without a leader. Sutherland imagined Christopher's team questioning Arias' man. The bastard deserved anything they did, just so they found Kelly.

He borrowed the driver's phone again and called his own home number. There was one message from Larry Adams, his architect, telling him he'd meet him in the lobby of city hall at 3:45 that afternoon.

"Damn it hell," he thought. "I forgot the zoning meeting." Then again, he hadn't planned the deadly encounter with Arias or Kelly's abduction.

For more than a year, he'd considered the town house project the key to his future. He wouldn't have dreamed of relying on anyone else to push it forward. That was before. Now he wondered what that future would be like without Kelly. He'd forfeit a hundred developments, a thousand down payments to see her safe. He called Larry Adams and told him he'd have to make the zoning presentation himself. What choice did he have?

"Are you all right?" Adams asked. "You're letting me do it alone?"

"You've done dozens of them," Sutherland said. "I've got faith in you." The words sounded strange. He couldn't remember saying them before.

They were nearing the Loop when he saw the sign for Western Avenue. They could be in Pilsen in five minutes. Who would know Arias better than his enemy? He used the driver's phone again and called Guadalajara Imports. A man said *señor* Rivera was in a meeting.

"Take the next exit," Sutherland told the driver.

A few minutes later, he paid the fare with his spare credit card and got out in front of Guadalajara Imports. He pressed the button by the front door and looked into the overhead camera. The time before, the young woman immediately buzzed him in. Things were evidently different when the boss was around. A man's voice blared from the speaker over the door.

"*Qué quiere usted?*"

"I want to speak with Alfonso Rivera. Tell him Doug Sutherland from the other night. Enrique Arias is dead, and I need to talk to him."

Would Rivera see him? Even though he helped them, he hadn't believed their story.

He stomped his feet and rubbed his hands. A stiff wind carried his breath away in shreds. It was below freezing, too cold for two sweaters to help much. The door finally opened and the bodybuilder who had frisked him the other night met him. This time, he wore a Western-style suit, boots, and string tie. He patted Sutherland down and then led him to the office of the *jefe*. On the way, they passed an open office with a five men in business suits around a conference table. They looked like expensive lawyers working on a deal.

Rivera sat behind a large stainless steel and glass desk while talking on the phone. With an impatient gesture, he waved Sutherland in. Rivera wore a black blazer and an open silk shirt. With his dark mustache and graying hair, he looked like a leading man on a Mexican soap opera. He finished his phone conversation with a brusque order to take care of it and hung up. When he looked at Sutherland again, he wasn't smiling.

"You joke with me?" Rivera said. "I take Arias very seriously." His gaze swept Sutherland from head to toe. "And you come looking like a beggar."

"I'm lucky to be alive. I don't joke. Arias is dead. It happened last night in San Miguel." Sutherland pointed to the chair in front of the desk. "Mind?"

Rivera nodded, scowling.

"Two of his men were killed with him," Sutherland said, sitting.

Rivera was silent as he stared at Sutherland. He finally said, "*De veras?* You killed him?"

"You can check. You must know people."

"*Por supuesto.* San Miguel de Allende?" Rivera picked up his phone and dialed a long number. He turned his back and after a few seconds, began talking. Sutherland couldn't hear what he said. After several minutes, he turned back and hung up. He looked dazed, shaking his head.

"*Increíble. El hijo de chingada* is dead." He took a deep breath. "I wish I had seen it. What happened?"

"There's no time for the whole story. Like we started to tell you, I found myself in the middle of one of Arias' deals. He came after me in San Miguel. It ended when I set off an explosion with him in it."

"You say deals," Rivera said. "You are involved in drugs?"

"Hell no. Arias stole artifacts from a ruin in Mexico. I accidentally got in the way. He would've killed me."

Rivera shook his head. "Artifacts." He looked up for a moment, apparently thinking. "Drugs are his main business. That gallery is a front. Why would he kill for artifacts?"

"Treasure was involved."

Rivera's eyes widened. "Now I understand. But you're not *policía*. Why you?"

"First, I wanted to save my mother, Gabriela Castellano. Now his men have kidnapped my *novia*. The police closed down Arias' gallery and warehouse, so she's not there. You know Arias. Where would his men hide her?"

As if he needed time to think, Rivera pulled a cigar from a drawer, cut off the tip with a pen knife, and lit it with a gold lighter. After he blew a gray cloud toward the ceiling, he looked at Sutherland and said, "Enrique was once like a brother. We made a lot of money. He wanted the drug business. For me, it brings too much attention and killing. When I refused, he took everything. He had the *biche cobarde* kill my brother." He pointed behind him to a television monitor on the credenza. It was sequencing scenes of the alley, sidewalk, and warehouse. "Do you know why this is like a fort? Do you know why my bodyguards carry automatics or why I keep one in my place? It's because he would kill me, too. This is my territory. He doesn't come here."

Sutherland didn't want background or history. He wanted Kelly safe. "Can you help me or not?"

"The restaurant is called *El Chapulín Verde*. That is where you will find her."

"Are you sure?"

"Knowing is how I stay alive," Rivera said, smiling like a man with a secret. "You need help? I owe you very much, *señor*."

"Thanks, but I have help. The feds have been after Arias for a long time. They may have talked to you. Agent Christopher?"

He shook his head. "I don't talk to *federales*." He stood up and came around the desk. "I would like to hear more and thank you properly, but I have a meeting. And you are in a hurry. Miguel will show you the restaurant." He pointed to his bodyguard standing in the doorway. "If there is anything you need, here is my private line. *Con confianza*." He handed Sutherland a card. There wasn't a name, only numbers. "It is the least I can do. The war with Arias was not business. It was personal."

"I probably shouldn't ask what business."

Rivera stood and extended his hand, brandishing a roguish smile. "You are a wise man, *señor*. *Muchas gracias* and good luck."

Sutherland shook his hand and turned for the door.

"Wait," Rivera said. "One more thing. Your father was the lawyer with charges against Arias, no? Enrique and I were *amigos* then. I am afraid I accidentally helped him defeat your father. I knew Gabriela in Guanajuato and told Enrique she married that ca*brón*, Emiliano Valdez." He shrugged, as if to say he was sorry. "Enrique got that drunkard Valdez killed to get himself released."

"That explains how Valdez found Gabriela. Arias said the redhead killed Valdez. Who is he?"

Rivera arched his brows. "Who knows? Enrique called him *el pelirrojo*, the redhead. I think he was in the freight business because they hijacked shipments together. When they attempted an armed robbery, Enrique was caught. The redhead escaped. After Enrique Arias was released, *el pelirrojo* disappeared."

Sutherland followed Miguel through the office and warehouse to the alley doors in the rear. A few cars were parked inside. Miguel directed him to a black Cadillac with dark glass all around. It had a CD player, phone, and GPS screen in the dash. The backseat had a bar and television set. When he closed the door, it felt and sounded heavy.

"Solid," he said to Miguel.

"It's armored. Bulletproof. The windows, too. We have two of them."

Sutherland tapped the side window. Whatever Rivera's business was, it was profitable. And dangerous. Miguel checked the television monitor next to the garage door. It showed an empty alley. He opened the door with his remote.

On the way down Eighteenth Street, Miguel said, "You are a lucky man, *señor*."

"How's that?"

"You have don Alfonso as your friend. He is a man of his word. The man who killed Arias will be his friend always."

"That's good to know."

"Now he has one wish. He wants the man who killed his brother."

"*El biche cobarde*," Sutherland said. "The blue-eyed coward."

"That is what don Alfonso calls him. We only know he's an Anglo with clear eyes. He wore a hood over his head, but the witness saw his eyes and heard him speak. He shot Alejandro, don Alfonso's brother, in the back."

It took twenty minutes on Western to reach Fullerton. Sutherland borrowed Miguel's phone and tried the number Christopher gave him for

Arias' men. He got the same unsuccessful result. On Fullerton, they drove west past the Logan Square neighborhood and made a right. *El Chapulín Verde* restaurant was a single-story building with a grocery store on one side and a bakery on the other. A Budweiser sign was lit in the window. They parked across the street and several buildings down.

A few minutes passed while they watched. How could he find out if Kelly was inside? She was probably guarded. Could the police rush in? Didn't they need a search warrant? There wasn't any time for that.

He tried the number again. This time, he got a grunting "hello." Sutherland didn't waste words. "This is Doug Sutherland. I've got the stone *señor* Arias wanted. I'll trade it for the woman."

He waited. Maybe the guy didn't understand English. "*Habla usted ingles?*"

"I understood," the voice said. "You have until six o'clock. Then, *adios* Kelly." If there was an accent, he couldn't discern it.

Sutherland glanced at the dashboard clock. "That's less than two hours."

"Should we wait, or kill her now?" the man said.

"Where?"

"Montrose Harbor. Far eastern end. Know it?"

"Montrose Harbor? I'll be there," Sutherland said. "You're bringing Kelly, right?"

"Come in a taxi. Alone." He hung up.

Miguel had been listening. "Where is this thing they want?"

"My office building," Sutherland said. "Madison and Clark. How long will it take?"

"Forty minutes."

"There isn't much time. Let's watch the restaurant a little to see if my call stirred things up." He was dialing Christopher's number while he spoke. He answered immediately. "They want to meet at the eastern end of Montrose Harbor," Sutherland said. "Can you cover me?"

"Just a minute." Christopher talked to someone in the background. While Sutherland waited, two men jogged out of *El Chapulín Verde* and headed for a white van parked on the street. Something was familiar about one of them. Had he seen him in San Miguel with Arias? The men hopped into the van and drove toward them. As it passed the Cadillac, Sutherland got the license number and another glimpse of the men inside.

Then Christopher came on again. "My team will be there. They'll be out of sight. How can we get a wire on you to follow what's going on?"

"Meet me in the lobby of my office building. Did you find out where they have her yet?"

"No luck."

"Ever hear of *El Chapulín Verde?*"

Christopher took a second to answer. "An Arias hangout. It's too obvious. I'll see you downtown. We're gonna get these bastards, buddy."

When Sutherland called Detective Duncan again, he wasn't in his office. His partner, another detective, told Sutherland they'd spoken to the DEA. Agent Christopher was on vacation and there was no offensive underway on Enrique Arias' operation.

"It must be confidential," Sutherland said. "Because Christopher and his men have sure been busy." He gave the detective the license number of the van, saying that Arias' men were inside. He told him that Kelly was being held in *El Chapulín Verde.* At this point, what difference did it make if he was wrong? Christopher said it was too obvious, but Rivera was pretty sure. Who was he supposed to believe?

While Duncan's partner made excuses for why they couldn't rush the restaurant, Sutherland had a flash. He remembered where he'd seen the man leaving a few minutes earlier. He was Agent Bradley, the man he'd hit with the bat. He hadn't placed him immediately because he wore a heavy coat and hat. In the van, he'd removed the hat. The crew cut and the square jaw gave him away. Why was Christopher's man coming out of Arias' place? He suddenly felt as if he'd fallen through a trapdoor.

Clues dropped into place like pieces of a jigsaw puzzle, especially nagging things he'd been too distracted to question. Christopher knew Sutherland went to Mexico and didn't take the stone. He knew Sutherland didn't shoot the professor and Mercedes because he said Sutherland killed three of them in the trailer, not five. Arias spoke English over the phone to a man called Diego who was searching Sutherland's office. Christopher didn't speak Spanish. Diego was Spanish for James. He'd known Arias' every move. Because they were on the same side. Arias was the bad guy. James Christopher the good guy. Sutherland had fallen all right, right up to his neck in *mierda.*

He checked the dashboard clock. There wasn't much time.

"I'll be inside," he said to Miguel.

# CHAPTER FORTY-SEVEN

▼

"Are you loco?" Miguel grabbed Sutherland's arm. "That is Arias' place."

Sutherland yanked himself free. "He's dead, and two men just left. I'm just gonna look." He pointed to Miguel's hat. It was the Western type, black with a silver band. "Can I borrow that?" It would hide the lump on his head and help him fit into the Mexican scene.

Miguel shrugged and handed it to him. It was a little big, but it covered more of his face that way.

"If I'm not out in ten minutes, call 9-1-1," Sutherland said before he slammed the door.

The sign over the door of *El Chapulín Verde* had a cartoon picture of a green grasshopper with a guitar and sombrero. He entered and quickly surveyed the interior—red plastic tablecloths, cheap glassware, and paper napkins. It was about as upscale as he expected. Two men and a woman were at a corner table. Two men were on stools. The bartender near the window was reading a newspaper. Paintings of pueblos, mountains, and beaches covered the walls. A large Mexican flag hung behind the bar. In the air, he heard barely audible *mariachi* music, and he smelled the aroma of corn tortillas and garlic. A corridor leading from the rear had a sign reading, "*Servicios y Teléfono.*"

Sutherland walked past the tables to the far end of the bar and eased onto a stool. The bartender looked up from his paper.

"*Buenas tardes. Qué quiere tomar?*" He was small and slim. His jet-black hair was slicked back into a ponytail.

"*Una cerveza, por favor.* Dos Equis." He set out a ten-dollar bill.

He had maybe ten minutes if he wanted to make it downtown, pick up the stone, and then meet Arias' men at Montrose Harbor. If Kelly was here, unguarded, he wouldn't need the time. The men at the table were in business suits. The woman wore a skirt and blouse. They were discussing spreadsheets and didn't look dangerous. The two men drinking at the bar were in a world of their own. The only worry in sight was the Latino serving him the beer.

Sutherland took a drink and then pointed to the corridor. "The telephone work?"

"*Sí.*" He wore a waiter's jacket and skintight jeans. His walk was a little effeminate, but the bulge under his arm said, gay or not, this *caballero* had a gun.

"Bring me a tequila," Sutherland said. "Herradura reposado. I'm going to make a phone call." He had to risk it. Worst case, if he was caught, he could still make the trade. He didn't want to think about an even worse case of him being too late.

After another swig from the bottle, he slipped off the stool and went down the passageway. Out of sight of the bar, he quickened his pace. The pay phone was on the left, and as he passed it he saw a kitchen on the right with a boy stirring a pot on the stove. Voices of Spanish soccer announcers echoed around the kitchen and into the hall. He then passed a unisex bathroom, a mop closet with slop sink, and stopped at a door marked "Private." He knocked and then tried the knob. It resisted. When he threw his shoulder into it, the latch popped open. Inside was a large office with desk, table, chairs, and couch. The table was cluttered with crumpled fast-food bags and half-eaten burgers. The large flat-screen television on the wall was showing ESPN. The two men he had seen in the street had left in a hurry.

He left the room, closed the door, and hurried toward the rear. The alley door had a keyed deadbolt and a burglar bar, also locked. There was no way out. The only other door had a sign that read, "PROHIBIDO ENTRAR." He opened it and gazed down a dark stairway.

He found a light switch and hurried into the basement. There was a long aisle with shelves on each side stacked with cans, boxes, crates, and liquor bottles. All were behind a padlocked chain-link fence. At the end of the aisle were three padlocked doors. He checked his watch. It had been two minutes since he'd left the bar.

He grabbed the crowbar lying on a crate of melons and ran to the first door. He knocked with the crowbar and yelled, "Kelly?" It was painful gripping the bar with his broken hand, but, with two heaves, the hasp tore free. It was dark inside, but he could see shelves piled with boxes of cigarettes. He saw Marlboro, Winston, and Kent, but no sign of Kelly.

Repeating the process, he broke open the second door. He had to blink twice and then turn on the light before he believed it. It was an arsenal. Boxes of ammunition were stacked neatly on shelves. A half-dozen automatic rifles were standing side by side in a gun rack. Arias was ready for war.

He pounded on the third door. As he pried off the hasp, he heard muffled cries within. The door opened to a large, windowless room.

"Kelly?"

As he reached inside for a light switch, he heard the groan again. She was here. When he found the switch, he saw her stretched out on the first of four beds. She was bound with duct tape and gagged. Her eyes were wide and wet.

Easing the gag from her mouth, he glanced around the room. Judging from the empty shelves, it had been a storage room, but they had added beds, a television, refrigerator, along with a toilet and sink in the corner. It was a barracks for Arias' men. Or were they Christopher's men?

Her mouth free, she exhaled, as if it was the first time in a day.

"Thank God," she said. "They just left me here. How'd you find me?"

"We're not outta this yet." He ripped the tape from her wrists.

"Anything's better than what I've been through. Sons of bitches." She was still in her running tights and windbreaker. Her ankle was the size of a grapefruit.

"Can you walk?" he said.

"I'll crawl if I have to." She tore the tape from her legs.

He checked his watch. The five minutes since he left the bar seemed like hours.

"Head for the stairs."

She hopped down the aisle while holding onto the fencing. He ran into the ammunition room and grabbed a box labeled "twelve-gauge." He ran with box and crowbar to a cage containing cleaning supplies, paper towels, napkins, and matches. With one heave of the crowbar, the lock sprang off with a loud crack. Inside the cage, he scattered napkins and paper towels in a big pile. Over that, he poured the contents of a five-gallon can with an inflammable icon on it.

"What are you doing?" Kelly said, hopping and skipping past him.

"Get to the top and wait." He placed the box of shells on the pile, stepped back, lit the match, and dropped it. The fire started with a whoosh. Kelly was halfway up when he caught her. In the corridor, he helped her into the mop closet and closed the door. Then he ran into the bar and frantically beckoned the bartender over.

"Smoke's coming from the basement," he said, gasping.

The young man stared, wide-eyed. As if on fire himself, he scrambled around the bar and dashed into the corridor. Sutherland waited a second and then followed. Seeing the bartender disappear down the stairs, he helped Kelly out of the closet. He wrapped her arm around his neck. She hopped and limped beside him into the bar. As he passed the trio at the table, he yelled,

"Fire! Get out of here! Call the fire department!" They looked up at him, eyes and mouths wide open. Sutherland didn't stay to see if they believed him.

He was sweating, and the cold outside hit him like a wake-up slap. He pointed to the Cadillac where Miguel was waiting down the street. With her unable to walk and an icy sidewalk, it seemed like a long way.

"How'd you do that?" he asked.

"I stepped in a hole when they were chasing me. They would have never caught me."

She winced with every step. He finally said, "I'll carry you piggyback." She jumped on his back, and he shuffled along the ice like an old man in a hurry. The pain in his hand and the wind made him tear up.

From behind, Kelly said, "Nice hat, cowboy."

"Smart-ass. This'll teach you to take my advice."

They were forty yards from the Cadillac when a white Acura skidded to the curb from behind. The passenger window opened and Christopher yelled, "Hurry up. Get in. They're coming back."

# CHAPTER FORTY-EIGHT

▼

The rear door of Christopher's car burst open, and a big man jumped out. He motioned Sutherland and Kelly into the backseat. There was little time to think. Christopher was the spider. His car was his web. Inside there was no escape, but they couldn't run. Rivera's Cadillac was at least forty yards away, and Kelly was injured.

"Don't just stand there," Christopher shouted through the passenger window. "They're right behind us."

Muffled shots broke out in *El Chapulín Verde*. It might have been the shotgun shells in the fire, but who knew?

"What the fuck was that?" Christopher said. "Get in!"

The man from the backseat bounded through the snow pile separating them. "I'll carry her." He grabbed Kelly's leg and, when she released her hold around Sutherland's neck, she fell into the man's arms. As if she weighed twenty pounds, he strode back to the car and eased her through the door. There was nothing Sutherland could do except follow. They were screwed.

Christopher, wearing dark aviator glasses, was in the passenger's seat. Another man wearing a baseball hat was driving. The big man squeezed in after Sutherland and Kelly. The car sped off and Sutherland saw Miguel's shocked face as they passed Rivera's Cadillac.

Christopher turned around, his face flushed with excitement. "You're amazing, partner. You pulled it off."

"How'd you know I was here?"

"You mentioned the place. Then the bartender called them. We were listening."

So much for his feeble disguise. Sutherland took off the hat and tossed it on the shelf behind.

"What now?" He had to keep up the charade until he saw a way to escape.

"We'll get you to a safe place." He smiled and gave Kelly a casual salute. "Nice to see you, miss. The last time was at your boyfriend's apartment. The night he coldcocked my man."

"Where's that guy now?" Sutherland asked.

"He's around," Christopher said, looking through the rear window. "I think we're clear for now. Where do we pick up the stone?"

"Let's get Kelly to an emergency room first," Sutherland said. "Her ankle's broken."

"And a bathroom would be nice," Kelly said.

"You're right," Christopher said. "We'll get the stone afterwards. Where do we go?"

"Why do we need it?" Sutherland said. "Kelly's free."

"If they get away now, we'll never find them. Besides, they might make a last shot. Let's put it in the right hands."

Now what? He could give him the stone, but he had to get Kelly clear first. Then he could work on saving his own skin.

"Let's stop at Northwestern Hospital. It's on the way to my office," Sutherland said.

Christopher turned around and frowned. "They searched there already."

"I know," Sutherland said. "My apartment too..."

"And your boat," Christopher said. "They saw the pictures in your office."

How did Christopher keep up the pretense? It was always "they." It was better this way. Everybody pretending they were on the same side. Everything friendly and nice. It wouldn't take much to change things.

"It's in the building, but not in my office," Sutherland said. "I'll show you. The exit for Northwestern is coming up."

"You are one smart son of a bitch." Christopher smiled broadly, full of bonhomie. "You knew they'd search your office. Okay, but let's pick up the stone first. I'll call to set up a guard at the hospital in case they try something." He didn't have any intention of letting her go.

"They're probably halfway to Mexico by now," Sutherland said, pushing his argument.

"Who said they were Mexican?" Kelly asked. "They wore masks, but they sounded like *gringos*."

Sutherland wished she hadn't said that. Christopher's smile dissolved into a tight-lipped line. The dark glasses masked his eyes, but he appeared to be thinking for a moment. Then he produced a gun with a silencer and rested it on the seat back.

"We'll do it my way," he said. "We'll pick up the stone."

Sutherland swallowed. The man beside Sutherland pulled out a gun and jammed it into Sutherland's ribs. There was no more being friendly and nice.

Kelly gasped and said, "What's…"

"It's simple," Christopher interrupted. "We get the stone. Nobody makes a fuss. You guys go free." Removing his glasses, he stared at them with deep blue eyes. "We okay with that?"

Sutherland hadn't any reason to notice the blue eyes before. Was this the man who killed Rivera's brother? The blue-eyed *gringo*? *El Biche Cobarde*? He had an idea.

"No problem," he said. "Well, maybe one. I don't have my ID or keys."

"Search him, Cal," Christopher said.

The man beside him patted him down while nearly impaling his side with the gun.

"Nothing," he said.

"No matter," Christopher said. "Cal doesn't need keys."

"We'll need building ID after five-thirty. Can I use your phone?" He reached into his pocket for the card Rivera had given him.

Christopher laughed. "Who do you want to call? That dumb cop Duncan?"

"The building manager. I can't get in after hours without a magnetic ID. He leaves at six."

Christopher looked at his watch, stared out the window a moment, and finally handed him the phone.

"Don't be stupid," he said.

Alfonso Rivera answered immediately. "*Dígame.*"

"This is Doug Sutherland, Mr. *Biche*. Suite 1510."

There was a pause. Then Rivera said, "You said *biche?*"

"I'm on my way to my office. I lost my ID. That guy at the desk, *cobarde*, can be a bastard. Can you call him?"

"You're saying you're with *el biche cobarde?*" Rivera said. "You can't talk?"

"That's right. This minute. Can you help?"

"You're heading for your office? Does Miguel know where it is?"

"Yes, he does."

"We'll try. *Gracias, amigo.* Good luck."

He returned the phone to Christopher who said, "Thinking ahead. Good boy."

They were driving down Milwaukee toward downtown. Sutherland wondered if he should try something when he was in the building. The metal detector in the lobby meant they couldn't take their guns. Sutherland could tip off a guard or somehow slip away. Taking them on wouldn't work. With a broken hand, he couldn't do much. Christopher's next words settled it.

"Here's how it goes. Our hero goes in with Cal. We drive off with the girl. When Cal gets the stone, you take a cab. We'll be in phone contact. If you don't come in twenty minutes, the girl won't love you anymore. You got a problem with that?"

"I sure as hell do," Kelly said. "Whose side are you on?"

Sutherland grabbed her arm and said, "They can have the stone." To Christopher, he said, "We've got no problem."

It wasn't what he thought. Christopher had no intention of letting them go. What would Rivera be able to do now? Miguel knew where his office was and about the plan for the harbor. But, with Kelly as hostage, Rivera's men were helpless, even if they arrived on time. If Christopher was waiting anyplace but the harbor, Rivera wouldn't find them.

"Good," Christopher said, turning to face forward again. "Now, everyone be calm and peaceful."

They were in heavy traffic when Christopher said, "Do you know what's interesting? You were smart enough to figure out everything except this."

"You want me to say how clever you are? Okay," Sutherland said. "By the way, are you really Christopher with the DEA?"

"Where else would I get the technology? But the money's better in trafficking."

"Why did you get involved in stolen artifacts?" Sutherland said.

"Arias' idea. I thought there was too little money in it. Turns out he stumbled on to something big."

When they pulled to the curb in front of Sutherland's building, Christopher said, "Are we clear on what happens if I don't hear from Cal?"

"Clear. But he can't get in with his gun."

"He doesn't need one."

It was ten minutes to six o'clock when they entered the lobby. As Sutherland thought, the sign-in process didn't start until six. They entered without a glitch. They went to the seventh floor and down the hall to his storage room. Cal had the door open in a minute with some kind of lock pick. They retrieved the backpack with the stone. Cal gave it a quick look and made a call. He only said, "Got it." After a total of ten minutes, they were out of the building and in a cab. The building security guard hadn't cared what the big man was carrying on his back.

"Where to?" the cabbie asked.

"Take us to Montrose Harbor," Cal said.

The cab driver reached for the meter and then stopped. "There is nothing there this time of year," he said.

He was a dark man with clipped English, maybe Indian or Pakistani. He was right. The marina would be empty. The boats would be gone. The food stand and yacht club were closed. Sutherland had seen fisherman around the deserted docks a few times, but few others ventured there in winter.

"We're gonna look at the view."

Cal sat behind the driver with the *lagarto* stone in the backpack on the floor. He stared straight ahead. The whole time he and Sutherland had been in the building, he had said two words. Those were to Christopher over the phone. "Got it."

Traffic was heavy as they made their way across the Loop to Lake Shore Drive. Snow was beginning to fall, and headlights reflected off the wet asphalt. The six o'clock news was on the radio, warning of a blizzard closing in from the northwest. The forecast was for six to eight inches before morning. Sutherland looked at his watch. Ten minutes after six o'clock, and they were nowhere near Montrose.

"We're not going to make your boss's twenty-minute deadline," he said.

Cal pulled out his cell phone and pushed one button.

"On our way. Traffic."

Why did they pick the harbor? It made sense for them to leave Chicago. With Arias' operation closed down, including the gallery, warehouse, and restaurant, what would keep them? That didn't explain a rendezvous on the lake front. Montrose, like most of Chicago's recreational harbors, usually froze over in January.

"Are you planning to escape on a boat?" Sutherland asked. "If you are, you're nuts. The harbor will be ice. And look at those whitecaps." He pointed out on the lake at the waves crashing against the seawall.

"You'll see," Cal said.

"There's a storm coming," Sutherland said. "It's suicidal."

He suppressed images of Kelly and him being tossed overboard into the icy lake, thinking instead of Rivera and his man Miguel. Sutherland had given him his office address. There had been no sign of them there. Miguel also knew about Montrose Harbor because he overheard the phone conversation with Christopher. Would they show up? If they did, what could they do with Kelly and him being held hostage?

They spent the next fifteen minutes on Lake Shore Drive. Sutherland's thoughts jumped between hope and desperation while a radio interview droned in the background and the taxi's windshield wipers thwacked back and forth. Through the darkness and snow, he watched Diversey and then Belmont Harbor pass behind them. In summer, these marinas sheltered hundreds of pleasure boats. Now there was only an empty expanse of frozen white. It was six-thirty when they turned off Lake Shore Drive onto Montrose. The snow fell harder now, slanting through their headlight beams and drifting across the road. The harbor, one-third of a mile in length and almost completely surrounded by land, was on their right. A line of whitecaps marked the opening to the lake. Empty docks, shadows against the icy moonscape, jutted from the banks like fingers. Nothing moved except falling snow.

"Past the bait shop. Go all the way toward the lake," Cal said.

Christopher's white Acura sat facing them on an otherwise deserted road. The street lamps were veiled in snow. Visibility was poor, but Sutherland had run there often and knew the area well. The road continued on a curving peninsula that sheltered the marina, dead-ending at its mouth. In the darkness to the east of Christopher's car, there was a broad field of prairie grass, a sand beach, and the lake. To the west lay the frozen marina.

Cal paid the driver and directed Sutherland toward the Acura before hefting the stone off the floor. Christopher got out of the front passenger seat and opened the back door. He had his ski jacket zipped up and a fleece hat pulled down over his ears. The driver had changed his baseball hat for a woolen watch cap. Kelly was in the backseat, her hands behind her back. She gave him an imploring look that said, "Please get us out of this." As he slid beside her, he saw she was handcuffed.

"Everything cool?" Christopher stood just outside the passenger door.

"Easy," Cal said. "This weighs a ton. Where you want it?"

Christopher opened the backpack and ran his hand over the stone's surface while Cal held it. "Looks like a piece of crap. No wonder Arias didn't know what it was." He pointed to the broken edge. "And this. A piece is gone." He closed the backpack and got in the front seat. Turning to Sutherland, he said, "Which brings us to the next thing. Where is it?"

Sutherland shrugged. "The professor had it. Look, you said you'd let us go." He hoped he sounded like he believed it. Their only hope lay with Rivera. Failing his help, they would trade for the missing piece. No one knew he'd left it with Gabriela and he didn't want to jeopardize her. He'd have to get creative.

Cal put the stone in the trunk and got in the backseat next to Sutherland. He put his gun in his shoulder holster while he cuffed Sutherland's hands behind him.

"I repeat," Christopher said. There was just enough light to see the sheen of the gun barrel on the seat back. "Where is it?"

"I've only got a photo."

"We searched you."

"It's in my carry-on bag," Sutherland said. "As you can see, I don't have it."

The gun jerked, as if Christopher was fighting off an urge to fire. "Where the fuck is it?"

"In the car that dropped me at *El Chapulín Verde*."

"A taxi?"

"Rivera's car." By bringing Rivera into the mix, Sutherland might buy some time and bluff through a trade.

That seemed to stop Christopher. He was silent for ten seconds. When he spoke again, his words came out slowly. "That's how you found the restaurant. Alfonso Rivera. I should have figured." He paused. "I should have killed him with his brother."

Rivera's involvement must have started Christopher thinking because he didn't say anything for several minutes. In the meantime, Kelly poked Sutherland and said, "Do you have it? If you do, give it to them. They're not fooling."

"I don't," he said. "Like I said…"

"There was no trace of it in Hidalgo's trailer," Christopher said. "Where would you leave it?"

"It was in the trailer," Sutherland said. Why had he left it with Gabriela? He should have buried it. "It must have been destroyed. The photo is all that's left."

"So I just call Rivera, right? Ask him to deliver the photo?"

"No, I do," Sutherland said. "He'll send me the bag. You get the photo."

For the past several minutes, the driver seemed increasingly agitated, looking out the window and fidgeting. An inch of new snow had already settled, and it was coming down hard. He finally said, "This shit's getting bad, Rusty. Can they make it?"

Christopher leaned forward to look through the windshield and then shrugged.

"He's been through worse than this. Desert sandstorms, for crissake."

"Where the hell are they?" Cal said.

"Don't worry," Christopher said. "We'll beat the worst of it."

Just then, a car drove toward them and slowed. It was dark and long, and from the silhouette, it looked like a Cadillac. As it passed them, all eyes in the Acura were on it. All guns were ready. Before anyone could react, the night exploded in light flashes, a burst of automatic fire and the sound of bullets pinging off metal. Sutherland threw himself against Kelly, forcing them both down against the far door. If this was Rivera's way of saving them, they were better off alone. Another burst split the air with more metal pings. The Acura slumped toward the gunshots, and it was silent again.

"Anybody hit?" Christopher yelled.

"The tires," Cal said. "They got both left tires."

When Sutherland looked up, the Cadillac was gone. No one had returned fire. All three were staring through the rear window. The Cadillac couldn't go far. The road dead-ended at the harbor mouth. It must have turned around because a few seconds later, it reappeared, a gray blur in the white. It stopped a few hundred feet behind them.

"What the fuck?" Cal said. "Who's that?"

"Look," the driver said. Another car had arrived, barely visible through the snow. It stopped in front of the Acura, 200 feet away. "It boxed us in."

Christopher seemed rattled for the first time. He looked behind at the one car and then forward at the other. There was no movement around either. They sat like shadows. "The automatics? Where are they?" he asked.

"The trunk," the driver said. "Should we make a run?"

Before he could answer, Christopher's phone buzzed. He picked up and listened a moment. "How'd you get this number?" After listening again, he said, "I'll get back to you. Meantime, try anything and they're dead."

"Who was that?" the driver asked.

Running his hand over his mouth Christopher said, "Rivera. He had my number from when our *amigo* called. He wants us to free them."

"Thank goodness," Kelly said.

"Shut up," Christopher said, his hand still rubbing his face. "I gotta think. Does he know who I am? His brother? Shit."

"Do we go after them?" Cal sounded eager.

"We wait," Christopher said firmly. "He doesn't know about the chopper." He looked at his watch. "It'll be here in a few minutes. They won't rush us with these two here."

That was their plan. The two men leaving *El Chapulín Verde* were taking the van to pick up a helicopter. Sutherland looked out the window at the field of fresh snow and grass between them and the lake. It was flat and deserted, a perfect place to land, pick up Christopher's men, and disappear.

Christopher leveled the gun at Sutherland. "I don't know how, but you did it again. Don't get your hopes up. Rivera's got a surprise coming. When the chopper comes, my men will blow them apart." He turned to his driver. "Phillips, back into that brush." He pointed at the field beside them. "That grove will give you cover to get the automatics. Spread out. Watch the flanks."

Without hesitation, the driver put the Acura into reverse. The car banged over the curb and backed through the snow, flattening the shrubs and grass stubble. Running on two tires that had been blown out, the car skidded and lurched across the ground. It stopped with a jolt against a small tree. Christopher smashed the inside overhead lights with the butt of his pistol. Phillips popped the trunk. Cal and Phillips piled out of the car into the darkness behind. Through the windshield, they could just make out Rivera's cars, two smudges in the white.

Christopher, Kelly, and Sutherland were alone in the car. The trunk slammed, and someone slapped the fender twice, a signal.

Christopher said, "They're ready."

"Now what?" Sutherland said.

"Enjoy the wait. It's all you've got left."

# CHAPTER FORTY-NINE

▼

"Rivera won't know what hit him." Christopher pressed a button on his cell phone. "What's your twenty?" He listened for a few seconds and bolted upright in the seat. "What?" He listened again and then said, "Don't let them search that van. Any trouble, eliminate them. Call me when you're at the chopper." He disconnected and exhaled forcefully. "Fuck."

Had Sutherland's message to Detective Duncan worked? Did the police put out one of those APBs?"

"Cops, huh?" Sutherland said. "Stopped the van?"

"Just a fucking trooper. They'll get out of it."

They waited. The car was getting colder. Sutherland and Kelly huddled together in the backseat. Christopher's men were somewhere outside, watching the flanks. Sutherland couldn't stand the silence. "What if the trooper calls for backup?"

"You don't know shit."

"What if Duncan put out an APB?"

If the possibility bothered him, Christopher didn't show it. From behind, Sutherland watched him turn his head from side to side, apparently checking for movement from either Rivera car. There was nothing to see. Just two dark hulks within firing distance.

"This was not the way Christopher had it planned," Sutherland thought. Everything was unraveling. That didn't mean they were out of it though. The cuffs cutting into his wrists were a constant reminder of who was in control.

Christopher looked at his watch and used his phone again. After a few seconds, he said, "Who is this?" He listened a second, then slammed the dashboard with the heel of his hand, emphasizing each strike while screaming, "Fuck, fuck, fuck."

The police must have overwhelmed the van, leaving Christopher without his escape route and desperate. Sutherland would have to be careful.

"If they're not coming, why not let us go? That's all Rivera wants."

"You think so?" Christopher said. "He'll never let me outta here." He lowered the window and whistled. A moment later, Cal was crouched next to the car. "Change of plans. You and Phillips take the car on the right. No prisoners, but we want the car."

Cal disappeared, and Christopher raised the window.

Sutherland waited until the two men would be too far away to be called back. "They don't have a chance," he said. "The car's armored."

Christopher lowered the window again and was slapped with a cold gust. It must have convinced him that calling would be futile. He raised the window.

"They're soldiers," he said finally.

They waited, watching snow cake the windshield and listening to the wind. Every few seconds, the car was buffeted as a cloud of white blew by. Christopher turned the ignition on long enough to let the wipers take a few sweeps, then turned it off again.

The fight started like a war movie on a wide-screen. Through the windshield, they saw a series of flashes to the right of the Cadillac accompanied by automatic gunfire. More flashes and staccato came from the other side. Metal clanged and pinged with each burst. Suddenly they heard a high-pitched crack, and something stung Sutherland's ear. A bullet through the side window sent glass flying. Why were they shooting at the Acura? Sutherland crushed himself against Kelly, pushing her to the floor. He could feel her hot breath on his cheek. He couldn't see anything, but he closed his eyes anyway, hoping it had been a stray bullet.

The shooting stopped and then started again. This time, different-sounding automatics joined in. Now and then, there were single cracks like pistols and louder bangs, like shotguns. Then the firing seemed to move farther away. Finally, after what must have only been a few minutes, there was only the wind.

Christopher's phone rang. "Yeah?"

While he listened, he trained the gun on Sutherland. "If you come close, they're dead." He disconnected.

"Let me guess," Sutherland said.

"Shut up."

They were a half -mile from the nearest apartment buildings and in the midst of a blizzard. As unlikely as it was, someone could have heard the gunfire. Rivera may have thought the same thing because one of his cars pulled away and disappeared toward Lake Shore Drive.

"They'll be watching for cops," Christopher said.

He shifted over to the driver's side, started the engine, and put it into gear. Under the roar of the motor, they could sense one tire spinning. The flat was tire thumping on its rim. The Acura rocked, lurched, and finally settled back into a rut. Christopher flicked off the engine. He sat there for a moment. Then he zipped up his jacket, pulled his hat down, and said, "Okay, miss. You're coming with me. They'll never see us in this shit."

"You carrying me?" she asked.

"Her ankle's broken," Sutherland said.

Christopher exhaled loudly. "Fine. Better you anyway. You can carry the stone. Turn around." He took Sutherland's cuffs off and told him to fasten them to her cuffs and the shoulder seatbelt. While he was closing the cuffs, she whispered, "Don't let him win, Doug."

"Trying not to," he said and kissed her cheek. At least she would be safe.

Sutherland wore only two sweaters, jeans, and running shoes. He didn't have any hat or gloves. When he stepped outside, his shoes filled with snow.

"Grab the thing from the trunk." Christopher pointed with the gun.

A dim trunk light came on when Sutherland raised the lid. He hoped Rivera's men could see it, signaling what Christopher was up to. In the snow, sheltered by the brush behind the car, it was doubtful. Sutherland struggled into the backpack and adjusted the weight on his shoulders. He was tempted to grab one of the pistols on the trunk floor, but Christopher was too close.

"Let's go." Christopher directed him toward the lake. Their path kept the Acura between them and the Cadillac. No one in Rivera's car could have seen them.

"What are we doing?" Sutherland said. "There's nothing out there but water."

"Just keep going."

They were slogging through new snow. Drifts were forming, some up to six inches already. By the time they made the rocks at the water's edge, they couldn't see the Acura or the Cadillac. Then Christopher pointed west along the lake side of the peninsula that hooked around the marina.

"That way. Double time."

Sutherland's hands were frozen, his feet wet and nearly numb. He didn't have much time. Christopher would kill him as soon as he didn't need a hostage and mule. Without the stone, Sutherland figured he could outrun him, but even in this poor visibility, Christopher could get off a good shot.

They were halfway out on the peninsula, half-plodding and half-jogging into the wind. In a few minutes, they would be stopped at the harbor mouth with fifty feet of water between them and shore.

"A dead end, just like what I'm doing," Sutherland thought. "I'm carrying the stone until I'm killed. Why do I keep doing this?"

"We're going the wrong way," Sutherland shouted. He was sweating from the pace and heavy load, but his face was so cold that his lips could barely move. "It's a dead end."

"That's why they won't guard it." Christopher turned, apparently reassuring himself that no one was following them. "They won't look for us cutting across the ice."

# CHAPTER FIFTY

▼

Crossing the ice was insane. Sutherland shielded his eyes and strained to see the harbor. What he could make out looked frozen, but that didn't mean it was safe. Didn't Christopher know people have fallen through and died out there?

The thought of being trapped under a roof of ice, drowning in freezing water, made his stomach clench. His legs, weary from jogging with the heavy stone, gave way. He fell to his hands and knees and threw up in the snow.

"Get up," Christopher yelled.

He looked up at Christopher's angry face. He knew he would to shoot him, but the fear of drowning was worse.

"It's not safe," he shouted into the wind.

"We'll go to the end of a dock," Christopher said. "Fifty yards max to the opposite wall." Then he grabbed the knapsack and dragged Sutherland to his feet.

Bent into the wind, Sutherland trudged to the first dock in their path. He wondered why he kept going. He was only postponing the inevitable.

The dock was wooden, maybe eight feet wide. A dozen or so gangways, slips for sailboats, jutted like fingers on either side. He made his way to the end and looked down. The ice was covered with snow. It could be one or six inches thick, the margin between drowning and living until Christopher shot him. As he crouched to get a closer look, he saw the surface wasn't solid. It had broken into a patchwork of large sections, a floe rising and falling in slow motion. Crossing it would mean stepping from one slab to another. If you made a misstep or slipped into a gap between them, it would be over. He wouldn't go.

"It'll hold," Christopher said. "Get down there."

"I gotta take this off." Sutherland struggled out of the backpack. "Test it first." His hands were so frozen that he could barely grip the shoulder straps. He hoped Christopher would come within striking range. Instead, he backed away, his gun ready. Seeing no option, Sutherland decided he'd risk the ice, but he'd hold onto the dock for security. Then he'd scramble under it, using it for cover while he made for shore.

He set the backpack on the edge and lowered himself to the surface three feet below. Touching down, he felt the floe move. It creaked as it ground against the pilings. He grabbed the dock with both hands. Before he could duck under it, Christopher dropped down next to him. The ice rocked, and water sloshed across it. Sutherland sidestepped away, still holding on.

"Not so close. It's too thin," he shouted.

"Get the pack, and let's go." Christopher backed up to give him room, his gun in his right hand.

Who could make it across with that heavy stone? Even now, the slab Sutherland stood on, the size of a double bed, was tilting with his weight. Freezing water crept over its edges into his running shoes. He had a flashback. He was in the car under the ice with water rushing in. He couldn't face that again. He'd take a bullet first.

His heart raced as he reached for the backpack. He fumbled with the straps.

"My hands are frozen!" he yelled. "Help me get it on."

He lifted it off the dock and the ice tilted like a rubber raft. Water washed over his ankles, so cold that it hurt.

Christopher inched closer. He kept his gun in his right hand. With his left, he held the shoulder strap for Sutherland's arm. They were too close. The ice was sinking under them. Sutherland wanted to scream, but nothing came out. With the stone as a shield, he lunged for Christopher. He saw bright flashes and heard two shots as they fell. Christopher landed on his back with his arm under the stone. Sutherland was on top, face-to-face with him. He smashed down on Christopher's nose. Then he rolled off and grabbed Christopher's gun hand with both of his. The gun went off like a thunderclap in his eardrum. He smelled gunpowder and felt water seeping under him. He finally wrenched the gun free and scrambled to his feet. He tried to grip it to shoot, but his fingers were too numb. Then he noticed his right hand was bleeding. He hurled the gun into the darkness and stumbled to the dock.

He hauled himself over the edge. When he turned, Christopher was on his knees wiping blood from his nose. Without his gun, Christopher couldn't do anything. He wouldn't catch Sutherland now.

Christopher got to his feet, glaring at Sutherland. "You think you won?" he shouted. "I can take you out any time."

Sutherland backed away down the dock. He was soaking wet. His skin was raw. His clothes were already stiff. He only wanted shelter and to be dry and warm. Christopher and the stone didn't matter anymore.

"You know what else?" Christopher yelled. "Gabriela has the broken piece. I'll finish what I started with Valdez. I should've killed her then."

Christopher lifted the backpack and shrugged himself into the straps. The ice under him tilted and he took a few steps to level it. He shifted the weight on his back and started across the floe. The far side of the marina was completely veiled in snow. As he negotiated the unstable ice, he teetered and listed like a wino on a bender.

Sutherland watched him go, stunned. Christopher was *el pelirrojo*. His hair was silver now, but it would have been red thirty years ago. It was red when he was nicknamed Rusty. Red when he was Arias' accomplice in the pawn shop murder. Red when he killed Valdez, drugged Gabriela, and left her to believe she was a murderess. Finally, it was red when he locked the four-year-old Sutherland in the closet that night. He wasn't just *el biche cobarde* who killed Rivera's brother. He was the man with the burning hair of Sutherland's nightmares.

Sutherland wished he'd found a way to pull that trigger a moment ago. Now the gun was lost. The only way Christopher could be stopped was to go after him. Sutherland wouldn't win a fight. He was frozen and weak. One hand was broken, and the other wounded. It would be a suicidal effort. If Christopher made it, he would go after and kill Gabriela. Could Sutherland live with himself if he didn't try to save her?

In the face of what he had to do, he screamed. It was primal, half from fear, half as battle cry, a long bellow swallowed by the wind.

He ran back to the end of the dock and dropped to the ice. The slab tipped and he sidestepped, leveling it. Christopher was barely in sight. Sutherland took a deep breath and followed. The snow was crusty underneath, offering traction. He teetered and balanced as the floe shifted. Several times, he had to jump wide cracks. Stinging water soaked him with each wrong step. He gradually found a rhythm, like a dancer, trying for the stable spots and quickly shifting his feet. With each glance, Christopher's dark silhouette grew closer. The heavy stone was slowing him.

Halfway across, with the far side vaguely in sight, Christopher looked back. Seeing Sutherland must have surprised him because he tried to run, stumbling to keep his balance. Every few seconds, he glanced over his shoulder. When Sutherland was within ten feet, Christopher stopped and turned.

"Stay away!" he shouted. "You'll sink us both."

Sutherland squinted into the blinding snow. "I don't care!" he yelled and moved closer. The ice rocked and leveled again.

"Are you crazy? What do you want?"

"Nothing." He was almost within reach.

Christopher unfastened the backpack and lowered it to the ice. The zipper was torn and the *lagarto* stone hung out a few inches.

"You want me?" He beckoned with both hands.

Sutherland had lost their clash in his apartment. This time, a draw would be good enough. His hands were nearly useless, but he dived for Christopher's knees and wrapped his arms around them. A sickening grinding followed the impact as they landed. A crack shot out at right angles to Christopher's body, the ice slab canted down and water gushed through the gap. He jackknifed to a sitting position. Sutherland still hung onto his legs.

Christopher kicked and pummeled Sutherland's head and shoulders. With a fierce chop to the temple, he made him let go. The shock couldn't have lasted more than a second. When he looked up, Christopher was on his knees reaching for the backpack.

Sutherland clambered closer, and his weight tipped the ice downward toward Christopher.

"You're not getting away!" he shouted.

"You'll kill us," Christopher cried. Water spilled over the backpack and around his boots.

Sutherland inched forward, ready to lunge again. The ice growled under them. Then, as if something holding it broke free, it heaved up steeply behind him. Sutherland flattened himself on his back and dug in his heels to stop sliding toward Christopher. On his stomach, Christopher slid backward, clawing at the ice with gloved fingers. He didn't stop until he was dangling over the edge, up to his waist in water.

Sutherland sat up. The backpack was at his feet. Part of the stone was sticking out from the opening. Christopher grabbed the shoulder strap and pulled on it, using it to haul himself onto the ice. As he pulled, the backpack peeled off like a glove, leaving the stone behind. The pack finally broke free, and Christopher slid back again. Only his fingers digging into the crusty surface held his head and shoulders above water.

"Help me!" he yelled.

Did he really expect help? Sutherland eased closer.

Christopher's head and chest were pressed against the ice. His arms were stretched out and holding on.

Sutherland watched, too exhausted and cold to do anything else. Christopher clawed at the snow crust, but the water made it more slippery. With each few inches gained, the slab tilted more, and he dropped back.

"For God's sake," he cried. "Help me."

Sutherland didn't answer. There was nothing to say.

"Fuck you," Christopher rasped. "Fuck all of you."

After a minute, he stopped trying. He just held on. Then he lifted his head and forced out the words. "I could have killed you…anytime. Gabriela too."

Sutherland strained to hear.

"The night I capped Valdez…" Christopher spit out some water and coughed. "Little shit. Screamed your fucking head off. You thought I was killing her…" He coughed out a laugh. "But I was…"

Sutherland didn't want to hear it. The memory flashed by in a whirl of red and gray. He saw a blank-eyed man in a pool of blood, a younger Christopher on top of the motionless woman. His mother.

The *lagarto* stone lay on the ice between them. Sutherland bent his legs, put both feet against it, and pushed. The stone hit Christopher's upturned face, knocking him backward with a splash. When he disappeared, he was hugging it in his arms, like a long-lost love.

Sutherland didn't have much time. He'd die of exposure if he didn't get off the ice. He forced himself to his feet and stumbled, teetered and finally crawled to the dock. It was only a few feet off the ice, but he didn't have any strength left. He would die here. Then he felt hands pulling him up and heard voices.

"Doug." It was Kelly.

"*Amigo.*" Alfonso Rivera.

Minutes later, he was in the backseat of the Cadillac under several overcoats. The car was moving. He tried to stop shaking. Kelly started to warm his hands with her breath and gasped. "You've been shot. Your finger."

"Don't feel a thing," he said, his teeth chattering. "It happened when I grabbed the gun."

Rivera held a flask to Sutherland's lips. "Did he get away?" he asked. "Is he alive?"

Sutherland took a sip, coughed, and said, "No."

Rivera shook his head. "Too bad." He closed his eyes halfway, as if imagining the type of death he had in mind for Christopher, the man who killed his brother.

"If it helps," Sutherland said, "I can't think of a worse way to die."

# CHAPTER FIFTY-ONE

▼

"We found his body." Detective Duncan took off his topcoat and sat in an armchair in Sutherland's living room. It was nearly six o'clock on Sunday. As darkness descended on the city, apartment lights came on randomly in the high-rise across the park. "Identified as James 'Rusty' Christopher," Duncan continued, consulting his notebook. "He was what he claimed, an agent with the DEA. They're doing backflips trying to get out of this."

"A crooked agent. The DEA guys are lining up to see me." Sutherland sat on his sofa and sipped tea from a large mug. On the table in front of him was a box of paper tissues and a bottle of cold medicine. He wore a heavy turtleneck under a fleece sweater. "Are you sure you don't want some tea? With honey?"

"No, thanks. He was a decorated Marine, too. Gives us a bad name."

"You a Marine?" Sutherland put down the mug and stifled a sneeze. His left hand was in a soft cast. His entire right pinky finger was taped and bandaged.

"*Semper fi.*" Duncan saluted. "Anyway, there's some things we gotta clear up." Duncan flipped pages in his notebook. "The two men who were killed near the harbor. You must have seen something."

"Like I said, they left the car. A couple minutes later, we heard all the shooting. We couldn't see twenty feet. You figure it was a drug war?"

Duncan shrugged. "If you and your girlfriend didn't see anyone, how'd you get home?"

"She flagged down a car. The guy took us to my place for twenty bucks." It was true except for the flagging and the twenty bucks. They would never have made it without Rivera. The storm was getting worse. Kelly could barely walk, and he was hypothermic.

"Did you get his name?"

"What for?"

Duncan frowned and turned a page. "For a guy so smart a few days ago, you don't know much, do you?"

"What do you mean?"

"Don't play dumb. You run around playing James Bond or Rambo. You don't tell me shit."

"I told you about Arias' gallery. I gave you the key. I told you where the shipment was. I told you about the restaurant and van. I told you where to find the body. What else you want?"

"Something's missing," Duncan said. "How'd you find that garage? How'd you know about the van or the restaurant?"

"You saw the key. It was like nothing else. A hardware store guy in Pilsen told me about the garage. As for the restaurant, I didn't remember at first, but Arias mentioned it. When I got there, I recognized one of them." He finished his tea. "He got in the van. What happened to it?"

"It skidded into a car in Wheeling. Patrol did a routine check, found the APB, and called for backup. Guys in the van tried to shoot their way out."

"Are they dead?"

"One. The other is critical. They had a fuckin' arsenal and kilos of coke." Duncan loosened his tie. His face was red, and his forehead glistened with sweat. "Is it hot in here?"

"Not enough," Sutherland tucked his hands in his armpits and winced with the pain in his broken left hand. "I've been shivering for two days." The cast and fever weren't his only reminder of what he'd been through. He was still sore where Arias kicked him. The bruises and scrapes on his face had yellowed and scabbed over.

"Lucky you didn't drown, too," Duncan said.

Sutherland stood up and walked to the thermostat. The temperature was only seventy-six degrees, so he turned it up four degrees. "Are we nearly through? I gotta go back to bed." He remained standing behind the couch facing the detective.

"Sorry, but there's more." Duncan wiped his forehead. "That stone."

"What's the question?"

"The Mexican Consulate sent an expert to check the shipment. That lizard thing wasn't there, but there was an empty crate. Somebody took it."

"Don't look at me. Where would I put it?"

"Enrique Arias thought you had it. Agent Christopher, too. Otherwise, why'd they want you? Why'd they kidnap your girlfriend?"

"They thought I was hiding it. I think the guys who shot Christopher's men have it."

Duncan closed his notebook and shook his head. "You know more than you're telling."

"What can I say? It's over," Sutherland said. "We're safe. The bad guys are dead, and their operation is finished."

"I'll tell you what matters. There's that missing artifact. Someone's out there with illegal weapons killing people, and you know who."

"How would I know people like that?"

"Don't give me that Innocent Joe crap. Nobody could've done it alone, especially what you did in Mexico. Two found dead in a mine. Five bodies burned in a camper. The Mexican police have questions, too."

"They'll get the same answers, but let me get better first." He sneezed.

"Whatever." Duncan stood and pulled on his topcoat. "I'm through for now, but there'll be more." They walked together to the door, and Sutherland held it open. "The artifacts will be returned to Mexico as soon as their museum team arrives," Duncan said. "You'll be hearing from them."

"I know," Sutherland said.

Duncan stopped halfway through the door. "How?" He shook his head. "Oh, never mind." He turned and stomped to the elevator and slapped the button with his palm. It would have been easy to explain, but he didn't want to spoil the effect. Gabriela was leading the archeological team. He wondered how she would react to the news that she hadn't killed Valdez.

Sutherland went to the kitchen and poured another cup of tea. When he turned around, Kelly was standing there on a pair of crutches. Her left ankle was in a cast.

"You hear it all?" he asked.

"I'll never believe anything you say again." She smiled.

"I just left out the parts with Rivera. You're my witness."

"Too true," she said. "I'm glad I didn't witness what happened in Mexico. I couldn't handle it."

The image of Mercedes' death flashed in his mind. He nodded and turned his back on Kelly, fussing with a tea bag so she wouldn't see his eyes. The last week had produced a lifetime of bad memories, but that was the worst.

Kelly put her hand on his shoulder and said, "She was a good person, wasn't she?"

He nodded again, his eyes burning. "And it killed her."

The telephone on the nightstand woke him. The clock said eight. It was dark, so it was the same day. Kelly sat in the corner, reading. He picked up the handset.

"Hello?"

"Doug, you're on top of my shit list." It was his ex-wife's voice, but the sultry whisper had an icy edge.

"Are you okay?"

"Why didn't you tell me? That detective scared the bejesus out of me."

"I tried to tell you. Just be glad it was a false alarm. Are you all right? Jenny?"

"What do you think? We've been hiding in a hotel for three days. I felt like a criminal."

"I'm sorry, Margo. Are you home now?"

"Damn right. And I'm sending you the bill. I ought to charge you for screwing up my week. Next time you're in trouble, leave me and Jenny out of it."

"No more next times. I promise."

"You can forget about Jenny meeting you in Colorado."

"We'll talk about it later, Margo. I'm glad you're both fine. Bye for now."

He hung up and turned to Kelly, speaking as if he was a concerned Margo talking to him. "Are you okay, Doug? Is Kelly safe? Were you hurt? How was your week?"

"I assume she didn't take it well," Kelly said.

"Par for the course. It's always good to have your decisions validated."

"You did the right thing."

"You're telling me." But the decision he'd alluded to was their divorce.

He'd just dozed off again when Kelly woke him and handed him the phone.

"It's Larry Adams, Doug," she said. "He says you'd want to hear."

Sutherland propped himself up in bed, expecting his architect had bad news. A denial or delay on the development would be ruinous. But until that minute, he hadn't thought about it. The exigencies of keeping Kelly and himself alive had taken precedence. He took the handset knowing that even the worst news couldn't diminish his gratitude for having both of them safe.

"Hi, Larry. Did the snowstorm screw up Friday's meeting?"

"Hell no. It might have helped. There were no objections. The project's a go. I would've called earlier, but the blizzard…"

Sutherland wanted to pump his fist, but his ribs hurt too much. "I knew you could do it, Larry. I had faith in you."

"It wasn't me," Adams said. "I think they wanted to get home before the storm hit."

When Sutherland hung up, Kelly said, "Had faith in him? Now I've heard everything."

The phone rang again before he could respond. It was the doorman. "Mr. Sutherland, someone just dropped off a letter for you."

"Can you send it up? I'm under the weather."

"Right up, sir."

Five minutes later, Kelly swung into the bedroom on her crutches. She held an envelope in her teeth and dropped it in his lap. "There isn't any perfume, so you're allowed to open it."

It was a plain white business envelope with his name on it and no return address. He opened it and pulled out a note card. It was short and all in Spanish. He read it and smiled.

"What is it?" Kelly asked.

"It's not signed, but it's from Rivera. A thank-you note of sorts."

"Let me see." She held out her hand.

"Wait." He tipped the envelope. A key fell onto the bed.

Kelly stared at it, cocked her head, and said, "Isn't that like the one Javier gave you?"

"Except it's a different number."

"That's thoughtful," she said. "A memento."

She didn't get it. The police weren't the only ones with divers.

Sutherland laughed and said, "He couldn't fit seventy pounds of limestone in an envelope."